The Vows of Silence

BY THE SAME AUTHOR

Featuring Simon Serrailler
THE VARIOUS HAUNTS OF MEN
THE PURE IN HEART
THE RISK OF DARKNESS

Fiction
GENTLEMAN AND LADIES
A CHANGE FOR THE BETTER
I'M THE KING OF THE CASTLE
THE ALBATROSS AND OTHER STORIES
STRANGE MEETING
THE BIRD OF NIGHT
A BIT OF SINGING AND DANCING
IN THE SPRINGTIME OF THE YEAR
THE WOMAN IN BLACK
MRS DE WINTER
THE MIST IN THE MIRROR
AIR AND ANGELS
THE SERVICE OF CLOUDS
THE BOY WHO TAUGHT THE BEEKEEPER TO READ
THE MAN IN THE PICTURE

Non-Fiction
THE MAGIC APPLE TREE
FAMILY

Children's Books
THE BATTLE FOR GULLYWITH

The Vows of Silence

A Simon Serrailler Crime Novel

Susan Hill

Chatto & Windus
LONDON

Published by Chatto & Windus 2008

2 4 6 8 10 9 7 5 3 1

Grateful acknowledgement is made for the quotation from *Four Quartets* by T.S. Eliot, reprinted by permission of Faber and Faber Ltd / The T S Eliot Estate.

First published in Great Britain in 2008 by
Chatto & Windus
Random House, 20 Vauxhall Bridge Road,
London SW1V 2SA

www.rbooks.co.uk

Addresses for companies within The Random House Group Limited can be found at:
www.randomhouse.co.uk / offices.htm

A CIP catalogue record for this book
is available from the British Library

Hardback ISBN 9780701179991
Trade paperback ISBN 9780701180003

The Random House Group Limited supports The Forest Stewardship Council (FSC), the leading international forest certification organisation. All our titles that are printed on Greenpeace approved FSC certified paper carry the FSC logo. Our paper procurement policy can be found at www.rbooks.co.uk / environment

Typeset by SX composing DTP, Rayleigh, Essex
Printed and bound in Great Britain by
Clays Ltd, St Ives plc

To
The Wedding Guests

Acknowledgements

I would like to thank Dr Robin Birts for patiently answering my medical questions, and in language I could understand. Carl Mee's assistance on the subject of firearms and the police was invaluable. Nick Peto told me all I could ever need to know about recreational shooting. Jessica Ruston's advice and eagle-eye were always spot-on. If any errors remain they are my own.

One

They had climbed for two hours. Then they had come into the low-hanging curtains of cloud. It had started to drizzle.

He opened his mouth to make some sour remark about the promise of a fine day, but, at the same moment, Iain turned his head a fraction to the left. Motioned with his forefinger.

Iain knew the hills and the weather of the hills, the subtle shifts of wind direction. Knew them better than anyone.

They stood, still, not speaking. There was a tension now. It hadn't been there minutes before.

Something.

The sun broke apart the cloud curtain, leaving it in tatters. The sun shone at first with a watery cast but then, like a man leaping out into view, full and strong. The corners of Iain's mouth twitched in a smile.

But still they stood. Motionless and silent. Waiting.

Iain lifted his binoculars to his eyes and looked from left to right, slowly, slowly.

And he waited, watching the set of Iain's head, waiting for the moment.

Their clothes began to steam in the sun.

Iain lowered the glasses and nodded.

They were above the deer, and for another half-mile he saw nothing. But they were there of course. Iain knew. They went carefully, keeping upwind. The ground was stony here, easy to slip.

He felt the old excitement. These were the best moments. When you knew. You were this close to it, this close to having it in your sights, this close to the whole point and purpose and culmination of it all.

This close.

There was the faintest outbreath from Iain's pursed lips.

He followed the line of sight.

The stag was alone, halfway up the lower slope immediately west of where they were standing. It had sensed nothing – that much was clear for the moment. Keep it that way.

They dropped down and began to crawl, the soaking ground against their bellies, the sun on their backs. The midges came on with a vengeance, to find their way unerringly through chinks in clothing, brushing aside the barrier of citronella, but he was so keyed up now he barely noticed them. Later he would be driven mad.

They crawled for another ten minutes, dropping down slightly until they were level with the stag and a couple of hundred yards away.

Iain stopped. Lifted the glasses. They waited. Watched. Still as the stones.

The sun was hot now. The wind had dropped altogether.

They began to inch maybe thirty yards further and the thirty yards took ten minutes; they barely moved. Just enough.

The stag lifted its head.

'The Old Man,' Iain whispered, so softly he could barely hear.

The oldest stag. Not as huge as those living on the lower ground, and without the vast antlers. But mighty enough. Old. Too old for another winter. He had too much respect for the beast to let that happen.

They were downwind and perhaps a hundred and fifty yards off. But then the stag shook its head, turned sideways, ambled a little way, though never turning its back. They waited.

Waited. The sun blazed. He boiled inside his wax jacket.

Then, casually, it turned and, in a breathtaking second, lifted its head and faced him full on. As if it knew. As if it had been expecting him. It positioned itself perfectly.

He unslipped his rifle. Loaded. Iain was watching intently through the glasses.

He balanced himself with care and then looked down the sights.

The old stag had not moved. Its head was raised higher now and it was looking straight at him.

It knew.

Iain waited, frozen to the glasses.

The world stopped turning.

He aimed for the heart.

Two

Dark blue jacket. Blue-and-white print skirt. Medium heels.

Scarf? Or the beads?

Beads.

Helen Creedy went into the bathroom and fiddled with her hair. Came out and caught sight of herself again in the full-length mirror. God, she looked – frumpish. That was the only word. As if she were going to a job interview.

She took off the skirt, blouse and jacket and started again.

It was very warm. Late September, an Indian summer.

Right. Pale grey linen trousers. Long linen jacket. The fuchsia shirt she hadn't yet worn.

Better? Yes. Earrings? Just plain studs.

There was a roar outside as Tom gave his motorbike its usual final rev turning into the drive. The roar died. She heard the clunk of the metal rest going down onto the concrete.

Just after six o'clock. She had hours – got dressed far too early.

She sat down on the end of her bed. She had been excited. Keyed up. Nervous, but with something like pleasure, anticipation. Now, it was as if the temperature had dropped. She felt sick. Anxious. Afraid. How absurd. Then she felt nothing but a draining tiredness so that she could not imagine ever having the energy to stand on her feet again.

The kitchen door slammed. She heard Tom drop his helmet and heavy leather gloves onto the floor.

Pale grey linen. New fuchsia shirt. She had even had her hair done. She wanted to lie down on her bed and sleep and sleep.

After another couple of minutes she went downstairs.

'Oh, good choice, Ma.' Elizabeth looked up from her French textbook.

Tom, as always when he got in, was at the toaster. Tom. He had said he was 'OK' about it. 'Fine' about it. But Helen still wondered.

She had nothing to worry about with Elizabeth, though – it was her daughter who had pushed her into this in the first place. 'It's six years since Dad. You won't have us here for much longer. You've got to get a life, Ma.'

But now she caught a look on Tom's face which was at odds with what he said. That he was 'OK' about it. 'Fine.'

'I thought you weren't meeting this guy till eight.'

'Half seven.'

'All the same.'

Tom scraped what looked like half a pound of butter and a dollop of Marmite across four slices of toast.

The kitchen got the evening sun. It was warm. Elizabeth's French books. Pens. Markers. Tom's Marmite pot, lidless on the table. The smell of warm toast. And bike oil.

'I can't go,' Helen said. 'I can't do this. What am I thinking?'

'Oh God, not again, we've been through all this. Tom, tell her, back me up, will you?'

Tom shrugged.

His sister snorted impatiently. Put her pen down on *Eugénie Grandet*. 'Right, let's start again. Is it just first-night nerves or what?'

First-night nerves? How did that even begin to convey what she was feeling, sitting at the kitchen table in pale grey linen and a fuchsia shirt she had never worn and at least an hour too early?

It was a couple of months ago that Elizabeth had said, as they were walking Mutley, on the Hill, 'I don't think you're meeting people.'

Helen had not understood. In her job as a pharmacist she met people every day.

'I don't mean that.' Elizabeth had sat down and leaned her back against the Wern Stone. It was July. Mutley lay panting.

Helen had hesitated, standing, looking at the view over Lafferton so as not to look at her daughter. She sensed that something was important, or that things were about to change but she did not know what or how. It alarmed her.

'Mum, don't you think you might . . . well, meet someone – I mean, someone else. After Dad. Sit down, I'm getting a crick in my neck here.'

Helen sat on the dry grass. Elizabeth was looking straight at her. She had always been like this. Helen remembered the night she had been born: Lizzie had looked straight at her in this same, uncompromising way, even though newborn babies were not supposed to focus. She had done it as a small girl when asking a question. That straight, blue-eyed gaze that held you and did not let you off. Here it was now.

'Before you know it I'll be at Cambridge, fingers crossed. Tom will be off with his weirdos.'

'And I'll be on my own and I won't be able to function is what you mean.'

'Not exactly.'

'What then?'

'I worry that you're missing out. You should have someone.'

'I don't want to be married again.'

'How do you know? You may not want to in theory . . . but if you met someone.'

'Well who's to say I won't?'

'Not stuck in a windowless cubbyhole full of pill packets you won't.'

'I like my job.'

'That's not the point. Look, I think you should take a more proactive approach to this thing.'

'There is no "thing". Come on, Mutley's too hot. So am I.'

She stood. But when Lizzie also stood, there it was, the direct gaze. Not letting her off. Helen had turned and started back down the Hill so fast she almost slipped on the stony track.

*

She had not wanted to think about it. She wouldn't think about it. She was perfectly contented. She had met Terry when she was twenty-three, married him a year later, had the children, been happy. When Tom was six she had gone back to work, part-time. Life had been good.

When Terry had been diagnosed with malignant melanoma she was told he would have a couple of years, maybe more. He had had four months. Any sort of relationship with any other man had been – was – unthinkable. She realised as she reached the last few yards of the track that she was angry, angry and in some sort of panic.

'I think –' Elizabeth said, catching up with her.

'Well, I don't. Leave it. It is not a conversation I am prepared to have.' She had spoken harshly but Elizabeth had simply gazed at her for a long moment without replying.

Two days later, a brochure came through the post.

'My name is Laura Brooke. I run the Laura Brooke agency for men and women wishing to meet a partner hand-picked for them. I do not believe people can be matched by computers. I act as a friend. I only take on clients with whom I feel I can succeed and I only introduce clients to one another after extensive interviews and my own personal and careful consideration. I give clients my time and expertise to find them . . .'

She had stuffed the brochure in the bin.

The following day in the hairdresser's, she was startled to find herself wondering if people really did meet successfully through agencies or via the Internet, if the whole thing was possibly not the con she had always assumed it to be. Sad people went to dating agencies, sad or sinister people. She could understand why you might join something or other if you were, say, new to a town and had no way of making friends – a club, a sports group, a night class. But friendship was one thing, this was another. She had friends. What she didn't have was enough time to spend with them.

She was forty-six. By the time she was fifty Tom and Elizabeth would have left home. She would have her job and also more time for her friends. She would have the St Michael's Singers and she might rejoin the Lafferton Players. She would volunteer for something.

Terry was irreplaceable. His death had devastated her and she still felt like someone who had lost a limb. Nothing would ever change that. Nothing and no one.

'I'm not going,' she said now. 'I can't do this.'

'You are and you can, if I have to push you there.'

'Elizabeth . . .'

'Once, you said, just once when someone seemed really worth meeting. And he does. We agreed. Tom, didn't we agree?'

Tom put his hands up. 'Leave me out of this, OK?' he said, banging out of the room.

'He doesn't like it,' Helen said.

'He doesn't like anything that isn't about his own peculiar world. Ignore him.'

'Why are you pushing me into something I don't want?'

'You *do* want it. You want to get out of here, you want to open yourself up to something new. You want a fresh start.'

'It's only one date.'

'Exactly!'

A part of her knew that Elizabeth was right. Helen had thought about it a good deal, once she had allowed the idea house room. She was fearful of being too much alone when her children had left home, she was too young to be in a rut, she needed to open herself to something new. All the same, to her, meeting someone through an agency or a dating website, or by answering an advert, was an admission of failure. And she wasn't sure she even wanted to succeed. Besides, there was a stigma, when someone of her age did this.

'Rubbish,' Lizzie had said.

Of course it was a stigma. If she did – by remote chance – meet someone through a dating agency, and that someone came to be important, she would never be able to tell anyone how they had got together. She would cut out her tongue rather than admit it.

'I don't get it.' But that was Elizabeth and she was her daughter.

'I'll send a text message and say I'm not well.'

'That is absolutely pathetic. For God's sake, Ma, this is a drink in a pub –'

'A bar.'

'A drink. A chat. You can leave it there. Oh God, we've been through all this – if you get the feeling he's a mass murderer, you send Tom a text and he'll be there in five.'

'I won't think he's a mass murderer. He sounds . . .'

'Like a nice bloke.'

'Yes.'

'Yes.'

'You must have wanted to go through with it earlier, you got ready hours ago.'

'Is this too dressed up?'

'No, it's great. That wasn't my point.'

There was a long silence.

'I do want to go. I want to. But I don't want to. I just haven't done anything like it before and it's so many years since I even had an evening out with a man . . .'

Elizabeth got up, came round the table and gave her a hug, bending over her as if she were the mother, Helen the child.

'You look great and it's going to be fine. And if it isn't – so what? What have you lost? One evening.'

'*EastEnders*.'

'Well, that's crap at the moment so there you are.'

Elizabeth settled down to *Eugénie Grandet* again. The room went quiet.

'Lizzie . . .'

'Mother – *go away*!'

She had retrieved the agency brochure from the waste-paper bin. But she felt uncertain about being interviewed by someone with the firm intention of matching her with a man on their books, particularly when she didn't even know if she wanted to meet anyone at all.

Which was how she had come upon the website *peoplemeetingpeople.com*. Because she would admit to that. Yes. She would agree that she was a person wanting to meet people.

It was quite straightforward. You joined the site for a fee which was not too expensive, not too cheap. She had done that finally one evening when she was on her own. You went step by step. You didn't have to commit yourself to too much too soon. She felt happy with that.

She put in her name – first name only – and age. The next stage was to narrow down the kind of 'people' she wanted to meet. *Age group*. That was surprisingly easy. Between forty-five and sixty. *Marital status*. She ticked *Widowed*. Then *Divorced*. Not sure about divorced but so many people were now, and the reasons were less – what? Sinister? Worrying? She did not tick *Single*. Few really eligible men were still single after forty-five.

She entered her geographical area. Narrowed it down a bit.

Occupation. Professional. Media-related. Public services. Administrative. Business. Farming and countryside. Almost any of those. She could probably find something to chat about even to a farmer. She ticked each box.

She had expected there to be more stages, more questions, but she was asked if she would now like to see photographs and brief details of anyone matching her outline.

She went to make a coffee. Somehow, photographs of people, real people, took it one big step away from being a game, made it serious, committed her.

No. It did not commit her. It was just photographs. And oddly enough, she was excited. Who would she see? What kind of men? They would probably all be bald. Or with huge bushy beards. Or small eyes. ('Never trust a man with small eyes.' Her mother.) Or bad teeth. Or . . .

She took her coffee to the table, set it down and decisively clicked on the 'Yes' button.

It was the first one. How do you tell that you like someone from a photograph? How do you know that you want to meet them?

He was fifty-two. He had brown hair. He had a warm expression. Slightly diffident smile. Nothing especially distinctive. But a good face. Good-looking? Yes, but not overwhelmingly handsome. It was his expression. Warm. Trustworthy. Yes.

She glanced at the others. One was out at once – the bushy beard. Another was too old. Perfectly OK but she couldn't believe he was sixty or under. The last one was fine. Nothing against him. But when she looked back at the first there was no contest.

'Click beside any photograph if you would like to know more about this person.'

She clicked.

'Phil is Head of History at a boys' school. He has been widowed for five years and has two grown-up sons. His interests include cooking, cricket, books and ornithology. He loves his job and has many friends but since his sons left home he has felt the lack of a special companion in his life.

If you want to send your profile and photograph to Phil, click HERE.

If you would like to leave a voicemail for Phil, click HERE.'

She clicked twice.

Three

'There is not any such word as plam.'

'There is *so* such a word as plam.'

'You're making it up. Uncle Si, isn't he making it up?'

'Mummy . . .'

'Don't ask me,' Cat Deerbon said, dropping a handful of walnuts into the salad bowl, 'you know I can't do Scrabble.'

'You don't "do" Scrabble, duh. You play it.'

'Sam, how many times have I told you, "duh" – and especially "duh" with that face – is incredibly insulting and you do not do or say it.'

Sam sighed and turned back to the board. 'Plam,' he said, 'is a word.'

'What does it mean then?'

'It's . . . the sort of way Australian emu birds land. They go "plam".'

Simon Serrailler stood up with a shout of laughter. 'Brilliant, Sam. I give you ten for Creative Cheating.' He wandered over to the other side of the kitchen and dipped his finger into the salad dressing. 'Needs more lemon.'

'I doubt it.'

'And a pinch of sugar.'

'Why not make it yourself?'

'Can't be arsed.'

'Mummy, Uncle Simon said –'

'I know, and it is a most unattractive expression. Don't say it again, please.' Cat glared at her brother.

'You've got bossier. That's Australia for you. Loud, bossy women.'

Cat threw a piece of lettuce at him. Simon ducked. The lettuce landed wetly on the floor.

'God, I love it. Love it, love it, love it.' Simon threw himself onto the old kitchen sofa. 'I wish you knew what it was like when you weren't here and those people were and I couldn't come and –'

'You told us,' Sam said, tipping the Scrabble letters into their green drawstring bag, 'how awful it was.'

'Yes, about a million zillion times.'

'So you missed us. That figures.'

'Si, will you open that bottle? Sam, please put the mats on the table. Hannah –'

'I have to go to the loo, I absolutely-scootly have to.'

'Mum, you have to stop her doing that, she's always doing it, she does it to get out of things, she doesn't need to go to the loo at all.'

'Stop whingeing.'

Simon rummaged in the drawer for the corkscrew. 'You know,' he said to Cat, 'it is "absolutely-scootly" typical of Dad. It really is.'

'He can see us when he gets back. Don't make a thing of it.'

Richard Serrailler, Cat and Simon's father, had announced that he was taking a holiday just when the Deerbon family returned from Australia.

'But he doesn't go on holidays. He hates holidays. And what's he going to do in Madeira for two weeks, for God's sake?'

'Soak up the sun?'

'He hates sun.'

'He just didn't want to make a song and dance about us coming home after nine months – he wants to pretend we haven't been away at all, and by the time he gets back it'll feel as if we haven't. Actually,' Cat put the salad bowl on the table, 'it feels like that already.'

'God, sis, am I glad you're home.'

She gave him a brief smile, before bending to take the fish out of the oven. 'Give Chris a shout, will you? He's probably fallen asleep with Felix. Chris does jet lag like nobody else.'

But Chris Deerbon walked into the kitchen as she spoke, rubbing his hand through his hair. 'I think I must have gone to sleep.' He looked puzzled.

'So long as Felix has too.'

'Half an hour ago.' He poured the wine into glasses and handed one to Simon.

'Here's to home.'

'In Australia, we had supper outside nearly all the time. We had barbecues on the beach. We had a barbecue in the garden, it went with the house. Everyone there has barbecues – they call them barbies, like Hannah's puke dolls.'

'Wish you were still there, Sam?'

'Sort of.'

'I don't,' Hannah said. 'I missed my friends and my pony and my bed and I missed Uncle Simon most of everything.'

Sam made a loud sucking noise.

Simon looked round the table at them all. He felt a burst of pure and extraordinary happiness.

'Do you get a lot more money being a Detective Chief Superintendent?' Sam asked.

'I get a bit more.'

'Do you get to do more interesting things? More important cases?'

'Some. My really important cases are likely to be with SIFT though.'

'Why?'

'We get called in precisely because they're important –'

'Serious Incident Flying Taskforce. I thought everything a policeman did was serious.'

'It is.'

'Then I don't see –'

'Eat your fish, Sam.'

'Is it because they've had no luck solving them, so you're their last resort?'

'Not usually. They might need more minds focused on something, if it's very difficult. They might need a detached point of view and a fresh eye, they might need us because their own resources are becoming overstretched – all sorts of reasons. The best thing for me about SIFT is that we're out there *doing*, not sitting behind a desk. The higher you get in rank, the easier it is to get trapped in an office all day.'

'In Australia, the police wear fleeces and baseball caps.'

'Ever seen your uncle in a baseball cap, Sam?'

'He'd be cool.'

'This,' Hannah said, 'is blah-blah boring talk.'

'Go to bed, then. You shouldn't be at grown-up supper if you get bored with grown-up conversation, you should be playing puke pink Barbies.'

Cat sighed. The bickering between her son and daughter had got worse in Australia.

Wondering now if it was to be a permanent and tiresome feature of their relationship, she turned to her own brother. 'Did we wind each other up like this?'

'No. Ivo wound me up. I wound Ivo up. Not you.'

Cat had spent two separate periods with their triplet brother, who worked as a flying doctor in Australia, and had come away each time feeling that they might well not be related at all. Ivo seemed to be from a different planet. He was brash, stubborn, opinionated, tough. She had left him both times with relief and some bewilderment.

'Dad,' she said now, her fork to her mouth. 'I suppose that's the answer. It was staring at me. Ivo is like Dad.'

'Could have told you that,' Chris said.

After the children had gone to bed, they opened another bottle and Mephisto the cat bumped in through the flap and settled on Simon's stomach.

'Did this boy take to strangers living in his house?'

'Apparently he was absolutely fine.'

'Traitor,' Simon said, stroking him. Mephisto half closed his eyes. 'How have they settled back to school?'

'Hannah strolled in as if she'd never been away. Sam a bit less easily. His class has split into different groups so he's lost some of his old friends and there are new boys . . . but he'll be fine. It's sport, sport, sport now anyway – he was rarely within four walls all the time we were in Sydney.'

'You?'

'Oh, I was within four walls. Chris and I were working, you know.'

'I mean coming back.'

'Good. Great in fact.'

'OKish,' Chris said. He had been the one to press for them to take the sabbatical in Australia, the one who had extended it from the original six months. The one who had been loath to return. 'But at least we've come back to find that, at last, the role of the GP is getting more recognition.'

'You mean double the money for half the work. No nights, no weekends, no bank holidays. Jolly nice – I take your point.'

Cat groaned. 'Si, this is an area where angels fear to tread. We've had so many arguments about it we've made a pact: Chris and I don't discuss the new GP contract.'

Cat had always been bitterly opposed to agencies covering nights and weekends for the practice, other than on a locum basis to give her and Chris an occasional rest. She had come back ready to do battle to retain her right to visit her own patients out of hours, only to discover that not only was Chris against their taking that work back in-house, but so was every other GP in the area. It was impossible for her to do out-of-hours by herself and so, resentfully, she had had to concede defeat.

'For now,' she had muttered. 'But I'll find a way. I hate leaving my patients to the mercy of some doctor flown in from abroad at huge cost to cover a few nights here or even worse, someone on call from fifty miles away. It isn't safe, it isn't right, it is also over-stretching the ambulance service and overloading hospital A & E and it is not conducive to patient welfare and peace of mind.'

But the arguments over it had become too angry.

She and Chris had agreed to go back to work and accept the status quo, focusing on catching up with changes and reacquainting themselves with patients, staff and all the routine of a busy surgery.

'Seen a lot of Dad?' Cat asked now.

Simon made a face. 'Took him out to a pub lunch a couple of

times. Dropped by, but he was often out. I hate going to Hallam House now.'

'I know you do, but with us away and no Mum he needed you a lot more.'

'Not so's you'd notice. I took flowers up to Martha's grave on her anniversary. I rang Dad – thought we could meet up. He wasn't in. He never mentioned it. I don't think he's thought about Martha since she died. Or about Mother come to that.'

'That's unfair, Simon.'

'Is it?'

Simon had been close to Martha, their handicapped sister, close to Meriel, their mother. Their deaths had been two blows from which he knew he had not recovered and probably never would.

It was easier for Cat. She had Chris, she had three children and she had escaped to Australia.

Escaped? He looked at his sister now, curled in the sagging kitchen armchair with her legs under her, holding a glass of wine. She looked well. But to call it an escape – for her – was wrong. He knew that if Chris had not pushed, she would never have left Lafferton. Cat was like him, a home bird. She seemed entirely settled and content to be back in the farmhouse.

Simon closed his eyes, stroking Mephisto until the cat's purr was like the throbbing of an engine. He realised exactly how miserable his months without the sanctuary of this house and this family had been.

He let out a deep sigh of contentment.

Four

She didn't have time to look around and take anything in – the people sitting at tables or standing near the bar – because as she went inside he was there, saying, 'Helen? Yes, of course you're Helen. Let's get out of here, it's packed, this was a thoroughly bad idea.'

And he took her elbow and guided her through the door. Outside it was a warm September evening. Dark. The *Old Ship* was strung with fairy lights.

It had taken ten days. She had sent him her details, received his, sent a voicemail message, got one back. It felt right. She was comfortable.

Phil had suggested they meet at this pub in the centre of Lafferton. She hadn't known it, but both Elizabeth and Tom had said, 'Oh, that place is OK. You'll be fine there.' So here she was.

'Let's get right out of Lafferton. Do you know the *Croxley Oak*? The food is good so it won't be empty but we should be able to hear ourselves think.'

'Shall I follow you then?'

'What? No, no, I'll drive us back here, you can pick up your car later.'

It wasn't the plan but she was swept along by him, across the car park, into a dark-coloured Peugeot, clicking the seat belt and then off, out of town, on the road, heading somewhere else. It had happened before she could disagree. The country road was dark. Once, a car overtook them too fast. Dark road again.

'Helen, I'm sorry . . . rushing you off like that. What must you think? I just can't bear overcrowded bars, but more to the point, some of my students were there. I wasn't going to meet you for the first time in full view of them.'

'No, it's fine. Fine.'

The car seemed new. Smelled new. She clutched her bag. Her mobile was safely inside it. After a few minutes she glanced at him sideways, very quickly. The photo had been pretty good. He was not as tall as she'd imagined, but he was not a small man either. She had a phobia about small men.

'What have you been doing today?' he asked. 'Tell me from the beginning.'

To her surprise, she did. They sped through the darkness, away from town, away from Tom and Elizabeth, away from everything familiar, away from the place she had told them she would be for the evening, and so, to quell the anxiety she felt riding at night in a fast car with a stranger, she talked through every detail of her day.

The *Croxley Oak* had the tawny atmosphere only some good country pubs acquire, mellow, with the pleasant hum of conversation. Helen drank lime and soda, then a glass of white wine; Phil had a single half of bitter and then went on to ginger beer. And they talked. After almost an hour, they ordered home-baked ham with chips and salad, and the chips came thick and hand-cut, the ham in chunky slices, sweet and lean.

He was talking about some difficulties with one of his school's department heads, how everyone had to handle her tactfully, how she upset students. It had arisen because Helen had told him about a colleague who had always been exceptionally conscientious and had recently become slack and careless, worrying everyone because it was so out of character. She told Phil she couldn't take an interest in cricket, though she had tried hard for Tom's sake when he had been in the school team; he expressed total ignorance of choral music when he learned she was a member of the St Michael's Singers.

Now, as he shook his head over a remark the department head had made that day to a pupil, Helen looked across the table at Philip Russell and felt an extraordinary sense of having known him all her life. It was as though he had been there, familiar, trusted, even while she had been married to Terry and bringing up their children, somehow living a parallel life which was interwoven with hers. The feeling startled her and in a second it had gone, to be replaced by the knowledge that she was simply enjoying her evening and his company.

'Would you like a pudding? Coffee?'

'I'd like some tea.'

'Good, so would I. Isn't it great that you can actually get tea in pubs now and no one thinks it odd?' He made to get up, then said, 'Helen, do your family know where you are?'

'They know I'm meeting you.'

She felt embarrassed. How could she say, Yes, and my son is sitting at home waiting for a call to tell him to come and rescue me? 'Why do you ask?'

He laughed, looking embarrassed himself, and went off to order their tea.

The pub was emptying before they paused in talk about their families – how her Tom was one of those teenagers struggling to find a meaning and a spiritual dimension in his life, and how she worried that most of his friends seemed to be so odd; how his elder son Hugh was spending a year teaching in Africa and the younger, also Tom, was at drama school – against his father's better judgement. 'But I'll support him all the same. I have to. You have to make up for a lot, don't you find? Make up for that huge gap in their lives.' His wife had been killed in an appalling electrical accident in the house. He had stated the fact in a way that forbade further enquiry.

'It's rather late,' Helen said.

'I know, but we're grown-ups. Nobody's going to tell us off.'

'Oh yes they are!'

He held open his car door. I am enjoying myself, she thought again. I haven't enjoyed myself like this for too long.

At her car, in the now deserted yard of the *Old Ship*, he said, 'Thank you, Helen. I'll phone you if I may?'

Turning out into the street and on her route home, glancing in her rear-view mirror as she drove away, she saw that he waited and watched.

Five

Melanie Drew was so happy. It was very quiet, very peaceful, and the early autumn sun was coming in through the window onto the table at which she sat with a packet of thank-you notes. She had written two and had worked out that she still had forty-two to go.

The previous day, a delivery van had arrived from the company, *everythingwedding.com*, with which they had had their list and it had taken two men the best part of forty minutes to bring all the parcels and boxes out and up the two flights of stairs to the flat. They had been perfectly cheerful about it, though, and after it was all done Melanie had made tea and given them each a piece of wedding cake and they had toasted her in the new blue mugs with white stars.

Now, she took an envelope and wrote on it – but not the address of the aunt who had sent them a hundred pounds.

She wrote:

Melanie Drew.

Melanie Drew.

Melanie Drew.

Mr and Mrs Craig Drew.

Mrs Craig Drew.

Craig and Melanie Drew.

Craig and . . .

What a waste of an envelope! But she sat in the sun looking at her writing and she couldn't stop smiling. She hadn't been able to stop smiling since the wedding two weeks ago.

Now, though, the honeymoon was over, Craig had gone back to work at the estate agent's yesterday, she had another couple of days off but then she would be heading for the reception desk at Price and Fairbrother. Tonight, they had more wedding presents to open. The flat suddenly seemed very small. The spare room was where Craig wanted to keep stuff like his Wellington boots and waterproof jackets and mittens. Now, it was so full of boxes they could barely open the door. And then there was a mountain of wrapping paper, tissue paper and cardboard to dispose of. Craig was keen on recycling and determined to find out the greenest way of binning it; Melanie had muttered about a bonfire.

'Do you know what you're saying there, Mel? Bonfire? You can't have a bonfire. It adds to the carbon levels in the atmosphere.'

'Oh. Right.'

'You should be more concerned.'

'I'm concerned about getting my spare room back, that's all.'

It had not been a row though. They never rowed. They agreed to differ.

She smiled now and wrote *Mrs Melanie Anita Drew* three times on the envelope.

The sun was warm as well as bright. The flat faced west so it would be like this when they got in from work and for a lot of the evening, right through the spring and summer. They had been lucky to get it, and for the price, though they had worked like slaves for the previous six months replacing the kitchen, taking up ancient lino and rotten floorboards, pulling down sixties wood-effect panelling, ripping out old gas fires, and redecorating. It had paid off. It looked fresh and bright and new and Melanie was delighted with it all. Married life, she thought now. Married life. She and Craig had known one another for three years but never actually lived together, so everything was new, everything was fun, as well as, occasionally, slightly scary.

She looked around the room. Then back to the envelopes. Thank you, thank you, thank you, thank you. Midnight-blue Le Creuset cookware, pale blue Nigella Lawson kitchenware, china with hearts and stars, soft white fluffy bathrobes and towels, desk lamps, cutlery, mirrors, clocks, and a massive chandelier made out of tooled wire and hanging crystal beads that she had put down on the wedding list because it looked fun but which was so expensive she had not really thought anyone would ever buy it. Her godmother, who was an actress and liked what she called 'a bit of OTT', had. The box it came in could have housed a new fridge. The moment it arrived Melanie had had misgivings. Craig hated it.

But it didn't matter. It was a laugh. It was daft and she was happy. Happy, happy, happy.

She put aside the thank-you notes and opened her laptop. The wedding pictures had gone up on the photographer's website and she had looked through them several times since they had got home, revelling in every detail. She was still surprised at how much she had missed on the day itself, and also, of course, how much happened that she had never got to see at all – Craig and his brother and ushers arriving at the church, the bridesmaids getting out of the car and her sister Gaynor almost measuring her length and her posy having to be reassembled. They had made a beautiful collage of the reception which by some clever trick moved and changed as you watched – so that every time Mel opened up the website she saw something she hadn't previously noticed. This time, it was the expression on Adrian's face, as he was waiting to make his best man speech: he looked as if he were headed for the gallows.

She also had two disks of pictures taken by friends, and she planned to post the best of these on the wedding-day-and-honeymoon website she had set up. That way some of the family on her father's side, who hadn't been able to join them, could share the day.

She had taken a lot of persuading to have a September wedding. May or June had been her choice, but she'd been shocked at how booked up everywhere got so far ahead and September was the earliest they could organise. Which had turned out well because most of May and June had been cold and wet and September, including their wedding day, gloriously sunny.

She sat back and closed her eyes and let the sun warm her face, remembering. It was odd. Time did strange things. The day had passed so quickly, in a flash really, and yet ever since it seemed to have expanded and grown so that she could relive it in slow motion, going over every little detail again and again. She thought that Craig probably didn't. Not that he hadn't enjoyed it, because she knew he had. But his attitude was: Right, that's that, it was great, so what's next?

If she was honest, it not only puzzled her, she was mildly upset.

'Well, he's a man, isn't he?' Gaynor had said. 'Get over it.'

If she didn't have to go back to work, she could imagine spending a great many more afternoons like this, looking at the photographs, unpacking and sorting the wedding presents, writing thank-you cards and then starting to get supper ready with all the new kitchen things. She enjoyed her job. They were a nice firm to work for, she liked everyone there and she knew perfectly well that once the novelty of all this had faded she would have gone off her head with boredom alone in the flat all day. All the same, just another couple of weeks would have been nice.

Meanwhile, there was tonight. She was making a Thai chicken recipe with three fresh vegetables and a citrus and walnut salad. Bread. Cheese from the new *Just Cheese* in the Old Market Square – Lafferton's latest mall of small shops which were very tempting and very expensive. She got up to check on the recipe to see how much longer the chicken had to marinate and discovered that she had forgotten to buy walnuts. That was the sort of thing you could do when you had the day at home to yourself – shop in a leisurely fashion and pop out again if you found you had forgotten something. The flat was less than ten minutes by car from the supermarket on the Bevham Road. She could get walnuts and a bottle of wine. Wandering round the supermarket at half past three in the afternoon was part of the fun of these last days off. Part of being happy.

Melanie laughed at herself as she picked up her handbag and keys. Being happy because you're going to the supermarket in the middle of the day – 'How sad is that?' as her teenage stepsister Chloë would say.

Chloë. Who would have thought that Chloë would have looked like that as a bridesmaid – her hair up, skin glowing and a smile like half a melon. Chloë, who had sworn she would die rather than wear sugar-almond pink and who had behaved like an angel and seemed to have grown up to become a stunning young woman – for the day, at least.

Melanie laughed again as she went out.

The street was quiet. The sun had made the inside of her car too hot and as she didn't have anything so fancy as air conditioning, she opened the windows and door and waited for it to cool down. It was while she waited that she saw him, loitering along the opposite pavement, in the shade. He stopped to light a cigarette, his head turned away from her.

It struck her that she might have forgotten to double-lock their front door. There had been burglaries in the area, a spate of them, though mostly of the detached houses and ground-floor flats. Had she double-locked it?

God, was she going to turn into one of those women who had to go back nine times to make sure they'd turned the gas off and another three to double-check that the light wasn't on in the bathroom?

No, she was not.

She started up the engine and when she looked again the man had gone.

In the supermarket she picked up a copy of the local paper to read over tea in the café. And there it was. She hadn't even remembered they had sent in the details.

The photograph was quite large on the page because there were only two other weddings. It was the one of her looking adoringly at Craig, the one which Gaynor had pronounced 'Yuck'. But Mel liked it. Her dress looked its best, the silver beading shining and the silver quills in her hair looking as original as she had hoped. She had never seen anyone else wearing them. Pity about the lilies which the florist had foisted on her. They looked huge and stiff, the stalks too long, and she hadn't known how to hold them, up or down or what. They weren't like flowers, they were like something man-made. In the newspaper photograph they jumped out at you. Otherwise, though, it was nice. It was very, very nice.

Melanie Calthorpe and Craig Drew

The marriage took place, conducted by Senior Registrar Carol Latter, between Melanie, elder daughter of Neil Calthorpe of Lafferton, and Mrs Bev Smith of Lancaster, and Craig, youngest son of Alan and Jennifer Drew of Foxbury. The bride wore a strapless dress in white jersey crêpe with a bodice encrusted with crystals and silver beading and silver quills in her hair, and carried a bouquet of calla lilies. She was attended by Gaynor Calthorpe, bride's sister, Chloë Calthorpe, bride's stepsister, and Andrea Stannard, bride's friend, who wore burgundy off-the-shoulder dresses and carried posies of ivory roses with silver-ribbon accents. Lily Mars, bride's god-daughter, was the flower girl in a silver satin and tulle dress and carrying a basket of burgundy rosebuds. Mr Adrian Drew, bridegroom's brother, was best man, Carl Forbes and Peter Shoemaker, bridegroom's old school friends, were ushers and the reception was held at the Maltdown Hotel. The couple honeymooned in Gran Canaria and have made their home in Lafferton, where the bridegroom works as an estate agent with Biddle Francis and the bride as a receptionist for Price and Fairbrother, Solicitors.

She read it twice, read it again, and on the way out bought six more copies of the paper. In the car, she sent a text message to Craig and then drove home feeling as she had felt when her father had pushed her on the park swings so high she had thought that if she let go of the chains on either side she would simply fly up and up to heaven.

She came out of the brightly sunlit street into the dark hall of the flats and could barely see. The light on the first-floor landing had gone again. Individual flat owners were responsible for keeping the lights working on their own floor, changing the bulbs when necessary. Mel was annoyed. The people on this floor always seemed to be leaving their landing in darkness and it was dangerous. She would have to ask Craig to tackle them about it again.

It was only as she reached her own floor that she realised she had left the newspapers on the back seat of the car. She paused. Go on in, put the shopping away and get them later? Go back now? No, go on in, dump the shopping and then run back down again.

She unlocked their own door. The hall was bright from the late-afternoon sun streaming in through the window of the kitchen opposite. She set the bags down. She would cut out two of the newspaper articles and post them straight off to Nan and to little Lily's family. Cut one out for her wedding book. She'd have time to do that later while she was waiting for things to cook.

She went out of the flat and down the stairs at a run, almost tripping on the top step of the landing without a light. She had found a parking space a few yards up the street. Fished out keys. Newspapers. Yes, on the back seat. Waved to the elderly lady who sat in her chair at the window of the bungalow opposite for most of the day. Locked the car. She was out of breath. Unfit. The swimsuit had better come out again. There had been so much to do in the run-up to the wedding she had let her daily swim go – and she felt the difference.

Back to the house. She reached up to the keypad. But the front door was ajar. The people in the bottom flat often forgot to make sure it was properly shut and it made her mad. What was the point of having a front-door security lock to which everyone had the pass number if half the time it was not properly shut?

She trudged up the stairs. Along the unlit landing again. On up to their own floor.

She wished she hadn't had those calla lilies, they just overpowered the photographs, great stiff waxen things. It wasn't like her to be bullied, but she had been at the end of her tether, trying to find the right shoes all day, and somehow the florist had found a chink. Maybe she got a special deal on calla lilies. There certainly seemed to be an awful lot of them about. She had hated them on sight, but it was too late then and of course they didn't spoil the day. They did spoil the photographs though.

'Oh get over it,' she said aloud.

Had she left the door of their flat on the latch?

It was odd.

When she pushed it open.

In that split second, Melanie Drew registered that it was odd. Minutes ago, when she had dropped the bags there, the sunlight had been flooding from the kitchen directly into the hall. Now it was blocked by something. There was a darkness. A shadow. There was no sunlight. Odd.

As she went nearer to the kitchen she registered that it was a figure blotting out the light. Then everything was brilliant in an instant, brilliant, shattering light, with a noise that exploded in the centre of it.

Then nothing.

Nothing at all.

Six

'Cat! I thought it was you.'

Cat turned from locking her car. Helen Creedy was a few spaces away in the Cathedral Close.

'It's good to have you back – the altos have sounded pretty thin without you.'

'I don't think! But it's good to *be* back.' Cat looked around the old buildings of the close lit by the lamps that lined the paths. At the top end, the house in which her brother had his flat; down here, the east front of the cathedral towered over them. 'I haven't sung anything for nearly a year.'

'How was it?'

'Exciting. Challenging. Strange.' They walked together towards the door that led to the New Song School where early rehearsals always took place. Tonight, the first of the new season, they were making a start on Bach's *Christmas Oratorio*, a favourite of Cat's.

'What have you been up to, Helen? How are Tom and Lizzie?'

'Oh, fine. Actually . . .' Helen hesitated in the half-open doorway. 'There's something . . . do you think . . .' She was confused, not knowing exactly what she wanted to say.

'Am I a doctor here?'

'God, no – if I wanted to see you like that I'd come to the surgery. No – look, forget it, let's find our places.'

'Helen . . .'

But she had gone on into the rehearsal room, crossing to the far side, hurried, embarrassed.

The Song School filled up, and Cat was greeted with shouts of welcome from right and left. They queued to get their music.

St Michael's Singers rehearsals always ended with a drink in the nearby *Cross Keys* pub, but as Cat made her way along the cobbled lane she noticed that Helen Creedy was slipping off down the snicket that led to the close.

'Helen, aren't you coming for a drink?'

Helen turned. 'I ought to get back.'

'Lizzie and Tom not old enough to put themselves to bed? Come on, live a little.'

Helen laughed.

'Live a little.' She squeezed into a space next to Cat on the bench. 'Funny you should say that.'

'You were going to tell me something.'

'Yes.' Helen took a slow drink of lime and soda. 'I don't know where to start. I don't know what I want to say.'

Cat looked at her closely. 'Helen?'

Helen's face remained composed but her neck flushed scarlet. A roar of laughter came up from the group of tenors at the bar.

'You guessed,' she said, 'sort of. Only I'm confused, I don't know what's happening . . . I think it's OK, but I need reassurance maybe.'

Cat sipped her ginger beer. She had known Helen Creedy for some years as a patient she rarely saw and as a pharmacist she occasionally had to consult by phone. She knew her best in the context of the choir. But she had also seen fourteen-year-old Elizabeth in the first stages of near-fatal meningitis. She remembered it now, walking into the house expecting to see a feverish cold – and summoning the ambulance within three minutes, praying for it to be quick. Lizzie had made a full recovery and Cat had seen little of Helen since, other than on these choir evenings. She was a nice woman, but unconfident and reserved. Not someone Cat felt she was ever likely to know well.

Now Helen said in a low voice, 'I've met someone.'

'Helen, that's great! How long's this been going on?'

'Well, that's the thing . . . no time. Just the other night. It isn't what I expected, Cat. It was Lizzie really – she pushed me into it. She kept telling me I should . . .'

'Get out more?'

Helen smiled.

'She was right.'

'If I told you what I did, please don't laugh.'

'Wouldn't dream of it. Does it matter how people meet? I met Chris over a corpse in an anatomy lab.'

'Can't compete there. I went to a sort of agency. On the Internet . . . it's called *peoplemeetingpeople.com*.'

'And you did.'

'I never expected anything . . . well, maybe a few new friends.'

'Was this the first one you followed up?'

'Yes. It just all clicked. But I feel as if it should have taken much longer, that I should have met half a dozen others first.'

'That's like saying you want half a dozen people to look round your house and not make an offer before a buyer comes along.'

'I never thought of it like that.'

'Well, you should. I'm pleased, Helen. Friend or more than friend – it's good.'

'You don't think it's a bit . . . I mean – doing it this way. I haven't told anyone else.'

'Why should you? No one else's business.'

'It isn't, is it?'

'Are you going to tell me about him?'

'We've only met once. And he phoned just before I came out tonight to ask me out again. We're going to the theatre tomorrow. It just seems to be rushing away with me.'

'Don't you want it to?'

'I don't know.'

'What's worrying you?'

'Nothing. I suppose I hadn't even thought I'd meet someone local – he even lives in Lafferton. I don't know.'

The choirmaster was pushing his way through the crowded bar to greet Cat. She said, 'Well, if you want to talk about it again ring me or we can meet. Sounds to me as if you just need someone to tell you you're doing the right thing.'

Driving home, Helen played a tape of the Dixie Chicks which Elizabeth had given her for her last birthday, 'to keep you up to date, Mother', and recalled the phone call from Phil. 'I really enjoyed myself. Can we meet again soon? Can I take you to the theatre tomorrow?'

Yes, she had thought, but not said. Hesitated. Pleaded a possible meeting with an old friend. Would have to check. Would ring him back. Had put the phone down and immediately decided she had been too cool, put him off, pushed him away. She wanted to go but did not know if she should.

When Elizabeth had asked if she was all right she had snapped; when Tom had made a joke about her evening out, she had rounded on him.

She turned into Dulles Avenue, taking a short cut. A house halfway down was floodlit. Police vehicles and white vans were parked up and the whole of the front was cordoned off behind tape. Helen slowed instinctively, glancing to see what was happening. A policewoman standing at the gate peered at her.

She sped away as the Dixie Chicks sang of a travelin' soldier.

Seven

He remembered the day. He remembered everything about the day. But the bonfire that had flared inside himself he remembered most of all.

'When can I go out on a proper shoot?'

'When you're twelve.'

And then he was twelve. He was twelve.

It was cold. His head ached with cold. His face felt as if he had lost a layer of skin because of the cold. His ears burned with cold. He was aware only of being cold and blissfully happy.

They had been walking since a little after nine, the spaniels running ahead, and they had an hour or so more before they would stop for lunch. They paused. There was a brief silence. A shot rang out. Another. The rooks rose in panic from the tops of the trees ahead.

You remember this, his father had said. This is the most dangerous form of shooting you'll know, until you get to shoot driven grouse. You're walking up and firing together. If you don't know what's *behind* what you're shooting at, you leave it be. Keep to the line. Watch and wait.

He had heard it like a lesson in church. *The most dangerous form of shooting*. He repeated the words to himself as he walked.

He was looking ahead but then something to the left caught his eye, a paler shape in a rough clump of grass. He stopped.

'All right, steady as you go. Watch carefully,' his father whispered. 'Is there anything behind it?'

'Hedge.'

'Keep walking. Keep watching.'

He did as he was told. Then the spaniel was there, flushing the rabbit out, sending it racing away and he was ready, aimed and fired and all in a second, his heart beating as fast, surely, as that of his quarry and it almost stopped beating too, almost stopped as dead as the animal he had just shot.

'Fetch.'

But the dog was there, retrieving, racing back across the field with the warm body soft in its mouth.

His hands were shaking. His father lifted the shotgun from him, safe in his own steady hands, but said nothing. Took the dead animal from the dog and slipped it into the bag. They strode on, catching up with the line.

He felt the cold again now. The wind had got up, whipping across the dry open field from the north-east, making nothing of thick jackets and caps. The rooks rose again above the trees, rose and fell, rose and fell. But he was kept warm by the hot fire of excitement and satisfaction burning up within him. He didn't need a word from anyone else.

He had looked up, scouring the winter sky for pigeons, the stubble for flocks of partridges, listening for the cackle and whirr of a pheasant getting up, determined to go one better. Prove something more. But not to them. To himself.

Eight

'Morning, everybody.'

Simon Serrailler went straight to the whiteboards on the far wall of the incident room.

Photographs.

Melanie Drew, alive and well, on her honeymoon.

The exterior of the block of flats.

Interior of the kitchen.

Craig Drew.

Melanie Drew's body. The whole body.

Melanie Drew's body. Detail of gunshot wounds.

Area map.

'Right, listen up. Melanie Drew. She was twenty-seven, married for just over a fortnight to Craig Drew. He works as an estate agent with Biddle Francis in Ship Street. Melanie worked as a receptionist. She had three extra days' holiday after they returned from their honeymoon. Craig had gone back to work. Now Melanie was seen in Tesco's on the Bevham Road at around three thirty. We have CCTV. She did a bit of shopping, bought a local paper, went for a cup of tea in the supermarket café. She then bought half a dozen more copies of the local newspaper. The folded copies were dropped on the floor of the kitchen just inside the doorway. They were bloodstained. CCTV has her leaving the supermarket at three forty-two and driving out of the car park. That's it. Her car was parked outside the flat as normal. Husband came home just after six – he cycles to and from Ship Street. On entering the flat, he found his wife's body. She was lying – here – inside the kitchen. Near the door. She'd been shot twice at close range, one bullet to the heart, one to the head . . . here . . . and here. Time of death is somewhere between four and six. No one was in the flat below, they were at work, and the owners of the ground-floor flat are currently away. No one saw Melanie Drew in Dulles Avenue. House-to-house hasn't turned up any reports of anything or anyone unusual, but most people were out – it's one of those dead streets by day. Not much traffic as it doesn't lead out directly onto the main road. This is, as they say, "one of those". Nothing was taken . . . husband can't think of a person in the world who would have any reason to attack his wife.'

'What about the husband, sir?'

'He's been interviewed. She sent him a text to tell him their wedding picture was in the paper.'

'Do we know what the gun was?'

'Yes. Ballistics have just come back with it.' He looked round. 'It was a Glock 17 SLP.'

There was a stir in the room but Serrailler went straight on. 'Right, I need background on Melanie Drew – work colleagues, family, everyone at the wedding. Close friends. Ditto on Craig Drew. As I said, we've done house-to-house in the avenue itself but we now have to spread that out into the adjacent streets – that's Caledecott Avenue, Tyler Road, Binsey Road and the cul-de-sac at the end of there called Inkerton Close. People hanging round, unfamiliar cars, all the usual. We've got nothing at the moment and I mean nothing. I'm doing a press briefing in an hour, we need them onside. Tomorrow we'll have posters, uniform will be at the supermarket handing out leaflets, we want to be sure anyone who was shopping there yesterday afternoon knows about it. Television news have it, Radio Bev has had it on several bulletins and they're running an appeal for info. I also want to go further back on Melanie Drew – previous place of work? We know she went swimming most days – I want someone up at the pool, talk to anyone who might have known her there. School. She went to the Sir Eric Anderson until sixteen, then to Bevham College of FE, so inquiries up at both – friends she had, any she still kept in with. OK, that's it for now, plenty to do. Thanks.'

'Needle in haystack, then?' DC Warren Beevor said on his way out.

'I know,' Serrailler said. He never minded brief groans and moans, as long as he heard them inside the building, not outside, and they represented a reflex reaction, not an attitude of mind. 'Get yourself a decent magnet.'

'You in all morning, sir?' DC Vicky Hollywell, small, plump, face folded into a perpetual expression of worry.

'No. I'm going back to Dulles Avenue. Why?'

'Nothing,' Vicky said anxiously. 'Just in case we need you.'

You would never believe, Simon thought, running quickly down the concrete stairs, that Vicky Hollywell was one of their best and brightest, who came up with original suggestions time after time. She only lacked the one quality which she would need to get her moving up the ladder – self-confidence.

He drove through Lafferton, thinking. He planned to talk to Craig Drew later, but first wanted to spend more time at the flat in Dulles Avenue. He had been there on the evening of the murder, before Melanie's body had been moved, but, in his experience, he could learn more from a solitary, careful assessment later when the crime scene had become less dramatic, less immediate and distressing. It would also be less busy. Too many people were around while a body was *in situ*, doing their very necessary jobs but lending the place a highly charged and unnatural atmosphere.

He thought about his recent dealings with appalling crime scenes, on his first case in command of SIFT. An area of rural Kent had been targeted by an arsonist. Four cottages on or near working farms, but in fairly remote locations, had been set fire to in the middle of the night. All had been occupied and a total of seven people had died including two children, all but one of the bodies burned beyond recognition. A fifth cottage had then gone up in flames, and another person had almost died.

After three weeks on that case, Serrailler had been glad to return to Lafferton and his new position as Detective Chief Superintendent, heading up CID. He had resisted a posting to Bevham, threatening – and half meaning – to look for another job outside the area if he was not offered Lafferton. Fortunately, the

Chief Constable had either taken his threat seriously or pretended to, and the Bevham idea was dropped.

He slowed as he turned into Dulles Avenue. A lot of the large houses here had been converted into flats during the past twenty years or so. It was a pleasant part of the town but not the most expensive, not like the Sorrel Drive area where the large houses were all still intact as single dwellings. In the sixties Dulles Avenue had been like that. Then it had gradually become run-down as the occupiers of the large houses died and many properties fell empty. When the houses were converted, it began improving again. Serrailler could see the police tape sealing off the crime scene. He parked on the opposite side of the road, well down from it, and began to walk, looking closely to right and left. Here, a spruce drive with white-painted fencing and a well-kept front lawn, a closed gate. There a scruffy drive with a badly parked motorbike. No gate. Here a house name – Belmont – next door to it just a number; after that, a house with half a dozen name slots beside an entryphone. A white cat sat on the wall, watching him as he approached. He stopped and put out his hand but the cat leapt away into some laurel bushes.

It was quiet. Most of the drives were empty, no one looked from front windows so far as he could tell. People were at work. Anyone could drive or walk up Dulles Avenue, stop, go into a house, come out again ten or twenty minutes later, and do so entirely unobserved.

He neared number 48. A solitary officer was standing on duty at the front door. A car came from the opposite direction, slowed, the driver peering at the house. The red-and-white tape moved slightly as it picked up speed again.

A few yards away Simon saw a Honda Civic parked, a man and woman sitting inside it. As he approached, the passenger door opened. 'Super?'

Adam Phillips from the Bevham newspaper. The woman would be a photographer.

Simon went over. He did not believe in being rude and obstructive to the press so long as they kept their side of the bargain.

'Hello, Adam. Nothing going on here, I'm afraid. I'm just

taking another look round, now forensics are out of the way, but I doubt I'll have anything to report.'

'Mind if I come in with you?'

Serrailler gave him a look. 'I'll be doing a briefing at four. I want to catch the local TV and radio news.'

'Anything you can tell me now?'

'Nothing. I would,' Simon said, turning away, 'if I could. Sorry. I'm not keeping you in the dark.'

Adam nodded and went back to the car.

But the DCS noted that the pressman did not drive away.

He ducked under the tape. Stood, looking around him. Tarmac drive. A couple of bushes in front of a low brick wall. Neat and tidy. Well-kept woodwork on front door and window frames. The door was open with more tape across.

He went into the communal hall. Again, it was well maintained. Clean. Staircase recently painted. Quiet. Unnervingly quiet.

There was a second uniform at the door of the top flat. Boring job, Serrailler thought. He remembered doing it years ago. Trying to stay alert, thinking of things to think about.

'Sir.'

'Morning. Nothing doing?'

'Not a thing. You going in, sir? It's not locked.'

'Thanks. Yes, I'm going in.'

The two flights of stairs to the top had rubberised treads so the noise of anyone coming up was slightly deadened. Not completely though. It would depend on the shoes.

The landing smelled faintly of pine cleaning fluid.

Melanie Drew had come up these stairs. Stood on this landing.

Serrailler opened the door. Silence came out of the empty flat, a blank, deathly, oppressive silence.

After a few seconds he went inside.

Any house, any room, in which there has been a recent murder, has its own atmosphere. He had learned that over the years and had experienced it often. There was sometimes a feeling of intense sadness and stillness, of melancholy. And sometimes of fear.

He remembered breaking into a luxury Docklands penthouse, accompanying the brother of a missing man, and the dreadful wave that had all but hit him in the face, the vivid sensation of pent-up violence and evil. They had both felt it, looked at one another and hesitated to go in.

The man had been chained and manacled, hung from a steel beam by leather cuffs and disembowelled. The atmosphere of the flat had lodged itself forever somewhere deep in Simon's mind.

Now, as he entered the bright, newly furnished flat where Melanie Drew had been shot there was a feeling of absolute emptiness. He went into the living room first. Then the main bedroom. The spare bedroom was full of boxes and packages, most of them labelled *www.everythingwedding.com* and 'Cream lamp and shade' or 'Navy towel bale X 2' or 'Casserole trio – Blue'.

His footsteps echoed on the polished wood floor.

Forensics had left their mark in the kitchen – chalked body outline, white circles, small stickers. The floor was stained with blood over a wide area, the walls splashed and spattered, as were one leg of the table and the side of a chair. But he had a strange sensation of – nothing. Nothing. No struggle, no fear, no presence at all. The flat might never have been occupied. It gave out no clue, not the slightest hint of who had been here and why.

It was the worst sort of case, the murder with no apparent motive, no witnesses, no public sighting of anything or anyone. Unless there was DNA from a person other than the victim and her husband. It felt cold, sealed, purposeless, empty.

Empty.

'Over 70 per cent of murders are committed by a partner or close family member,' Serrailler said to the waiting constable, who nodded and said 'Shall I close the door, sir?'

'Thanks. Do that.'

Outside, he rang the station and the new DS. 'Graham? Where's Craig Drew?'

'Staying with his parents, sir. He left the address as 6 Oak Row, Nether End, Foxbury.'

'Meet me out there in half an hour?'

'Sir.'

Graham Whiteside had been in Lafferton for a little over six months, having joined from the Thames Valley force. Simon did not know him well and had not yet formed a detailed opinion of him. He needed to. Since Nathan Coates had left, he had not sustained a close working relationship with any other CID officer and he felt the lack of it. He was someone who liked to work and plan and think alone, but out in the field he needed a good colleague who was bright, on his wavelength, loyal and reliable. Nathan, now an inspector in Yorkshire, had been that. He and his wife had a son, Serrailler's godson Joe, and were expecting a second child. He must get up there to see them, but at the moment Yorkshire might as well be the moon.

It was twenty past eleven. Indian summer. The leaves were duller but still thick and barely changing colour. He drove out of Lafferton into the country. Foxbury. Nice village, one of the last with a couple of working farms, some vegetable growing, not much in the way of new building.

Oak Row was on the very edge of it, six cottages together, in the past housing for workers on the adjacent farm. Similar to the first cottage torched by the arsonist in Kent. Serrailler remembered the acrid smell of the burnt-out building, the sight of twisted and blackened beams and rafters. Two people had died there.

But these cottages were whitewashed and spruce. Number 6 was actually two, Numbers 5 and 6, which had been knocked into one. Beyond were freshly ploughed fields leading to a view of Starly Tor.

The garden was colourful with dahlias and chrysanthemums, a rose in late flower. Two cars were parked outside. As Serrailler pulled in behind them he caught a flicker of movement at an upstairs window.

DS Graham Whiteside's car turned down the lane.

Nine

The back room of the cottage had an old-style sun lounge extending onto the garden. The door was open, the small enclosure hot under its unshaded glass roof. Beyond the long stretch of grass, with flower beds on either side, was a hen run in which half a dozen bantams were scratching around and what had probably been a ferret cage. Over the fence, fields, hedges, trees and Starly Tor.

Craig Drew sat on the wicker sofa, staring out as if looking at the garden and the view, but Serrailler knew he was seeing nothing, that his views were inward, tunnelled and dark. He had thick, tangled curly hair, a narrow face. His eyes were deadened, sunken down into the sockets. He was unshaven. His hands hung between his knees and the nails were bitten down. The DCS had seen him in his wedding photographs, happy, with his arm round Melanie's waist, wearing a morning suit and silver waistcoat, dark blue cravat. A good-looking, confident young man.

His father had brought them mugs of coffee and a plate of assorted biscuits which were on the rattan table in front of them, pink icing and chocolate coating already melting stickily in the heat. He was a man of fifty who looked twenty years older. His skin was weathered. He looked shrunken inside his open-necked shirt and trousers. He had set down the drinks and gone out again, touching his son on the shoulder as he passed. Two well-trained spaniels stayed close to his heels.

Somewhere in the far distance, a tractor turned the earth, droning steadily into earshot and out of it again.

'I don't understand this,' Craig Drew said without looking up. 'I don't understand any of it.'

'Mr Drew, I'm sorry to have to come here and question you again. I do know how distressing this is. We want to find out who killed your wife. That's why I'm here. It's the only reason. Do you understand that?'

Silence.

'You are not under arrest, you are not under caution. You are free to ask us to go at any time and we will leave. But it is in your own interests to try to answer.'

The young man sighed, a long, desperate, agonising sigh. He wiped his hands over his face, back over his hair. Sat up. He did not look at either Serrailler or the DS, but ahead out of the window, still into nowhere.

'I told the others. Didn't they write it down? – no, hang on, they taped it. Why don't you listen to the tape? You'd find it all out from that.'

'I need to ask you some things myself. I have listened to the tape but sometimes things are better understood in a personal interview. And you may have remembered something.'

'I wish to God I had.'

He leaned forward to pick up his mug of coffee but his hand shook so hard that the drink spilled and he set it down again.

'I'd just like you to remember again how your wife seemed that morning. I know it's painful but it is important. Was everything as usual?'

'She was fine. It was fine. She was – we'd only been married a couple of weeks.'

'I know.'

'She was wishing I didn't have to go back to work – she had another three days of holiday herself. I was wishing it. We'd have liked to go into Bevham together, there was some stuff she wanted to look at – curtains and . . . we wanted to have a day like that. But there wasn't anything else. She was fine. Lovely. My wife was lovely.'

'Did she have a serious relationship immediately before she

met you?' Graham Whiteside had barked out the question without warning.

Craig looked at him in bewilderment. 'I – she'd had boyfriends. Well, of course she had.'

'No, I mean what I say – a serious relationship?'

'I don't know. Not just before. She'd broken up with a guy called Neil . . . but it was months before. I think. I don't know. You'd have to . . .' He dropped his head suddenly, stared hard at the floor. His hands were still trembling.

You'd have to ask her, Serrailler filled in for himself silently. He was furious with Whiteside, but he let him run with his style of questioning.

'Why did you have to go back to work before her?'

'I said. She had a few more days owing.'

'That wasn't my question. Why did *you* have to go back? Surely you could have arranged more time off, as well?'

'All right,' Serrailler said sharply, 'I think it's quite clear.'

The sergeant gave him a sour look and reached for another biscuit.

'Craig,' said Simon gently, 'I know you have been over and over this in your mind but I do need to ask you again . . . is there anyone who would have had the slightest reason to harm your wife? Anyone from the past, the neighbourhood – from some time ago even? Had she ever mentioned being afraid of anyone?'

He shook his head, still looking down.

'What about your neighbours in the house? Do you know who lives in the other flats?'

Craig was silent for a long time. Then he looked up slowly. He seemed to have been miles away. To have been deeply asleep. He looked as if he did not know who the men were, where he was, what had happened.

But he said, 'No. There's an older couple in the ground floor. I don't know their name.'

'Brian and Audrey Purkiss.' The DS had his notebook and flipped over a page. 'That them?'

Craig shook his head.

'You don't know? Not even the name? Isn't it on their doorbell? Haven't you noticed that? How long ago did you buy the flat?' He was battering the young man with questions, they were coming at him like rapid fire.

Serrailler jumped in again. 'We've talked to your neighbours. No one was at home that afternoon. Brian and Audrey Purkiss were away. The house was empty. But whoever came in and went up to your flat, either had the security number to open the front door by the keypad or rang the apartment bell. And Melanie either let him in from upstairs or she came down to let him in.'

'She wouldn't,' Craig said, at the same time as the sergeant said, 'Or her. Him or her.'

Serrailler ignored him. 'Craig?'

'Who would she open the door for?' Craig said.

'Well, a friend. Her sister? Or stepsister? There must be plenty of people she would be happy to have come up to the flat.'

'Yes, but . . . of course there were – but not anyone who would kill her. Not anyone with a gun.'

'She wouldn't know, would she? She wouldn't know that the person ringing the doorbell had a gun.'

He shook his head again.

'I'd like you to go on thinking back . . . we need to know the slightest thing that might come to your mind as seeming relevant. Or odd.'

'What sort of thing?'

'Something she may have said. A person she may have mentioned. Or it might be an incident she referred to.'

'I don't know.'

'Keep thinking, Craig.'

'Where's your office?' Whiteside asked.

'Ship Street.'

'There all that afternoon, were you?'

'Most of it. I've told them this.'

'You haven't told me. Were you there all afternoon?'

Craig Drew looked across at Serrailler now, like a child looking to a parent to rescue him.

'Craig, please understand that we need to know everything – if only to get it out of the way. Did you have lunch in your office?'

'Yes. I went out to Dino's, the café in the next street. I got a sandwich and a coffee. I bought a banana as well if you want to know. I took them back and ate at my desk.'

'Anyone else there with you?' Whiteside asked.

'Yes. Three – no, four of us. We generally stay in the office over lunch . . . occasionally someone is out showing a client round a property . . . Stephen was. The rest of us were in.'

'Later on?'

'I caught up – I'd been away from the office, I'd missed what had been sold, what had come on . . . you have to keep up. Your own properties, other people's . . .'

'All afternoon? You're telling us you were there *all* afternoon?'

Why the aggression? Serrailler wondered. Why was Whiteside treating Craig Drew like a prime suspect? There were times for belligerent questioning. This was not one of those.

'No. I went out to meet a client – to show a property. It was on the new estate at Ciderholes.'

'What's his name?'

'She – it was a Miss Bradford . . .'

'And Miss Bradford will confirm this?'

'I don't know . . . I suppose so . . . I don't know what happened.'

'Happened?'

'She didn't show. I went there and waited half an hour and she didn't turn up. I couldn't get hold of her on the phone, so I went back to the office – it was getting on for half past five then. I just picked up my bike – I cycle to work – and went home.'

'How did you get to Ciderholes?'

'I borrowed one of the cars – we have a couple of company cars. I couldn't cycle all that way and back, and anyway, it doesn't look professional.'

'I bet. Funny this Miss Bedford –'

'Bradford.'

'Ah yes, Miss Bradford – sounds like she might be going for Miss UK, doesn't it? Funny she didn't show, didn't leave a message, you couldn't get hold of her. Odd that. Don't you think?'

'No. It happens. We get time-wasters.'

'Ah, I see. So this is what she was? This invisible woman?'

Simon Serrailler had never in his senior police career shown up a junior officer in front of a member of the public. He tried not to do so even in front of colleagues, though occasionally it was necessary. But he came as close as he ever had by nearly giving Graham Whiteside a dressing-down now, in front of Craig Drew and Craig's father who had come to offer them more coffee and to hover in the doorway when they refused.

Craig looked across at his father. He had tears in his eyes. His face was flushed. But above all he looked bewildered. He did not understand why he was being harangued, what the questions meant, what he had done wrong.

Nothing, the DCS wanted to say, you have done nothing wrong at all. Because he believed it. Craig Drew had not killed his wife. If there had been any doubt in Simon's mind earlier – and it had been a shadow of a doubt only – there was none now. Craig Drew was not a killer.

He got up. For a moment, Whiteside remained seated, eating yet another biscuit.

'We'll leave it there, Craig. Thank you for your cooperation and I'm only sorry we had to come. You understand that we may need to ask you further questions when any information comes to light? If we have any news at all I will contact you of course. We have a photograph of your wife and there's a poster going up as we speak. You may find that upsetting but it could help us a lot. People think when they see a poster, they remember things and they often come forward.'

'You've got to do it,' Craig Drew said clumsily. 'You've got to. I know that.'

'Thanks. Thank you for the coffee. Oh, and if you need to talk to me or there's anything you think might be useful, this is my card, these are my phone numbers, work and mobile. Don't think twice about contacting me.'

Whiteside's hand was reaching to the biscuit plate, but on seeing Serrailler's glare, he pulled it reluctantly back and followed him out of the cottage.

Ten

They had arranged this afternoon together over a month ago. Lizzie finished school at three on a Thursday, Helen had booked the day off.

She spent the morning sorting out her clothes. She ended with three piles: what she never wore, what she occasionally wore and what she often wore. Eventually, there were three bags for the charity shop, one for the clothes recycling bin, one for the dry-cleaner's. The rest, brushed and rehung, went back into the wardrobe where a large new space waited promisingly.

She met Elizabeth at the school gates, for the first time in goodness knew how many years, and they drove into Bevham. Three hours and many carrier bags later, they were back in Lafferton and having coffee and toasted teacakes at the new brasserie in the Lanes.

For the entire time, Helen had managed to keep the conversation on clothes and shoes with brief mentions of university entrance and the girl who was doggedly pursuing Tom.

The brasserie was quiet. It had been an immediate hit with local shoppers, office workers, young people, women meeting up for lunch, busy from the first coffee servings at ten thirty through to a lot of afternoon teas. It would be busy again after seven. Now, only a few people were drinking at the bar. They had got a table on the dais in the window which had a view down the Lanes towards the cathedral, and Helen was feeling pleased

– pleased to be with her daughter, pleased with her purchases, pleased.

'Right. Spill the beans,' Lizzie said, spooning up the froth from her cappuccino.

'What beans?'

'Well, something's happened. Come on.'

No point in stalling. Lizzie knew her too well. Lizzie had been the first one to say, 'You liked him, didn't you? It worked out, didn't it?' a couple of minutes after Helen had stepped in through the door after her first evening out with Phil. 'Good,' she had kept saying. 'Good,' as she had heard more.

She had also come home the next day and announced that a friend whose brother was at the school where Phil taught pronounced him 'Decent' and 'Not dumb'.

'Don't get excited. This is so daft I'm not sure he was serious.'

'*What* is?'

'He's asked me to go with him to the Jug Fair!'

'Oh. My. God. You are joking!'

'Apparently not. Since he rang again ten minutes later to say he hadn't been. Joking that is.'

'Actually . . . I think it's rather sweet. In fact, definitely it is. You can eat candyfloss together and hold hands on the ghost train and he can win you one of those pink rabbits with goofy teeth on the duck shooting.'

'Thanks a bunch.'

'You are going, aren't you?'

Helen had asked herself the same question several times, without coming up with a final answer. It was not the Jug Fair. That would be fine. A fair was a fair, whoever you went with, and if she couldn't enjoy herself at one she was a lost cause. But she sensed that if she went with Phil, she would be taking a definite step over a line between a single friendly outing and . . .

And whatever she had signed up on the Internet for.

'Mum?'

'Well, of course I'm going,' she said, wiping butter from her mouth. 'And I'm having another espresso too.'

Eleven

He was excited. He went to bed with the sick feeling of excitement he had had as a small boy on Christmas Eve. He had woken with the same thump in his gut as he remembered what day it was.

The perfect weather went on and on. The huge moons. The misty dawns. Hot days. Chill set in after six.

They were out at the grounds on the Clandine estate, fifteen miles to the west of Lafferton. Always were for the last shoot of the season. The woodland setting, the hill behind, the drop to the lake, everything was perfect. The hospitality was second to none. The sponsors were generous. But it was more than that. Everything came together at the last shoot. For him, it was more than a day out, a good lunch. He set out to win. He always set out to win. He had set out to win from the first time he shot at clays.

He was there early. They were still setting up. It was an English sporting layout of eight ten-bird stands and a hundred-bird team flush off the newly installed high tower. The best you could hope for. The birds would simulate high pheasant, very high pheasant, crossing pigeon, flushing partridge and various others incoming and going. There was no challenge like it.

People working for the sponsors were stretching a banner between two posts. The catering marquee was up. Land Rovers full of girls and cutlery baskets drove across the field.

He went back to the car. Stood leaning on the bonnet, looking,

looking, checking the atmosphere, the sight line, the backdrop, looking, looking. Getting his eye in.

A couple of members drew up beside him. He nodded. Went back to looking, looking. In a minute, he would walk from the tower, a hundred yards, out and back. Looking. He swung his arms. Turned his head from side to side. Keep loose. Keep flexible. Keep easy.

He used a 32-inch over-under. The same he had used for the past three years. The years he had won.

He began to walk away from the car. Pace evenly towards the tower, looking, looking. Swinging his arms.

But he was careful to go into the marquee afterwards, get a breakfast bap, hot bacon and mushrooms, from the smiling blonde girls, take it to a group table, talk, laugh, socialise. He didn't want to be labelled a loner. Loners weren't liked. Not trusted.

Not loners with guns.

He bit into the soft fresh bread and the salt bacon taste made the juices run inside his mouth.

'Champion again this year, then?' Roger Barratt said, clapping him on the shoulder.

He swallowed. Shook his head. 'Someone else's turn. I reckon I've had mine.'

They all laughed. He hadn't taken anyone in.

They were looping back the sides of the marquee already. It was going to be hot. Clear. Blue sky. Shooting to the north-east. Perfect.

He walked out, easy, relaxed, calm. Confident.

Twelve

'Raffles!'

But the dog was at the door before him, quivering. Phil Russell laughed as he unhooked the lead and put his hand on the door handle. Paused. The retriever looked at him, frozen, knowing but hardly daring to admit that, yes, he was home, yes, they were going on a walk. Yes!

Phil opened the door.

During term, Phil took the dog with him on a two-mile run every morning. A neighbour came and walked him again after lunch. But it was this occasional late-afternoon outing man and dog enjoyed most of all, into the car and off into the country beyond Lafferton. It kept them both sane.

Now, he turned onto the main road and east towards Durnwell. The river ran this way. The bank was fringed with pollarded willows.

He had come here a couple of times a week for years, with Raffles and with his previous dog. Once he had grown used to life without Sheila, Phil had enjoyed his own company. In any case, he saw enough people during the working day. Nothing was different.

Everything was different.

He stood for a while on top of a slope overlooking the river and threw the ball. He was training Raffles to the gun. The dog raced and dived, retrieved and returned, and it was only when he began to slow down on the way back with the ball in his mouth, panting with pleasure and tiredness, that Phil sat down on the grass. Raffles lay companionably beside him, the wet ball tucked beneath his chin. It had been another hot day. The midges seethed over the water.

Everything was different.

He did not know if he believed in a *coup de foudre*. It had taken him months to be sure of his feelings for Sheila, though once he was sure marriage had been the next and easy step. It was only in the last year that he had entertained the idea of looking for someone again and he had usually pushed it straight out of mind.

It had been the thought of winter that had troubled him, winter alone, now that Hugh was in Africa and Tom so wrapped up in his acting. Phil had resources. There was much that he could enjoy. Winter was the time for pheasant-shooting. But 'alone' had begun to read 'lonely'. The thought would not leave him.

He had walked into the pub to meet Helen Creedy hoping to have a friendly drink and to find a companion for the theatre from time to time. Helen Creedy. He had seen her and known, in a way he had never known anything since Sheila, that she would be important. Would change his life. Would . . .

Stop. He watched as a heron flapped up from the water and flew away, legs dangling, ungainly in the air as it was graceful at rest.

Stop.

Helen Creedy. What? He tried words in his head, watching the letters move about and come together, words like Enjoy. Friend. Pretty. Fun. Intelligent. Good. Talk.

Like Gentle. Sympathetic.

Like Company. Good listener.

Like Attracted.

Love.

Stop.

What was love? He had loved Sheila. Of course he had, though love had changed every year, as love did. Early love. Surprised love. Warm love. Protective. Married. Parent. Everyday. Companionable. Happy. Frightened. Anguished. Desolate. Bereaved love. Grief.

He loved Hugh and Tom. That was different.

What was this now? Attraction. Liking. Enjoyment. Pleasure.

Love?

The shadows were lengthening. The cloud of midges thickened and jazzed closer to the surface of the water.

Marriage.

Company. Like friendly. Relief.

Marriage. Partnership.

Love.

He stood up and offered to throw the ball again but Raffles wandered away.

Love.

He had rung Helen to ask her to the Jug Fair, an impulse, for fun. She had laughed. Agreed. For fun.

The Cocktail Party was at the Bevham Rep next week.

'I haven't seen a T.S. Eliot play for years.'

'They don't do them much.'

'Like Christopher Fry, out of fashion. Pity.'

'And John Whiting.'

'I loved John Whiting! No one has ever heard of him now.'

'*The Cocktail Party* then?'

'Yes please.'

Love?

Something was different. Something. He thought about Helen as he drove home, with Raffles asleep on the back seat.

Love?

He was bewildered. Something which had begun in a half-hearted way, something he had dared himself to do, had turned him inside out and he had no experience, no knowledge, no emotional resources to draw on for help. He felt churned up, with anxiety, confusion, regret even at having started this in the first place.

He had not wanted complication, he had wanted someone to enjoy the theatre with now and again.

The theatre and all the fun of the fair.

Thirteen

'Are you telling us you don't have any suspects at all?'

Serrailler had never felt there was anything to be gained by lying to the press though he had occasionally asked them to conceal a truth for a good reason.

'Yes.'

'The husband's not in the frame then?'

'No.'

'Are illegal firearms a growing problem in Lafferton now?'

'Not especially. On the other hand, illegal firearms are a growing problem throughout the country.'

'And it was definitely a handgun that was used? Do you know what type?'

'Yes, but I'm saying no more yet. Right, that's it for now. I'll let you know the moment we have any further news and, meanwhile, your cooperation is appreciated. Please try and keep the murder of Melanie Drew up there – someone has got to know something, or to have seen or heard something. We want to jog their memories. Thanks a lot.'

As he left the briefing room, Serrailler caught a glimpse of Graham Whiteside pushing his way through the media pack towards one of the reporters from Bevham who sometimes sold info on to the nationals.

'Will someone ask DS Whiteside to see me in my office?'

'Sir.'

As he went up to the CID room, he was planning what he would say. Whiteside would not like it. But he got no further. A DS came fast up the stairs.

'Sir, there's been a shooting at a house in May Road. Man holding woman hostage. Call just came in.'

'Let's go.'

She drove. Serrailler used his phone. By the time they were out of the station car park, an armed response vehicle was en route.

'What do we know?'

'A passer-by heard shouting from the house – then a scream. One shot. Man came to the window waving what looked like a gun. He had his arm round a woman's neck. Then he dragged her back. That was it.'

'Any names?'

'No, sir.'

'Who lives in the house?'

'Rented property, owned by Mr Theo Monaides.'

'He owns a lot of property round there. Tenants?'

'A Joanne Watson. Been there for a couple of months.'

'Alone?'

'They're still checking. Monaides' office says yes, alone, but a neighbour says a man has been seen coming and going.'

The car went round a corner on what felt like two wheels. Serrailler made a face. But the DS was a highly trained police driver. She spun expertly out into the main road and overtook two buses. The DCS closed his eyes.

There was the usual circus when they reached May Road, half a dozen streets away from the house in which Melanie Drew had been killed. Outside a semi, in the middle of the street, the press were already hovering, kept back behind the tape.

'Neighbours haven't been backwards in picking up the phone,' Serrailler said as he got out of the car.

Three uniform were holding the fort and the sergeant looked relieved to see Serrailler.

'You SIO, sir? We've had no further sighting, no more gunshots – if it was a gunshot.'

'Who reported it?'

'A woman, walking her dog. Lives over there, at number 17.

Seems reliable. She flagged down a motorist, he saw the man at the window with the gun and then, a few seconds later, with the woman. Used his mobile to phone us.'

'Has he opened a window, shouted anything out?'

'No, guv.'

'DCS Serrailler?' The sergeant in charge of the ARV was at his side, the vehicle pulled up a few yards back.

Simon filled him in.

'What do you want to do?'

'Wait. Just to see if there's any communication.'

'OK. Give us the word.'

Simon stepped back and looked up at the house. Then he walked off in the opposite direction, to think.

Inside the Armed Response Vehicle, six men waited.

'Always the bloody same,' Steve Mason said. 'Go like a bat out of hell then sit cooling your heels.'

'Probably a water pistol,' said Duncan Houlish.

'Somebody's shadow.'

'His own arm.'

'Kids. Often kids.'

But they were tensed as they waited, on the ready, pepped up and wanting to go. They were trained for it, trained to do, yet 90 per cent of their time was spent not-doing.

Clive Rowley looked at his feet. 'Get on with it,' he said under his breath.

'Could be linked with the other one,' Steve said.

'What? Melanie Drew?' Clive looked at him.

'Once you've got a lunatic with a gun out there . . .'

'What's to say he's a lunatic?'

Clive picked at the skin on the side of his finger. They yammered on. He preferred to stay quiet. Ready. Not that the others wouldn't be ready, but they talked too much.

It was hot inside the vehicle.

Steve's chewing gum went to and fro, round and round, with a wet clicking sound.

'Liverpool to win three–nil,' someone said.

'Be a draw. They haven't got the strikers.'

The talk shifted. Shifted back.
'Need air conditioning in here.'
'Your wife due her baby this week, Tim?'
'Next. She's had enough. Heat gets to her.'
'What's that, three?'
'Three up.'
Clive Rowley's right foot itched inside his boot. It was the kind of thing that could drive you mad, itching where you couldn't get at it. But the minute he unlaced the boot the balloon would go up.

Five minutes later, as Serrailler was walking briskly back, plan made, the door of the house opened and a man came out, hands up, shaking his head. A young woman followed him, clinging to his hand, crying that it was all nothing, he hadn't done anything, it had been a row about nothing.

The weapon was a popgun belonging to the woman's five-year-old son.

Inside the ARV the mood was deflated and irritable. They were trained for it. Up for it. Tensed for it. Swore liberally at another false alarm, another shift spent hanging about.

Outside the house, two PCs wound up the tape. The street emptied. The circus moved on.

'They should fine people like that, for wasting our time. A grand would do it,' the DS said, on the way back to the station.

'"People like that" don't have a grand. More to the point, a young woman was murdered and we haven't found her killer. You think we should have ignored this?'

She sighed. 'Trouble is, everybody gets twitchy. A popgun for God's sake.'

He decided to leave it. They would all be grumbling for the rest of the shift, not least the AR officers. They all knew that there were likely to be a lot more incidents of the same kind until Melanie Drew's killer was found because no one was going to be taking chances, anything halfway suspicious would get an overreaction.

He went up to his office. There were new files on his desk and he had to write up his report on the afternoon's incident. It was twenty past six. The report would take him fifteen minutes or so and the files could wait till tomorrow.

His father had returned from Madeira the previous evening. Simon thought he ought to go over there, offer to take him out for a drink which might lead on to a congenial dinner – in the unlikely event that Richard Serrailler would be feeling mellow in the aftermath of his holiday.

Fourteen

When he was four he had told his Mam he was going to marry her and when she'd stopped laughing and said he couldn't because she was already taken, he said he'd marry Stephanie then, only his sister had said she hated boys and hated him the most so that had been that, until he'd met Avril when he was fifteen.

He'd pined for Avril Pickering. He'd worked out how long before he could ask her out, then how long before he could get a job and start saving, how long till they could get engaged, how long till he had enough to rent a house and they could be married. He'd put it all down, figures in columns, everything. On paper it had looked all right to him. Fine. Then Avril Pickering had gone out with Tony Fincher. He'd seen them, walking down Port Street holding hands. He'd hated Avril Pickering. Not Tony Fincher, oddly. It wasn't his fault. It was hers.

He had planned to do something to her, make her regret it, but before he had worked out what it was going to be, it was the summer holidays and when they went back to school in September Avril wasn't there. The Pickerings had moved away. Scunthorpe, somebody said; London, somebody else. No one really knew.

He had gone out with a few girls after that. Four or five girls. The usual sort of girls. Nothing special. He began to wonder what the fuss was about. He told Stephanie. She laughed. He told Dad, one day when they were shooting. His dad had given him a look and said he'd got something there. What was all the fuss about? Right.

Then he had met Alison, introduced by Stephanie's fiancé, as he was then. Soon to be husband.

And everything had changed. Alison.

He sat nursing a pint, on his own, remembering, because there was a new girl on the front desk and her name was Alison and it had all clicked into focus again. Vivid. Seeing Alison. Hearing her. Watching her. The tiniest things. He could rerun it like a film going through his head.

Not that he'd ever forgotten. But when something happened, the same name, a little link, it went full on. Colour. Vivid.

He drank the rest of his pint slowly and steadily to slake the anger that always blazed up. Sparks. A breath of wind. A fire, running out of control, and for years nothing would dampen it down.

But then he found it.

Fifteen

Hallam House. It was dark when he approached it down the lane. The lights shone out onto the drive.

Simon stopped. It was still hard. He still hated coming to the house knowing that he would not see his mother, that Meriel would not be pruning or weeding or cutting something back in the garden or else visible in the kitchen or at her desk in the window of the small sitting room. He saw her now. The shape of her head, the way her hair was done, the way she glanced up and her expression when she saw him.

She had not always been there if he had called unannounced. Even though her busy life as a hospital consultant was over and she had stood down from several committees, she was still on the board of this and a trustee of that, often out. But when she was there, she made time for him at once, sat down, listened, caught up with news. Family first, last and always, she had said.

Simon missed her with a strength of sadness that was still raw and painful. He thought about her, had meant to say this or that to her, ask about someone or something.

He looked again at the house. The lights on and welcoming. But his father had never learned the knack of making his family feel especially welcome.

The kitchen curtains were not drawn and as Simon got out of the car, his heart lurched because she was there, he saw her, saw her standing beside the dresser, her arm raised to take something down, saw her as clearly as he saw the two stone urns filled with the white geraniums she had always planted in them, beside the front door.

He looked away quickly, terrified. How could his dead mother be there?

And when he looked again of course she was not.

'Simon? Have I missed a message from you? I don't remember your saying you were coming.'

'I wasn't far. Thought I'd drop by and see if you enjoyed your holiday.'

'I did indeed.'

As he followed his father into the kitchen, Simon caught a glimpse of her again, her back to him. Only the way she had done her hair was new. Meriel had always worn her hair upswept. Elegant. She had always been elegant. Even in old gardening clothes, elegant.

Meriel was dead. Meriel had been dead for –

'Hello.'

She turned round.

Her hair was quite different and she was far younger. But she was tall, like his mother, and with the same way of speaking. Odd.

'I don't think you've met. Judith Connolly: my son Simon.' Richard paused and his voice took on its usual faint edge of sarcasm. 'Detective Chief Superintendent Serrailler. He's a policeman.'

'I know,' she said. Smiling. Coming over to him. She held out her hand. 'Hello, Simon. I've been wanting to meet you.'

There was a smell of cooking. Something simmered on the stove. Since his mother's death, the kitchen had lost some of its warmth and the small touches that had made it special. There had always been flowers and flowering plants on the window ledges; there had been notes pinned to a cork board, reminders about meetings written in Meriel's striking italic hand and bright blue ink; there had been a row of musical scores on a shelf next to the cookery books, and photographs of them all as children next to new ones of Cat's sons and daughter, stuck up everywhere. But the plants had died and never been replaced, the music had gone to Cat; some of the photographs had fallen down or curled at the edges. The noticeboard was bare. Simon hated going into the kitchen. It was the one room where he missed his mother beyond bearing.

Now he noticed some scarlet geraniums on the ledge, neat in their pots with saucers beneath. There was an unopened bottle of wine on the table. Glasses.

Who was this?

'I take it you've seen your sister,' Richard said.

'Of course. They're back and fully functioning. It's brilliant.'

'I'll telephone Catherine tomorrow.'

'Don't you think you should drive out there, Richard, not just telephone? They'll be longing to see you.'

Simon looked from the woman to his father and back again. Richard said, 'Oh, I doubt that.' But he was smiling.

'Will you stay for supper, Simon? I've made a chicken pie that will feed half a dozen. I always cook too much.'

Who was this? What was she doing, cooking in his mother's kitchen, inviting him to supper, telling his father where he should go, who he should see? Who was this?

She handed him the bottle of wine. 'Would you open this?' Smiling. She had a warm smile.

She was – what – late forties? Tall. Light brown hair with some careful, fairer streaks. Straight. Very well cut. Pink shirt. Necklace of large almond-shaped stones. Large mouth. Slightly crooked nose. Who was this?

His father said, 'Should we eat in here or shall I lay the table in the dining room?'

'It's so comfortable in here. Simon, do stay. We don't have any holiday snaps to bore you with.'

Holiday?

His father was avoiding his eye.

Simon picked up the bottle and went to the drawer for the corkscrew but she had it in her hand. Held it out to him.

Her look said, Don't ask now. Later. He will tell you later. I will see to it.

He took the corkscrew. She smiled.

Tall. But not like his mother. Not his mother.

In his mother's place. In her house. Her kitchen. Cooking in her kitchen. Not his mother.

He wrenched the cork hard out of the bottle.

Sixteen

The evening air smelled of bonfires. Cat Deerbon walked towards the east door of the cathedral in the gathering dusk and the woodsmoke drifting on the air was nostalgic of childhood, school satchels, her first year as a junior doctor, running across to the hospital from her room to answer a bleep when the groundsmen were burning the leaves. And her mother in the garden at Hallam House, tall and elegant in jeans in her mid-seventies, pushing the debris of the summer borders into the glowing heart of a small, neat and well-controlled bonfire.

Cat stood for a second catching her breath at the vividness of the memory, wishing she could go there now, make a mug of tea, chat, catch up.

The cathedral was still and almost empty at the end of the day. Two vergers were changing the candles in the great holders on the high altar. Someone was brushing the floor at the far end of the chancel with a rhythmic scritch-scratch of bristle on stone.

There was no service. Cat had had to drop in a letter to the New Song School and she always took the chance to sit in the cathedral for a few moments when she could, centring herself, reflecting, bringing some of her patients and their problems with her to leave in the peace and holiness of the building. She had only just returned to the practice. There were new patients, old ones returning with new problems, nothing dramatic yet. Her energies were going into opposing some changes, learning to work with others, battling the system. Chris, still not fully recovered from a lengthy jet lag, was refusing to argue, refusing to compromise, unusually irritable. But she was determined to win on one front, determined to do some nights on call, seeing her own patients when they needed her most. It would all settle down.

She closed her eyes. Her mother was there again, rekindling the bonfire with a handful of sticks and weeds.

'What would you do, Ma?' And the voice replied, 'What your professional conscience dictates, of course – tempered by common sense. And don't call me Ma!'

Cat smiled. Footsteps down the aisle beside her pew. She looked up and nodded to the verger. The smell of guttering candle wax reached her as it wove its ghostly way down the nave. She bowed her head, prayed for a few moments, then left, pausing as always to look up at the glory of the fan-vaulted roof, the stone angels on the tops of the columns blowing their gilded trumpets.

She had missed a lot of things during their time in Australia and this cathedral perhaps the most.

As she walked out into the warm evening, her phone beeped for a text message from the surgery.

Urgent ring Imogen Hse re Karin M.

Karin McCafferty. The last time she had spoken to Cat was before Australia, but she had sent a couple of emails. She was fine, she had said, still fine, scans all clear, two years after her diagnosis, the oncologist at Bevham General was 'surprised but delighted'. 'Dare say that goes for you too!' Karin had ended.

Karin had refused all forms of orthodox treatment for a late-diagnosed and aggressive breast cancer and had embarked, against Cat's best advice, on a journey through all things holistic, naturalistic, alternative – both familiar and what Chris called 'wacky'. Karin's husband had left her to live with another woman in New York, but her business as a garden designer and horticulturalist had flourished and so had she. Against the odds and the medical advice, she had got well and stayed well.

Chris called it a statistical aberration, Karin called it a triumph. Cat had been both delighted – and furious. She had found it hard to talk about – and had replied only briefly to Karin's last email.

Now she stared at the message on her phone.

She went back to the car, texting as she walked. A message to Chris that she was going to the hospice, *Get curry out freezer*.

How strongly did a doctor want to be proved right when being right meant a patient's terminal illness and death? How much had Cat wished for Karin to be both wrong, totally and utterly and profoundly wrong, and yet cured? What would her mother have said? She desperately needed to know, but Meriel's image was no longer vivid in her mind. Meriel had faded. She was leaving her to sort this one out by herself. 'You don't need me,' she heard her say.

Oh God but I do, Cat thought, as she stood, afraid to drive to the hospice, not wanting to find out what was happening to Karin, smelling the last faint smoke from the burning of the leaves.

Imogen House. There was change here too. The new wing was complete, the old senior sister had retired, a couple of other nurses Cat had known well had moved on, new ones had arrived. But Lois on the reception desk for evenings was still there and greeted Cat with a look of pleasure and a warm hug. It was Lois who was the first face of the hospice when patients arrived at night and were apprehensive as well as desperately ill. Lois who welcomed relatives who were afraid and in distress, Lois who made every one of them feel at home, in safe and loving hands, Lois who was cheerful and positive but never too chirpy, Lois who remembered every name and who absorbed what she could of the anxiety and dread.

'Karin McCafferty?' Cat said.

'Came in last week. She's been refusing to see anyone at all, but this afternoon she asked if you were back.'

'How is she?'

Lois shook her head. 'Be prepared. But it's more than her physical state, which is actually better now they've sorted out her pain control. She seems very angry. I'd say very bitter. No one can get through to her. Maybe you'll have some luck.'

'I might. I can guess what's making her angry. Surprised she wants to see me though – Karin's very proud, she won't want to lose face.'

The telephone rang. 'People,' Lois said to Cat, before she answered it, 'behave unexpectedly. You know that as well as I do. There's no second-guessing how it's going to take anyone. She's in room 7.

'Imogen House, good evening, this is Lois.'

The sense of calm and peace Cat always experienced walking through the quiet corridors of the hospice at night met her as she left the reception area, though there were voices from some of the wards, and lights were on. Whatever their beliefs about death, Cat thought, no one could fail to be affected by the atmosphere here, the lack of rush, the absence of noise and bustle that was the inevitable part of any other hospital.

She turned into B wing. Here, rooms 5 to 9 were grouped around a small central area which had armchairs and small tables, and double doors that led onto a terrace and the hospice garden. Patients who were well enough sat here during the day or were pushed out in wheelchairs and even beds, to enjoy any fine weather. But now the doors were closed and the room empty.

Or so it seemed. But as Cat went across to room 7, someone said, 'I'm here.'

Karin McCafferty was sitting in the chair closest to the darkened windows. The chair was high-backed and turned away, towards the light. Cat realised that she had failed to see her not only because of that but because Karin, who had never been tall, seemed the size of a child curled up in it.

Cat went over and would have bent to hug her but Karin made a movement to lean back and away from her.

'I was afraid I'd die,' she said, 'before you got home.'

Looking at Karin in the light from a lamp in the corner, Cat understood that this might well have been so. The flesh seemed barely to cover her, her skin had the transparent gleam and pallor of the dying. Her fingers on the chair arm were ivory bones interlaced by the blue threads of veins. Her eyes were huge in deep sockets sunk into her skull.

'Don't gloat,' she said, looking intently at Cat. 'Don't crow because you won.'

Cat pulled up one of the chairs. 'You think very badly of me,' she said. 'I'm sorry.'

Karin's eyes filled with sudden tears and she shook her head furiously.

Cat took her hand. It lay almost weightless in her own. 'Listen – everything fails. Sooner or later. Everything. We don't know nearly as much as we pretend. You did what you believed in and it gave you time – good time too, not time recovering from awful side effects, not time without your hair and being sick and exhausted or recovering from major surgery. You had the courage to reject the orthodox. And, for you, for a long while, it worked. What do I have to crow about? You could have had surgery and chemo and radiotherapy and been dead in six months. Nothing's guaranteed.'

Karin smiled slightly. 'Thanks. But it *has* failed. I'm angry with it, Cat. I believed, I really and truly believed, that it would cure me for good. I believed that more than I have ever believed anything, and it let me down. It lied to me. They lied.'

'No.'

'I'm dying nevertheless – and I wasn't going to die. I was going to stay well. I thought I'd beaten it. So I feel totally betrayed and if anyone asked me, should they go down the road I took, then no, I'd say, no, don't bother. Don't waste your money or your energy or your faith. Put your faith in nothing. None of it's any good.'

The tears splashed down onto Cat's hand, and now Karin leaned forward so that she could be held.

No one can get through to her. Maybe you'll have some luck, Lois had said.

Cat felt Karin's frail body shake in a fury of crying. She said nothing. There was nothing to say. She simply held her and let her cry her tears of weariness and pain, disappointment and fear.

It took a long time.

In the end, Cat helped her to bed and sent a text message home, fetched tea for them both and came back to find Karin lying, white as the linen of her high pillows, exhausted but calm.

'Have you been in touch with Mike?'

Karin's mouth firmed. 'No, I have not.'

'Maybe he'd want to know?'

'Then he'll have to want. I've moved on from all that.'

'OK. It's your call.'

'There is . . .' Karin hesitated. 'I want to talk about it. About dying.'

'To me?'

'Do you know what happened to Jane Fitzroy?'

Jane had been the chaplain to Imogen House and a priest at the cathedral.

'No, but I could find out. She went to a convent – I had an address before we went to Sydney – and if she isn't there any more they'll probably know where she went.'

Simon might know, she thought but did not say.

'I liked Jane. I could talk to her.'

'I'll do whatever I can.'

'I'll try not to die first.'

Cat stood up. 'Do you want me to come and see you again?'

'If you can bring Jane.'

'And if I can't?'

Karin turned her head away.

After a moment, neither saying any more nor touching her again, Cat went quietly out of the room.

Her phone buzzed the receipt of a text message as she crossed the courtyard.

Feel crap going bed. Si here mad as hatter. Hurry up. Xx.

Seventeen

Ten past six. This end of town is quiet. Offices shut. Shops shut. And the *Seven Aces* not open till eight. Plenty of time.

Timed it right. Perfectly calculated.

The floor of the old granary looked dodgy but he'd been up twice and it was better than he expected. He'd walked on the beams and the boards. Tested. There was woodworm. Dust flew. But it wasn't about to give way under his weight.

The evening sun had warmed it. There was straw and white splattering where the swallows had nested in the summer. They'd found the holes in the roof. He came up the old fire escape at the back. He wore trainers with the soles covered in thick wedges of polythene foam. No prints.

It smelled of wood and dust and dryness. There was a FOR SALE sign on the temporary fencing at the front. DEVELOPMENT POTENTIAL. Half of Lafferton. The Old Ribbon Factory. The canalside buildings. The old munitions store. Now this. Lafferton was changing. Apartments, boutique shops, smart offices.

He didn't mind. Not sentimental. Wasn't born here anyway. Nowhere near. Safer that way.

He'd come up here three days ago, at this time. Looking down onto an empty street. The odd car, but the granary wasn't on the road to anywhere and this end of town was still run-down. Not for long. But run-down now. Which suited.

He left the door open behind him.

He'd already done the run twice, silently across the open granary loft, slip through the door, close it, rope secured over the fire-escape rail. Quickest. He was good at ropes – no one knew that – ropes and the beam, from being seven or eight. Small. Agile. Strong arms.

Behind the old complex of buildings there were two ways he could take. The path leading to the canal, overgrown, trees and shrubs in the way, so he'd pushed through it half a dozen times. He'd go that way, make a narrow track through, and then along the towpath, running. Easy. The other way was a gravel path leading to the street.

The van was parked in the next, Foster Road, halfway down. D.F. STOKES. PLUMBING. CENTRAL HEATING. CORGI REGISTERED. 07765 400 119.

All over the house, girls were dressing up. Miniskirts, nurses' aprons, schoolgirl blouses, St Trinian's ties. Claire Pescod was Lady Godiva, her own hair but with extensions, a flesh-coloured leotard. Her chief bridesmaid-to-be was dressed as a lady vicar, another girl as a cowgirl, shrieking with laughter, fighting for the mirror.

Claire's mother, laughing. 'I spent my hen night in the pub. Your dad and his best man turned up just before closing time.'

'Mum!'

'Didn't matter. We had a good time.'

'We're having a good time. When's the limo coming?'

'Ten to eight.'

'Too early.'

'Mum, Page says ten to eight's too early.'

'Well, you can't change it now.'

'Oh help.'

On and on, mascara, glitter, lip gloss. Fake tattoos. Badges with 'Claire's getting wed'.

Seven. Seven thirty.

'Good God!' Claire's dad, skirting round them in the hall. 'Don't come near me, I stink of oil.' Off to the shower. 'Have a good time, girls. And behave.'

Half the street out to see the stretch limo. White. Black windows. Champagne. Confetti. Chauffeur.

'Behave.'

'Be good.'

'Be careful.'

The limo backed, slow and stately, inch by inch, down the road. Cars stopped for it. Hooted. A man got off his bike. An Alsatian went mad on the end of a leash.

Champagne.

'Here's to you, honey.'

They showered her with rose petals, concealed in skirts and pockets, inside the car, shrieking with laughter, looking out at Lafferton through darkened windows.

He had waited for two hours. Calm. Unworried. Occasionally checking the sight lines through the space a few inches to the left of one of the boarded-up windows. The boarding-up was split, and worm-eaten as well. He had brought nothing to eat, a single can of drink which when finished he crushed up small and put in his pocket.

It was warm. Snug. He was alert. Ready. Tense but not anxious.

Occasionally he had walked the length of the loft and back.

At first it was quiet but in the last half-hour or so it had grown lively outside. The *Seven Aces* opened at eight. The fluorescent and the neon went on outside the club and on the boards and hoardings. The pavement turned blue and green. Faces were orange. He had worked it out to the second. Took the rifle down from the false cupboard behind the ceiling boards. Left the front panel off to replace it quickly afterwards. Loaded.

Positioned himself. The sights were perfect. Take a stag at three hundred yards. More.

He waited. Only now his heart began to beat faster. As it should. But he was cool. His hand was steady.

The white car glided to the kerb outside the club, caught in the whirling lights, now blue, now green, now pink, now gold. The doors opened and they started to spill out, laughing, shrieking, arms waving.

Claire Pescod.

He had her in his sights.

Aim for the heart.

But a split second and the girl in the silly cowboy hat stumbled and reached out.

The shot glanced off the cowgirl before hitting Claire, too, but not in the heart, not clean.

Outside, the screaming rose and rose.

Chaos.

But not here.

Here he reached up and stowed away the gun, replaced the panel and then went surely, lightly, across the broken rafters and through the door. Dropped the wooden bars. Turned for the metal fire escape and the rope and slid, fast.

At his back the screaming increased until it was like the crying of a thousand seagulls following him away.

Eighteen

'Mummy it's going to be the Jug Fair, it's going to be the Jug Fair.'

'Mummy, we can go, can't we, we always go to the Jug Fair?'

'And I'm old enough to go on the big rides now.'

'Don't be stupid, you're not, you wouldn't be allowed, you'll be on the teacups again with Felix, nuh nuh nuh.'

'Mummeeeee . . .'

She could deal with her own squabbling children easily enough. But not Simon.

Simon was leaning against the dresser with a mug of coffee in his hand.

'OK, what's that face for? – as Ma would have said. Sam, stop winding your sister up. Have you finished your homework? No, don't answer that, just go and do it. Didn't Dad make you?'

'He went to bed with his jet lag.'

'Good excuse! Hannah, don't whine. Now GO. You on duty, Si?'

'Yes and no.'

'What's that supposed to mean? Well, I'm having a glass of vino. Are you staying to eat?'

Simon shrugged.

'For God's sake, I can't cope with three of you *and* Chris's everlasting jet lag. What's happened, Si? Oh, before I forget, do you have an address or a number for Jane Fitzroy?'

Simon looked wary.

'Karin McCafferty is in the hospice. She'd like to see her.'

'Bad?'

'Bad.'

Cat slipped out of her shoes and lay back on the sofa with her drink. She closed her eyes and centred herself back home, winding down, gathering her resources slowly to cope with supper, the children's bedtime. And her brother.

'Dad's got a girlfriend,' Simon said.

She opened her eyes. 'Ah.'

'Is that all you can bloody say?'

'Er . . . I could do "Good" if you prefer.'

'How can you possibly say that?'

'Good. There, said it again. Take that look off your face. Good. Good. Good. If Dad has got someone to be with, good. Why shouldn't he have?'

'You read *Hamlet*?'

Cat sighed and got up. She poured a glass of wine and handed it to her brother. 'If your phone rings ignore it. They can manage. Now get that down you and stop being ridiculous.'

'I knew you'd take that line. I just bloody knew.'

'Dad is alone, he is lonely – though he would bite out his own tongue rather than admit it. He misses Ma, it's over a year since she died –'

'Exactly. Only one year.'

'Time enough – if he thinks it is. Anyway, how do you know?'

He told her. 'I couldn't bear it . . . she was in the kitchen, at the stove, getting things out of the cupboards . . . she was in Ma's place. I couldn't bear it.'

'Get over it. This isn't about you, it's about Dad. Who is she, anyway?'

'Some woman called Judith Connolly.'

'Don Connolly's widow?'

'No idea.'

'If so, she's lovely – God, what a brilliant outcome. Don Connolly was one of the cardiologists at BG and, ironically, he died of a coronary.'

'Bad advertisement.'

'Nice man. Judith's delightful – quite young. She was his second wife.'

'Making a habit of it, then.'

'Oh shut up. Come on, Si, look at it another way. It might take the pressure off us – not that there's been a lot.'

'How do you know? – you haven't been here.'

'Well, has there?'

Simon shrugged again.

'God, I could hit you. You're behaving like Sam.'

'Drop it, then. I just hated it, Cat. It was . . . I saw her in the kitchen through the window. It was a bad moment.'

She put her hand on his arm. She knew. Simon and their mother.

His mobile rang.

While Simon was outside where he could get a better signal, Cat went upstairs. Sam was sitting at the small desk in his room reading a comic. Hannah was in bed, asleep, fully clothed. Felix was in his cot looking grubby.

Everything blew up inside her at once and she went into the bedroom, furious that Chris could not organise his children properly, dismissive of his continuing jet lag, but as she reached the door Simon called up the stairs that he had to go.

'Another one,' he shouted.

'What?'

'Another shooting. I'll ring you.'

The front door slammed. Good, she thought, take his mind off Dad. But then she pulled herself up short. Someone was probably dead, and they had still not found the killer of the young woman in Dulles Avenue. There was nothing good about it.

Sam had slithered past her, hoping to prove invisible.

'Sam, if you've finished your homework it's –'

'*Mummy*, come here!'

You didn't ignore anyone who called out like that.

Sam was standing, frozen, in the bathroom doorway, and as she came up behind him he turned to her, his face puckered with fear.

Chris was lying awkwardly. He was banging his head on the floor, his eyes were rolling back and a line of froth was bubbling out between his half-open lips.

Nineteen

The ball cracked into the pins. Four down.

Phil groaned.

'Right, stand back.' Helen bent, swung her arm back. Tried to look as if she knew what she was doing. It was her first visit to a bowling alley and she was enjoying herself but uncertain if her lower back might not be agony the following day. She smiled. So what, so what? She cast a glance sideways at Phil. Yes, she thought, and sent the ball down fast.

'Eight.'

'You have done this before.'

'No, honestly not. Beginner's luck.'

'Quite.'

'I'm still winning.'

It was the fourth time they had been out in ten days. Luck. Yes, speaking of luck.

'Is that your mobile?'

'No.'

'Well, it's coming from your bag.'

The phone was playing 'Love Changes Everything'.

'God. Elizabeth! She must have reprogrammed it. It used to play "Oranges and Lemons".' But as she dug around, the ringing stopped.

'My turn. Got to do better than eight.'

'Hang on.' *Lizzie* it read. 'I'd better call her back.'

'You won't get a signal in here. Phone her outside.'

She headed for the exit, and as she got into the air of the forecourt the phone rang again.

'Mum?'

Lizzie. Sounding unlike Lizzie. Sounding ten years old again.

'What's the matter?'

'Mum . . .' Her voice came through shuddering breaths.

'Where are you?'

'There's been a shooting. At the *Seven Aces*. We were waiting to go in. We're in the street, everyone's in the street, they wouldn't let us leave, there's police, they won't let us leave –'

'A *shooting*?'

'Two girls. It was a hen party going in, they were going into the club, we were in the queue . . . Mum, I think one of them is dead, they both might be dead . . .'

'Don't move. We're coming.'

'They won't let us move, the police won't let us move, there are armed police, God, there are two ambulances –'

'We're coming, OK?'

The signal died as she ran back through the entrance area to the bowling alley, screaming for Phil.

Mobile ringtones fighting for attention in the narrow street. Sirens.

Simon's own phone rang as he got out of his car. 'Can't talk. It's a shooting.'

'Oh God, Chris is on the bathroom floor, he's having a fit.'

'Sir?' The armed response command came up and Simon cut Cat off.

They had done a good, quick job on the scene in front of the club. Those who had been queuing were inside the foyer area, the public held back, tapes in place. The ambulances were there, a couple of paramedics inside treating for shock, four or five behind the screens which had been set up.

Simon went through. One body lay on the ground, covered, blood seeping. Another was concealed by the huddle of green-suited figures, drips held up. DOCTOR. Fluorescent yellow letters on green jackets.

'One dead, one badly injured. They were part of a hen party going in together. A couple of the others are inside being treated but they're not critical. Just shocked. That one is too bad to move.'

'Any ID?'

'Yes. The other girls told us. Dead one was Claire Pescod.'

'Any idea where the shots came from?'

Bronze Command pointed to the buildings opposite the club. 'Either somewhere in there, but it's a semi-derelict building –'

'The old granary.'

'– or next door . . . offices – top floor unoccupied, no one there at this hour.'

'Night security?'

The armed officer shook his head.

'Any sign of the gunman?'

'I've sealed off both buildings and they're secured. We'll go in after we've completed the exterior check. If he's in there, he won't be going far.'

'How long's it been?'

'Twenty minutes. We've been here ten – the second ARV followed straight on.'

'Right. Thanks. I'm going inside. Who else is here?'

'DS Willis, DC Green.'

The paramedics were lifting the injured girl steadily, slowly, drips still held high, crowded round the stretcher.

'DC Green?'

'Sir?' Fiona Green turned from the club doorway.

'Go in the ambulance. Doesn't look as if she'll be in any fit state to talk but we need anything you can get. Let me know.'

'Sir.'

'David?' Simon spoke to Sergeant Willis as he went into the foyer of the club. 'I need to set up a temporary incident room here. Is there an office?'

'The manager's already handed his over to us, guv. He's with the rest of the staff. They're waiting in the bar.'

'How many uniform have we got?'

'Four outside, two in.'

'That'll do for now. Right, let's get on with it.'

Twenty

He was not out of breath. He had walked steadily for a couple of hundred yards. Got into the van, moved off, driven out onto the Bevham Road. Speeded up on the bypass.

Three miles. Turned left. Country road. Drove at forty. Turned right into the old airfield.

Rabbits fled away in the sweep of the headlights. It was a warm night.

Doused the lights. Switched off the engine. Torch. It took a couple of minutes to peel off the panel.

D.F. STOKES. PLUMBING. CENTRAL HEATING. CORGI REGISTERED. 07765 400 119.

He rolled up the plastic and slipped it under one of the corrugated-iron panels of the hangar, between the metal hoop and the struts. Seven struts down. It was completely hidden.

He was back on the road by nine ten. Heading in.

Twenty-one

'Send the ambulance away,' Richard Serrailler said.

'Dad, he needs to go to hospital.'

'You heard what your father said. Send the ambulance away. You heard what I bloody well said. Just do it, why can't you?'

Cat knew that this was not Chris, equable, cheerful Chris, not the Chris who was her husband but some other man, some irritable stranger leaning back on the sofa with a pillow at his head. But she was hurt in spite of what she knew.

She had telephoned her father and the ambulance, and her father had arrived first, with Judith, who was now upstairs with the children. Chris had come round slowly from his fit and she had managed to help him downstairs. The paramedics had tried to take over but Chris had lost his temper and sworn, and only agreed to sit here under sufferance. He had been going to take a shower, he said, and he planned to continue.

The green-suits stood by, waiting for a decision. Cat got up and beckoned them outside. 'I'll persuade him,' she said, 'and then my father and I can bring him in. I'm sorry about this.'

'So long as you can manage, Doc. But you should try to get him to come with us, it'd be safer.'

'I know. But you heard him.'

Their bleeper went for another call and they left. Cat watched the ambulance turn in the driveway. Not wanting to go back into the kitchen, not wanting her medical mind to throw information at her which she wasn't ready to deal with.

She headed upstairs.

They were on the big bed, Judith and all three children, Felix asleep on his tummy, the other two leaning against her listening to *The Fantora Family Files*. Hannah had her thumb in her mouth but she pulled it out as Cat appeared.

'Is Daddy dead?'

'Has Dad gone in the ambulance?'

Cat sat down beside them. 'No and no, he's on the sofa having a glass of water and Grandpa is with him. When he's feeling up to it, we'll drive him to the hospital.'

'Why? That's what the ambulance does, it drives people to hospital.'

'Daddy will be more comfortable in the car.'

'Going in an ambulance is cool.'

'Yes and uncomfortable.'

'I'm happy to hold the fort here,' Judith said.

'Thank God you could come.'

'Yes, thank God you could read to us, you're a good reader aloud,' Hannah said, wriggling closer to her. 'She'll be able to look after us, we'll show her where everything is and what we do.'

'And what time you're supposed to be asleep, which is *now*.'

'Right,' Judith said. 'End of this chapter and then I learn how to put the Deerbon Three to bed.'

'Felix is easy-peasy, you just dump him down.'

'And I put myself to bed so there's only the baby-waby girl.' Sam dived for cover.

Judith closed the book with a snap. She said nothing but both children went quiet.

Cat slipped out.

Chris was sitting as she had left him, his colour better, his expression mutinous.

'I'm not going anywhere,' he said. 'You heard. Now bugger off, the pair of you.'

Twenty-two

'Serrailler?'

'It's me, I'm at . . .' But Cat could hear the sirens and voices down the phone. 'I'll talk to you later. I'm at the hospital with Chris.'

'Hold on.' Simon walked a few yards away up the road. 'It's just a scare . . . some kids letting off fireworks but some woman thought it was a shooting. What's wrong with Chris?'

'We're waiting for an MRI scan. I tried to tell you. He had some sort of fit.'

'When? Why?'

'I don't know. Dad's here with me.'

'Guv?'

'Got to go. I'll call you as soon as I'm free. Text me.'

'Yes.'

'Cat? Chin up. It'll be fine.'

'Will it?'

'Yes. Chris is tough.'

The woman had gone to hospital as a precaution, shocked but unhurt. The rest of the street had calmed down.

In the armed response vehicle they were preparing to leave, after another abortive call-out.

'What *is* all this?' Clive Rowley said. 'As if we didn't have enough, with a real killer out there. Flaming kids.'

'Didn't sound like kids. Men, that woman said.'

'She wasn't thinking straight.'

'Hardly surprising.'

'Probably cap guns. You ever have a cap gun, Clive?'

'No.'

'My dad's still got his. No caps though. He says they smelled of sulphur . . . give out quite a crack though.'

'Could have been caps. Could have been fireworks.'

They had scoured the streets but whoever had terrified the woman and whatever had made the gunshot noise had long gone.

'You on training this weekend?'

The ARV was backing.

'Yes. All of Unit 3.'

'Tim?'

'No. Baby should be here by then. I'm off from tomorrow.'

'My back itches,' Clive said.

It itched right in the middle, beneath the body armour and his shirt, driving him mad, but he'd have to wait until they had checked in and been stood down before he could get at it.

'What do you reckon?' he asked Duncan. 'Nuts?'

'This lot? More like malicious.'

'I meant the other one. The one earlier this evening. He's killed three women now.'

'Two. Two dead. Tonight's was a deer rifle with telescopic, Dulles Avenue was a Glock. Doesn't have to be any connection.'

'Course there's a connection. Got to be.'

'Why? Coincidence.'

Clive shook his head. 'I don't buy that. No one's heard a gunshot in Lafferton for years apart from that bloke who topped himself and then we get three women shot in three days. Got to be a connection.'

'You heard if forensics came up with anything at the old granary?'

'Not a sniff. Not yet. Give it time. I don't think he was in the granary at all, me, I reckon he fired from the roof of that office block next door.'

'They'll have to go all over that as well.'

'What makes you say that, Steve? That he was on the roof? They found that rope by the fire escape.'

'He jumped across. Easy enough. From the roof he'd a clear sighting down onto the street.'

Clive Rowley shrugged and twisted about, trying to get at the itch and not succeeding as the vehicle swayed round a corner. False alarms were going to happen until everything settled down. Women thinking they'd heard gunshots, kids messing about – inevitable. Frustrating.

But there were two good days coming up – training days were always good. They reminded you what it was all about, what you were there for, what might happen and how you dealt with it. They kept you up to the mark, sharpened you. This time round they were training on the old airfield. Best of all. 'Kids,' his sister said, 'you're like a load of bloody kids, running round playing goodies and baddies.'

He was off tomorrow. He might go up there. See her, see her kids. He hadn't been for a couple of weeks. Let her wind him up about being a big kid himself. The van pulled up outside the station. Clive was the first out. Couldn't wait to get processed and then strip to sort out his flaming itch.

Twenty-three

'You know too much,' Richard Serrailler said, 'inevitably.'

The radiography waiting area was empty, quiet for the night. The plastic tiles had been mopped and a bright yellow V-board planted in the middle. DANGER OF SLIPPING. WET FLOOR.

'I know what people mean,' Cat said, 'when they say they can't stand the smell of hospitals. You don't notice it when you work inside one all day but when you come in like this, it's unbearable.'

'Listerine,' Richard said. He was standing, looking at a poster about tuberculosis.

'I wish I didn't know anything. Right now, I wish I was waiting for a neurologist to come and tell me good news and I wish I was able to hang on to it.'

'You can do that.'

'Can I?'

He went on reading.

'I rang Simon,' said Cat.

'I hope Simon is busy catching people who shoot young women dead.'

'Dad . . .'

Anyone else would have helped her out, turned, smiled, made some gesture, but her father was not like that. She had something to say so he waited to hear what it was. He was not unkind, not unfeeling, as Si believed, he was rational. 'Simon was a bit surprised to meet Judith. But don't hold it against him. He wasn't expecting it and he misses Ma more than any of us.'

'How can you be the judge of that?'

'Sorry. But you know.'

'And you? What do you feel?' Now he did turn to look at her.

'I miss Ma, of course I do, I miss her now, I wish she was here now more than anything.'

'I meant what do you feel about Judith?'

Cat looked at her father. I have never understood you, she thought, never known what makes you tick. None of us has – almost certainly Ma never did but she found a way of living with you, and I have always felt that you and I had a good relationship in spite of it. Simon is the only one who does not, cannot and probably will not. Yet at this moment you might as well be a rather unsympathetic stranger.

'I like Judith,' she said. It sounded lame but exhaustion and anxiety hit her like a fist in her gut so that she felt suddenly faint.

Richard did not speak, he simply walked away, out of the waiting area and down the corridor.

Cat thought nothing. She was beyond thought. And perhaps it was easier to be here alone.

He returned with a plastic cup of coffee and handed it to her. 'Difficult,' he said. 'I know it's difficult.'

Cat sipped. It was black and sweet.

They had not talked in the car: Richard had driven and Cat had sat in the back with Chris, who had grumbled for a short time that he had no reason to be going to hospital and had then fallen completely silent until they arrived. He had remained silent, not meeting her eye, responding curtly to the immediate questions, nodding agreement to the scan.

'He knows,' she said now. 'He knows the score as well as we do.'

'He knows the options but it is always harder to make objective judgements about oneself.'

The door of the scanning suite opened. How could she have sent so many patients here and never had any real idea of what it was like for them to go inside, and for their families to wait out here, wait for the news, wait for someone in a white coat to start talking to them in language they did not know, give them news they could not interpret? Not yet. Not here.

She stood up. The registrar was a young woman.

'Shall we talk here or do you want to come into the office?'

'Is my husband . . . ?'

'He's going onto the ward. I need to admit him at least for the rest of tonight and Dr Ling will see him tomorrow, if you're happy with that?'

Christina Ling. Consultant neurologist.

'May I see the scans?'

'Yes of course. Dr Serrailler?'

'I am not an experienced interpreter of MRI pictures,' Richard said.

'Come with me all the same,' Cat said. She did not need her father for emotional support, she would not ask for his shoulder, she needed to draw on his detachment, his professionalism, his ability to rationalise, even with his own family. It was a sort of strength.

The screen glowed neon blue, the strange, impersonal image like an illustration in a textbook.

Cat stared. The cross section – the slice, the layers of this image inside the bony cavity – was the inside of her husband's brain, Chris, the father of her children, Dr Chris, the man she loved and had been with for fourteen years. Chris. Chris's brain.

Dr Louise Parker, the badge read in black letters on pale blue plastic. *Neurological Senior Registrar*.

She was leaning forward, pointing at the screen with the cursor.

Richard Serrailler cleared his throat.

'Yes,' Cat said. 'I see it.'

It was always the way. You knew, but you pretended you did not; you feared the worst, not because you were a pessimist but because you knew the medical facts. It was your job.

She had known.

'The lesion is here,' Dr Parker said, highlighting the shadowed area. 'It's already quite large. He must have had symptoms, but they can grow pretty rapidly as you know. The pressure just reached a point where it triggered off some electrical activity, causing him to fit. It would explain the mood changes – personality changes.'

'Yes,' Cat said.

'Has he complained of headaches?'

'He has, but he didn't imply they were severe – I put it down to the stress of packing up and travelling. Jet lag. He's been very tired – I should have realised. I should have known it wasn't prolonged jet lag.'

'Easy to miss. He says he's vomited a couple of times in the last few days.'

'He didn't tell me. Why didn't he say anything?' She looked at her father but could not read his expression because there was none. He might not have heard the conversation.

Chris's brain. She looked at the shadowed portion, trying to assess exactly where the tumour lay in relation to the rest, to assess the prognosis, to behave as if she were a doctor and this were a patient's scan. To behave like her father.

'It doesn't look good,' she said at last.

'No. Dr Ling will look at it first thing tomorrow and talk to you about the options.'

'May I see Chris?' I am a helpless relative, she thought. Everything has changed.

'Of course. I'll take you along. Dr Serrailler?'

'I'll wait in the car. No point in crowding him.'

Chris was in a side ward. The lights were dimmed. Three other beds, one with a prone figure, one humped over. One with the curtains drawn. Murmured voices. Drip stands. Cat felt a swell of fear.

He was propped up on a pillow rest. Hospital gown.

'I'll go and see if someone can find him pyjamas,' the registrar said.

Hospital pyjamas.

But he was Chris. He looked no different. Somehow she had expected him to have changed.

He looked at her. Looked away.

'Why didn't you tell me?' She hadn't meant to accuse. 'You must have known it wasn't just jet lag.'

'I used to have migraines – in my teens. I thought they'd come back.'

She put her hand on his.

'Seen the scan?'

'Yes. MRI diagnosis is for the experts. You'll see the neurologist in the morning.'

'Where are the children?'

'With Judith.'

'Who's Judith?'

'Dad's friend. You've had a sedative, don't worry.'

Chris was silent. Drowsing? Thinking?

She moved to get up but he turned his hand quickly, pinning her own down. Cat leaned over and stroked his forehead. 'I'll come in early.'

'If it's a grade-four I want you to give me a morphine overdose. Promise me.'

'Don't try and diagnose yourself.'

'*Promise me,* Cat.'

She was silent. She could not promise. She could not begin to think of what it would mean if he was right. But he wasn't right.

'A glioma. Anything above a grade two. Please.'

'Try to sleep. But you know there are plenty of other brain tumours. Don't leap straight to the worst. Don't think about it any more tonight.' For God's sake, she thought, how stupid. How stupid, stupid, stupid. *Don't think about it any more*. As if.

She leaned over to kiss him.

Chris turned his face away.

'Strange,' Richard said as they turned out of the hospital car park. 'The symptoms are contradictory. The epileptic fit and the drowsiness indicate a brain stem tumour whereas the mood changes are consistent with one in the frontal lobe. Glioma, would you say? Has he had eye problems? There's certainly no ataxia that I could see.'

Cat struggled to reply. The car seemed to be airborne, streaming ahead down the bypass. Her father had always been a careful, safe and very fast driver. Her mind was a swirling mass of images and nothing would stay still.

'What did Chris have to say?'

She meant to reply that he had been sedated and not very

communicative. She said, 'He made me promise that if it was a grade-four I would give him an overdose.'

'Ah. Interesting.'

'*Interesting?*'

He did not reply.

'For heaven's sake, there are dozens of possibilities, aren't there? It could be benign, in which case it might be amenable to surgery and he'll make a full recovery. It could be amenable to radiotherapy. It may not even be a tumour. An MRI is hard to read, you said so yourself.'

'Not that hard.'

'My God, you are a comforter. I'm struggling here, Dad. I need you to help me.'

'Of course I'll help you. What on earth do you expect?'

'You sound so clinical.'

'I'm a clinician. So are you. Just because I'm talking like a medic doesn't mean I am without any feeling. I'm extremely sorry for Chris. It is not a road I would wish anyone to have to travel.'

'How can someone ask his wife to kill him?'

'He spoke only of one particular circumstance.'

'In any circumstance.'

'Easily. I would do the same.'

'Never ask me.'

'Martha,' Richard said now, as they stopped for a set of red lights, 'would have asked for it, if she'd been able to. I see that now.'

'Martha?'

'As it was, your mother had to take the burden on herself. At the time, I was horrified. I was blinded by grief to the truth, which was that it was the right thing to do. I was unable to think rationally – to see reason. Your mother had to see it for me.'

The lights changed and a motorcyclist roared across their path as Richard accelerated. He braked and swerved and the bike vanished into the darkness in a trail of exhaust smoke. They turned right. They were on the country road. Three miles or so from Cat's home.

'What is the statistic for the deaths of young men on motor bicycles?'

'I want you to stop. I need you to tell me what you mean.'

'No need to stop. It was perfectly clear.'

'No, it was not perfectly clear.'

'Don't shout at me, Catherine.'

'I don't understand what you just said. About Mum and Martha. You have to tell me.'

She looked at him as he drove. His narrow face was set in a neutral, calm expression as he watched the road. I do not know this man, Cat thought, but I do understand why Simon feels as he does.

'I would probably never have told you. But now you know. Your mother gave Martha an injection of potassium. She could not bear to see her existence continue in that way. She told me and I agreed to say nothing to anyone else. Until now I've kept that promise. But as the subject arose again it seemed appropriate to tell you. I presume you agree we should keep this between ourselves?'

Twenty-four

It was very late. Judith sat in the Deerbons' friendly kitchen and thought about the day her husband had died.

She had been making notes for a case conference about a child they thought they would have to take into care. There had been a cat then too, huge and grey with scarred ears. Gasper, named by David. Fifteen years before. A scrap of pathetic fluff found in a puddle by her daily help and brought to them in a duffel bag. Now David was in the Congo saving lives, Vivien in Edinburgh doing her vet training and Gasper was spreadeagled in a patch of late sunshine on the kitchen table beside her, one paw occasionally reaching out to scratch half-heartedly at her file. Don had gone fishing, leaving at dawn. He never woke her. She had come downstairs just after seven but he had been long gone to his favourite stretch of the Test.

The Deerbon cat, Mephisto, was on the chair opposite her, a tight, neat ball, paws tucked away.

She remembered making a pot of tea and looking at the clock to work out when to put the casserole in, thinking about her case, worrying about it as she always did. Taking a child from its parents was never easy, she never felt other than anxious about it, that was why she had been reading the case notes again.

She remembered the child's name. Campbell Wild.

Don should have been home by eight. There had been the sound of the car a little after seven. Good, she had thought, I can go for an early bath and Don can peel the potatoes after he's sorted out his fish. Assuming there are fish.

And then there had been the sound not of his key in the door but of the bell. Ringing, ringing.

He had managed to struggle to the bank before falling onto it, face down, as the pain of the coronary hit him, and had lain there half the day before a couple had come by, walking their Labradors.

It had been her husband's registrar, who had turned up one Sunday morning a month later and simply told her that he was going to drive her there and that perhaps she might want to pick some flowers to take with her. He had been the week before, he said, on a recce. Knew where to go, found the spot. He had been gentle and firm, a nice boy with a strangely domed forehead, rimless spectacles. When they reached the exact place on the riverbank, he had gone away and left her alone for about twenty minutes. Afterwards, they had gone to eat a steak in a nearby pub. He had sussed that out in advance too.

Mephisto stirred and yawned and burrowed more deeply back into sleep and then there were the lights of the car swinging into the drive.

But it was Simon who came into the kitchen, and then stood looking at her, glancing around then back at her again, and she saw that his initial surprise and disapproval had been quickly shuttered. His expression blanked to nothing.

'What happened?'

Seeing him, tall and pushing his white-blond hair off his face in a gesture she recognised even in this short time, she felt intensely sorry for him. She saw not a man of nearly forty and a senior police officer but a boy.

'Simon, I'm sorry – first you find me in the kitchen at Hallam House and now here. I know what it looks like.'

'Oh. What does it look like?'

Children react like this, Judith thought, remembering how David had been the same. The best way was to carry on as normal and let them come round. Or not. She filled him in.

'The children have been fine. They're all asleep now. Can I make you tea or something?'

'I'll do it. I'll make coffee. You?'

'Thanks. Yes, I would like some.'

He opened cupboards, took out the cafetière, set the kettle to boil, all with his back to her. She stayed on the sofa, stroking the cat. Waiting. There was no point in saying more and making things worse. He minded. She had been in his mother's place, and now she was here.

'Are you on duty?' It seemed all right to ask.

'Yes. Everyone is on alert at the moment.'

'The shooting, yes. Has there been another?'

'Yes. One girl shot dead, another hurt. And a false alarm. The town's wired up with it. Every time someone coughs in a quiet street we get an emergency call.'

'All women. All young. And shot. For what? Dear God.'

She watched him pour the boiling water on the coffee grounds. There was something about the way he bent over, the set of his head, that made her feel for him even more. Richard had every right to be seeing her. She had every right to see him. But that would not be the way it seemed to Simon. He set the coffee down. 'Budge,' he said, shifting Mephisto. The cat turned, rearranged himself into the small space between Simon's leg and the chair arm and closed his eyes again.

I shouldn't be here, Judith thought. I am an unwelcome intruder. She felt, as she had often felt as a widow, ill at ease and out of place in the midst of someone else's family, another person's home. It was the loneliest and the bleakest of feelings.

Twenty-five

There were six of them round the table. The Chief Constable, Chief Superintendent Gilligan, Armed Response Gold Command, a DCS from Bevham and Serrailler with one of the DIs from the Lafferton force.

Simon had already done a briefing that morning. The wounded girl had died during the night without regaining consciousness. The team was out on house-to-house, questioning everyone who had been in and around the *Seven Aces* club, visiting the workplaces of the murdered young women. It was the usual routine, painstaking police work which might lead somewhere.

The Chief was grim-faced.

'Simon, are you a hundred per cent sure there is no connection between these young women killed outside the nightclub and the one . . .' she glanced at her papers ' . . . Melanie Drew, murdered at her flat?'

'No. Of course I'm not sure. How can I be? But at this stage the only connection we've made is that they were all at the Sir Eric Anderson school. The nightclub girls were best friends. Melanie Drew was older. We're still talking to people and we're still checking everything – churches, sports places, societies they might have joined, even pubs and restaurants they could all have frequented. We've checked out Melanie's husband and Claire Pescod's fiancé but found no link at all.'

'So it's coincidence?'

'Coincidence happens, doesn't it, ma'am?' The DI spoke. 'This is a lunatic with guns. He likes shooting. Doesn't care where or who.'

Andy Gilligan shook his head. 'That sounds casual and careless, and he's neither.'

'Or she.'

'Unlikely, but all right if you want to be correct. The murder of Melanie Drew was carefully timed. Not many people about, she was alone in the flat, it may well be that it was being watched. The club shooting was from a carefully prepared spot, probably from the roof of Bladon House, though possibly from the old granary next door. There is absolutely no trace of anything or anyone – forensics are still going over it but there isn't even GSR. Someone who is a good marksman, someone who has prepared a getaway meticulously . . . this isn't a lunatic roaming round Lafferton with a pistol; this is a clever, cunning psychopathic killer.'

'Who will kill again.'

'Almost certainly.'

'But if there is no connection between his victims how can we second-guess where he will be next?'

'We can't,' Simon said, taking a swig of water. 'We can't cover the entire town. We don't have the justification.'

'Or the resources,' the Chief put in.

'This isn't a terrorist.'

'And no warnings? No demands?'

'Not a thing.'

The Super leaned back with a groan. 'The worst bugger of all.'

'Young women,' Paula Devenish said. 'Let's think of places where young women congregate. Let's try to get one step ahead of him. Schools. The college. Where else?'

'There are two gyms and there's the swimming pool.'

'The ice-rink.'

'Any more clubs?'

'There's a place called *The Widemouth* in Monmouth Street . . . it's a bar with dancing, though, not really a nightclub, and it's more upmarket than the *Seven Aces*. It's popular with the twenty-somethings. Stays open till midnight.'

'Any place opposite that a marksman could hole up in and get them in his sights?'

Serrailler and the DI said, 'The multi-storey,' as one voice.

'Right. Let's have some visible patrolling up there and in the streets around, especially when they're spilling out at the end of the evening.'

Simon sat bolt upright. 'The Jug Fair,' he said. 'That's coming up – weekend after next.'

'Why would he stake out the Jug Fair?'

'Why not? Plenty of young women, crowds, lots of noise to cover the sound of shots.'

'Well, it's possible.' Andy sounded doubtful.

'There's always a strong police presence there,' Simon said. 'We've had some yobbishness, drunken louts causing trouble. I wonder if he would take the risk?'

'Better have ARV on high alert, even so.'

'We're on it already, ma'am,' Andy said.

'Now, as there are two items on the agenda for this meeting, let's move on to the second. As you know, the Lord Lieutenant's daughter is getting married in the cathedral on the tenth of November and there are royals on the guest list. Security is tight, as always of course, but in view of all this, it'll have to be even tighter. Royal protection will come from the Tactical Unit but Clarence House have noted the shootings and want a meeting. Eleven o'clock next Tuesday morning in my office – you too, Simon. Meeting with Sir Hugh Barr – the Lord Lieutenant and father of the bride – his PA, someone from Clarence House, someone from royal protection, the Dean and myself.' The Chief got up. 'We could do without a high-profile wedding with royal guests.'

'At least they'll pay for their own protection.'

The Chief looked over her shoulder on the way out. 'We should be so lucky.'

Twenty-six

'Dr Deerbon?'

Short. Dark, close-cut hair. Clipped voice. She glanced at Cat. 'And you are Dr Deerbon's partner?'

'Wife.'

'Please sit down. Just give me a moment, would you?' She flipped open a file. Turned over a couple of sheets. Looked for some minutes at one, then a second. Turned to address Chris. 'And you came in last night by ambulance to A & E?'

'No, I brought him – well, my father and –'

'Why?'

'Why?'

'Why on earth did you bring him by car? He needed an ambulance. With symptoms like that in a car without any paramedics . . .' She shook her head.

'I'm a doctor. So is my father.'

'GP?'

'I am – Chris and I both are. My father is a retired consultant.'

'Neurologist?'

'No.'

'Right.' She pursed her lips and was silent again, reading the file, turning the sheets over and back.

She was mid-thirties. She had not smiled. Always smile at the patient, Cat thought.

'I have the scan results here. Are you experienced at interpreting an MRI?' She looked at Chris but did not wait for him to answer. 'It's the best tool we have. It's pretty watertight. How long have you had symptoms?'

He shrugged.

'He didn't mention anything. We've been in Australia,' Cat said.

The doctor ignored her.

'Hard to say.' Chris looked at his hands. 'I had a headache. All the last week we were in Sydney, but we were packing up, it was hot. I didn't think anything of it.'

'Visual disturbance?'

'Slightly. I thought I might need stronger reading glasses.'

'You make it sound very vague. It can't have been. Not with a scan like this.'

'I suppose I was trying to ignore it.'

'Not a good plan.'

'If it's a grade-four glioma it wouldn't have made any difference.'

'But I don't think it is. Grade-three, possibly. Not a four. And though I think it's unlikely to be benign, we need a biopsy to be sure. I could be wrong.'

But you think that is almost out of the question, Cat thought. Self-belief is your speciality.

'Thanks.' Chris stood up. 'Not a lot more to say, is there?'

'Treatment. There's that to say.'

'There is no treatment. Don't take the piss.'

'If you'd sit down, I could go through the options. You may not be up to speed. GPs rarely are, I find. How long is it since you diagnosed a grade-three glioma?'

'About two months ago, as a matter of fact. Thirty-six-year-old man, six foot six, bronzed and fit, swimmer, diver, one of Australia's many outdoor sports fanatics.'

'So in that case you know that in many situations we can operate to relieve pressure.'

'Depending on the site of the tumour.'

'This one looks possible.'

'There's no point.'

'You won't say that when the headaches become more intense, which could be any day now. We'll also give you the maximum number of radiotherapy bursts – ten I should say. That will keep the worst of the symptoms at bay for a time. I'll put you down to start next week. We want to get on top of this. It won't wait.' She stood up. As she did so, Chris turned to Cat as if he was about to say something but instead was suddenly and violently sick.

In the car park he said, 'Remember.'

Cat did not need to hear more. 'Chris, don't ask me. I would do anything to help you, to get you through this.'

'Anything except what I want.'

'You can't ask your wife or anyone else to kill you – I can't, I won't and you shouldn't even think it, no matter what's happening to you. I don't want to have this conversation again.'

He sat beside her in silence all the way home. Dear God, Cat prayed silently, get us out of this.

She made an egg salad and coffee and set the table on the terrace. It was as warm as June, the wasps sailing insolently close to their plates, but the stems of a dogwood at the far end of the garden were already turning red, blazing in the sun. The grey pony came ambling across the paddock to the near fence.

Chris said, 'I didn't understand what patients meant when they said, "I can't take it in. I haven't taken it in." Well, I do now because I can't.'

'No.'

He put down his fork. 'Tell me what to do, Cat.'

She reached for his hand. The feel of his skin and flesh and bone, the utter familiarity of this man's hand, was unnerving. She was thinking of it as the hand of someone dying, a hand she should not love too much because it was going to be taken away from her. It was unimaginable.

'I think you do as she said. She was a bitch. She should be in a lab, not dealing with people – God knows how other patients cope with her, totally bewildered by everything in there, not only by what might be happening to them but by the jargon and the procedures. She should never have to speak to a patient again for the rest of her life. But she was right. You have to do what she said. You know that.'

'Is there any point? How long is it going to take – six months? Max. Do I want to spend that time recovering from brain surgery, exhausted by radiotherapy? I'm not sure I do.' He sounded infinitely weary, even at this stage, too tired to bother with any of it.

'Yes. They need to do a biopsy. They can reduce the size of the tumour.'

'To buy me time.'

'What's wrong with time?'

'Oh, nothing whatsoever from where I'm standing.'

'Surgery and radiotherapy will buy you time – and good time, Chris. Maybe quite a long time. And if the biopsy is good –'

'It won't be. They never are.'

'Rubbish and you know it.'

'Do I? What do we doctors say? Listen to the patients, they'll give you the diagnosis. So listen to me.'

She smoothed her fingers over the back of his hand, memorising the feel of it. She said, 'Why didn't you tell me?'

'No point.'

'Chris, I'm your wife.'

'You were going to find out. Why spoil the last bit of Australia, why put you through it before it was inevitable?'

She looked at him. Brown hair. Brown eyes. Long nose. Wide mouth. Flat ears. Not handsome. Not ugly. Not a face that stood out in a crowd. Not a face anyone would see and be unable to forget. Chris's face.

He lifted up her hand and pressed it to his cheek.

'The thing is,' he said, 'it's not only that I don't want to leave you and I don't want to leave the children. I don't want to miss them growing up. I don't want not to be here, doing what we do, in this place. The thing is . . . it isn't even that I don't want to die.'

She felt the stubble on his skin. She thought that if she tried she could even feel the flow of the blood beneath it.

She said nothing. Waited. Whatever it was, he had to say it. To tell her. Whatever it was.

But he was silent. He held her hand to his face a little while longer, then let it go before getting up and wandering away across the garden towards the paddock. Cat watched him and as she watched saw that his gait was odd, uneven and slightly unsteady. She closed her eyes, knowing why, too terrified to watch any more.

Twenty-seven

The grounds of the hotel ran down to the river. There was a small hooped wooden bridge beside willow trees where almost everyone had a photograph taken – the bride and groom standing romantically together with the willow branches bending over them, the water gliding by. Photographers were clever with reflections. The bridegroom would hold up a branch of willow for the bride to pass under. They would stand hand in hand, leaning over the bridge rail looking down. It never failed.

Amy Finlayson, Events Manager and Wedding Coordinator for the Riverside Hotel, stood on the lawn watching the gang erect the marquee for the following day. The double doors of the dining room would be open onto the small flight of stone steps, the marquee entrance just below, and with a bit of luck, they could open up the back too so that people could see the lawn leading to the river and stroll down there later. This lot were having fireworks at ten. The team would set them up in the paddock. She'd earned her bonuses and the extra tips this year. People were generous when a wedding went well, they were lavish with gratuities. By the end of October she'd be taking her holiday in Canada.

'I don't understand you,' the manager had said. 'Why don't you go for sun and a beach? Why not somewhere like Mauritius?'

'Because Mauritius means one thing,' Amy said. 'Bloody weddings.'

*

From where he stood, concealed behind the thick stump of a pollarded willow, he had the perfect view – the woman pointing, the marquee men. The line of sight was ideal. Up the lawn, through the tent to the open French windows.

He looked carefully around him. Behind, a wooden fence into a field. He could climb over easily enough but the field was fully open to view from the hotel. The footpath beside the river was also open and visible. Only if he went left did he have any chance of slipping away unseen and it was a risk because although there were screening trees and a hedge, both had significant gaps. It was also a long way to the road. Too long. There was nowhere he could safely hole up, either.

No. It would be clear exactly where any shots had been fired from. The patrol cars, especially just at the moment, would be fast on the scene. He had no chance. Unless . . .

He smiled. Unless.

It was so obvious he could have worked it out as a ten-year-old boy.

What kept you? he thought.

Alison had dreamed of a marquee – the inside had been designed in her head for years, with pink and white ribbons tied round a maypole, a pink and white awning and swags of flowers. It had all come together in the weeks before. Cost a fortune. Her mother paying. Paying for a grand wedding.

It was what she wanted and what she wanted was fine by him.

Alison.

He drove home feeling the sparks of anger, that always smouldered, rekindle and burn hard. When something reminded him, it affected his breathing. He felt a tightness in his chest. Even his vision sometimes changed, clouding a little.

Alison.

He put the car away and locked it, then went out again, a quarter of a mile to the pub he preferred because no one was interested in anyone else, no one behind the bar wanted to chat.

He bought his pint of keg, hating the sweet thick taste of the real ale they tried to push, took it to a corner with the local paper and a biro in case he needed to mark anything out.

It was full of the shootings. Three deaths. No leads. No clues. Lots of blether filling page after page but nothing real. Nothing that troubled him.

Twenty-eight

Simon Serrailler lay on his back on the floor and rolled first to the left and then to the right, left and right, left and right. He was a tall man and his back had been giving him trouble but in the past two weeks he had been working fifteen-hour days and although he knew he should go to the physio for treatment there had been no time.

He rolled over left to right a dozen more times and then lay on his back again, arms behind his head, in the quiet of his living room. Before long the bells would start to ring. Thursday night was full practice night. But for now, only the floorboards creaked occasionally, settling back after he had disturbed them with his exercise.

Exercise also helped to clear his mind. Work he could deal with. He had been in the game too long now to carry it home in his head. Earlier that day he had said, 'We'll get him and I'll tell you why. Because he'll make a mistake. Yes, he is clever and cunning, yes, he is planning carefully. But with firearms there are any number of mistakes he can make and sooner or later he will make one of them and give himself away. I don't mean we sit and wait for him to do it. We're being as proactive as possible on this one. But I'm confident that when he does cock up, in however small a way, we'll be there and we'll have him.'

He believed it.

He had closed his eyes. Now he opened them and looked around his room, drawing from its calm order. Then he stood up, twisted this way and that a few times, and went to fetch himself a whisky. He was spending the evening in, alone, watching a documentary about Italy and reading Simon Sebag Montefiore's biography of Stalin. It was time he desperately needed, time he had been looking forward to, limited enough for him to relish every moment. He wanted to go through his sketchbooks of his spring break in the Faroes where he had gulped in lungfuls of crystal-cold air and walked among seabirds and grass-roofed houses and felt both invigorated and deeply peaceful. He had an exhibition next year, half of which would be of these drawings, the rest of portraits, many of his mother. He wanted to sift through them, place them in perfect order which would take a long, careful time.

He stretched out on the sofa. It was not only time which he did not have. He needed a calm emotional sea and he could not see when he might get one.

His brother-in-law had a brain tumour. Simon knew enough to be aware that his chances were slim. He was very fond of Chris, he would find it hard if he were not around, but it was his sister he had most in his mind and in his heart. Her future, with three young children and a stressful job but without her beloved husband, was unimaginable. She would need Simon. He would need to have strength and time and love for all of them. There was no one else.

The cathedral bells started up. Simon went to the window and looked down on the close.

Not true, a voice niggled, not true and you know it. There is Dad. And now there is Dad and Judith.

Judith Connolly.

She is a nice woman, the voice niggled. She is warm and kind and seemingly straightforward and she will do your father a power of good. What possible reason is there for your being so antagonistic towards her? None.

While work was muddied and turbulent, while Chris was ill and very probably dying, and Judith was in his mother's place, he could settle to nothing here, could not take pleasure from his drawing and planning his next exhibition, could not relax and simply be.

The phone rang.
'Si?'
Cat.
She was crying.
'I'll come,' Simon said.

It was another mild night, another day had stretched out the long decline of summer even further. The close was empty, the bells ringing on through the evening. Simon stood for a moment listening. He was neither musical nor spiritual – he left that to Cat. She did music and God for both of them, she had once said. But he thought about Chris, facing a horrible illness, and a horrible treatment and very possibly a horrible death, and his thoughts were as close to prayer as he ever came.

If a SIFT case came up now and looked like taking him away from Lafferton for any length of time, he decided that he would ask to be left out. He was needed here, not halfway across the country after an elusive and anonymous murderer, though if he wanted one of those, he didn't have far to look.

As he sped through the narrow town streets, his mobile rang. He ignored it. Right now Cat came first.

Twenty-nine

'Jamie, be quiet and go to sleep.'

He was a good sleeper. If he hadn't been, Bethan Doyle would have gone off her head. He woke before six but in any case they had to be ready to leave the house at seven so it didn't matter. She walked to the nursery, then caught the bus to Bevham to be there at eight. Mornings were death but she'd rather that than depend on Foster, rather be independent, rather have no money. Not that she had much money now by the time she'd paid for the nursery and her rent. But she was her own woman. And if her wedding-dress business took off she might even give up the day job.

Jamie wailed. She closed the door and switched on *Corrie* but the wails came through the wall. There wasn't anything wrong with him.

The television wailed too, the *Corrie* signature tune, drowning him out for a minute. Bethan went into the kitchen and switched on the kettle, but when she came out, Jamie's cries were so loud that next door were banging.

She went into the dark bedroom. His cot was in one corner, her bed in the other. Poky little room. She suddenly wanted to throw things around, she hated the pokiness so much. And the street it was in and the people next door and the rest of them all round. She was on the council list but they'd only offered her on the roughest estate in Bevham and she wanted to stay here. Lafferton was a step up and it was away from Foster. When the time came the schools were decent. If she could get a job here so she didn't have to fork out for fares, it would be even better.

She had plans. It all took so long but she did have plans. Jamie hadn't been planned, far from it, but he was here so the plans had to be for them both. Children grew up, it wasn't forever. Her plan was to go to the college, do dress design and business studies and move from sewing at home to opening a wedding shop. Already her ads had brought in some work. She had a beautiful beaded dress on the go now. If she could just go out there and shout at all the girls as easily led by boys as she had been. If she could force them to *see*. But she'd make it. She was sure.

She pushed Jamie's damp hair back from his forehead. It was close in the room. That was probably why he couldn't get off.

Bethan drew the curtains back and opened the window a notch. A warm breeze blew in, ruffling Jamie's blanket, which hung on the end of his cot, and making him laugh. Blowing in the smell of chips too.

She could have killed for a packet of hot fish and chips but that was another thing you didn't know about, how you were completely stuck, tied to them. Some mothers would have left their babies, run out to the chip shop a couple of blocks away. Some would stay out for a drink as well. Some would leave two or three kids together with an older one supposedly responsible enough to look out for them, aged all of ten or eleven.

The smell of chips was taunting her.

'Jamie, lie down. Come on, it's night, it's sleep time. Lie down.'

He had been on his knees but now he pulled himself up and held out his arms to her, a big fat smile on his face.

'Jamie, come on, lie down. Look, here's Mousey.'

There was a ring at the bell. Jamie began to bounce up and down waving Mousey with one hand, holding onto the end of the cot with the other.

She wouldn't go. It would be someone collecting or selling or just kids. Kids were a pain but she didn't blame them. They were bored.

Jamie was still standing up and now he was banging on the side of the cot. Sometimes he banged his head there which woke her up. That was worrying. Why would he bang his head so hard it must hurt? She had mentioned it to the doctor when she had taken him for his jabs but the doctor hadn't seemed interested, just shrugged and said, 'They do it sometimes. One of mine did it.' Bang bang bang.

Then the bloody bell again.

She left the bedroom door open so that Jamie could hear her. If she closed it he would bang his head and shake the cot bars even more.

The chain was across the door. She was always careful, locked the windows at night, kept the chain on whenever she was in by herself, which was usually.

She shifted the Yale and opened the door the short distance until the chain tightened.

'Hello?'

Silence.

Bloody kids.

She didn't let the chain off, just put her head out a bit further.

The noise of the shot made Jamie sit down suddenly in the cot. He stared through the bars, to where his mother had been standing in the hall and was now lying there, and then he began to scream.

He screamed for a long time. The front door had been pushed shut and his mother still lay. Jamie banged on the cot bars. No one came. After a time, he sat and looked at his feet, then he crawled across and reached for Mousey and lay down pressing the toy to his face. He shouted once or twice, but Mousey was there, soft and comforting, and at last he fell asleep. The hall light stayed on and after a while it rained in through the open bedroom window onto the sill. The child stirred and woke and tried to get under the blanket but sleep came over him again.

He woke twice, and once he stood up and banged the cot, first with his fists then with his head. He banged for a long time. His mother still lay on the floor and would not come to him and the light stayed on. The rain was heavier now, soaking the curtain.

In the end, the darkness thinned to grey and the child fell across the cot and slept, Mousey beneath his body. He slept past six o'clock and seven, and did not wake until after eight. But nothing was different. The rain beat on the windows and the light was still on and his mother still lay on the floor in the hall and the child began to cry quietly now, realising the pointlessness of shouting and banging the cot, hungry and dirty and cold.

But still nothing happened. Nothing changed. No one came and his mother did not get up.

Thirty

Jane Fitzroy drove slowly up the long drive between the rows of swaying poplars whose leaves lay in soft golden heaps on the grass. The convent buildings had not yet come into view. There were just the mown fields on either side, and the trees of the park. The trees, of course, had grown and been cut down and others planted and matured, but in the same places, so that the parkland could not have changed much since the eighteenth century when it was laid out. The main house and a hundred or so acres had been bestowed on the abbey fifty years later and was theirs in perpetuity. Which in itself was a worry, Jane had found out within a short time of arriving there. Once there had been 120 nuns in the community. Even thirty years ago there had been over seventy. Now there were twenty-two and more than half of them well into their eighties. New postulants arrived occasionally and a few made their vows and remained. But, in ten years, there would not be enough nuns to justify the upkeep of the house and grounds. There probably were not enough now but they had a generous benefactor. When she died, no one knew what would happen to the abbey or the nuns.

Jane stopped the car and got out and the amazing silence washed over her. There was a ripple of sound from the breeze in the poplar branches and a slight rustle as it shifted the piles of leaves, but otherwise, nothing. Silence. The most astonishing, palpable silence she had ever known. It filled her with a sense of calm now, as it had done every day of the six months she had spent here. The silence had become part of her for that time, had lodged inside her, and something of it had remained for her to draw on even after she had left. Now, as she breathed it in and let it fill her again, she felt that she was topping up her inner store, to see her through the next few months. If it had only been a question of simply living with this silence, she would be here still.

It was ten past eleven. The abbey would be at work. She got back in her car, drove up to the side of the building, parked and wandered back into the grounds. No one was about. Deer grazed in the distance. A squirrel raced up a tree trunk and peered down at her. Jane walked on, to the oak with the bench around its base where she had sat so many times, reading, thinking, saying the office. And struggling with herself. Now it felt pleasant to sit here free of the struggle, decision made. It had been painful and messy but she knew now that however happy she was to be back as a visitor she had been right to leave.

Life had been a confusion of plans made and unmade, sadness and above all restlessness – for over two years, she realised now. It had begun when she'd gone to Lafferton, which had turned out to be the wrong place for her in some senses, the right in others. But in Lafferton things had been frightening and unsettled. She had been naïve, she had antagonised some people, not given others a chance. Even before she had been ordained as a priest she was fascinated by the monastic ideal, had read extensively about it in the past and present and some part of her longed for the cloister. She had come to the abbey in an emotionally vulnerable and fragmented state and her time here had given her healing and a measure of peace. It had restored her to herself, put many things into perspective and, in a strange way, helped her to finish whatever growing up she had had to do. She had been content and the time had been satisfying and absorbing. But from the first week, although she had clung to her dreams, and known that she was gaining a great deal from this place and the people in it, she had also known that the life was not for her. Not permanently. The reality, she saw now, was not so much too rarefied as too mundane, and what had unsettled her most had been the claustrophobia of living with a small group of other women in confined circumstances. Because the convent routine was utterly confining, in spite of the house being huge and the park and gardens being free and available, Jane had missed the outside world. She realised she had romanticised monasticism and mistaken her own capacity to live it. The truth had come as a shock and a lesson in humility. She had been ashamed and crestfallen, but the other nuns had treated her with admirable and exceptional kindness and common sense. 'You're not the first and you won't be the last,' the abbess had said. Sister Catherine was a realist.

Jane got up and wandered back and entered the paddock where the chickens were pecking about the grass around their wooden coops. There was the sound of a machine. She went through the gate. The last runner beans had been harvested. One of the sisters, wearing boots and ear-muffs, habit carefully tucked up, was going over a large strip of ground with a rotavator. Jane watched until she reached the far end, turned expertly and came towards her, glanced up and then began to wave madly. The nun stopped the machine. There was a rich smell of freshly dug soil.

'Jane! I'd have known that hair anywhere! How lovely to see you. Have you come to stay? Have you come for lunch?' Sister Thomas opened her arms and wrapped Jane in a warm hug, then held her at arm's length, smiling. 'You look so well. The world suits you. You'd grown peaky in here, you know, and look at you now. No one told me you were coming. Look, when you left I was sowing and now we've harvested almost everything and I'm turning the ground for the autumn broad beans and the sprouts are well on. Come on up to the house, does the abbess know you're here, she'll be thrilled, everyone will be pleased to see you and looking so well, the world suits you, did I say that? Yes, well it's true and we miss you but I think it was for the best, looking at you now, Jane, you were needed elsewhere. Tell me now, where are you, what have you been up to?'

Sister Thomas, kind-hearted and enthusiastic, had always chattered nineteen to the dozen during the periods when they were not in silence, as if everything was pent up in her for hours and came pouring out when the stopper was removed. Others spoke little at any time, as if they had forgotten how to, had lost words, so locked were they in their world of silence and contemplation.

All nuns were allowed to speak freely to visitors at any time. Hospitality and making guests feel at ease came first. It was a civilised rule. A lot of what was here at the abbey Jane had found far more civilised than she had expected. It was one of the things she missed, this and the habitual, mutual courtesy and consideration. Here, people automatically put others first. It was a way of life. The contrast with the outside world was brutal. Most of the nuns, who had not been beyond the abbey walls since their first admittance, would not survive outside. The abbess went out. She knew exactly what the world was like and was remarkably unfazed by it. But then, the abbess was an exceptional woman.

They went towards the back door where Sister Thomas shed her boots, and then on into the house. 'You won't mind coming this way, Jane, I know, otherwise we have to go all the way round, and look, we've mended that window there at last and this corridor has been painted freshly, you can probably still smell it.'

They went from the domestic regions down the newly painted corridor and then they were in the more formal part of the abbey. The smell of the paint was submerged in the smell that struck Jane again as her most vivid memory of the place – that and the abbey sounds, of bells and of footsteps pattering along corridors in sequence as the nuns went swiftly and silently to chapel.

The smell was the smell of boarding school as well as convent – floor polish with undernotes of cooking.

The door of the sewing room was open and an electric machine whirred. From an office came the soft tap of fingers on a keyboard. Jane's rubber-soled driving shoes squeaked on the tiles as they rounded the corner, past the chapel, past the double doors to the refectory, round a second corner beside a tall clear window flooding sunlight through onto a silver vase of lemon-coloured chrysanthemums before a wooden cross.

*

When Jane had begun to doubt if the religious life was for her, Sister Catherine had listened, made an occasional remark, but never pressured her to decide either way or to rush her decision.

'You are welcome to stay here as long as you need to,' she had said. 'Give it time. No one is going to ask you to leave until you are ready to go. Or to stay.'

Jane had felt better at once. The abbey was a different place from the one she had expected and thought that she wanted. Life was routine and, in many senses, dull routine. She had loved the silence and the stillness, the measured, calm way in which the women went about their daily business. But she had missed the stimulation and challenges of the outside world. Not the buzz, not the rush, but the novelty of every day. Here, novelty was almost entirely absent. That was part of the point and she was surprised how much she missed it.

The prayer life was not a problem to her, even though she found it easier to say her own office than to take part in the communal services, easier to spend time praying alone in the chapel of her room. Her room. She had laughed at herself. Her room had been one of the major problems – and how ridiculous that sounded. But it was true.

Her room was more like the uninteresting and functional one in a B & B than a monastic cell. It was sparsely furnished but not uncomfortable. It looked over the side garden. It was dull and it had never felt hers and never had any atmosphere whatsoever. A single bed with a pale blue cover, a light wood wardrobe, 1930s style, a small desk with a dark wood chair – and somehow the clash irritated her; a plain dark wood dressing table without a mirror. An armchair upholstered in beige moquette of the sort common in old people's homes. An anglepoise lamp which kept falling apart. A crucifix on the desk. A reproduction of a Renaissance painting of *The Banishment from Eden* on the wall. A miasma of depression had fallen on her when she had first entered the room and had never left but fallen again and again every time she returned to it. A hermit's cell carved out of a rock or one with whitewashed stone walls in a medieval monastery, with its own strip of garden, a high wall round it, a straw mattress on the floor. Had these been what she had craved? She had faced her own false and laughable expectations almost with embarrassment.

On the day before her departure, she had shared a simple supper on a table by the window, organised by the abbess, who believed firmly in one-to-one encounters and conversations over food and drink as the way to sort out many problems and difficulties within her community. It had been pleasant and the talk had roved over a wide variety of topics – world affairs and politics, the plight of the Third World, the place of the monastic life in modern society, education, the role of women in the Church. The abbess was not a priest. None of the nuns was ordained, and Jane had been touched by the respect for her status shown by the older and more senior woman.

When coffee had been brought by the sister in attendance, they had moved to the pair of armchairs set by the open window overlooking the park and Jane had said, 'I don't belong here. I didn't belong at home. I didn't belong in Lafferton. I'm afraid I will never belong anywhere, Sister.'

'"Our hearts are restless till they find their rest in Thee." That means something to you, Jane, unless I have got you very wrong. You've not found what you are looking for here but the reasons have nothing to do with lack of faith or loss of it indeed.'

'No. Being here has confirmed my faith. I'm sure of that if I'm sure of nothing else.'

'I'm glad. But inner tranquillity and assurance are so valuable that if you have faith, as you do, finding your real place in life isn't going to be difficult.'

'No?'

'No. It may be time-consuming. You may go in several different directions – but those will all add to your experience. If I know anything, I know nothing is wasted. Not ultimately.'

'Yes. But what direction now?'

'When you came here, one of the things you mentioned was the desire to go back to some sort of academic work. I know you spent a lot of time in the library here. Has that been helpful?'

'Oh, yes. I loved it.'

As well as reading and studying and thinking on her own

there, she had been put to work in the library, and her time spent there was among the best she had known during her stay. Her other work had been in the laundry, which she had also rather enjoyed, and the sewing room which she had hated with all the passion of her teenage years in needlework lessons.

Now, the smiling abbess got up from the desk and came towards her, both hands outstretched to take Jane's.

'Jane, what a pleasure! How very good to see you.'

'It's good to be back.'

She meant it. It was good to know that this place was always here. She knew that she would always be able to come back if she needed a place of prayer and quietness, even though she also knew, as she had walked in through the door again, that she would never want to stay.

'Do you feel like a walk, Jane? I could do with stretching my legs and a change of scene.'

They made their way towards one of the iron benches. The deer were further off now, grazing in their herd towards the sloping banks of the river, a section of which wound through the park. The gnats jazzed in the air.

'Unseasonable,' Sister Catherine said, 'but welcome. It's a long winter.'

Jane glanced at her. She was a handsome woman, probably in her fifties, and she had spoken with the faintest touch of – melancholy? Wistfulness? How difficult would it be if you doubted your vocation or even your faith, or were simply weary of convent life, and yet were head of your community? The temptation to do nothing, stay quiet, not admit any of it even to yourself, to live out your life in a not-unhappy routine, would be considerable.

Doubt was not a subject Jane could raise with the abbess.

'So Jane – you look very well and you have a more settled air. From our point of view I'm sorry to say it because we so wanted you to come to us – but I'm very glad you obviously made the right decision. In fact, I never doubted it, you know.'

'You mean you didn't think I'd be a success here?'

'Oh, what is "success"? No, I simply mean I always knew it wasn't right for you.'

They sat in silence for some time, a companionable silence. The sun slanted through the autumn trees and the deer wandered towards them. Jane was in no hurry. She was driving straight from here to Cambridge, a journey of a little over an hour and she had no appointments for the rest of the day, just her own work. She had a job as an assistant chaplain at a hospital in Cambridge, another as a locum chaplain at St Stephen Martyr's College, filling in for someone who had gone to do missionary work. She was also working on a PhD in medieval monasticism. The abbess had roared with laughter when she had been told. 'That'll suit you far better, Jane,' she had said. 'You'll enjoy the privations of twelfth-century northern England, when monasteries were really monasteries!' Ruefully, Jane had agreed.

The abbess got up. 'I must get on,' she said, 'but do go and see the others, everyone will be so pleased, and Sister Thomas will have the coffee pot on.'

But on the way into the house, they met Sister Monica, bustling out of her office, spectacles swinging from the cord round her neck.

'My dear Jane, what an extraordinary thing. Ten minutes ago I took a call asking for your whereabouts and I was just wondering if we had a current address when I looked up and there you were. I couldn't believe my eyes!'

'Who on earth would telephone me here?'

'A Dr Deerbon from Lafferton. Do ring from the office, my dear.'

Thirty-one

'What the hell . . . ?' Serrailler looked out of his office window to see a crowd of television vans in the station car park. The area was taken over by trailing cables, people with cameras and other people talking into them, vehicles with open doors revealing engineers and equipment.

'Get the press officer up here.'

'Sir.'

As the door closed the phone rang.

'Simon, what's going on? I've got press coming out of my ears, I've had the chairman of the Police Committee in my office, I turn on the radio and I hear someone talking about an uncontrolled shooting spree in Lafferton. Talk to me.'

'Well, ma'am, the car park here is stuffed with television vans.'

'Sort it. We have four dead women, three separate shooting incidents, and not the faintest idea who's responsible. Am I right?'

'Pretty much.'

Elaine Dimitriou was new, charming and, Simon thought, under-powered when her job as press officer became, as now, more than local routine.

'I'm really sorry, they just arrived and started setting up. It's the baby, sir. They all want to run stories about the baby. I've issued a press release but they're being quite aggressive.'

'Have you got what you gave them?'

Simon scanned it. 'This tells them what they know and it more or less says we haven't a clue. Come on, Elaine, this isn't going to satisfy them. Call a conference for four o'clock. I'll talk to them and I'll take questions. Public confidence is draining away and I'm not having that. Get on with it.'

Elaine fled.

'Sir? I've got something.'

DS Graham Whiteside looked smug. He'd had that smug look ever since he'd rescued Jamie Doyle from his cot.

'Yes?'

'Someone reported a man on a bicycle. Yesterday.'

'Go on.'

'He was cycling past Bethan Doyle's door and wobbling because he was going slowly and peering at the house. The duty PC noticed him as well. Apparently he almost fell off into the road he was that busy looking.'

'Plenty of people doing that. Cars slow down. People walk their dogs past the crime scenes. People hang about. Voyeurs. Gives them a kick.'

'Got a description.'

'Go on.'

'Fits Craig Drew. Medium build, brown hair, thirties, pale. They remarked on the paleness.'

'Fits Craig Drew, fits half the male population of Lafferton.'

'Not on bikes in Millingham Road. Craig Drew's got a bike.'

'A lot of people have got bikes.'

'I think I'll go and talk to him again.'

Simon pushed his hair back from his forehead a couple of times, thinking.

Craig Drew. There was a perfectly likely reason for him to be cycling past another house in which a young woman had been shot dead. He had probably cycled past the *Seven Aces* club and his own house too, a dozen times. It was what people did when they were in shock and a state of disbelief.

'We haven't got anything else, sir.'

'Not a good enough reason for pulling in Craig Drew. Might as well bring in anybody.'

'I think you're wrong. Sir. I think we should look at Drew. Hard.'

'You made that plain the first time we went to see him.'

'I didn't believe anything he said.'

'What? Nothing?'

Simon pushed his hair back again. Fact: he disliked Graham Whiteside, and had been angry at his tactics in the first Drew interview. Fact: if there was the faintest chance that Drew had shot Bethan Doyle, in front of her eighteen-month-old son, the angry press pack would sniff it out. Fact: the public was alarmed and baying for blood.

'All right, but don't go wading in.'

The DS half nodded.

Simon went into the CID room.

'Vicky here?'

DC Hollywell was staring at her computer screen with a far-off expression and jumped when the boss walked over to her desk.

'Found any relatives for Bethan Doyle?'

'Not yet, sir. I was just looking again, actually. The ex-partner is the only name we've got and he's working in a bar in Ibiza – police there have tracked him down, they're talking to him.'

'The little boy . . .'

'Jamie. He's in care.'

'I can't believe he has absolutely no living relatives apart from an absentee father.'

'We're trying, sir.'

'I know. Bethan seemed a solitary girl without family and without friends, did her job, came home, picked him up from nursery and stayed home alone with him. Was that it?'

'It appears so.'

Simon shook his head. 'I don't buy it. Get on to neighbours, go to her work, go to the boy's nursery . . . everyone. There has to be someone.'

'There was.'

'What?'

'Well, there was someone who killed her. Or was it random like the others?'

'Were they random?'

'I don't know, sir.'

'Nor do I, Vicky, and it's driving me nuts.' He turned round. 'Listen up please. I'm doing a press conference this afternoon. I've got to give the buggers out there something. I want to defuse this. We need them onside and at the moment they're not. Meanwhile, as you go in and out don't say *anything*. Be polite and carry on. I want everyone in the conference room at four. Show of solidarity.'

His mobile rang. Cat's number. He went into his room and closed the door.

'Where are you?'

'Office. What's happened?'

'Chris has gone into BG. They're operating this afternoon. They think it's a grade-three glioma.'

'That's good, isn't it? I mean them operating.'

'It's to relieve the pressure. He went blind in one eye and the headaches are awful. They'll try and take some of it out, but it's in a difficult place.'

'Oh, love.'

'He'll have radiotherapy. One course, it's just palliative.'

Cat sounded cold and mechanical, removing herself from her emotions, setting aside the fact that she was talking about Chris.

'I'll try and come over tonight. It should be OK after the press conference.'

'It's all right, Dad and Judith are coming over so I can go and see Chris.'

'Oh? You don't need me then.'

'Christ. Of course I need you. I need everyone. Simon, don't have tantrums, I can't cope.'

Someone knocked.

'Have you talked to the children?'

'Tried. I never realised how hard it was just to explain, just to get them to understand even a little. Sam can. In a way. But he doesn't want to. He put his fingers in his ears.'

His door opened. Elaine.

'I have to go. Hold on in there. I'll come later.'

He looked up.

'Sorry, sir, but the Chief's here. She went into the CID room but I thought you'd want a heads-up.'

'Thanks.'

Another head round the door. Vicky.

'The Spanish police came through. Foster Munday, Bethan Doyle's partner . . . left his bar job five weeks ago. Left his apartment as well.'

'And?'

'Took a flight to Birmingham.'

'When?'

'Two days before Melanie Drew was shot.'

'Right, we want photographs, full description, get on to the airport, taxis, railway, car hire. I want him in here yesterday.'

Vicky turned and crashed into the Chief Constable. Simon caught a glimpse of their faces, Vicky scarlet and horrified, Paula Devenish thunderous.

'Ma'am. I'll get someone to go for tea.'

'I don't need tea. I need some small scrap of evidence that you have moved forward in this investigation.'

Thirty-two

DS Whiteside pounded the front door of the cottage with hammer blows. Inside, dogs barked.

When Craig Drew's father opened up he looked terrified but said at once, 'You've got some news? What's happened?'

'Can we come in?' Whiteside barged through the front door as he was asking. The DC with him, Louise Kelly, hesitated, apologetic.

'What's happened?' Alan Drew asked her.

She shook her head.

'OK, where is he?'

'Craig? Upstairs, I think. What's happened?'

'Call him down, will you?'

The DS prowled round the living room, looking at a picture, picking up a photograph, turning the corner of the mat over with his toe. Louise stood in the doorway. He was a sergeant, she was in her first six months as a DC but she knew that the way he was behaving was out of order. She wanted to say something but if she did he would take it out on her later. She knew a bully when she met one, knew what you should do with bullies but felt powerless. Whiteside brushed her aside and went to the bottom of the stairs. 'Drew! DS Whiteside here. I want a word.'

'What's going on? What's happened?'

'What's he doing up there?'

A lavatory flushed. Craig Drew came running down the stairs, still doing up his belt. 'Have you got him?'

'I was hoping you were going to tell me that.'

'Sorry?'

Craig stared.

Poor bloke, Louise thought, poor bloody bloke, he doesn't know what time of day it is. His wife of two weeks was shot dead, he's a mess of emotion and dread and questions he can't answer and we're here to ask more.

'You've got a bike, Craig?'

'Cycle. Bicycle. Yes.' He looked bewildered. His father stood beside him. Protective, Louise thought. Even at his age. Fat chance my dad would protect me like that.

'Been out and about on it, have you?'

'He cycles most days,' Alan Drew said. 'He needs to get out of here.'

'Where do you go, Craig?'

'I don't know . . . all over. Anywhere.'

'You don't know. All over. Anywhere.'

'I just go out.'

'Lafferton?'

'Yes. Or – just around. Villages. Nowhere in particular.'

'Dulles Avenue?'

'I went there.'

'What for?'

'We – I live there. I went to my flat.'

'On your bike?'

'Yes.'

'Can't carry much on a bike, can you?'

'I didn't have anything to carry.'

'Didn't go to pick anything up, stuff you needed, clothes and so on?'

'I'd have taken the car.'

'I'd have gone with him as well. What's this about, Sergeant, what's with all these bike questions?'

'Know the *Seven Aces* club, Craig?'

'No. I mean, I heard about it, those other girls. It's the same thing, isn't it? Someone just shooting for no reason.'

'How do you know it's the same?'

'Well, I thought . . . it's got to be the same, hasn't it?'

'Has it? We haven't said so.'

Craig Drew looked both confused and as if he were about to cry. He glanced desperately at Louise.

'Do you know the *Seven Aces*, Craig?' she asked gently.

Whiteside shot her a look.

'No.'

'Have you ever been?'

'No. We – I . . . clubs are not where I go. We don't. Mel didn't like that sort of place. It's new, isn't it?'

'You're telling me you've never so much as been past it?'

'I don't think I have but I can't swear to it. Of course I can't, can I?'

'Why not? I'd have thought it was perfectly simple. Have you been past the *Seven Aces* or haven't you?'

Craig sat down and dropped his head.

Whiteside went on. 'Did you read about Bethan Doyle, Craig?'

'Who's Bethan . . . Oh, God, her, the one with the baby. Christ.'

'You know about it, then?'

'You'd have to live on the moon not to know about it, wouldn't you?' Alan Drew. He had crossed the room to stand beside his son, put a hand on his shoulder for a second.

'Craig?'

'Yes.'

'Know where she lived, do you? Where it happened?'

'Yes.'

'Not far from your place.'

Silence.

'You went down there, didn't you, Craig?'

'No.'

'Really? I heard you did. Biked along the street. Had a good look at the house where it happened. Didn't you?'

Craig looked up, his eyes seemed to have sunk back into his head, still bewildered.

'I might have. Yes. I did. I was on the bike round there. I was trying to take it in. I can't take it in, you see. I keep expecting her to walk in the door here and she doesn't.'

'Melanie?'

'Yes.'

'Why would that make you cycle past Bethan Doyle's place?'

'It didn't. I mean, I don't know why. I wanted to see. I suppose. Maybe it would help me take it in. I just don't know.'

'So you did cycle past the house where Bethan Doyle was shot in front of her eighteen-month-old baby?'

Craig shrank back into himself as if warding off a blow.

'Craig?'

For one second they were all of them frozen in the small room but to Louise the second went on for hours, became timeless, as if the shutter on a camera had stuck, keeping them all there.

Then Whiteside said, 'Get your coat. I'm asking you the rest down at the station.'

Craig Drew looked up. The bewilderment in his eyes had become fear.

'What?'

'You heard. Coat.'

Alan Drew moved. Froze again. Looked from one to the other for an answer. Found none.

'I'm sorry,' Louise said, so quietly they probably didn't even hear her.

'I don't have one.'

The DS turned from the doorway.

'A coat. My wax jacket's at Dulles Avenue. I don't have a coat. I don't need a coat.'

Whiteside jerked his head towards the door.

Don't go, Louise thought, don't be bullied, you've got rights.

But Craig Drew, head down, got up and walked meekly out of the room, Whiteside behind him.

Thirty-three

'Hey, petal, how you doin'?'

'Don't call me petal.' DC Louise Kelly waited for the machine to pour its coffee sludge into the plastic cup.

'Didn't think you were one of those feminist birds.'

'I'm not.'

'Right, well, petal is only what my teacher would have called a figure of speech.' Clive Rowley watched while she struggled with the cup which had stuck in the grip of the metal holder. 'I'm afraid to offer help, now.'

Louise sighed and stepped back. 'Please,' she said.

He snapped open the holder and wriggled the cup of hot liquid out sideways. 'There's a knack, you see.'

'Thanks, Clive. I'm sorry, didn't mean to take it out on you.'

'What's up?'

'It'll pass.'

'No, go on. Better out.'

'Not here.'

The corridor was a busy thoroughfare.

'Come in here then.'

They stood in a lobby beside the stairwell.

'What's up?'

'Bloody DS Whiteside.'

'Been chatting you up or what?'

'Oh, I can cope with that.'

'I bet. Quite scary, you.'

'Seriously. He's a bully.'

'So am I. We're coppers. It's what we do.'

'Not like this.'

Clive watched her closely as she told him. Pretty. Fair hair. Small features. Small hands and feet. Neat little thing. He looked at her hands. No rings.

Was she his type? Might be. Ask her out? Might do.

She stopped talking and drank the coffee.

'You see my point?' she said, looking round for somewhere to throw the empty cup. 'He was bang out of order.'

'What about this Drew guy? He done it?'

'No. Absolutely not.'

'All the same. He's in the frame, isn't he?'

'No.'

'The DS did right to bring him in.'

'Straws. Clutching. At.'

'Fair point. Where is he now?'

'Interview room, I imagine. Look, what should I do?'

'Nothing.'

'I can't.'

'Yes. Nothing. Don't stir it up. Don't make a complaint, it'll backfire. Only if he starts on you, tell me. I can deal with the Whitesides of this world.'

She laughed. 'It's not me I'm worried about. But thanks.'

'Stay schtum. OK?'

He winked at her and walked off towards the Armed Response Unit room.

Louise watched him go. Cocky, she thought. He doesn't walk, he swaggers. Maybe AR are always like that. Maybe it goes with the territory. She didn't take Clive Rowley seriously. Not like Whiteside.

She went upstairs to the CID room.

'What's been going on?' another DC asked as she went past.

'What have you heard?'

'Craig Drew's been brought in.'

'Then that's what's been going on.'

'No way.'

Louise sat down at her desk and clicked to restore her screen.

FRIENDS REUNITED. SIR ERIC ANDERSON COMPREHENSIVE SCHOOL. LAFFERTON. 1995.

She went on scrolling down the list. Maybe somewhere in here was a friend of Melanie Drew, née Calthorpe, someone who had something against her, and against the three other girls, something bad enough to have rankled all these years until it blew up in his head and he shot them all dead. Maybe. She leaned back. But this was how you found it, patient detail, plodding through, looking for a connection. This was how she was going to be the one who found it. She would take the tiny scrap of a lead to the DCS and he would agree, she would be given a team, they would track him down, Craig Drew would be freed, Whiteside would be reprimanded . . .

'Briefing in ten,' someone shouted.

Louise came to, embarrassed. But no one knew.

Maybe.

It had been raining and the conference room smelled of steaming clothes.

Serrailler held up a sheet of paper. 'This,' he said, 'came in, posted in Lafferton yesterday, addressed to me. It's up on the screen – here.' The letter was blown up so that they could read it, a single sheet of ruled A5, lettered in crude capitals.

WATCH YOUR BACK I'LL BE WATCHING YOURS HAVE FUN AT THE FAYR YOU WONT SEE ME IM 2 CLEVER 4 THAT SYMON.

'Someone's been reading too many Agatha Christies.'

'This is a wind-up, sir.'

There was a murmur round the room.

'Probably,' Serrailler said. 'I get enough of those. But it serves to focus our minds on next weekend. This will go to forensics of course, who won't find anything on it.'

'Of course.'

'But we can't afford to take a threat like this – and it is a threat – too lightly. Not with four women already dead. The Jug Fair. There'll be a heavy uniform presence, ARV on standby, all of that, but I want everyone in here at the fair as well, eyes and ears open. Suspect everyone, watch everything, be everywhere. You're looking out for a clever, ruthless gunman, you're not there to have fun, no wives and kiddies in tow.'

'What, no candyfloss?'

'Good cover, a gob full of that pink Brillo pad.'

'There'll be a ground plan – I'll brief a couple of hours before the fair opens. I don't know about this,' he waved the letter, 'but it's a heads-up. I don't want carnage at the Jug Fair.'

'Think of the headlines,' Beevor said.

'Think of four people already dead, DC Beevor.'

'Sir.'

'Sir, is it true Craig Drew has been arrested?'

'It is not. Graham brought him in for further questioning, that's all, and he is not under arrest. The press is still out there in force and I don't want them getting hold of the wrong story. Mr Drew is not, repeat *not*, under arrest.'

'He's still under suspicion though?'

'Until we get something new,' Serrailler said, 'almost everyone is under suspicion. Including you, DC Beevor.'

The room exploded into jeers and laughter.

Thirty-four

From the *Lafferton Gazette*:

TANYA AND DAN HITCH A LIFT

When six-year-old Tanya Halliwell was a maid in attendance to the Lafferton Jug Fair Queen in September 1988, she cannot have guessed how she would ride on the float again not once but twice in the future.

In 1998, Tanya was the Jug Fair Queen herself and last week she took to the float yet again – this time as a bride.

She and her husband, Dan Lomax (a page in 1987), left their wedding at Lafferton Methodist Church on the float which was specially lent for the occasion and decorated by Claudia's Florists, where Tanya works. Her two bridesmaids and two pageboys rode with the newly-weds to their reception at Selby House Golf and Country Club. Later, Mr and Mrs Lomax left for the first stage of their honeymoon on the float, this time lit by lanterns and guided by flares. The float is owned by the Wicks family of Selby Farms and was kindly loaned by Michael Wicks, a cousin of the bride.

The couple plan to return from their honeymoon cruise in time to enjoy this year's Lafferton Jug Fair on the last weekend in October.

Thirty-five

The rain began to fall quite gently as she drove away from the abbey but by the time she had been on the road for half an hour the sky was blue-black, the clouds heavy-bellied and the rain was sheeting down. Jane switched on her lights and the radio. Flood warnings. Severe weather warnings. Storm warnings.

The country road crossed and recrossed the river several times before running along the valley. The last thing she needed was to be stuck somewhere or to have to turn back, losing precious time. Cat had made it clear that time would count. 'Karin hasn't long to live,' she had said in a steady voice. 'She has secondaries in her spine. She mentioned your name twice.'

The traffic coming towards Jane was slowing down and a couple of cars flashed their lights. Lightning was jagged across the sky immediately ahead and then she hit the water which was flowing fast across the middle of the road. It shot up on either side of the car and she slowed, got through it, then pulled in behind several others. It was half past one and almost pitch black, the clouds boiling over.

She wondered if it was safe to use her phone – assuming there was a signal. Could mobiles be struck by lightning? She thought not and the car had four rubber tyres which would presumably negate the effect in any case. But there was no signal.

The road had turned into a river and was gushing beneath the cars.

*

Half an hour later, the worst of the storm seemed to have moved away and she was going again, heading for the slip road of the motorway. The surface was treacherous, warning lights slowed the traffic down to 30 mph which became a 5 mph crawl. The rain lashed down. The radio issued solemn warnings not to travel unless absolutely necessary.

It was quarter to three and 120 miles to Lafferton, assuming it was possible to take the direct route.

Karin McCafferty came into Jane's mind, as she had last seen her, glowing with well-being and determination, confident and strong.

And then Chris Deerbon. Cat had told her before she hung up. He had a brain tumour. They would operate. After that they would know more.

Jane had told the abbess the bare details of the conversation. Karin and Chris would be in the abbey prayers night and day from now on.

'That's our job,' Sister Catherine had said. 'Yours is to go and be with them.'

Jane had expected to be in Lafferton by late afternoon but the storms caused such traffic chaos that she was still on the road well after eight, inching forward in a queue several miles long. It gave her time and solitude in which to pray but, inevitably, she also had time to think. Lafferton meant many things to her, some of them extremely painful. But she had made some warm friendships during her time there and she hoped they would be enduring ones.

She had also met Simon Serrailler.

She had run away from Lafferton and she could admit now that Simon had been one of the main reasons for her flight. Simon had assumed an importance, had somehow got under her wire, in a way she had not yet fully acknowledged.

The traffic did not move. She switched off the engine and took her Bible out of the glove compartment. At odd times such as this, she liked to rediscover the Books she did not know well and which were not a familiar part of the church services.

'The word of the Lord came to me saying, Jeremiah, what do you see? And I said, I see a branch of an almond tree.'

She loved the Bible when it was at its most direct and matter-of-fact, when it spoke of everyday. *'I see a branch of an almond tree.'* It scarcely mattered what you believed or did not.

She was still reading, occasionally looking up, over an hour later and by then she had found a notebook and jotted down comments on the text.

When the lights of the car in front showed red and it began to move, she was relieved not only to have studied all of Jeremiah, but to have put Simon Serrailler firmly out of her mind.

He came back to it as she drove on, free of the traffic eventually and taking side roads and short cuts, to try and make up time. She tried to picture him. Tall. White-blond hair. Long nose. But his whole face would not click into place, he hovered somewhere, shadowy and vague. Why was she trying to remember exactly what he looked like?

She switched on the car radio and tuned in to a discussion about Chinese babies abandoned in the countryside. The story might have been biblical.

She drove on down the dark roads.

Thirty-six

At first they had all been cut out and stuck into a scrapbook and the scrapbook was still there, to be consulted, in a box file on the shelf, but lately he had bought a scanner and scanned the pieces straight onto his computer. Easier to organise.

He had a routine. When he got in he went straight to the shower, then changed into clean clothes, usually combat trousers and a T. Tonight the T was an old olive-green one with a faded picture of Che Guevara. Retro. He hadn't much idea who Che Guevara was.

Food. Lamb chop, carrots, peas, fried up mashed potato from the day before. Banana. Apple. Four squares of chocolate. Two mugs of tea. He liked his food. He ate well. Always cooked. You were what you put into yourself. Too much putting in of junk – that's what did for them. Did for their brains and their behaviour and their attitude and their bellies.

He watched the news. Watched half an hour of random sport on Sky. Pulled the ring off a can of lager. Opened up the computer. Switched on the scanner.

FORTHCOMING MARRIAGES

The wedding between Andrew Hutt and Chelsea Fisher, both of Lafferton, will take place on Saturday 22 October at Our Lady of Sorrows Catholic Church, Dedmeads Road, Lafferton, at 2.30 p.m. All friends welcome at the church.

He filed it under 'Additional'.

NOTICE

The Dean and Chapter of the Cathedral Church of St Michael, Lafferton, give notice that the Cathedral Close and the area of Cathedral Lane, Old Lane and St Michael's Walk will be closed to the public and to through traffic between 1 p.m. and 4 p.m. on Saturday 10 November. Diversions will be clearly marked. The Cathedral Close will remain accessible to residents.

Which was filed under 'Primary'.

He pressed Save, closed the files. Changed the password, as usual every evening.

Tonight's was 'woodcock'.

Time scale, detailed plan, schedules, routes – were in a second box file, marked 'Tax Receipts', kept in the wooden chest on which the television stood.

The chest was locked. The key was in the freezer buried in a full tub of margarine. If it took five minutes to get at it that didn't worry him. Precautions. Plans. Schedules. A routine.

That way there was less chance of anything going wrong.

Thirty-seven

Simon left his office and ran.

He was stopping for nothing and for no one. He had been on duty for fourteen hours. Bethan Doyle's former partner had been questioned and was in the clear. Whiteside had taken it upon himself to drive him to see his baby son. Craig Drew had been driven back to his parents' house by Louise Kelly. Simon had never been up against so many blanks. He felt as if he was wading through clouds. The one thing he could get his teeth into was the job of giving the Jug Fair the highest police profile it had ever received. The Chief was certain the fair would draw the gunman. 'Nothing,' Paula Devenish had said, 'and I mean nothing, can be allowed to happen.'

Simon got into his car and dialled from his mobile.

'This is the Deerbon residence, who is speaking please?'

'Hi, Sam.'

'Oh.'

'Are you OK?'

'Yes. Only Dad's had an operation. On his brain. So I'm not really OK.'

'I'm coming over now, I'm just leaving the station. Will you tell –'

'Mummy's upstairs with Felix and she's crying a lot. Grandpa and Judith were here but they've gone to the hospital. Hannah's on a sleepover. So there isn't anyone.'

'Ten minutes, Sam.'

'In your own car?'
'Yes.'
'Oh. No siren.'
'No. But I'll screech the tyres round the corners.'
'Cool.' Sam put the phone down.

He was at the door as Simon drew up. He looked suddenly older; his legs were longer, his face was changing, the baby softness firming and sharpening. His resemblance to Chris was clearer. Not long ago he would have raced to Simon, arms outstretched, ready to be lifted up and swung round. Now, he waited, his face serious.

'Hi, Sam.'

'Mum's still upstairs. How's the shooting investigation coming along?'

'We'll get there.'

They went inside.

'I saw you on the telly. How old do I have to be to come and do work experience with CID?'

'Sixteen.'

'That's not fair.'

Simon heard Cat's footsteps on the stairs. 'Many things aren't fair,' he said.

Sam had the new Alex Rider book but he was reluctant to be left, asking anxious questions about Chris, chattering pointlessly about whether dogs could see in the dark and if his brother would grow up to get better marks than he had in maths. His eyes moved between Simon and Cat, looking for reassurance. They sat with him, talking, answering. In the end, he had simply opened the book, turned away from them and said, 'I'm going to read now.'

Felix was asleep, face down on the pillow, knees drawn up as if he were about to crawl away. Simon laughed.

'Yes,' Cat said. 'They keep me going. Sam is so sharp, he susses too much.'

'But you have told them?'

'As much as they need to know. Which is probably all there is to tell.'

Simon went to the fridge and found a bottle of white wine.

'No,' Cat said, 'I'm not. Not just now.'

He put the bottle back and went to the kettle. 'They can't take everything but I can, you know,' he said.

Cat leaned her head back and closed her eyes. She looks older, Simon thought, like Sam. Her face has changed, too. Something like this happens and we slip down a rung or two and we can never go back. He wanted to draw her.

'Peppermint tea,' she said. 'It's in the blue jar.'

'How did the operation go?'

'They took quite a lot of the tumour out, but of course they can never get it all – too dangerous. They did the biopsy. It's a grade-three astrocytoma. They'll give him a course of radiotherapy.'

'Which will help?'

Cat looked at him as he handed her the tea. 'For a while.'

He sat next to her. There wasn't anything to say. He couldn't produce platitudes.

'You're staying off work?'

'Oh yes, I have to. He'll be home in a week and then he'll need me all the time. There isn't much of that. You know, when patients used to tell me they couldn't take in what I'd just told them, I didn't really know what they meant. But I sat there this afternoon listening to the neurosurgeon explaining everything and he was talking Greek. I couldn't understand it. It didn't go in. When I came out of the room I stood in the corridor and repeated what he'd said to me. "Your husband has a grade-three astrocytoma, I have removed what I could. That will relieve the pressure for a time and we'll give him ten days of radiotherapy. It will buy him time. But this is only palliative, you understand." I actually said all that to myself aloud. A couple of people went by me and . . .'

Cat set her cup down carefully on the table and started to cry.

Cat. Crying. Simon remembered when she had cried after falling off a horse and breaking her arm, and at the funerals – their mother's, Martha's. But they had not been tears like this, not tears fetched up from somewhere he could not reach, tears of despair and pain and desolation. He sat, his hand on her back as she leaned forward sobbing into her cupped hands.

Chris would die. Cat would stay here, bring up the children, resume her job eventually. The world would go on turning. Nothing would change.

Everything would change. Chris. He loved his brother-in-law, had always got on easily with him, had taken his presence for granted over thirteen years. Chris was not a complex man. He liked his life, loved his family, did his job, could be contrary. An ordinary man. And now, an ordinary man with something eating into his brain. Lying in hospital tonight after his head had been sawn open.

The ground seemed to shelve away in front of Simon, exposing a crater.

Thirty-eight

She'd sounded odd. Not herself. But he hadn't been able to put a finger on it.

'Can we go another night?' she had said.

'What's wrong? You not well?'

'No. Yes. I mean, I'm not ill, just a bit – I'd rather go another night. Or just have a drink.'

'But I've booked.'

She had sighed. There had been a silence.

'Come on, do you good, you'll feel better for it.'

'Where is it anyway?'

'Somewhere you'll like.'

'I don't like surprises.'

'You'll like this one.'

Silence. A long silence. He hadn't been able to make it out.

'Alison?'

'Yes, yes, right. I'm sorry. Fine, it's fine, of course, we'll go.'

'You sure?'

'I just said.'

'I want you to like it. I want you to enjoy yourself, it's special.'

'I will. Sorry. What time do you want to go?'

'Pick you up at seven.'

'As early as that?'

'There's things to look at, then we can have a drink and then we'll eat.'

'Is it far, this place, wherever it is?'

'Twenty minutes.'
'Oh. Right.'
'I'll pick you up at seven.'
'Right. Fine. See you then.'
'Love you.'
But she had already gone.

He sat, now, over his tea, Scotch egg and green beans, plums and cream, hearing the way her voice had been. In his head. He'd known but he hadn't known. Of course he hadn't. They were engaged, they were getting married in six months. She'd got a cold coming or the curse.

He'd known.

He stared at the egg on his plate. Neatly halved, the pale crumbly yolk, the rubbery grey-tinged white, the sausage meat, the orange crumbs.

He'd known.

When he'd got there she hadn't been ready and her sister, Georgina, had been there, looking at him and then looking away. Afterwards, he realised that Georgina had been embarrassed. Because Alison had said something.

But he'd ignored it. Of course he had. Nothing was wrong. How could there be? They were engaged. They were going to be married. There was no one like Alison who had ever been born. That was how he felt, the extent of it. No one who had ever been born.

She'd come into the room and the sun had come out. It's what happened, what she did. She wore a blue frock and a white jacket and her hair was down, floating round her head somehow, gauzy hair. The light showed through it as she came into the room.

Alison.

Georgina had looked at her. Alison hadn't wanted to catch her eye.

There was something.

But when he pulled away from the kerb, he could have laughed with happiness.

*

'The Compton Ford Hotel,' she had read aloud as they drove through the gates and up the drive. The gravel crunched under the wheels. 'I've heard about this place.'

'You'll like it. I came and sussed it out.'

'What for?'

'Us. You wait.'

He handed her out and she had looked round slowly, taking everything in, the inch-thick gravel and the lawns, the stone urns full of white flowers, the terrace and avenue between the trees.

'Come on.'

'It's very smart here. It's got to be expensive.'

'So what?'

The staircase curved round and there was a marble floor in the entrance, a glass-roofed dining room, with doors open onto the lawn. White tablecloths. Waiters in long white aprons. Flowers.

'Look at the flowers,' Alison had said, her voice a whisper.

'You wait – they'll be yours. Ours.'

'What do you mean?'

'Our wedding.'

'We can't get married here!'

'Why not?'

But she had turned away. She had gone to the Ladies while he went to order their drinks and find a table on the terrace in the evening sun. He sat, imagining it, picturing her. The garden full of their guests, Alison in the centre of it all.

She came back after what seemed a long time.

'I asked for a brochure,' he said, 'when I came before. The sort of things they do. You can have anything you want. You ask, you can have it.'

She had looked at him and looked away quickly. She had picked up her glass of wine and taken a small sip and put it down.

'What do you think?'

He could still see the way the sun had been shining on her face and on the table and her glass and his glass, and feel the warmth from it. A few other people had come in. Behind them there was the soft sound of someone putting cutlery down on linen.

'I've got something to say.'

That was all. Odd. That was all he'd needed. 'I've got something to say.' And his world had fallen apart. He'd watched the pieces of it floating away slowly like leaves down and down and out of sight and all there had been was a dark hollow space and a cold wind blowing.

Just that one thing she had said and the way she had looked, but not at him, the expression on her face. *I've got something to say.*

The pale gold lager and the paler wine had soured and curdled in the glass and his fingers had turned to ice.

He had heard her out and said nothing. Nothing at all. Just got up and paid the bill, cancelled the table. 'Not feeling too good.'

'Say something, please say something. I'm sorry. I'm really sorry, I don't know how it happened, I didn't mean it to, only it did, I'm really sorry.'

On and on. She was sorry. Didn't know how. But it had happened. He had said nothing.

It wasn't that he had not heard her or taken it in. He had. She was not going to marry him because she wanted to be with Stuart Reed. His friend Stuart Reed. Now her lover Stuart Reed.

'I'm sorry.'

He had not driven too fast or carelessly. He had gone straight to her house, walked round, opened the car door for her. She'd stood on the pavement outside the house, her eyes big, mouth working.

Alison.

'Say something, for God's sake.'

But he had simply stood and, in the end, she had walked unsteadily towards the gate, not looking back.

He had caught sight of Georgina. Looking down from the window upstairs.

Georgina. She knew.

He had got back into the car and driven off, driven for a long time and as he drove, he allowed the anger to seep out of the place where he had penned it. Drop by drop. He could not let it come too fast because it was so strong and so deadly, so concentrated. It would have set the car on fire.

*

The grief came much later and was so confused in his head with the anger that he barely recognised it for what it was. What shocked him was how the love he had felt for her had shrivelled to nothing and been burned up. He still felt passion but in a way which had twisted inside out, turned in on itself.

He sat beside a railway line watching the trains which flashed by every twenty minutes and pictured her lying on the rails. Her eyes were open and she saw everything and knew that he was watching her die under the wheels of the train. In the time he spent there, an hour or more, he planned what he would do and when and how he would do it and where he would go afterwards. He planned it so meticulously, in such careful steps, that he knew that he would succeed. He could not fail.

And none of it would be his fault. He would not be to blame and he would explain that to anyone. He was not to blame. She had done it. To him. To herself.

Alison.

It had taken two days and then he had woken in the night crying. He cried for her and for himself and what he had lost, knowing surely that he would never love again as he had loved her. It had taken him so long. Others did it so easily, girlfriends, partners, wives, but he had never got it right, never had the knack. She had been his miracle and he had never quite believed in her. Maybe that was it, he had thought, lying in the dark, maybe she had not been believable. Maybe it had not been true, as he had felt it. He had always been amazed that she had responded to him but then, why not, he'd got lucky, it was bound to happen, people had always told him so.

So now? Go to her. Go and ask and plead and beg.

No way. It had been hard enough. He wasn't about to risk that, losing his pride as well as everything else.

He knew what he had to do. He had thought it all out, hadn't he?

He knew.

He had turned over and slept but in his sleep the tears still came.

*

He stared at his plate. Then he took up his knife and fork. He gouged out the hard-boiled yellow iris of the Scotch egg and dissected it into minute crumby pieces on his plate. The white of the eye came next, prised out as a single flabby half-moon. He cut that into slivers. The rest, the sausage meat and the outer crust, he mashed with the back of his fork, pressing it down hard and flattening it onto the surface of the plate.

He did the same with the other half of the egg until the whole was a turgid mess, the iris of the egg and the white mashed together and stirred round and round, round and round.

He sat there for a long time, remembering. Reminding himself. Angry.

Thirty-nine

Helen put down her fork. 'The thing is – given the play discusses such serious issues, it always surprises me how funny it is.'

'Have you seen it before?'

She shook her head. 'I used to belong to the Lafferton Players.'

Phil made a face.

'All right, I know . . . It was all very am-dram and I left but I did get to know some brilliant plays, like the David Hare trilogy. I thought then how funny some of *Racing Demon* is.'

'Funniest line?'

'Easy. When he's challenging God, telling him He's not up to much, He's like some low-down football team.'

'Accrington Stanley.'

'Yes, and the supporters are like those who sort of support God but it's OK "because they're Accrington Stanley in their daily lives – they just don't go to the games".'

'Do you?'

'What, go to the Accrington Stanley games?'

'No, to God's.'

It was not a subject that had arisen in their half-dozen meetings but after seeing the Hare play about clerical crises and the state of the Church of England, it was inevitable one of them would raise it and Helen had known it would not be her. She had almost declined the theatre outing just because of it.

She ate more of her saltimbocca, very slowly.

'Is that not all right?'

'It's delicious. I'm savouring the last mouthfuls.'

'Right.'

She had to tell him about Tom. Of course she had to. And why not? She would defend her son to the gallows. But it was difficult. She'd veered away from it. But this was Phil. She looked at him across the table. He raised an eyebrow. Phil. The Phil she was growing to like very much, whose company she loved, who . . .

She put her knife and fork together and drank the last of her wine.

'Wonderful.'

'You needn't worry.'

'What about?'

'Maybe we shouldn't talk about it. Religion and politics, you know.'

'Well, we've done politics.'

'We have.'

They were both Gordon Brown Labour voters, both glad to see the back of Blair, both from families who in the past had been militantly left wing. As a student, Phil had sold the *Socialist Worker*, he said, had even become a Trotskyite for two terms.

'But you grow up, don't you? Real life breaks in.'

The waiter came to clear and bring the dessert menu. Phil ordered another glass of wine for her and more mineral water.

'I couldn't eat anything else,' she said.

'How disappointing. I could.'

He ordered a pudding for himself, then said, 'I'm an atheist. I cannot understand how anyone of intelligence believes in a God. It baffles me. I also think religion is dangerous. A force for ill. And if you're a Scientologist we'll have to agree not to mention Thetans, that's all.'

'So . . .'

'So?'

'Oh, I'm just getting my head round being a person without intelligence.'

'You believe in God?'

'I think so. Anyway, I sing with the cathedral choral society. I go to the Easter service, Christmas, the Advent carols . . . That's about it, though, I'm not a very good churchgoer.'

'Ah. Accrington Stanley in fact.'

'It's Tom you should know about. Not that I mind, not that it makes any difference at all to . . . anything.'

'Tom. Tell me.'

He leaned closer and put his hand on top of hers on the table. 'What is so dreadful about Tom?'

'No, not dreadful . . .' She sighed. It was difficult and it ought not to be but she still felt uncomfortable sometimes with what had happened.

'When he was sixteen one of his friends asked him to go on holiday with him and his family. Tom said yes and then it turned out to be some sort of Christian holiday – in tents on a showground. Anyway, by the time Tom realised, he said he'd better go as he'd said he would. It would be a laugh and there were bands, he'd get through it. There were beaches nearby for surfing, which he loves. It was in Cornwall. So off he went. Lizzie and I went to walk in Northumberland – Hadrian's Wall. We laughed a lot about how poor Tom was coping. But when we all got back he'd coped by joining up.'

'You mean they brainwashed him?'

'Not exactly. But the atmosphere was so highly charged and emotional and he was under a lot of pressure. He said it was like a light going on. He did nothing but read the Bible and go off with these people. They have very extreme, fundamentalist beliefs and they're pretty ferocious about everyone who isn't one of them. I was angry. I tried to talk to him. But you can't. Their brains seem to be rewired and you can't get through. Lizzie gave him hell. But I assumed it would fizzle out, like all these teenage things.'

'And it hasn't.'

'On the contrary. And I've been trying not to tell you.'

Phil started to laugh.

'Not funny. It really isn't. You should hear him – he's so earnest and serious about it. He isn't the Tom I know, Phil – he never talks about anything else, he has hardly any other friends. He went to one of their conventions in America this summer and he came back quite terrifyingly right wing and even more fundamentalist. We've had to agree not to talk about it at all. I find it pretty difficult to live with.'

'So would I.'

The restaurant was emptying. Phil had finished his pot of wine-soaked cream. They agreed to pass on coffee. Phil asked for the bill. But what he had said seemed to drop heavily onto the space between them. *So would I.*

Helen got up and went to the cloakroom, furious that she had had to tell him, furious with Tom. Now everything would go wrong. Fall apart.

She looked in the mirror. 'You love him,' she said.

Lizzie was at a friend's. Tom's motorbike was in the passage.

'I won't stay,' Phil said. 'Come to my place at the weekend.'

'No. Come in now. I'm not going to have my life ruled by my son.'

Phil touched her arm. 'It won't be. But I've a long teaching day tomorrow.'

She watched until his car had turned the corner. Tom's light was on, and the lights downstairs.

Helen looked up at the half-moon. The air smelled cold, with a touch of winter. So now he knew. It seemed hopelessly wrong that it was not drugs or bad company, not drink or giving up on school, but a narrow sectarian religious faith which divided her from Tom, made life with him difficult and might drive Phil away. Would she be scared off, in his position?

No, she thought. No, actually, I wouldn't. I'd say what Phil said. That it was Tom's life and she shouldn't let it affect hers.

But that was easily said.

Tom was at the kitchen table eating a bowl of cereal, a booklet propped on the milk jug.

'Hello.'

Tom grunted. 'Good time?'

'Very. The play was excellent and so was the Italian dinner. So yes. Tea?'

'No thanks.'

Helen glanced sideways at what he was reading. 'Is that something they're keen on then? Chastity?'

'No sex before marriage.'

'Same difference. Goodness.'

'What?'

'Oh, just – goodness. Not very fashionable.'

'No, fashionable is promiscuity, fashionable is casual sex, fashionable is gay, fashionable is at the root of social breakdown. The Bible says –'

'Ouch!'

He looked up.

'Sorry – splash of hot water. It's fine.'

She wished she hadn't started the conversation, but what conversation with Tom could she start which didn't head in the same direction?

'Don't expect too much of people, Tom.'

'I don't.'

'Not everyone has your take on it. And when you meet a girl you're very keen on you might see things differently.'

'I'll make sure I don't. Anyway, we all see it the same way.'

'We?'

'My friends. We don't compromise.'

How had the sturdy, pragmatic but gentle little boy who had been Tom turned into this narrow and unfeeling person who read pamphlets entitled 'Satan Works Through Sex'? What kind of people had him in thrall?

'Do you give them any money, Tom?' she asked suddenly.

'Give who?'

'Your – the church.'

'Of course. How do you think we fund our outreach? How do you think the Word is spread? It costs.'

'Right.'

He got up from the table.

'Put your bowl in the dishwasher, Tom.'

She looked at his long, thin back, the blades of his shoulders through his T-shirt, his pepper-coloured hair. Terry's hair.

'You should come,' he said. 'You never have. You go to Lizzie's orchestra, you go to your choir. You never go to my things. How do you know what it's about? You'd be fired up. You'd see everything differently.'

'That's what I'd be afraid of.'

She was ready for bed but she didn't go. There was a tension about Tom, a nervousness. She waited, fiddled about putting things away and wiping down the work surfaces. In the end he said, 'Might go back to the States next year.'

'See some more of the country? Good idea.'

'Thing is, we've got this college in Carolina. A kind of Bible college. For training.'

We.

'I can train there.'

'A training college. I get it.'

'Don't wind me up. I want to be an outreach minister, it's what I think I'm called to do. To bring others in – to spread the faith.'

She said nothing. The questions that came to her lips could not be asked. What would your father have said? How are you going to pay for this? Don't you think you're too young? Are you sure?

'Mum?'

'Yes. Well, it's your life, Tom. But just think hard about this. It's a big commitment.'

'I think hard and pray about it all the time.'

She wanted to hug him, tall, bony, worried-looking, something of the ten-year-old still lingering on his face.

'Goodnight, love.'

'Mum . . .'

She waited.

'This Phil guy.'

'You have to meet him. Lizzie has. You'll like him.'

'Thing is . . . I know I was cool about it to begin with . . .'

The kitchen was quiet. Wait, Helen told herself. Just wait.

'I just think maybe you should watch yourself. What's he like? You don't know really. He might be anyone.'

'He's Phil. He teaches history. I've been out with him half a dozen times. I've been to his house. What's to know?'

'Just think you should be careful.'

'At first. I met him over the Net so I was careful. But you know that, Tom. I honestly don't think you've anything to worry about now.'

'OK.'

'No, it's obviously not OK with you so talk to me.'

'What if he wanted you to go and live with him? Or get married?'

'I'd think about it very carefully.'

'He could be anyone.'

'But he isn't. Tom, next year, Lizzie will be off to Cambridge, we hope, you say you'll be in America. That leaves me here.'

'Doesn't mean you have to hitch up with someone.'

'Please let me make my own choices.'

'I could have found you someone. I'd have picked the right person.'

'What, from that sect of yours?'

'It's about truth. It's about being on the inside, not out there.'

Helen sighed. They had reached the brick wall again.

In her room she found that she was shaking. Tom wanted to pick a partner and presumably a husband for her from the sect, to make sure she was saved, 'on the inside' as he put it. Presumably Phil, like Lizzie, would never be 'on the inside'.

How could this have happened to Tom in one summer week, how could his mind have been so altered, his whole view of life tampered with, by these people? Lizzie had said it was like living with an alien and Helen had been angry, made her take her words back. Tom was her brother. But Lizzie was right. This new Tom was alien.

Helen lay awake for a long time, distressed and troubled, longing for the old, easy-going, cheerful Tom, the Tom who mucked about. The Tom who laughed.

Forty

They were crammed into the conference room.

'OK, guys and gals, Lafferton Jug Fair, Saturday 27 October.'

Armed Response Bronze Command pointed to the map on the wall.

'Timing first. The fair set-up commences on the Friday evening, goes on till midnight. We have a list of fairground operatives – that's official ones, those who travel with the fair, family members mainly, the ones who come year in, year out. There won't be a problem there, it's the casuals, odd bods who might get one-off employment, cash in hand, no names, no pack drill. Every fairground operative on the list has been given an ID badge. Whether they'll wear them or not is another matter but uniform will be trying to enforce. Normally the fairground is open to the general public at any time but this year the entire venue will be closed off until one p.m. on the Saturday. Barriers will be up, uniform will be attending. No vehicles other than fairground authorised, of which we have a list of reg numbers. One o'clock the barriers come down – can't be left any later on safety grounds, we don't want them charging in like a herd of elephants or we'll have kiddies and old ladies crushed in the stampede. The procession is due to arrive in the square at four twenty-five, Jug Fair Queen and retinue first, floats behind. Assembly for departure from the rec. Entering down here. Four thirty, the fair is officially opened, the Fair Queen and the Mayor get onto the merry-go-round at four forty for the first ride. Then it's everything go. I wouldn't anticipate any trouble there but we will have Vehicle B on standby. As soon as the procession moves off, so does Vehicle B and follows at the back. Now you've all got smaller versions of the map, shout if you were away with the fairies and didn't pick one up as you came in, sorry about the quality, printer cartridge was running out.'

'When isn't it?'

'True. Right, heads down and take a long look, at your own map, at the map on the wall. I want everyone more familiar with the fair site than with the proverbial back of. I know some forces do this with fancy PowerPoint presentations but I haven't the know-how and in my experience the old-fashioned way is the best – it gets it engraved on your minds which is what I want. This has to be as familiar to you by Friday afternoon as the layout of your own houses. I want you to be able to go in there blindfold and find your way about. This is Map One – we'll look at Map Two in a mo – which gives us the position of every fairground ride and stall . . . it's always laid out to exactly the same plan as any of you who went to the fair when you were five and went again last year will know. But here you've got the area as it is today. It will be like this from midnight on Thursday – i.e. there will be no parked cars, in fact no vehicles at all.'

They looked down at the familiar street names in the Old Town area. The Jug Fair was mainly centred on St Michael's Square and a couple of the lanes which rayed out from it in the direction leading away from the cathedral towards the town. The wide pedestrian-only New Moon Street led to and from the fair.

'If our marksman tries to take a vehicle down there he'll be stopped by the barriers.'

'If he has a vehicle.'

'Well, it's probable. He needs to conceal his rifle, get away quickly . . . he can't walk through the streets carrying it without being spotted. Right, the square is sealed off here and here – those two lanes are only ever pedestrians and cyclists anyway. This is the layout of the rides and the stalls . . . the big Ferris wheel at this end, the merry-go-round at this.'

'I used to love them Jinny horses when I was a kid. Couldn't go on them enough times.'

'Bag of chips in your hand.'

'Or a hot dog.'

'Nah, candyfloss. You have to ride on them with your candyfloss.'

'No wonder the square's awash with puke by midnight.'

'Shut up, Clive.'

'The kiddies' rides are all out of the main square, up here. Teacups. Peter Rabbit ride. Ribbon Lane is all stalls – here up this way and here. Coconut shies, bobbing ducks, that stuff.

'Ghost train and the scary rides this side. Along here, more stalls . . . plus your food stands. We are going in down New Moon Street and parking up – here. And the second ARV is at the other side, here.'

'Bit prominent, aren't we?'

'That's the plan. High-profile armed response.'

'Ah, public reassurance.'

'Don't sneer, Rowley.'

'Wasn't sneering, sir.'

Houlish looked at him. Clive Rowley's face was blank.

'Right, well, don't. Like I said, high profile. These shootings have made the public very jittery, as well they might, and as you may possibly have heard we have caught a lot of flak from our friends in the media, so there's uniform crawling all over the fair, there's plain clothes, there's us. Nothing is going to go wrong. We're at the ready from the minute we're in position. OK, let's look on the screen again please. From the shooting of the two young women outside the *Seven Aces* club we're sure this is a skilled and cunning marksman. He knows what he's doing. The guy who shot Melanie Drew and Bethan Doyle confronted them at close range from their front doors with a handgun. It may not be the same guy as the *Seven Aces* killer and it's the latter we're worrying about here. If he's going to target the Jug Fair for whatever perverted reason he's unlikely to be confronting members of the public at close quarters with a handgun. He'll be using a rifle – he's a sniper. Right, let's have some guesses here. Westleton, Rowley, be the sniper, where do you fire from?'

'Top of the helter-skelter.'

'How do you get up there with a rifle without being spotted?

When? How do you stay up there out of sight when there's a queue of people climbing up and flying down? Think again.'

'He has to get into position unnoticed,' Clive Rowley said, speaking slowly and with concentration. 'There's always a load of people setting up, no way could he lurk in the fairground without being seen . . . so it's got to be buildings around. Empty buildings? That's where he was when he shot the girls outside the *Seven Aces* – either in the empty granary building or in the office block. So I reckon we've got to look at what's *around* the fairground site, not at the temporary structures.'

'Right, let's think along those lines. What have we got?' Houlish took the pointer. 'Let's take the square first. East side. High wall. Iron gate. Nothing there. North side. The courthouse building. Victorian. Six storeys. What do we think?'

'Good view – unobstructed.'

'Roof's hidden behind that crenellation. Not sure if it's flat or not.'

'It's not.'

'Wouldn't matter,' Tim said.

'Access . . . building's in use during the day. Various offices. We'll sweep the whole thing at the end of the day.'

'What'd be his exit route?'

'Rooftops,' said someone. 'Or he'd hole up till morning.'

Clive Rowley was silent. He was known to work things out before speaking. 'Is there a security guard?' he asked.

'No. CCTV and that's it.'

'Better get them to check it actually works.'

'Why don't we get in there ourselves, guv? Stake it out. Great vantage point.'

'Because this isn't an ambush. Too many people around, too dangerous.'

'What? We're sitting doing cat's cradle in the vehicle all night?'

'I didn't say that. Next door to the courthouse building we've the run of terraced cottages, half a dozen of them, all offices, then the war memorial, then there's two four-storey buildings which are being renovated.'

'There's scaffolding and the frontage is covered in plastic. He could hole out there without much trouble.'

'He's probably got a rifle with telescopics – he doesn't need to be that close.'

'What if he isn't using his rifle? He could be walking about with a handgun. Very difficult to suss that out in the sort of crowds we get at the fair, especially after dark,' Clive Rowley said.

Bronze Command shook his head. 'He'd have no chance of getting away. This guy's not a nutter who shoots to give himself up. He's cunning. His close-range killings have been in places where he's made pretty sure there'd be no witnesses and he could make an easy getaway. That just wouldn't be possible here even without all of us. OK, let's go back to the plan. There will be our two ARVs and Bevham are lending us one for backup. Here . . .'

Clive sat back and watched the pointer go over this entrance and that exit, this danger point and that. Steve Mason had slipped down into his seat and looked as if he was asleep with his eyes open.

'That's it. We'll have another briefing in here nine a.m. on Friday. Until then, don't shove it out of the way, get that plan in your head. Brood on it. Come up with a bright idea, shout. You're the sniper. Think like him. He's clever. We've got to be cleverer.'

Ten minutes later they were filing out for refs. In an hour they would be on the way to the airfield for a training session. It was drizzling outside.

'What do you reckon?' Steve said, standing in the queue.

'Nothing'll happen. Too obvious.'

'I'm not so sure. He could cause mayhem in five seconds . . . he'd love that, shooting at random,' Clive said.

'No, he's got a reason for these killings. I reckon they're personal.'

'Large tea, bacon and tomato bap, thanks. He must be a bloke with a hell of a lot of grudges then. Don't think forensics have established any links, have they?'

'Come on,' Ian Dean said, piling four warm sausage rolls onto his plate, 'no way are these random. There has to be links.'

'I don't see it. I don't see any of it, to be honest. I can't get a handle on this guy.' Clive set his tray down and moved the sauce bottles out of the way. 'I just think – putting half the county force onto the Jug Fair is a waste of resources. He's not going to show.'

'A fiver says he will.'

'You're on,' Clive said, taking a swig of tea. 'That fiver's got my name on it.'

Forty-one

Lois was there as ever on night-duty reception. Lois, pleased to see her and ready with a warm hug of welcome.

But then Jane caught her expression. 'I'm too late,' she said.

'Yes. Karin died about an hour ago.'

Jane sat down. She felt tired, cold and frustrated. The storms had caused such appalling delays and rerouting that she was here at ten when she should have made it by five.

'Come into the kitchen, I'll make you a hot drink. Have you eaten?'

'No, but I'm not hungry. I should go and see her.'

'Have this first. No hurry now.'

No. No hurry. Karin had waited for her as long as she could but Jane had let her down. It was not her fault, of course it was not, but she felt guilty nevertheless.

The fluorescent lights hummed as Lois switched them on and poured water into the kettle.

'Poor Jane. Nothing more upsetting.'

'I wanted to be with her. She wanted me to be with her.'

'I know.' She did not give out false comfort. Lois was a realist.

She set down a mug of tea and a plate of biscuits. 'Dunk one,' she said, 'I know you said you weren't hungry but somehow a dunked biscuit always goes down.'

It was true. Jane followed her out to the reception foyer. From the far end of the corridor she heard murmured voices, saw a light. A door closed.

'Do you know about Dr Deerbon?' Lois asked, back behind her computer.

'Yes, Cat told me. I was hoping to see her but I can't very well go up to the farmhouse at this time of night.'

'I should think you of all people probably could. Why don't you ring now?'

Jane hesitated.

'She might be glad of it, you know.'

'Has she heard about Karin?'

'Not my place to ring her.'

Jane wondered what she could say to Cat, out of the blue, at ten thirty at night. Looked at Lois. Lois nodded.

'Look, go into the relatives' room, I'll switch the phone through.'

It was picked up on the second ring.

'It's Jane,' she said. 'I'm at Imogen House.'

Ten minutes later she was sitting beside Karin McCafferty. The nurses had not yet moved her body, though the syringe pump and drip stand had been taken away. The lamp was on. They had closed the door.

Karin looked like a moth under the bedclothes, her skin fine, and almost transparent over the bones, her hair brushed and tied back, lying on the slightly raised pillows. Jane took her cool hand and put it to her own cheek.

'I know you won't blame me, but I should have been here. I wish I had been. I'm sorry.' Karin's eyelids were faintly blue, like those of a newborn baby. She was beautiful in death, as she had been in life, but remote. Sometimes, Jane had been with the dying and the newly dead and had had a powerful sense of their presence. But not now. Karin was as far away as it was possible to be and had left no trace of herself behind.

Half an hour later, she was sitting with Cat beside a low fire in the farmhouse sitting room, a whisky in her hand, the rain lashing against the windows.

Cat was leaning back, eyes closed, her face drained of everything but exhaustion.

'A patient who was nursing her mother at home said to me, "I'm way beyond tired." And this will get worse. It's like lying down while someone rains blows on you but somehow each blow hurts in a different way.'

'How are the children?'

Cat shook her head. 'The saving grace there is Judith Connolly. My father has been seeing her and she is amazing – calm, strong, easy-going, got the measure of him perfectly and fantastic with all three of the children. She's fast becoming my rock, in the absence of Simon.'

Jane took a swig of her whisky. 'Absence? But I saw him on the television news.'

'Yes, you did. That's one reason for his absence and obviously the chief one – it's tough for him. But what makes me mad is his stupid attitude to Judith. Si was always Mum's blue-eyed boy but Mum is dead and he can't take someone else being at Hallam House.'

'Doesn't he see that it's helping your father?'

Cat snorted. 'He doesn't choose to see. It's a good job he's so tied up with work and I've got Chris to worry about or I'd really lay into him.'

Jane said nothing. She had not been sure what she would feel, coming back here, hearing about him. Everything ought to be overshadowed by Karin's death and Chris's illness. She was acutely aware of Simon, nevertheless. He was associated so closely for her with this house and with his sister. Jane's memories were more vivid than she ever expected.

'I never knew what happened exactly with you two,' Cat said now. 'And feel free not to tell me.'

Jane set down her whisky glass. 'I ran away,' she said. 'That's what happened.'

'You sure? Only it's usually the other way round. Simon is the one who runs.'

Jane shook her head. 'I ran. I didn't know what I felt. I was in a very confused and fragile emotional state and I couldn't cope with another factor being added to the mix. It ought to have helped but it made things worse.'

'A lot had happened to you. Awful things.'

'I needed to sort myself out.'

'And have you?'

'Not altogether. But I think I am slowly working my way towards it – whatever *it* may be. I thought it was going to be the abbey. I really did want to make that work, but I knew straight away that it wouldn't. I knew when I lay in bed in my room there on the first night. I struggled on for six months and I'm glad I did.'

'One down, so to speak.'

'Yes. I feel much more confident about the next move. I want to do more academic work.'

'You mustn't bury yourself in a library, Jane, you're too good with people. A library is as bad as a convent.'

'But a library combined with students and a hospital is about right, don't you think? I don't deserve my luck.'

'As to that, which of us deserves what we get?' Cat shook her head, her eyes filling with tears. She got up and pushed the last of the logs together so that they burned up bright again. 'Australia is as far away as a sunlit daydream.'

'Did you like it?'

'Not really. But we were happy together, and it was different, which always shakes you up. Looking back, it seems idyllic, frankly.'

'How is Chris coping? I don't mean physically.'

'I don't know. How strange that sounds. But I really don't. At the moment, he's just pretty doped and getting through the days, sleeping a lot, waiting for the radiotherapy to start. Everything else is just beyond him. And you know Chris . . . he doesn't philosophise, he just gets on with it. The worst thing is, I can talk to patients about dying. I do talk to them. I think it's important. I get them to tell me what they feel, I get their relatives to do the same. But I can't do it with Chris. We talk about what's going to happen medically, but otherwise . . . I can't and he doesn't. We have never ever had anything we couldn't talk about, even if we argued. We often argued. But now there is this. It's frozen us, somehow. I feel as if I'm acting a part. This isn't me, this isn't Chris, this isn't us.'

'It's strange. Karin believed so passionately in alternative medicine that she rejected everything you and I would accept – and probably Chris too.'

'Definitely Chris. He's an evidence-based man. He won't consider anything else. When it comes down to it, you know, not many doctors do.'

'What would you blame for Karin's death? That she refused orthodox treatment?'

'Cancer is what I blame for her death, Jane. It's what I will blame for Chris's. But the longer I'm in medicine, the more I see of it, it becomes clear that what we know about cancer goes on one line that reads as follows: "You get it, or you don't. You get better, or you don't." There's another thing . . . I feel it ought to be me, I feel guilty. But inside, I'm just relieved that it isn't me. That it's someone else again, even if the someone is my husband. I've escaped. There now, I've said it.'

'But that's what we all feel, isn't it? The bullet missed me. Phew. No, that's not the best analogy just now.'

'Are you going to see Simon, now you're here?'

'I don't know. Probably not. I have to go tomorrow, and you say he's tied up with this investigation.'

'Stay with us for a few days. The children would love it and I won't have much time for friends once Chris comes out of hospital.'

Jane was silent for a moment. She wanted to stay and she had no reason to be back in Cambridge yet. She might also see Simon. Did she want that? Yes. Should she?

'I'd like to very much. But I don't think it would be a very good idea.'

It was Cat's turn to say nothing.

Forty-two

It was chance. A beautiful chance. Roadworks had held him up for so long he'd tried a side route, taken a wrong turn off the bypass and found himself in Dedmeads Road.

One end led into the new Ashdown estate, a large and still growing area of private housing, interlacing cul-de-sacs off a main avenue. The completed houses were furthest away. From Dedmeads Road it was still a building site, half-finished houses and garage blocks, unmade roads, scaffolding, pieces of scrub which would be turfed as the final job. Of the completed houses, many were still unsold. Developers' flags flew outside a couple of show houses.

At the north end, down which he had just come, one road of identical 1960s houses led to the bypass and away.

He stopped. Got out and looked around. He had the very dirty silver Focus. You saw a dozen of them every half-hour.

It was nine ten. School was in. Workers in. Dedmeads Road was empty apart from a few mothers with toddlers and push-chairs gossiping in a cluster outside the row of shops.

He got back into the car and drove on down. Parked near the shopping block but not near enough to have anyone pay attention to the car or the number plate.

The mothers huddled closer as he walked past and into the post office-cum-newsagent's, and bought a paper and a packet of chewing gum.

'Morning. Thanks.'

'Going to rain for the weekend again.'

'Right bugger then.'

'Eighty pence. Cheers.'

'See you later.'

He walked out, reading the front page of the red-top. The shopkeeper had forgotten him before he reached the door.

Newsagent's. Chinese fish and chip shop, closed. Launderette, two people inside, busy at the machines, not noticing him as he glanced through the windows. Late night grocer. Louise, Ladies' Hairdresser. He walked straight by, looking at the paper; the place had a venetian blind down, slats open. No one saw him. Empty shop. Empty card-display stands pulled into the middle. Dirty windows. Piles of junk mail on the floor below the letter box.

That was it. He walked on, past a block of semis. Then the low brick wall. A gravel car park. Bit of grass. Three or four trees. Blue sign. Gold lettering.

Our Lady of Sorrows Catholic Church

Times of Mass: daily at 8 a.m.; Sundays and Holy Days. 8 a.m., 9 a.m., 10.30 a.m., 4 p.m.
Confessions: Saturdays and Thursdays, 6–7.30 p.m.
Priest: Father G. Nolan, The Presbytery, 40 Dedmeads Road.

Bare-looking 1960s brick. Bright blue, yellow and green stained glass on either side of the light oak doors. Three shallow steps up. Wide gateway. Low iron gates, open and hooked back against the wall.

On the other side of the road, semis and a single detached house quite low down at the bottom of steep drives. Outside the detached, a sign. *Dedmeads Veterinary Surgery*. Three or four cars.

Hours: Monday to Friday 9–11 a.m. and 3–5 p.m.; Saturday 9–11 a.m.

Perfect.

Everything was perfect. Chance. A beautiful chance. He had to take it. Things fell out the way they did for a reason, he knew that.

He got back into the dirty silver Ford Focus and drove unobtrusively away.

At six that evening the Focus was stowed away in the lock-up he rented in Canal Street and he was in the van on his way to the airfield. It was raining heavily. Traffic was light and he knew he wasn't being followed because no one had any reason whatsoever to follow him. No one. He turned on the car radio to a local newsflash about the body of a teenage girl found in a ditch. She'd been missing for over a week. So why had it taken so long to find her? What had the police been farting about at? She'd been assaulted and strangled. Who did that sort of thing? Some animal. He shuddered, thinking of her, daft as teenage girls were, full of herself, cocky. Or some sad, lost kid, broken home, abused already and now again. Gone off with a stranger for a bit of fun and attention. Affection.

How did parents get through all that, girl not arriving home, mobile not answering, friends saying she'd left them hours before. Waiting. Dreading. Hoping. Desperate.

What kind of animal did that?

He knew nothing about that sort of behaviour.

His were completely different.

A clean kill.

The airfield was full of potholes and the potholes were full of water. Rain streamed across the headlights. He doused them as he drove up to the hangar and used the torch when he opened the doors. He drove the van inside and closed the doors again, took out the mechanic's lamp from the boot and plugged it into the battery.

Which was when he heard the sound. He froze. Outside the hangar? Or inside? He waited. Nothing. He waited again, counting. Two minutes. Three minutes. Nothing.

He relaxed, picked up the torch again and trained it on the place where the rolled-up plastic was hidden. Waited again. Nothing.

He stepped on the cement blocks he had manoeuvred there weeks ago and reached for the space behind the strut. As he did so, there was a noise again, far back inside the dark recesses of the hangar.

He jumped quickly down and walked towards it, holding the torch out. His trainers made no sound.

The noise was odd. It might have been a human groan, or an animal snuffling. There were foxes out here, his headlights had picked them up.

He moved slowly forward, though now the noise had stopped he was unsure if he was heading towards it. The torchlight picked up scuffed papers and broken concrete rubble on the ground, and the sides of the hangar when he moved it higher. Nothing else.

It came again. Animal. Had to be.

The next minute, something moved, his torch picked up a series of shapes and shadows, and then a man was lurching blindly towards him, hand up to his face against the powerful beam.

'Whatsitwhositwhatthefucksgoingon?'

He stopped. The man was a few yards away, still dazed by the light.

He trained it straight into his face.

'Bloodygerritoffwhatthehellyoufuckingplayingat?'

'Turn round.'

But the bundle of old clothes and filth that was the man who had been disturbed from his drunken snoring in the corner of the hangar took another lurching step forward.

'Turn round.'

The man did so, swaying a bit. 'Allrightallrightwhatyou doingsfuckinnightnothurtinganyonefuckincopsyourenotsafean ybloodywhereforgodsake –'

He slumped at the first blow to the back of his head.

Two minutes. Three. Four.

He hadn't moved.

The torchlight showed blood down the filthy matted hair and on the old raincoat.

Leave him or drag him back into the corner?

Leave him.

It took a few minutes to select the piece of plastic and stick it to the side of the van, roll up the rest and replace it carefully. Then he unplugged the mechanic's lamp from the battery, and stowed it behind the false panel in the back. Drove out. Closed the hangar doors. Took off his gloves and stowed those away.

It was still raining. He went slowly over the rutted ground – there was always the chance of getting a puncture here and he didn't want to hang about changing a wheel by torchlight, risking being seen from the road. As he neared the gates, a fox slipped across in front of him, yellow eyes gleaming, caught in his headlights.

Forty-three

'I feel guilty,' Cat said.

The *Croxley Oak* was pleasantly busy, with half a dozen people at the bar, two-thirds of the tables full and the first log fire of the autumn. A waiter went past carrying a loaded tray. There was the chink of glasses.

Simon looked at her across the table. They were both exhausted, both in need of exactly this. He didn't bother to reply.

'Chris should be here.'

'Yes, he should.'

'Will he ever have this sort of quiet evening out again?'

Simon shook his head.

'He might. When he gets over the operation. The radiotherapy will reduce the rest of the tumour for a time, then he'll get a remission, it might be quite a decent one and we can come here.'

'You should. Do everything you can.'

'Yes.'

'You said we weren't going to talk about it.'

Cat's eyes filled with tears.

'Come on.'

The menus were chalked on blackboards at either end of the long room, specials on another board behind the bar. It was one of Simon's favourite eating places and he hadn't been here for months.

'Let's make the most of it. Oh, good, they've got mussels.'

*

Moules marinières and fresh sardines, French bread and a bowl of olives were on the table when Cat's mobile rang.

'If it's home answer it, otherwise ignore it.'

'I don't recognise the number. All right, ignore.'

'When is Karin McCafferty's funeral?'

'I've no idea. Do you know that apart from her bastard ex-husband I don't think she had any family? She never mentioned them. I wonder who'll make the arrangements? I've known very old people have funerals at which the only attenders were me and the district nurse but that just meant they'd outlived everyone. Karin was only in her forties. I'll talk to Imogen House, see what they know.'

'You went to see her when she was alive. That's what matters. Don't have regrets.'

'I don't. Jane is the one who has those.'

'Jane who?' He looked blank for a moment.

'Jane Fitzroy. God, it's been so long since we've talked.'

'Tell me about it.'

'Are you on call now?'

'I'm always on call at the moment. What about Jane Fitzroy?'

'Oh, you do remember her then.'

Simon picked a mussel carefully out of its shell with the prong of his fork and put it into his mouth. He did not look up.

'By the time she got here she was an hour too late. Not her fault, but it upset her.'

'She rang you?'

'She stayed the night.'

He poured her another glass of wine.

'Don't you want to know any more?'

He shrugged.

'She asked after you.'

'Cat. Leave it.'

'Why?'

He shook his head, wiping bread round the plate to mop up the sauce.

'You liked her.'

'Well, yes. So did you.'

'That's different.'

'Just leave it.'

Cat recognised his expression and his tone of voice. He meant it. The portcullis had come down. She would get no more out of him.

'You're your own worst enemy, did you know that?'

But the waiter came to take their plates and Cat knew better than to pursue the subject further. For now, she thought. For now.

'Are you taking the kids to the Jug Fair?'

'I think so. Chris will be back home but Dad said he would stay with him. Felix is a bit young. He can stay too.'

'Will you join up with someone else?'

'I'm sure we'll meet a load of people but Judith said she would come with me. And please do not put on that expression.'

'What expression?'

'Get over it, Si. She's lovely and she's good for Dad. Don't put yourself out in the cold.'

The waiter came towards them with braised lamb shank and pan-fried black bream.

'Simon,' she said, after the vegetables were on the table, 'thanks for this. It's what I needed. I didn't realise.'

'Trust your brother.'

'Hmm.'

'What?'

'Oh, I do. On some things.'

She picked up her knife and fork, but as she did so she remembered, remembered the full horror and awfulness of what was happening, remembered Chris lying in bed that afternoon, eating a spoonful of scrambled egg very slowly, his head bound with bandages, eyes tired and defeated. He had already seemed to be receding from her, living a twilight life in a place she could not go to, a place he had to inhabit entirely alone. She swallowed and stared at the food on her plate.

'It's OK,' Simon said.

But it was not and the tears spilled onto the back of her hand as she tried to wipe them away.

She got up. 'I'm going to the cloakroom. When I come back, just talk to me. I can't. Just talk to me.'

Simon waited, separating the flakes of moist lamb off the bones and eating them slowly, thinking. The bar had filled but they were in a corner at the end, not overheard.

She was a long time but when she returned her face was tearless, her hair brushed back.

'Right,' Cat said, putting the last of the vegetables onto her plate.

'Do you think I'll ever find the right person to marry?'

She stared at the food piled onto her fork, trying to take the question in. He had never asked anything like it before, had always veered away from the subject when she had raised it. Cat thought she had given up trying to fathom her brother but now she realised that she had not.

'I know you want me to talk about Jane but I'm not sure I can. I'm not sure about anything.'

'I suppose,' she said carefully, 'the first thing to know is, do you actually want to be married? Do you see yourself as a husband and perhaps a father, living in a house with a wife, having a totally different domestic set-up from the one you have now?'

'Why? Why would all that have to change?'

'Because now you are a bachelor, you have a pad for a bachelor, you live a solitary life, mostly at work, sometimes away with your sketchbook, occasionally with us. But that would change.'

'Not necessarily.'

'You expect a wife to fit in round the corners? You carry on as you are?'

'No. But you make it sound as if my life would change completely.'

'And you don't want that?'

'No. Of course I don't. I love my life.' He knew as he said it that it was profoundly true.

'Then you would have to have either a very remarkable wife or a very unusual marriage or probably both. It wouldn't change all at once, but in the end it would have to. Marriage is a new life and it's always a compromise . . . you just have to make sure that you both want the same compromise.'

'Yes. So perhaps I need to forget it.'

'I'm not saying that. You do have to be sure – perhaps more than most people. They marry for the person but maybe also because they are ready to change and develop and have a new sort of life. They want that actively. You don't. But you're not quite forty, Si, you're not old enough to be so set in your ways.'

He finished the last of his lamb without replying.

Cat thought about the women he had known – the ones she had been aware of at least. Diana, the older, spasmodic mistress – that had worked as far as Simon was concerned because Diana had not changed his life, though Cat knew she had wanted to. Freya Graffham. Yes, he had thought he might be in love with her, even more so when she became unobtainable. Before Diana, there had been one rather fleeting affair with a young woman barrister whom Cat had not liked. Eleanor someone.

And then Jane Fitzroy.

But Jane had been vulnerable, confused in most areas of her life and suffering under the blows which had fallen on her one after another during her short time in Lafferton.

'What is it that you want, Si?'

He was about to say that he wanted what she had – her happy married life, her farmhouse, her family – but he stopped himself. Cat without Chris, Cat facing her husband's death, Cat on her own bringing up the children, Cat who needed him far more than he needed her, the reverse of the way it had always been – he tried to imagine it and could not.

The waiter took their plates and brought the chalk board of desserts, propping it against the next-door table. They were both glad of it.

'Sticky toffee pudding,' Cat said, 'and ice cream. And mint tea.'

'Twice,' Simon said.

Later, driving back to the farmhouse, he said, 'Perhaps it's safer.'

'What is?'

'Like this. Women who aren't available. Is it that?'

'Cod psychology. It could be, if you don't want to change.'

'So what do I do?'

'For God's sake, Simon, I don't know! You're putting too much on me here.'

'Sorry.'

'We're lucky. Work helps. Think if you were stuck in a widget factory watching a conveyor belt all day.'

He sighed. 'Instead of failing to catch a particularly vicious gunman.'

'You'll catch him.'

'Nothing says we will.'

'You won't let this one go. I know you.'

'I tell you something, Cat. It's getting to me and when it gets to me it's personal. Like the child abductions got personal. Like the arsonist got personal. I begin to think he's doing it to defy me. How paranoid is that? But it's how I feel. I feel taunted. Come on, Serrailler, stop me, I challenge you.'

'Why? He's killed women.'

'Oh, I don't mean he wants me dead. But once they get lucky two or three times, once they start getting away with it, then it does become a thing between the two of us, however many others are involved – dozens in this case. Something connects between me and this unknown out there. I have to get to him, I have to stop him.' He banged his hand on the steering wheel.

'Are you sure there's only one?'

'No. It's possible the sniper who shot the girls is not the same as the man with the handgun who killed Melanie Drew and that young mother.'

'What do you really think?'

'Oh, I really think it's the same guy. I'm sure of it. Gut feeling.'

'And gut feeling says he'll do it again?'

'Yes,' Simon said quietly, 'I'm afraid it does. I want to get there first but get where? Where is he going to next? Why? I've no idea about the why, nothing links, nothing fits, Cat, and until something does, I'm blundering about in the dark wearing a blindfold.'

They saw the lights of the farmhouse shining out to them from the far end of the country lane.

'So be careful, always,' he went on. 'This is important. Don't answer the door if you don't know who it is and never let the children answer it, keep the door on the chain.'

'You're serious?'

'You leave doors unlocked, you leave windows open . . .'

'OK, OK, and I've got enough, don't start telling me about men with guns waiting to blow out my brains or those of my children when I open the front door.'

'It's happened. I'm reminding you.'

'Thanks. Aren't you coming in?'

'No, I'll head for home, get some sleep in before someone disturbs it.'

'You just don't want to see Dad and Judith.'

'That too.'

'God, you make me furious.' Cat slammed the car door hard and walked away.

'Don't say thanks for the lovely dinner or anything,' Simon shouted after her. But she had gone inside.

It occurred to him, driving his new Audi fast through the dark lanes, that an argument with Cat could end like this, with both of them cooling off under their respective roofs. An argument with a wife was one you would find it hard to escape. He did not blame his sister. She had enough to cope with and if she had to let fly at someone it might as well be at him. One of them would ring the other during the next couple of days and the whole thing would be over before it had begun.

If he were married he would not be able to return to a quiet, peaceful flat and life as he liked it.

He was better off on his own.

Forty-four

'You're pathetic. I don't get you. Why are you doing this? Why do you want to ruin it for her?'

'I don't.'

'You do. Obviously you do. Have you listened to yourself?'

Tom had barged into Lizzie's room and flopped down on her bed, then got up and roamed around, opening cupboards and shutting them, kicking his foot against the wall, taking a book off the shelf and putting it back. That had gone on for several minutes before he had finally said, 'I don't like him. He's all wrong. I just don't like him and he's got to go, she's got to see.'

His sister had been furious. As far as Lizzie was concerned, her mother looked wonderful, shining with happiness, enjoying life, having fun, sharing things. All of which was because of Philip Russell. Besides, Lizzie liked Phil. He was exactly right and she couldn't get over the luck. The chances of Helen Creedy meeting a series of disastrous men, wrong men, weird men, had been high, instead of which she had met Phil, bang, first time.

'What do you mean? Put that down, will you?'

'Jesse Cole told me. Phil Russell teaches his brother so I asked him.'

'Asked him what? What could Jesse Cole's brother know?'

'I said, he teaches him, he's been teaching him for two years.'

'And?'

'He said he's an atheist. He preaches it. He preaches there isn't a God when he's supposed to be teaching history, he makes cracks about it all the time, sarcastic remarks, he sneers, he talks to them about that Dawkins book.'

Lizzie sighed and turned back to *Henry IV, Part One*. Once Tom started on religion she didn't want to hear.

'He's bound to talk like that to her.'

'Mum's got a mind of her own.'

'I don't want her having anything to do with him.'

'Perhaps I should get him to talk to you like that. Time someone got you into a reasonable argument, showed up your sect for what it is.'

'It's not a sect.'

'OK, cult.'

'It's not a cult.'

'Go away, Tom, I've got to finish this. Go and pray with your friends.'

'If you came with me you'd see it wasn't anything like you think. You think it's the Moonies or the Scientologists or something. I dunno. Mormons, Plymouth Brethren.'

'Whatever.'

'It matters, it's about being on the right side, it's about having Jesus come into your life and change everything, it's –'

Lizzie stuffed her fingers in her ears.

Tom sat back down on the bed. He looked unhappy. She saw him as he used to be, moody but free, laughing, taking the mick, mucking about. A good mate. Not any more. Now he was either spouting the Bible or he looked unhappy.

'Leave her alone, let her enjoy herself. You've got to get over it, Tom. Once I've gone to uni, you can't rant and rave at Mum the entire time, it'll do no good and it'll make her miserable. And if you break them up I'll kill you.'

'I wish you'd see it like I do.'

'I can't. I never will. I don't know you any more, I haven't a clue what goes on in your head.'

'Yes, you do, I keep telling you, I try to make you see. It's really, really important, it's the only important thing.'

Lizzie got up and opened her door. Tom looked at her. Again she saw his face when he was six or seven. Not this face, now. His old face.

'I've got to finish this.'

'Lizzie . . .'

'Please.'

She held his look. Then they heard the key turn in the front door.

'Hi!'

'OK, she's back from her book group, go and make a cup of tea and don't you dare say anything, Tom Creedy, don't you bloody dare.'

After a moment of sitting, staring at the floor unhappily, Tom unwound his long frame and got up.

In his own room he sat on the window ledge looking out, as he had done when he was small and needed to think. The street below was quiet. People went to bed early.

He wondered if he should talk to Pastor Evans. Phil was a problem and Tom knew he had to solve it before his mother did something stupid like marry the guy. It wasn't that he minded her marrying. He'd sorted that out early on. Lizzie banged on about how lonely she was since Dad died, how it would be good for her, how she needed someone, and she was right, he'd never really had a problem with that. He hadn't now. She ought not to be by herself once he and Lizzie had gone. It was Phil. Tom used to get vibes around people when he was younger, that there was something not right about them, but more recently he'd tried to ignore them when the pastors had said that sort of thing could be the Devil whispering in your ear or even lodged in your brain. New Agey stuff. Still, secretly, he knew he'd often been right and he didn't like to ignore the vibes altogether. He'd had them when he'd met Phil, strong ones. He didn't like disagreeing with any of the pastors, they'd guided him the right way, he ought to listen. But about Phil Russell he knew best, and in any case, it wasn't only the vibes, it was what he'd been told, real stuff.

He went downstairs.

His mother was sitting at the kitchen table with a mug of tea, writing in her book group notebook.

'Hello – it's freshly brewed.'

'No thanks.' Tom got a can of Coke from the fridge and stood with his back against the worktop drinking it. He wanted to say something now but where to start, how to start?

'Good meeting?'

Helen smiled. 'Fine thanks.'

'Interesting book?'

'Yes thanks. *The Kite Runner*.'

'Right.'

'Do you want something, Tom?'

'No. Why would I?'

'A sub for instance?'

'No, I'm good thanks.'

'Oh. Fine.' She looked down at her notebook again, waiting for her son to say whatever it was he was finding difficult to talk about.

'You going out this week?'

Ah. She wrote a couple of words while saying, 'Yes. Thursday. And then we're going to the Jug Fair. Daft but fun.'

'Right.'

'Thursday Phil has tickets for the ballet. I'm not that keen on ballet but there you go.'

'Why?'

'Never seen the point. I always think they'd find it so much easier if they just started talking.'

'No, I meant if you don't really like it, why go? You don't have to.'

'No I don't. But I probably owe it to ballet to give it one more try.'

'I don't see that.'

'No, you probably wouldn't.'

Silence. He drank two or three times. The washing machine started its spin cycle.

'It is OK about the States, isn't it?'

'About you going? You live your own life, Tom, you know what I think.'

'It's really important. I've got to do it.'

'It may be important now. I just don't want you to gear your whole future to this church thing.'

'I'm not.'

'Seems like it from here.'

'It isn't the church thing, as you call it, it's giving my life to

Jesus, that's what it's about. If I go to the Bible college I come out ready to serve and bear witness.'

'You sound like a pamphlet.'

'Sorry.'

'Just don't be swayed by other people, Tom. Especially not by oratory. I know, they get up there and preach and it's mesmerising, but when you come down to earth –'

'Phil's an atheist.'

Tom had gone scarlet. He swigged the last of his Coke hastily and dropped the can into the bin.

'I know. Does that worry you a lot?'

Tom mumbled. His mother had put her pen down and was looking him full in the face, which always made him uncomfortable.

'Because while I can understand that it might, I don't think it's really your concern. You're going away, so is Lizzie soon. This is about me.'

'Not only.'

'Yes, only. Or rather, Phil and me.'

'I have to worry, don't you see?'

'You mean if I marry him?'

'You going to, then?'

'I've no idea. We're fine as we are for now. But if I go to hell I'll do it in my own way and take responsibility, it won't be your fault.'

'Only it will. It'll mean I could have done something and I didn't.'

Helen laughed, until she saw the pain and anxiety on his face and stopped.

'Don't worry. I've listened to you, I understand how important it is to you and if I reject it that is really not your fault. I'd stand up in your church and tell them so if it'd help.'

He shifted from one foot to the other. Helen's heart went out to him. He was too young for all this, trying to save everyone from damnation, trying to convert the world. He had been carefree, relaxed, a force for good, and now he was tense, troubled, endlessly striving, measuring himself against those she privately thought were not worth a hundredth of him. Whoever they were, they made her angry.

'Do you like Phil? That matters to me.'

'Don't know him really.'

'What you've seen of him?'

Tom shrugged.

'He's a good person, Tom. By most people's definitions of what good means, he is.'

'If you say so.' He turned away.

'I do. But you matter to me most – you and Liz. If this really upsets you, I won't see him.'

He looked at her again, his face open and alarmed. Then he came over and gave her a quick, hard hug. 'You've got to,' he said. 'You go for it. Doesn't matter what I think.'

He fled from the room.

For a second she made to follow him but stopped herself. Tom worried her because he had changed so drastically. His conversion to this Jesus sect had come in a rush and within months he had spoken of little else, dropped old friends, spent his spare time with new ones from the church, become obsessed with 'saving and converting' as Lizzie had said with scorn. But his new-found belief did not seem to make him happy or fulfilled. On the contrary, he was anxious and tense most of the time. The old Tom had been laid-back and cheerful, untroubled by most things.

She made another cup of tea, wondering if she could talk to Phil about it. But this was not his concern. Her children were hers, as Phil's sons were his.

She went to bed and lay awake, worrying about Tom, and for the first time in some weeks longed for Terry to be here, sorting it all out calmly, talking to Tom, reassuring her as he always had.

She was asleep when Tom slipped out of his room and out of the house without switching on the lights and pushed his motorbike halfway up the road before starting it, for fear of disturbing her and having to answer questions.

Forty-five

'There's a woman applied for the vacancy,' Ian Dean said on the way to the airfield. 'Lucy Fry. Know her?'

'Seen her around. Short dark hair?'

'Lezza,' Clive Rowley said.

'So?'

'Only saying.'

'I could report you for that.'

'Report me for what?'

There were three of them and a vehicle full of gear and it was an hour to the end of shift. It was driving rain.

'What was I thinking? I don't need the overtime this bad.'

'Hour, tops,' Liam Westleton said, spinning the van round a corner and sending up a sheet of spray.

'Right, and it's your round.'

'I don't mind having a woman, best shot I ever worked with was a woman.'

Clive made a noise in his throat.

'What?'

'Be PMT every time we have a nasty situation.'

'You want to watch your attitude, Rowley. Anyway, I only said she'd applied. Right, here we go. Which one are we picking?'

There were five hangars.

'Far one on the left,' Rowley said.

'Why?'

'Dunno. No good taking the nearest, we need a bit of a run.'

Westleton started to plough through the water-filled potholes and muddy grass towards the hangar. It was just after lunch. No one about.

'One day we'll come out here for training and the place'll be full of demolition men and builders. Got to be housing here sooner or later, it's a waste.'

'Think it's a contaminated site, Ian. No one knows what to do with it. Meanwhile, let's get on with it. Only this one's no good, the roof's half caved in.'

He reversed and drove back, the van lurching and swaying, to the second hangar.

'This one's too near the road.'

'None of them's near the road and what does it matter anyway? Save the suspension.'

Clive shrugged and went straight round to the back of the van when they stopped. Westleton went to the metal bar that held the hangar doors and lifted it.

'One of the other lot must have been out here,' he said, coming back. 'Thought that would be stiff but it came up sweet as a nut.'

'Fire service come up here for training.'

'Right. Better check when we get back then, make sure they haven't got a session clashing with us tomorrow.'

They were hauling the gear out of the van, long wooden and metal poles, a steel-mesh rope ladder. The smaller gear, mainly hand tools, came up with them on the day. The training day happened every six weeks, occasionally out here, with team exercises, climbing practice, breaking down and entering. Westleton and Rowley dragged out a couple of old doors from the van, set one down and carried the other towards the hangar. They would be building a makeshift entrance with the doors suspended on poles.

'Ian, bring the box of padlocks from under the bench, will you?'

Padlocks and chains to hitch round some of the girders, another kind of obstacle to be broken through.

The grey light of a sodden autumn afternoon filtered a short way through the open doors but the recesses of the hangar were dim. They would rig up makeshift lighting in the morning but some of the session would be in darkness with the doors half closed.

'OK, let's have this stuff up against the side here, cover it with the sacks. Not that anyone's going to be interested.'

They lugged things in and out, saying little. The rain slanted across on the wind into the hangar.

They stashed the last of the wooden poles and doors, covered them with tarpaulin and were making to go when Rowley said, 'You hear that?'

'Nope.'

'What?'

'I thought I heard something over there.'

'Birds. You get birds nesting in here, up in the roof.'

'Right.'

'You spooked or what?'

'Nah. Be my ears want syringing. See the ME if it gets any worse.'

But as they swung the hangar doors together, Liam Westleton turned and looked back inside.

'What?'

'Was it like a whistling sound?'

'Yeah, and I said, it's my ears. Forget it.'

'Come on, I want to get home, I've got footie training.' Ian Dean played for the county force first eleven.

They slammed the doors, dropped the bar across, piled into the van. The rain had eased but the sky was oyster-coloured, the wind whipping across the water-filled potholes and ruffling the surface.

Westleton had his hand on the starter, but then he hesitated.

'Come on, come on.'

'If there was something, we'd better check it out.'

'There wasn't.'

'All the same. I'll drive the van right in, scout the place with the headlights. Apart from anything else, I don't want that lot nicked.'

'Be a fox,' Ian said. 'Foxes all over here, you can smell them when it's drier.'

'Get the doors open again.'

Clive Rowley got slowly out of the van again and stumbled as he caught his foot. 'Shit.'

'Get on with it.'

'Twisted my ankle.'

'You're not hurt.'

But Rowley was hopping on one foot, leaning against the side of the van.

Westleton sighed. 'Get him back on board then. Leave it be.'

'Probably nothing, Sarge.'

The other two helped Clive Rowley up the back step of the van and onto the bench, where he sat rubbing his ankle and muttering under his breath.

'Ears. Ankle. You got a pencil. Better write the ME a list.'

'Ha ha.'

Liam Westleton turned the van and headed off towards the road.

Forty-six

It had taken him a week to plan everything. She hadn't been in touch at all, not a word, not a note. She hadn't and not one member of her family. He felt as if he hadn't existed as far as they were concerned, as if they had airbrushed him out of their lives and their memories.

He wasn't having it. But he didn't rush anything. His anger had been a flaring bonfire, but he waited until it had shrunk down and become a small, spinning, red-hot core which he knew he could control. You needed control. He went running, he walked it off up on the Moor, he went into Starly Woods and shot pigeons, and after the pigeons, he took half a dozen empty tin cans and set those up, shot at those until he could do the row, one to six, without missing. Every time one went down, it was one of them. Her father. Mother. Sister. Grandmother. Kid brother. Then her. She was the last each time. When he'd shot them all down he set them up in the same row and shot them again.

A week.

He had waited until teatime, half past six, when he knew she'd be home from work. She was always home then.

It was a beautiful evening, warm, still, sweet-smelling even in the middle of the town. He'd parked the car higher up and strolled down. A couple of kids had been doing wheelies in the middle of the road near her house. He'd waited a bit but in the end he'd told them to scarper. He didn't want kids there even if he was only going to frighten her. Frighten them all. Kids oughtn't to be involved.

He could trust his anger now. It was under control. He'd frighten her but nothing more. He wanted to see her face, how she'd look at him, what she'd try to say. Then see the fear.

As he'd walked he'd wondered why he was doing this because, in spite of it, he loved her. He had never thought he would feel as he had felt for Alison, as he still felt, and his ball of anger was a part of the same feeling. He had walked all the way down one side of the street, looking at her house as he had passed it, and then back on the other side. The gate was painted blue, quite bright. He could see the blueness staring out at him.

He had slowed down, slowed and slowed until he was hardly putting one foot in front of the other as he had approached the blue gate.

There was no car in the drive.

He'd stood there, hand on the gate, swallowing his anger down. Then he'd seen the movement in the window, behind the curtain. He had pushed the blue gate open.

She must have run down the stairs and been waiting because as he lifted his hand to knock she opened the door wide.

Georgina.

He could sense the fear on her. She was holding it back, behind defiance, but her eyes were everywhere, at him, away from him, over his shoulder.

'She's not here.'

'I don't believe you. I want to talk to her, Georgie. Tell her.'

'I said. She's not here.'

'I want to come in and see for myself.'

'Well, you can't. She doesn't want to see you anyway, she doesn't want anything to do with you, she told you that.'

He tried to push her out of the way but then there was someone else, a man he had never seen before, right behind her.

'This is my Uncle Gordon,' she said. 'Tell him Ally's not here.'

The man wasn't tall but he was squat and muscled, like a small thick barrel, arms crossed. He could have dealt with him easily enough but that wasn't what he'd come for.

'Alison,' the uncle said, 'isn't here. Can't you take that in?'

'I want to see her, that's all. I've a right to an explanation.'

'You've had one.'

'If she isn't here, where is she then?'

'Mind your –'

'No, it's fine, Uncle Gordon, I'll tell him. I think he ought to know.'

'Know what?'

She moved away from the door a few yards down the path and he followed.

'Look, she's not here and that's the honest truth. She hasn't been here for a few days. She's gone away and she isn't on her own. She's with Stuart. So you'd better leave.'

'Where is she? Where? Where?' He felt himself start to shake, felt the rage burst out of its strict confines. 'I've a right to know.'

'No,' Georgina said, 'no, you haven't. I'm not saying any more and don't come here again.' She turned.

He grabbed her arm. 'If I write a letter to her, will you pass it on?'

'I don't know.'

He hesitated. He didn't want to hurt Georgina. He didn't want to hurt Alison. But others would suffer. Others. Others would never taste happiness.

He pulled himself up. 'Thanks,' he managed to say, 'thanks, Georgie.'

He walked down the path, closed the bright blue gate behind him and went fast up the road, and now he was shaking, now he almost lost it, almost knocked over an old woman who was going past him, almost pushed her to the ground. He was angry with himself. He shouldn't be thinking like that. He needed to get himself under control.

He passed his car and walked on, walked fast and steadily, for a couple of miles, in and out of streets at random, talking to himself, bringing himself down, reining himself in slowly. It was like trying to get hold of a mad horse, but in the end, he felt that he was getting there.

He walked until he came to a corner pub and went in. Half of him wanted to drink himself into a stupor. He bought a pint of Guinness and sat down. He drank it slowly, making it last. His hands were shaking but he made that stop too.

When he was halfway down the glass, he started to think, coolly, rationally, point by point, trying to make a clear plan. He had the beginnings of it by the time the glass was empty.

He didn't allow himself another.

Forty-seven

It was thundery. The narrow road that wound up the slope to the crematorium was slicked with rain making the cars move even more slowly. Three cars.

Jane Fitzroy waited, sheltering under the overhang, the rain slanting across the lawns. The hearse. One other funeral car behind it. And Cat Deerbon's dark green Peugeot. And then, much further behind, just turning into the gates, a small battered van.

The hearse crunched slowly towards her across the gravel. Drew up beside her. The pale wood coffin had a small white posy, a wreath of red and gold, and behind those, a vast display of lilies and dark green ivy, commanding and extravagant.

Jane glanced at the card as the coffin was sliding out of the car. '*Dearest Karin, Our love and thanks for all the wonderful things you created for us and for your warm and loyal friendship. Too soon to leave us. Cax and Lucia.*'

An elderly couple got out of the car behind the hearse. Then Cat. Then a young man, awkward in a suit, from the van.

Jane hesitated. A large crowd at a funeral did not necessarily mean they were a crowd of loving friends, far from it, but this group seemed pitifully small. Karin had left a note about her funeral. The pieces of music. The hymn. The reading, from the garden writings of Christopher Lloyd. 'If it is you taking the service, Jane, I know you'll pick the right prayers.' She hoped that she had.

She turned and went inside to the first notes of 'Jesu, Joy of Man's Desiring'. As she did so, she heard a car come fast up the approach road. She hoped Karin's ex-husband might have thought better of his decision not to be here, but she walked on into the small, bland chapel, not glancing round.

She delivered the opening prayer, but as Cat got up to read a passage Karin had chosen from *The Well Tempered Garden*, Jane looked up and directly at Simon Serrailler. He was gazing at her. She turned her eyes quickly away, to Cat, to the flowers on the coffin, to the floor. He had slipped into a seat in the second row.

Cat read well, carefully and slowly.

Jane looked steadily at her as she finished, acutely, furiously conscious that her own face had flushed scarlet. But she kept her voice steady.

'Karin wanted the hymn "The King of Love My Shepherd Is". It isn't always easy to sing when there are so few voices, so we have chosen a recording of a congregational version and we can join that. I hope it doesn't seem too much like karaoke.'

Strangely, it did not. The voices from the tape took up the hymn and the real and present voices were clear above them. It was a compromise but better that, Jane thought, than a weak, thready rendering to embarrass everyone.

The rain drummed on the roof of the chapel as the hymn finished. It was hard to focus and she felt ashamed of that, angry that she was so disturbed by Simon's presence, wishing he had not come, wanting to remember Karin. And what would she have said? A picture flashed into Jane's mind: Karin looking amused. Yes, she would find it amusing, yes, she would have had something teasing to say. But if Karin was smiling, Jane could not.

'God our creator and redeemer, by your power Christ conquered death and entered into glory. Confident of his victory and claiming his promises, we entrust your servant Karin to your mercy in the name of Jesus our Lord, who died and is alive and reigns with you, now and for ever.'

She hated cremations, hated the anonymity of these identikit chapels, hated the lack of beauty, hated the terrible curtain and the sound of the coffin sliding away. For her, a burial had dignity, though she knew plenty of fellow priests who disagreed.

She looked once more at Karin McCafferty's coffin, the white flowers, the flash of brass on the handle in the dark chapel. Then she bent her head and began the committal prayer.

Cat had her eyes closed but made no attempt to brush the tears from her face. Andy Gunton stood rigid, swallowing hard. He had worked with Karin, spent part of almost every day with her in the gardens at Seaton Vaux, the Caxton Philips's estate, learned from her, laughed with her and, not knowing what to do or say when her illness took a final grip, had kept away and was ashamed of the fact now, despising himself for being the kind of person who crossed the road to avoid an uncomfortable encounter.

'Amen.'

Simon heard his own clear voice bridging the short distance between himself and Jane Fitzroy. He had not known what his reaction would be to seeing her again and had been taken aback by it.

The coffin slid forward and Cat caught her breath. Chris, she whispered, oh God.

Simon looked at her but her head was bent. Chris, he thought.

'Karin asked for some music now. It meant a great deal to her. Please listen to it and think of her with gladness, remembering her brave and vital spirit.'

So often, Cat thought, there is a dire moment at cremations when the canned music blares out 'My Way', 'Somewhere over the Rainbow', 'I will always love you' . . . But when 'Blowing in the Wind' came in, it was right after all. Cat smiled.

'God, I hate these places,' Simon said, touching Cat's shoulder as they came out to the porch. The thunder was rolling away but the rain was still heavy, the sky blue-black as a fresh bruise.

'I'm glad you made it.'

'Didn't think I would.' He looked round quickly, then said, 'I want to have a word with Andy Gunton. Now there's an old lag who turned out well.'

'I think Jane would like to see you.'

'I have to scoot then, sorry.'

She gave him a look, said nothing, as he went up to Andy who was standing uncertainly to one side.

Jane was talking to Karin's relatives. Cat waited, hearing the last of the song, sounding melancholy in the empty chapel behind them.

Simon ran through the rain to his car, followed by Andy. As they moved off, another funeral party was making its way up the drive. The undertakers had placed Karin's flowers in the porch and the scent of the white, waxen lilies was exotic. No lilies, Cat thought. No lilies, no crematorium. It was something she and Chris had always disagreed about. He was not a believer, though he respected her faith, and he was firmly on the side of cremation, for rational, practical and what she now saw as heartless reasons. She knew what he would want.

Jane had seen the relatives into the funeral car, and was coming towards her. It was a little after three o'clock.

'I'll drive us into town,' Cat said. 'Let's go and have tea and toast in Karin's favourite café.'

Jane smiled. 'I can take my surplice off in the car.' She glanced round the car park.

'He had to scoot,' Cat said. 'As he put it.'

Forty-eight

When he had walked up the road past the Catholic church he had paced out the distance from the kerb and then from the road by eye. That night he had drawn out a plan and also downloaded the map of the area, zooming in on the narrow section of Dedmeads Road which included the church and the vet's surgery opposite. Then he traced the route down which he would come and his exit. He reckoned he could be onto the bypass in fifty seconds, maybe less. Once there, he was away.

He cut himself a corned beef sandwich, made a mug of tea, and went back to the plan. This one was a challenge. If this one went wrong, that was it. The others had been easier, though he'd sweated a bit looking down onto the *Seven Aces* club, going over and over in his mind the images of the fire escape and the lane behind. But it had worked. It had worked every time but he knew the one thing he couldn't afford was take a chance, go into something without a careful recce and a well-thought-out plan. That was for idiots and idiots got caught and so they bloody well should.

One thing though. He scoured the local paper and watched the news, listened to Radio Bevham obsessively, but there'd been nothing about the bloke in the hangar.

He switched on the television again now and waited for the news. Nothing. It was fine.

He had forty-eight hours and everything had to fit, everything had to be perfect, the timing, the distance, the gun, everything.

He'd leave it now, sleep on it, knowing that it was in his head and printing itself on his memory. He'd look at it tomorrow and go over it twice, inch by inch, on Friday night. After that, he would trust himself, like he always did. Always had.

You couldn't trust anyone else.

Forty-nine

'Right, guys, two of you out to the airfield, pick up the stuff you left behind. Change of plan.'

'What change of plan?'

'Bloody wedding.'

'What bloody wedding?'

'The one with royalty coming. November.'

'Lord Lieutenant's daughter.'

'That's the one. OK, Clive and Ian, out to the airfield, load up. Make it snappy.'

'We need three.'

'Tough, there's two of you.'

'Where's Tim?'

'Wife went into labour this morning.'

Clive Rowley and Ian Dean went out to the van, grumbling.

'You ever worked a royal protection job?' Ian said, turning out of the yard.

'Yeah, couple of times. Nothing happens. The dogs have it sussed well ahead.'

'Be a bit tighter this time. Plenty of hiding places for our friend the sniper.'

'Nah. I said, they'll have worked it all out, got it covered. He wouldn't dare.'

'What royals is it anyway?'

'Charles and Camilla, was what I heard.'

'Be air exclusion zone as well then.'

'Blimey, who pays for that?'

'Who pays for any of it, Clive? We do. We pay for the lot of them.'

'Right. Only what else do you want? A president like in America?'

'Don't care what there is, doesn't affect me. Mind you, my old mam wouldn't agree. Royal mad she is. Got the Queen on the teapot.'

Clive Rowley laughed.

The sun shone. The potholes on the airfield were drying out.

'Look at that . . . dog fox running along the back fence there.'

'Cheeky sod.'

'Had my gun, I could finish him in one.'

'Yeah, but why bother? Let him go. What's he done to you? Shoot a few human thugs before I'd hurt a wild animal, me. Come on, let's be having this bloody gear back then.'

They pulled back the doors. The sun was behind them, shining into the hooped space of the hangar.

'Right, doors in first?'

'What's that?'

'What?'

Ian was walking ahead, past the stacked poles and wooden doors, towards the far side. 'You got the torch?'

Clive hesitated. 'No. Come on, give us a hand, we're supposed to be back there before we've done.'

'In the van. Get the torch from the van.'

'What you poking about for? You watch out, there's generally rats.'

'This isn't rats. Get the torch, I said.'

'Yesssir.'

Clive wandered out to the van. The old dog fox was still there, sitting in the sun on the far side warming himself. Clive watched him. He didn't stir, not a muscle. Clive could understand why.

'Get yourself in here with that light!'

Eventually, glancing over his shoulder at the fox, he went.

'Fuck it, where'd you get to?'

'Leak.'

'Here, over here.'

'What?'

Ian stuck up his arm and Clive put the torch into his waiting hand.

'He's dead,' Clive said.

'Jeez.'

'Been dead a couple of days by the look of it.'

Ian squatted and looked at the pile of old mac and trainers. The man was filthy. The raincoat was thick with clots of dark dried blood. Ian shone the torch closer. He wasn't very young, it was hard to tell, probably a drunk or a druggy. He leaned forward and felt the pulse in the neck.

'What the hell happened to him? What was he doing in this hole anyway?'

But Ian had got up and was walking quickly to the entrance, on the phone as he went.

The ambulance came bumping across the field half an hour later.

Fifty

Outside the high wind tossed the trees and rattled the fence. It rained in bursts against the farmhouse windows and then was blown away.

'Are you warm enough?' Cat asked.

'Fine.'

'I can stoke it up a bit.'

'I said I'm fine.'

'Sorry.'

'No.' Chris shook his head and winced.

He had come home the previous day, looking anxious, walking carefully, as if he was afraid to fall. 'It seems different,' he had said more than once. 'Everything looks weird.'

Sam and Hannah had gone to Hallam House for the night. 'Break you in gently,' Cat said.

'I don't need that.'

'I can get them back if you like.'

'Leave it, leave it.'

She could not get used to this touchy, irritable person in place of easy-going, laid-back Chris. Some of it was because of the tumour, some the aftermath of the operation and the drugs. Would it change? Would she have Chris back? She had no idea. The consultant had no idea. 'Every case is different.' The operation had removed enough of the tumour to relieve the intra-cranial pressure. But there was far more which they didn't dare touch. She looked at him. He had his eyes closed. He seemed smaller, very distant. His skin was pale, his face altered beneath the shaving and the bandages. Who was this?

'I feel like a revenant,' he had said.

The radiotherapy had started. She would drive him in for nine more sessions. The maximum. After that, nothing.

'Shall I make some tea?'

'Why?'

'I thought you might like some.'

'Have a glass of wine. That's what you do in the evening.'

'I don't want to drink without you.'

'Better get used to it.'

Cat turned her head away.

'Is your father going to marry her?'

'Judith? No idea. You know Dad, I can't ask questions like that.'

'I like her.'

'Oh, so do I. But he's so bloody contrary, if I tell him that he might change his mind about her altogether.'

'And then there's Si.'

'Oh, Simon.' She got up. 'I lose patience. I think I will have a drink.'

'Quite right.'

'Do you need any painkillers?'

'No.'

'Sure?'

Chris didn't answer. Why would he? He had said he didn't need them but she had asked again. Why had she? Because she didn't know how to help him, how to talk to him, how to behave towards him. I would have done better with just about any patient, she thought, no matter what was wrong with them, I would have been able to handle it better.

The truth was that she was a doctor. Just a doctor. She knew no more about how to cope with the person she loved dying of a brain tumour than anyone else, possibly less because she knew too much, looked for signs, interpreted everything. I should just get on with it. Get on with it, take it as it comes. Isn't that what I say? *Just take one day at a time.*

She put the wine back in the fridge. On the worktop above it, a box of Chris's medications. Later, she would take it upstairs.

She knew what rooms came to look like when people were dying in them, the clutter of medicine bottles and oxygen cylinders and syringe pumps. Would that happen here? Would Chris stay? Could she cope with that? Could the children?

The wind raced across the paddock and battered against the kitchen window and the headlights of a car fanned out across the drive. Then Simon dived into the kitchen, brushing off the rain.

'Hey, Chris, good to see you home. How are things?'

Cat held her breath, waiting for some explosion of anger, a withering remark. She held out the bottle of wine but Simon shook his head, flopping down on the sofa next to his brother-in-law.

'So-so,' Chris said. 'Better for being here. Bloody hospitals.'

'Be a lesson to you to stop sending people in there then.'

'You could say that. But since you ask, my head's a hell of a lot better. It works, lessening the pressure. I thought it would be more painful post-op than it is. Shows they can saw your skull across with little ill effect.'

'I'll remember that.'

'I get sick but there's good medication for nausea. I get tired but so what, no one stops me from going to sleep. So all in all, yeah, I'm doing OK.'

Why? Cat thought as she drew the curtains across to shut out the storm. Why can't he talk to me like that? Why didn't he tell me? Why can he say those things to Simon, no problem, and not to me? I don't know what's going on here and I mind. It hurts.

'Any coffee?'

She nodded.

'How's crime?' Chris was asking.

They talked on in the way they had always talked, easy with one another, and hearing Chris, laughing, swearing, needling her brother, hearing but not seeing him, made it seem as if nothing was wrong after all, as if he were well and things were as they had always been. Nothing had changed.

It was only as Simon talked about police anxiety over the gunman, still somewhere out there, walking free, planning God knows what next, that she glanced at Chris and saw his face, drawn and gaunt, and with a strange, troubled expression.

'We're stretched to breaking point, we have to cover the whole of the bloody Jug Fair full of families with kids, we have a cathedral wedding with royals coming and this damn gunman is giving us the complete runaround. I don't often lose sleep over things but I'm waking in the small hours. We have got to stop him.' He banged his hand on the arm of the sofa. 'We have got to get him.'

There was a short silence, before Chris said, 'What are you talking about? What gunman?'

'Does a brain tumour affect your memory?' Simon said easily.

Cat waited, horrified, expecting Chris to turn in anger, as he had done to her several times that day, over less, far less.

But he only shrugged and said, 'Apparently.'

He went to bed shortly afterwards, his face drained of colour, so exhausted that Cat had to help him wash and undress. He curled into the bed and groaned softly as he fell asleep.

'Can you stay?' she asked Simon, who was flicking through the television channels in the den when she returned.

'Not a hope, but I'll have another coffee.'

'Judith and I are supposed to be taking the children to the fair but I wonder if it's safe.'

'You'll never be safer. We'll have everything covered. Never mind the sniper, you won't so much as stand a chance of getting your pocket picked.'

'Hope you're right. Do put down that bloody remote.'

'Sorry. Chris looks bad but he seems in decent spirits.'

'To you.'

'What do they say?'

She shrugged. 'They won't. Can we talk about something else?'

'Depends.'

'Oh, you won't want to, but you're going to listen. Two Js. Judith Connolly. Jane Fitzroy.'

'Nothing doing, old girl. Do you want another glass of wine?'

'Sit down.'

But he was out of the room. She heard the sounds of kettle being filled, glass of wine being poured, cupboard doors banging. No, she thought, he'll duck out of it, as ever. And suddenly, she didn't care. She'd had enough. She was weary. Let Simon look after himself and let him think what he liked about their father.

He came back.

'Talk me through what kind of person shoots at random. It has to be a madman or someone with a grudge, but what grudge?'

Simon gave her a calculating glance. Drank. Said nothing. No, Cat thought. Nothing doing, as you said.

'We don't know for sure it's only one.'

'What, two gunmen?'

'Could be. The police are keeping an open mind, as they say. I think it's one man. He can use a rifle, he can use a handgun. He can shoot at close range and at a distance. The Chief wants us to bring in a profiler. I'm against it, I think they're useless. I can profile this bloke as well as anyone. Man. Loner. Gun-savvy. Grudge against women – it's young women he's shot. Clever. Cunning. Athletic. Good sight. Doesn't stand out in a crowd. Local – knows the area well. Psychopath. Clear-headed – not on drugs, probably doesn't drink, or not much. Good at covering his tracks. Easy when you know how. Now find him.'

'What are you going to do?'

'Wait till he slips up. Try and keep one step ahead – think like him. Difficult that.' He shook his head.

'You love it.'

'Yes. You didn't hear me say it, but yes . . . this is the sort I like. Am I warped and twisted?'

'No. Fascinated by human nature and up for a challenge.'

'Right. I'd better go. God, I can't take this in. This family doesn't deserve another –' He stopped.

'Death. You can say it.'

'Yes . . .' He put his arms round her. 'Might he be OK?'

'No,' Cat said, holding onto him tightly for a second. 'No chance.' She moved away from him, walked to the television and switched it off. Looked round. Say it, she thought. Say.

'Don't leave it, Si. Don't duck your feelings. It doesn't come round again.'

But he turned away without replying, as she had known he would.

Fifty-one

There was a single note on the organ, the sign for everyone to turn and look round and of course, she was beautiful, Chelsea Fisher, the most beautiful bride in the history of the world, as every bride was. Her mother had wanted to make the dress, said it was a waste of money to buy off the peg, but this wasn't off the peg, was it, this was Designer, she and her sister-in-law had been to London to the showroom. It had taken four fittings. Never mind what it cost, no one had to know, least of all her mother, and if it was the same price as half a new kitchen, who cared? No one, at this moment. Not her mother. Not Andrew, gone scarlet and then chalk white in the face as he watched her. No one.

It was tight, skimmed her so she could hardly walk, and it had a fishtail and a long train like a mermaid and she shimmered like one too, the fabric was some sort of gleaming, glistening, clinging magical substance that blended with her, merged with her skin almost. The top was like silver snakeskin wrapped round her, but her long pale arms were bare, her shoulders covered with a wispy shrug of what felt like goose down. She had looked at herself in the mirror, looked at the tiny glittering tiara and the soft foaming veil, and floated away, then floated on Uncle Ray's arm, floated in front of Lindsay and Flick and little Amy up the aisle towards Andrew and Father Brenner, grins a mile wide. Floated past them all, the hats and feathers and fascinators and pink georgette and lavender crêpe and black and white and purple cravats. Floated. Andrew's mother had tears pouring down her face. Reached out her hand to touch the floating silk and gossamer and goose down as it drifted past.

Floated.

Andrew's cravat looked odd. The pin was askew. She wanted to reach out and straighten it and her hand was shaking, the baby's breath trembling at the edges of her bouquet. Andrew smiled.

Father Brenner beamed. There was a bumping and banging as everyone sat down behind her but she floated. Still floated. Behind her, little Amy whispered, asking what she had to do now. Lindsay whispered back. Andrew touched his hand to his cravat.

She went on floating.

The priest made them feel like the only people in the world and certainly the only ones he had ever married. He looked into their eyes and he smiled and when he said his few words, he made everyone laugh. Warm, Chelsea thought, it was a warm service, as if you were being embraced by happiness and laughter and then, when he pronounced them man and wife, they turned round, embraced by the applause that pattered round the small, light church.

The thing that took her by surprise, holding tightly to Andrew's hand as they started to walk down the aisle, was how quickly it was over. The months and weeks of preparation, the planning that had gone into the service, the printed sheets with the silver swans on the front, practising it a couple of times – and it was over, flash, gone and they were married. The doors at the back were opened and beyond them she could see bright sunlight shining on the white wedding car. They walked towards the brightness and it was as if they were walking towards their bright future. Everything was right.

Behind her, Amy's new shoes slithered on the polished floor and she almost fell but, somehow, someone pulled her up and righted her and spoke to her to stop her making a fuss. Little Amy, who carried a rag doll dressed in the same outfit as her own.

There were a few people looking over the wall. You were not allowed to throw confetti but Andrew's sisters surprised them with bubbles, pink bubbles blown out of the little wire wands, and the pink bubbles floated up into the air and burst softly, silently onto Chelsea's hair and her dress and fell onto the gravel and rested there, iridescent, caught by the sun. Then everyone was coming out and crowding round, laughing and kissing and snapping small cameras and feathers bobbed on heads and a few of the men went a yard or two off and lit cigarettes. From behind her, Chelsea heard the last bars of the organ music and then the church went quiet.

What happened next happened so fast it was like a film speeded up so that afterwards no one remembered it properly and everyone remembered something different.

Chelsea was beside Andrew but he had stepped forward and little Amy was pushing her way out to be in the front, to be seen and admired and photographed, and someone had given her a bubble pot and wand and she was trying hard to blow, but the bubbles wouldn't form, the liquid simply spattered down her dress and onto the gravel. There was shouting – 'Andy, turn round, get closer to Chelsea . . . Andy, look this way . . . Chelsea, over here' – and then a roar, a motorbike racing by. The rider . . . who saw the rider? Yes. Black leathers, helmet . . . he skidded up and seemed about to stop but as he stopped he was accelerating again, and in between, the split second of the flash, sunlight on metal, the loud bang and the flare and blaze and Andrew was spinning round and grabbing hold of his shoulder with the other hand. And Amy was falling slowly slowly slowly to the ground and her face and dress were pouring blood and the blood splashed out onto the gravel and splashed up, onto Chelsea's wedding dress.

And people were screaming, screaming and in the midst of the screaming, the motorbike roaring away, wheels spinning and kicking up dust.

Someone was running. A couple of the men who had been standing by the wall smoking. They were running together, jackets flying, down the road fast the way the motorbike had gone.

Running.

Chelsea's dress was covered in so much of Amy's blood that

everyone thought it was her. Someone screamed, 'The bride's been shot . . . the bride's been shot . . .'

But it was not Chelsea who was lying face down on the gravel, one hand stretched out and holding a rag doll. Beside Amy, the tub of bubble liquid spilled out slowly onto the gravel, mingling with spilling blood.

Fifty-two

'Breakthrough!' DC Louise Kelly threw her pencil in the air.

A small cheer went round the packed room but Serrailler shook his head.

'I know how you feel and I don't want to rain on the parade but it's a chink of light, not a breakthrough.'

'More than anything so far, guv.'

'It is – small mercies and all that.'

'So what exactly did these guys get?'

'Right. Three men, two of them wedding guests, one a passer-by. One of them ran all the way up Dedmeads Road after the motorbike. Got as far as the junction with the bypass where he lost it. But two of them who are into bikes give it as a Yamaha, probably an FJR 1300. Black. Looked fairly new. Plate concealed. One of the men noticed a small yellow strip on one side, possibly fluorescent. Biker wore black leathers and helmet, no distinguishing marks, but he was seen leaning down to his right as he neared the top of the road, possibly stowing the gun into the pannier.'

'Anyone see him actually drive up to the church?'

'It's confused. One person heard the noise. Motorbike engine very close – startled her and she turned but then there was a shout for the bride to turn towards a camera so she looked there. It happened very fast. The bridesmaid who died was pushing in front of the bride exactly as the shot was fired.'

'So he wasn't aiming for the little girl?'

'Hard to say but probably not. We have to wait for ballistics to report on the likely line of fire but they think he was aiming to hit the groom. Andrew Hutt. There are some skid marks on the path and an oil mark. Forensics will report. Meanwhile, Dedmeads Road is cordoned off and I want an inch-by-inch search-hands-and-knees job. Traffic are on full alert throughout the county and surrounding. Now although I wouldn't dare use the word breakthrough, DC Kelly is right, this is the first time he's been sighted and once he gets bolder he'll start to make mistakes. He thinks he's several miles ahead of us and he's cocky.'

'He's going to have another pop, isn't he?'

'We have to make sure he's caught before that happens. Second-guessing a gunman like this isn't easy but I feel confident that a pattern is starting to emerge. So eyes everywhere, think, think, think, wherever you are – might he be here? Could this be the scene of his next attempt? Don't rule anywhere out. Check out every bike, house to house down Dedmeads Road and surrounding. Shops, vet's surgery opposite the Catholic church, garage at the end . . . Posters go up this afternoon. Leaflets are being printed. There will be four officers in the church area tomorrow handing them out and we've got a mobile point in the church car park where people can report anything they might have seen.'

There was a rumble as chairs were moved; one or two people got up.

'Sit down, I haven't finished.'

He stood waiting for silence. He believed in being open and relaxed, leading but not dominating. Now, though, his expression had changed and they recognised it. The room went still.

'This man has now killed five people.' He spoke quietly. The eyes of everyone were on his face. 'One of them was five years old. He's on a mission and he will kill again. I want him stopped. Every single one of you – heads-up. Every single one of you may be the officer to see this guy when he makes his next attempt. Get out there. Don't let me down.'

There was silence before the room broke up as everyone started to leave. The usual jests and sotto voce remarks were absent. The mood had changed.

Ten minutes later, the canteen was full, the atmosphere charged. The usual bursts of ribald laughter replaced with heated conversations.

'We've got a real chance Friday/Saturday. He'll think he's God now, he'll be planning to shoot into the crowd.'

'Jesus, I hope not.' Clive Rowley washed a mouthful of bacon roll down with his tea. 'Forecast's good for the weekend, the fair'll be heaving.'

'Difficult in the dark though.'

'True. But think of the chaos, think how easy to get away in that lot.'

'I reckon they should call it off.'

'Oh no,' Louise Kelly looked dismayed, 'it's a great thing, the Jug Fair, they can't. I think he won't dare. He's clever, like the Super said, he'll know there'll be more police there than at a Hendon passing-out parade. No way will he take a chance then.'

'I agree.' Vicky Hollywell stirred her coffee round and round, round and round. 'There'll be a lull now. He'll go quiet. Wait till we've come down from red alert a few rungs. Then he'll take another pop somewhere we can't possibly have anticipated.'

'Mind you,' Clive said, getting up, 'keeps us awake. Bet we're on higher alert than the anti-terrorist squads right now.'

'And that's what you like, is it, Clive?'

'Better than washing the bloody ARV every morning and there's only so much target practice you can do. Let's get out of here.'

Fifty-three

Jane Fitzroy walked onto Saunders Ward late in the afternoon. She had spent the previous hour with the family of a teenager recovering from meningitis, against all the odds. Now she had been asked to see Nancy Lee after her seven-hour brain operation. Early in the morning she had been called to baptise a newborn premature baby who was not expected to live more than a few hours. Nothing had really prepared her, she thought, for being on the edge as a hospital chaplain, time after time.

The ward clerk looked at her strangely. 'Can I help?'

'Nancy Lee – is she back from theatre?'

'I'll check. You're new, aren't you?' She did not seem especially pleased to see a chaplain – perhaps she thought they got in the way.

Jane smiled at her. It did not do the trick.

Intensive care was humming and bleeping with the usual machines and lowered voices.

'Bay three.'

'Thanks. Is Sister Wicks on duty?'

'Yes, but she's very busy.'

'OK, I'll catch up with her later. Thank you.'

No response.

Bay 3 was off to one side and Sister Wicks was there. Fourteen-year-old Nancy Lee lay attached to the monitors, tubes and drips, eyes closed, head swathed in bandages. Her mother sat beside her, holding one of her hands in both her own. But when Jane went quietly in and she looked up, she smiled, an open and beautiful smile, full of joy and relief.

Sister Wicks said, 'Good news,' nodding to Nancy.

'Yes?'

'The tumour wasn't malignant and they removed all of it. Outlook very good.'

Jane's eyes filled with tears. That morning, when she had come in to say a prayer before Nancy had gone down to theatre, the prognosis had been grim, the tumour thought to be malignant and difficult to remove.

Nancy's mother said, 'It's a miracle. It's just the most wonderful miracle.'

'It's certainly good news,' Jane said. She felt uneasy when people claimed miracles, especially too quickly after major surgery or early on in a serious illness. What was a miracle anyway? She thought of Chris Deerbon, for whom there was no good outlook, no surprise, no miracle. She glanced at Nancy's young face. She looked infinitely distant, infinitely frail.

'Will you say a prayer of thanks? God has been so good, he keeps his promises.' Nancy's mother was an evangelical Christian, entirely sure of her Bible-based faith, shining with righteousness as she held her daughter's hand.

It is more difficult than this, Jane wanted to say, it is never so simple, we can never claim an easy answer. But she could say no such thing. She put her hand lightly on Nancy's head and gave her a blessing.

'I'll come in tomorrow morning,' she said. 'See how she's doing then. It is early days you know.'

'She's going to make a full recovery. We can trust in that.'

Jane smiled and slipped away.

On the way back to the college she worried that she had sounded too negative or had seemed to deny the mother's sure faith. What was she doing being a priest in the Church of England if she did not accept that miracles happened and prayers were answered? She believed in the power of prayer. Miracles, though – what were they? Rareties, that was sure. A medical diagnosis which turned out to have been too pessimistic, with the result being better than everyone had dared to hope or expect – that was explicable and something to be glad and grateful for but not a miracle. The hospital saw good and bad outcomes all the time – she had seen both herself in the course of that day. Yet she had seemed to reject one woman's faith and she blamed herself for it.

She parked the car and walked thoughtfully across the college quad. It was quiet. The air smelled autumnal though it was quite warm and there were little clouds of midges and gnats dancing here and there. She knew how lucky she was, to have the privilege of a set of rooms in college, a part-time chaplaincy both here and at the hospital, and a doctorate to study for. She had made too many mistakes, taken wrong turns, didn't believe herself to be cut out for her previous jobs. Now, she had time and space. She hoped she would prove good enough – enough to justify the trust people had placed in her, 'yet again' she thought. She wondered why the confidence, which had been so strong when she first determined to be a priest, had weakened so much.

There was a note pinned to the door of her rooms. '*Dear Jane, would you have tea at four thirty with me tomorrow? I hope all is well and you are settling in comfortably. Good wishes, Peter.*' The courteous wording, from the senior chaplain, and the 'tea at four thirty' made her smile. Some things did not change.

A few people were in to dinner and she stayed talking in the combination room until just before ten. She barely knew anyone but introductions were easy in a college and she felt more cheerful as she went back to her rooms, planning to work for an hour and also to ring Cat Deerbon. But before that, she switched on the television to catch the news. As the picture came up, Simon Serrailler's face filled the screen. Jane stood staring at him, startled by the odd mixture of his closeness, here, talking to her, and his complete remoteness.

He looked calm and in control, but grim-faced as he took questions about the Lafferton shootings. It was easy enough to tell that Simon was on the spot and hard not to sympathise with the public outrage that a gunman was on a killing spree while the police appeared to be doing nothing to stop it. But after a moment, Jane saw Serrailler not there, under the television lights, giving a press conference, but outside the bungalow in which she had been held by a man driven mad with grief, Simon talking to him, trying to calm him down, and later, when she had finally been released, waiting for her, reassuring her. She remembered the evening they had spent together. She had cooked a makeshift supper. She had enjoyed his company but, at the last minute, rebuffed him, backed off, uncertain and confused, still in shock after what had happened to her. She had not been able to give Simon a chance and she knew that because he never found closeness easy, he had been both surprised and hurt at her behaviour. He had not understood why, having taken such a risk, he had found himself rejected.

Later, after leaving Lafferton and during the last weekend before going into the abbey, she had written him a long and careful letter in which she had tried to apologise and to explain.

She had never posted it.

The phone rang for a long time before Cat answered.

'It's Jane.'

'Sorry, I was upstairs with Chris.'

'That's why I'm ringing. How are things?'

Cat sighed. 'Hang on, let me sit down. I'm so glad you rang.'

'Good, but you will always say if it's a bad time or you can't cope with talking about it, won't you? I don't want to intrude.'

'You absolutely do not. But yes, I will always say. He's feeling pretty bad . . . his mood swings are quite strong and he sleeps a lot. He's on massive medication of course and he's had three radiotherapy treatments.'

'Any help?'

'Hard to say yet. I have my doubts.'

'Have you told the children?'

'Oh yes. As much as I can. Sam understands . . . he's very quiet about it. But he sidles up to me and hangs about rather a lot. Hannah – I don't know. She's such a bouncy little thing, I'm not sure she's taken it in. I can't tell them he's going to die, Jane . . . I've said I'm not sure if he's going to be well but that isn't the same. Sam looks at me. I know what he's thinking. Felix is too young of course, though he notices that he can't crash about all over Chris as usual. I have to keep him away, he's so boisterous. Dad has been here today. Blunt as ever. Judith didn't come, she's gone to Edinburgh for a few days to see her daughter. I could have done with her, she takes the edge off Dad. But Simon came and he's the one person who has the knack with Chris . . . nothing fazes him. They just talk. He can say anything and Chris takes it.'

'I just saw him on the news.'

'I missed it – Chris needed a sick bowl. How was Si?'

'Very professional. Grim.'

'They're in a mess. They haven't a clue, Jane, this guy's running rings round them. Have you been in touch with him?'

'No.'

'I think he'd like it.'

'I'll see. Maybe when they've got this one cracked.'

'That might be never. How's Cambridge?'

'Wonderful. Love it. Love everything. It's right, Cat . . . I just want it to stay right. I've made too many mistakes.'

'Not your fault.'

'Whose then?'

'I have to go, Chris is calling. Ring me again. I'll need you.'

Jane went to the window and opened it. The air smelled moist and earthy. One or two lights were on but it was almost silent.

She could not get Simon out of her mind. His face on the television screen. His face as she had looked up and directly into it at Karin's funeral. His face all that time ago as he had told her he wanted to see more of her, as he had sat in her kitchen in the Lafferton bungalow after supper.

But she had fled a long way across the country, to get away from him, to start a new life. She wanted that new life. It felt right. She did not want to go through her days with the image of Simon Serrailler hovering at the back of her mind.

Fifty-four

'This is bloody ridiculous,' Clive Rowley said. 'This is the sort of thing the public complains about. If the media gets hold of this –'

'Belt up, would you?'

'I'm saying, they've every right to ask questions. I'm asking questions, you should be asking questions.'

'Well, I'm not. OK, let's head round onto the Starly Road, see who we can catch using their mobile while driving.'

Clive snorted. They were on traffic.

'Not like the old days then,' Liam said.

'Bloody isn't. I mean, we're highly trained firearms officers, what are we doing doubling up as traffic?'

'Resources.'

'Plenty of money when they have to find a load of it to look after the bloody royals.'

'To be fair, not all of that's down to our force and it's only the once.'

'No it's not, it's every time we have one of them opening this or unveiling that.'

'I heard the wedding counted as private so they paid for their own policing.'

'Yeah, right.'

'God, you're a cynic, Clive.'

'No, I just want to be doing the job I was trained to do. With an armed lunatic running round, you'd think it would dawn on them we ought to be on permanent standby.'

'Playing cards, you mean. That one looks dodgy . . . bet he hasn't got insurance – look at him.'

'Stop him?'

'Why not? Doesn't look safe to be on the road.' Liam switched on the lights and warning siren and speeded up to get in front of the boy driving an ancient resprayed Fiesta. 'OK, laddo, let's be having you.'

They slewed to a halt in a lay-by and got out. As they walked towards the Fiesta, a motorbike shot by going so fast the tarmac smoked in its wake.

'Come on, come on,' Clive Rowley said, 'let's get after him.'

Liam shook his head. 'He'll be long gone.' He spoke into his radio, giving their location and reporting the speeding bike, then politely asked the boy, who looked no more than fourteen, to get out of the Fiesta for him.

On the outskirts of Starly, a patrol car returning from interviewing a shopkeeper about the theft of some stock came up behind a motorbike, forced to slow down at a traffic hold-up, and revving impatiently. As all motorcyclists were currently under greater scrutiny than usual, they pulled him in.

Ten minutes later, a DC put her head round Simon Serrailler's office.

'Guv? Someone's bringing in Craig Drew's father.'

'What for?'

'Doing eighty in a fifty limit.'

'What's that got to do with us?'

'He was riding a black Yamaha motorbike.'

Simon went back to his screen but he had lost track of what he was doing. Motorbikes. Craig Drew's father. The wedding.

He called the team into the conference room.

'Motorbikes. It's thin, to be frank, but it's our first definite line of inquiry. Black Yamaha motorbike, 1,000cc probably.' He wrote on the whiteboard. 'I want a check on how many of these are registered to the area, excluding our own bikes obviously . . . anyone with the slightest link to any of the gunman's victims, log it, copy everyone in, put it up here. When you've got a connection, if you get one, think, think, think. We'll interview but' – he tapped his forehead – 'make this work. What's the connection, is it coincidence, is there any personal history, firearms? Anything.'

'Is this just Lafferton, guv?'

'For the moment. The rings will spread outwards. He hasn't come from far – we won't be looking on the other side of the county. This is a local man, local knowledge – I'd be surprised if he comes from as far as Bevham. Now, funerals. You know the theory – the killer likes to see the job finished so he sometimes goes so far as to attend the funeral of his victims. The bodies of Melanie Drew, Bethan Doyle and the girls who were killed outside the nightclub are being released on Friday. Once we have funeral details, we'll mount a discreet presence at each one. ARV will park up nearby. We're taking no chances. We'll have uniform in the cemeteries or the crematorium and outside the churches . . . in any case, there'll be an official police presence at each one. But I want CID mingling with the mourners in the pews and at the gravesides, at the wakes if they have them . . . everywhere. Looking and listening. Detail, detail, detail . . . connections, connections. And motorbikes first. Thanks.'

A mile away from the station, in the Dean's office at Lafferton Cathedral, the Chief Constable, Paula Devenish, was in reassurance mode.

'All leave is cancelled. The cathedral, the grounds and the close will be sealed off from the Friday morning – only those with photo ID and passes will be allowed anywhere near. Two armed response vehicles will be on standby and officers from two others will be in position from five a.m. on the Saturday morning.' She nodded to the AR Gold Command.

'The sniffer dogs will go into the cathedral twice, on the Friday morning and again on the Saturday. They will also go over every delivery as well as the flowers. We know our job and we'll do it. Please trust us on this.'

'Thank you, Chief Constable, but given the number of

shooting incidents – fatal shooting incidents – I'm sure you understand only too well how concerned we are.'

'Of course I do.'

Royal Protection coughed. 'There hasn't been a lot of, er, progress, has there?'

'If you mean there hasn't been an arrest yet, no. That doesn't mean lack of progress.'

Royal Protection's face was a mask of politeness.

'It isn't,' the Lord Lieutenant said quickly, 'as if we don't quite often have royal visitors to the county. We've always looked after them well and kept them safe, I think.'

'You haven't always had a sniper in your midst,' Royal Protection said.

'So what do you propose?' Paula Devenish spoke sharply. When her force was under attack from outside she defended it aggressively, no matter what she might say in private. It was one of the things Simon Serrailler liked about her.

'I propose that Their Royal Highnesses do not attend.'

'Oh but you can't!' The Lord Lieutenant's face was puce. 'My daughter will be so upset. The Prince of Wales is her godfather, and a very attentive one. He came to her confirmation.'

'Well, perhaps he will not be coming to her wedding. I'm sorry, but this is what I will be recommending to His Royal Highness's office.'

'Well, I will be speaking to His Royal Highness himself, never mind his bloody office, and I think I know what he'll say. He'd be appalled if he thought he was seen to run away. Good God, man, the royal family face a possible sniper's bullet, to name but one threat, every time they appear in public. It's thanks to the police that they have all remained safe to do their jobs among us and I deplore your suggestion that our own force cannot continue to guarantee their safety. This . . . gunman has made no specific threat to the royal guests – not so far as I am aware.' He looked at the Chief Constable, who shook her head.

The Dean had been silent, biting the side of his finger occasionally. Now, he sighed. 'I do hope this is not going to cause a falling-out amongst us,' he said unhappily. 'Do please reconsider.'

Royal Protection frowned. 'I have to act as I see fit, and I do see a problem here, frankly. But let's look at the updated plan and the proposed arrangement of armed officers.'

Gold Command stood and unrolled a map smoothly, laying it on the table and securing it with brass paperweights and a candlestick.

'ARVs will be parked here, here and here. An armed officer will be positioned here, here, on the tower here, on top of the New Song School building here, in the organ loft, and in the roof space above the fan vaulting. There will also be armed officers at the east door, here –'

'Just a moment,' said the Lord Lieutenant. 'I can't say I like the idea of our guests arriving and there being officers with machine guns clearly visible.'

'Most of them will be concealed, sir . . .'

'I hope and trust you're not allowing the public into the close, are you, Chief Constable?' said Royal Protection.

'We were planning to allow a cordoned-off area opposite the east door . . . the public would like to be able to have some sight of the wedding.'

Royal Protection shook his head vigorously. 'Out of the question.'

'But only yesterday I was watching the Queen doing a walkabout among a crowd in Southampton –'

'Southampton doesn't have a killer on the loose – or at least not as far as we know. As far as I am concerned this area of yours is a no-go zone for the royal family until you catch him.'

He stood up. 'If you will excuse me, I have a meeting in the next county in an hour and a half. I'm sorry to disappoint you, Lord Lieutenant, but I will recommend that Their Royal Highnesses do not attend your family wedding. Unless there is an arrest, of course.'

Royal Protection glanced across at the Chief Constable, who barely met his eye.

Fifty-five

'Candyfloss!'

'You can't be serious.'

'I am perfectly serious. I love candyfloss.'

'But it tastes like sugar-coated wire wool.'

'Does it? I've never eaten sugar-coated wire wool.'

Helen exploded with laughter and let Phil pull her by the hand towards the candyfloss stall. The smell of burnt sugar mingled with the diesel fumes of the generators and the burning oil from the burger stalls on the smoky night air. It was eight o'clock and the Jug Fair was packed. Helen looked up at the Sky-Dyve plunging giddily down and at the sparks and crackles from the bumper cars and felt like one of the kids.

The candyfloss queue snaked round and back and mingled with the queue for hot dogs and another for toffee apples.

'God, this is fun. I haven't been since Tom and Lizzie were in single figures.'

'Place is knee-deep in cops.'

'Not surprised. This is just the sort of event where a gunman could run amok. Look around . . . all those points a sniper could stand.'

Helen's eyes were drawn to the Sky-Dyve. If a man . . . at the top of the helter-skelter. If . . .'

A gun cracked loudly not far away.

Phil put a reassuring hand on her arm. 'Shooting ducks. He

wouldn't take the chance. Here.' He handed her a shocking-pink cloud of candyfloss. 'Flowers for the lady.'

He put his arm round her and they wandered off in the direction of the rides.

Sam Deerbon steadied himself and waited for the row of ducks to bob past him four times.

'Hurry *up*, Sam. What's wrong with you? Can't you do it or something? I could do it easy-peasy, they don't go very fast, hurry *up*.'

He ignored his sister. The ducks bobbed by again. He steadied himself again.

'Sam, are you still there?'

Crack. Crack. Crack. Crack. Three ducks out of five went down.

Hannah turned away in disgust.

'Well done, Sam!' Judith said.

Sam smiled a small, satisfied smile and chose a pink porcelain piggy bank from the prizes on the stand.

'What do you want that for? What a stupid prize. You could have had that big blue elephant and given it to Felix, you could have had a mega box of sweets, what do you want a stupid piggy bank for?'

'To save money in.'

'What do you want to save money for?'

'To leave home with.'

Hannah's eyes widened slightly and she looked up at Judith.

'So I won't have to live with you, stupid.' Sam turned towards the fish-hooking game, examined it and came away.

'Too easy,' he said.

Cat returned carrying four paper cones of chips.

'God, I hate this fair. It's packed, they rip you off, it hurts your ears and it smells.'

'It's GREAT.'

'I knew you'd say that, Sam. Have some chips.'

'Think what the men are missing.' Judith Connolly bit into a hot chip and winced.

Chris was at Hallam House with Richard. He had felt like a

change of scene and the radiotherapy had begun to bite, giving him better days. Judith would pick up pizzas from the Italian restaurant, on her way back from the fair.

'I just saw Si on the far side of the square talking with a couple of CID. Never seen so many in one place.'

'Makes it safe. I hear they're not letting the royals come to the cathedral wedding though. Seems a pity.'

'They daren't risk it at the moment . . . only think.'

'I suppose so. But you shouldn't let this madman change the way you behave. Some people thought this fair ought to have been cancelled.'

'Mummy, can we go on the dodgems, please, please?'

'Not yet.'

'Why not?'

'Because you'll go in a car with me, I'll drive and I'll bang you into so many other cars you'll puke up all your chips and all your ice cream and –'

'Sam!'

Sam smiled and folded his empty chip cone into smaller and smaller triangles.

The sky above St Michael's Square was orange. AR Bronze Command stood in shadow looking round, up, down, to one side, to the other side. He had assumed that the sniper wouldn't fire from anywhere not providing him with a clear escape route. What if he had been wrong? They had discussed and dismissed several times the idea that he might now be on a suicide mission and therefore be trigger-happy at the fair, unconcerned if he was caught at last. He looked up at the top of the helter-skelter. Someone could have climbed the spiral stairs and be hanging about at the top. No. Only a kamikaze shooter would do that. The direction of the shots would be easy to see and there was no way down other than by sliding on a mat. And if he did that, they would be waiting for him at the bottom.

The floodlit cathedral tower commanded the fair. They had been up there, locked the bell tower, locked the door to the observation platform, and a couple of men were patrolling below. But he felt uneasy. Something niggled at the back of his mind and he was annoyed that he did not know what.

The square was heaving with people, the noise of rival music and machinery and generators most likely to muffle the sound of shots, and besides, shots were going off all the time as people queued at the rifle ranges. Maybe they should have closed those down for tonight?

He looked around him again. And up. And down. To this side. To that.

Tanya and Dan Lomax were on the Jinny horses, trying to hold hands across the gap between them as the merry-go-round picked up speed until it was a dazzling whirl of music and lights streaming through the night. She seemed to have been on the Jinny horses half her life, as a maid, as the Fair Queen, and now as a bride. The Jinny horses meant being happy and Tanya was happy. She tried to see Dan's expression but they were going too fast. She wanted to shout, with laughter and excitement and pride and happiness.

'I have decided,' Sam Deerbon said, coming back to the spot beside the fortune-telling tent, where Cat had told him to meet them. He had been given the choice of his last ride. Hannah had already chosen the teacups and been sneered at. 'The teacups are what babies go on – Felix could go on the teacups, I should think. You're a scaredy-cat.'

'Right, what's it to be, Sam, and don't say the Sky-Dyve, you know you –'

'No. It's in the square. Come on.'

They moved slowly through the crowd.

'Hold onto my hand, Hanny, don't let it go.'

Sam shoved someone in the back.

If Chris were here he could have had one of them on his shoulders, Cat thought. Even Sam. Even now.

They shuffled forward, Judith in front, trying to weave in and out.

'There's Uncle Simon! Uncle Simon!' Hannah yelled but she wouldn't have been heard, and in any case, Simon was out of sight again, somewhere in the crowd.

'There!' Sam said.

TAKE A TRIP TO GHOUL TOWN ON THE GRAVE TRAIN.

'I'm not going on that, I'm not going anywhere near that.' Hannah pressed herself into Cat's side.

'You're too little anyway, you have to be as tall as that gate and you're not. Can I?' His eyes shone.

'I'll go with him,' Judith said quickly. 'If you're dead sure, Sam.'

'Dead, dead sure.' Sam laughed. 'Good joke, Judith. Come on, quick, the queue's moving.'

'Judith, if you . . .'

'It's fine,' Judith said, as she was pulled away, 'honestly. Why don't you and Hannah go on the wobbly staircase into the hall of mirrors. Go on, I'll treat you.'

'Thanks! Would you like to, Hanny?'

'Yeah!'

They separated. When Cat glanced back, Sam and Judith were at the ticket booth, ready to go.

Clive Rowley, Paul J and Paul C pushed their way through the ten-deep crowd surging towards the Sky-Dyve. No one moved for them.

'Like ambulances,' Paul C said, 'people used to move aside for them but they don't now.'

'Yes they do. Always. Where've you been?'

'He could shoot anyone here – have the gun in his pocket, straight into the back, no one would know.'

'Not that easy. Besides, he won't do that.'

'How do you know?'

'Because,' Clive said as they reached the vans on the other side, 'he's a planner is our marksman, not an opportunist.'

'You've been reading too much profiling rubbish.'

'Why's it rubbish?'

But the generator behind them started up again and Paul J's reply was drowned out.

Simon Serrailler looked over his shoulder as he began to walk away from the fair. The high-profile police presence was working. CID were everywhere, standing in queues for fish and chips and rides on the dodgems, wandering about among the bobbing ducks and shove-halfpenny stalls, standing in pairs near the fortune-telling booths. Uniform were making a point of chatting to children and teenagers, joshing with the elderly, arresting a couple of pickpockets. AR were on the perimeter and on relief parked up in the vans. He had a good feeling. No gunman would take a chance here tonight.

He had tried to find his sister but the crowd was too thick. He'd catch up with them later but, for now, he was heading out of the melee, towards the back lane that led towards the Cathedral Close. In five minutes he intended to be drinking a whisky and reading the final chapter of the last Michael Dibdin Inspector Zen novel, which had more twists than the Jug Fair helter-skelter.

Sam Deerbon's eyes gleamed full of life and excitement as their car shot through the plastic curtains and into the silvery half-dark of the ghost walk and at once a couple of skeletons rattled down from the roof, almost touched them and swooped back up again. The tannoy let out terrible screams and shrieks as they hurtled into pitch blackness. Judith felt Sam nudge very slightly nearer so that his leg was just touching hers. The car dropped down and a gravestone opened up just ahead. A plastic bat was slippery and cold like seaweed waving in their faces.

'OK?' she asked, but a ghoul emerged from the walls of the tunnel, its terrible amplified groaning louder than her question, louder than the shrieks and screams of the people in the cars in front and behind.

They slowed down and then went suddenly very fast again and the tunnel swerved sharply to the right. This time, Sam grabbed her hand, and in the car two back, Helen squeezed Phil's, alarmed in spite of herself. She saw his face in the green phosphorescence, artificially pale, his teeth flashing as he roared with laughter.

There was a crescendo of noise as they plunged hard down into the darkness, and then, suddenly, down again, faster and faster until the car was rocking to and fro violently and the rails seemed to be rearing up in their faces. Helen screamed. The green lights were out and the place was both black and a hell of noise as metal and timber buckled and canvas ripped and the entire ride began to crumple, the top level crashing down through into the next and the bottom of the whole edifice collapsing under the weight and pitching forward onto the crowd below.

Simon Serrailler heard the noise and for a split second thought not one shot but a barrage of gunfire was resounding through the square. Then he turned and saw the ghost train toppling forward and crumpling like a pack of cards. Heard the unbelievable noise of tearing metal and wood and the exploding generator and the screams that rose and rose in terror, mingling with the lights and the smoke and rising, rising up to the great cathedral tower and so on up and up into the darkness.

'Sam!' Cat screamed. 'Oh God, no, no. SAAAAM.'

She tried to push forward but a wall of people was pushing her back and she almost fell over Hannah and they were forced to go the way they were going, to get out of the way of the falling debris. 'My son's in there, I have to get to my son. Oh God, please let me get back. Sam . . .' Someone was grabbing her arm and pulling her sideways and then she was pushed against the merry-go-round and a girl in a bright pink quilted jacket was pressed up to her so that the quilting was in her face, she could smell the shiny oily fabric. The fairground noise was dying down. The music was stopping, as the loudspeakers were switched off one by one, and then the generators began to fade, and after a while the only sounds were of the still-cracking, crushed ghost-train building and of human voices, shouting, calling, barking orders from somewhere behind. And screaming. Screaming.

Serrailler, pushing through the crowd and shouting 'POLICE', reached the fallen ride at the same time as a dozen other officers and St John Ambulance paramedics. Sirens were now sounding in the distance.

The smell of burning and dust and oil was acrid, the whole structure had toppled in on itself so that it was impossible to tell what had come down, what had been beneath. Fairground workers were already hauling at great beams and crippled girders and dragging them away, while uniform took over crowd control and also began to rummage in the broken mountain for trapped bodies.

Simon's mobile rang as he was clambering onto part of the broken carriage runway.

'Simon, Jesus, where are you? Sam was on the ride, Sam –'

'OK, I'm up there now. Where are you?'

'I don't know, on the other side, by a stall, I'm up against a stall, we're all pushed together –'

'Stay exactly where you are. Don't move. There are a lot of us here and everything is on its way. Stay there, Cat.'

He clambered over the rigging and canvas, a couple of armed response men behind him. There were shouts and cries from all around them, from underneath, from inside.

'Watch out, guv, it isn't stable, watch where you're putting your weight.'

'Wait for the fire crews. Listen, there's someone just here, Paul, shove this plastic sheet out of the way, hold me steady.' Clive Rowley balanced on a broken piece of rail at an angle.

'Shut up. Listen.'

They stood in the small pocket of silence they had constructed out of the noise crazy all round them.

'Left, to your left and then down, Clive.'

'Hold this steady.'

'Watch yourself. You need an axe.'

'Haven't got a fucking axe. Hang on. Hold it steady, will you?'

He squatted and began to rip the plastic sheeting apart. It came away easily in his hands, revealing a cavern of black twisted metal, with a wheel broken off and sticking up into the air. Below it, someone was crying softly in pain and fear. He put his foot forward. Beside him, Paul C held the girder fast.

Clive reached his hand and then his arm into the dark space beneath him and felt around.

'Hello. Where are you? I'm Clive, I'm a police officer. Can you hear me?'

The moaning went on without a pause but it was near, almost at his feet.

He got down on his knees, testing the surface cautiously, then inched along and put his head to the hole.

'Can you hear me?'

'Help me, help me.'

'Gotcha. OK, we'll have you out of there in a minute. I'm reaching my arm down. Can you lift a hand up?'

A moan.

'Try lifting a hand and feeling round for mine.' He half turned his head. 'Get a torch, can you? I need to see in here.'

The sirens were in the square now, vehicle after vehicle turning in and stopping, the flashing lamps still going. Firemen, ladders, lights, hoses.

'Get me a torch.'

A torch was in his hand from somewhere behind.

'Steady, watch that wooden platform on your left, Clive, duck down. It's moving.'

There was a creak and a splintering sound but Clive held steady and the girder did not move. He waited. He felt round again in the blackness and then managed to get the torch in but all he saw was a mess.

'Can you still hear me?'

No reply.

'Reach your hand up.'

Silence.

He wiped the sweat off his face.

'I'm still here. I'm Clive. Can you hear me?'

From below, someone shouted and a woman was screaming, 'Oh my God, oh my God. Oh Jason, oh my God.'

Then, without warning, Clive felt something touch his hand and move an inch up to his wrist and, for a second or two, grip.

'Yessss.'

Gradually, arc lights began to come on and now the ladders were being run up the fallen stands, one after another. A child was crying in the blackness deep down under the broken girders.

'I'm Clive,' he said. 'Can you reach my hand again?'

After a moment, he felt his wrist gripped weakly. He crawled forwards cautiously an inch or two, set the torch down and reached both his arms into the hole.

'Grip,' he said. 'Grip hard and hold on. Can you move?' He thought the voice was a woman's. 'Are your legs free?' A groan of pain but then a movement and a sudden cracking sound. 'Be careful. Slowly, do it slowly. Can you move your legs?'

He felt the grip tighten on his wrists. He held fast. Someone had his legs behind and there was a ladder beside him.

'You can do it,' he said into the hole. 'You're nearly there. Just try and free your legs very carefully. Do your legs hurt?'

He could not make out the words. Sweat dripped from his face onto his hands and onto the hands that were gripping his wrists. A beam shone and caught the black hole and held it and in its vivid white light he saw the tangled wreckage, the wheel, and the woman's hands on his wrists. Further down, he could see a green jacket. Dark hair. Her legs, one free, the other angled out of sight. His wrists were burning and his back felt as if someone were pressing a weight of cement onto it but gradually, very gradually, he began to move the woman up out of the dark pit, painfully slowly. Then, other arms reached out and took the strain with him.

'Don't pull too hard, her left leg isn't free. Watch it, watch it.'

But after hours of the night and another lifetime beyond those, her head and then her shoulders were up and into the cool air and the brilliant arc light and someone was cutting away the metal and wood below to free her left leg.

'Clive,' she said faintly.

'That's me. Nearly there. Be out of it any second.'

'Leg's free, leg's clear. Be careful, she may have a broken ankle there.' The noise of cutting stopped, though they could hear it going on all around them, above them, below them, as the firemen worked on the wreckage.

'God, it hurts. God.'

'You're doing brilliant. You're doing great. Come on.'

'Clive? You're Clive? Oh God, thank you.'

She was pulled up, gently and slowly, by the others behind them, onto a flat section of the wooden stand. The letters 'GHOU' were painted on the wood in white and blood red.

'You're OK,' Clive said. 'It's over.'

'You're Clive?' She was dazed.

'Yup. Who are you, love?'

'Helen,' she said.

Fifty-six

'This is Radio Bevham. We're interrupting the late-night phone-in for some breaking news on a major accident at Lafferton's Jug Fair. One of the rides is reported to have collapsed and there are a large number of casualties. We don't know yet how many or the degree of seriousness. Emergency services from three counties are on the scene, and speaking from there is our reporter Cathy Miles.

'Cathy, I gather you were actually at the site of the accident this evening, is that right?'

'Hi, David, yes, that's right. I live just outside Lafferton and I was at the Jug Fair which occupies the whole of the area around the cathedral . . .'

Simon switched off the car radio and for a moment or two sat in the dark car. He took several deep breaths in and slowly out and felt the tension flow from him. It had been an alarming and exhausting night but as always in a major incident the adrenaline had kept him, kept all of them, at peak performance, hyped up and working as a team. He had driven from the scene of the accident straight to the hospital where Sam and Judith Connolly had been taken. Cat had gone in the ambulance with Hannah but had sent Simon a text soon afterwards to say that Sam was fine, only badly bruised on his shoulders – the falling platform had missed his head by millimetres. Judith had a broken leg and was in shock. By the time Simon had arrived Sam was ready to be discharged. Judith was being kept in overnight. He had taken his sister and the kids back to Hallam House before returning to the accident, by which time Paula Devenish was on the scene. Now, six bodies had been brought out of the rubble but it was thought unlikely there were more, though the search would continue. The injured had been ferried off in ambulances, the press briefed several times.

Just before he came away, the Chief had found him again. 'I don't know which is worse,' she had said wearily, 'this or the shooting we dreaded.'

'Accident or design? On balance I'd rather deal with an accident but . . .'

'But we would rather have neither. Of course. Do you think there was going to be a shooting, Simon? Was he here and was he going to cause mayhem, only the collapse of the ghost train got in the way?'

'I'd put money on his not being here. He'd never have taken the risk.'

'Does your bet hold for this blasted wedding?'

Simon had wiped his face with his sleeve and the sleeve came away filthy with the dust and dirt that had been released into the air by the crash. From the moment of the collapse until now, he had not given a thought to the gunman. Where had he been tonight? Among them, watching, waiting, looking for his opportunity, or miles away? It was a terrible game and they were only distracted now because of a random catastrophe.

'I don't know,' he said at last. 'But probably. He doesn't take risks beyond a certain point. He isn't a chancer, he calculates.'

'He could be calculating this one.'

'He could. We've got to make sure he decides the risk isn't worthwhile, or if he takes it, that we have him.'

'I'm going to make a fuss . . . press conference pointing out how secure this wedding is going to be, massive armed police presence and so on.'

'Good.' He had looked across at a fireman, poised on a girder. 'One of our armed officers deserves a medal,' he said.

'Clive Rowley? Yes, I heard. He wasn't supposed to pre-empt the fire service of course, he might have made matters worse.'

'You're not serious, ma'am? AR are not trained to clamber

about trying to drag people out of debris? Health and Safety? Oh please.'

The Chief raised her eyebrows. 'Officially, Superintendent, officially.'

He felt all the energy and control begin to drain out of him.

'Go home, Simon. You've done as much as you can here. Leave them to it.'

'I'm fine.'

'Are you safe to drive?'

He gestured in the direction of the close. He had left his car in front of the flat after returning from Bevham General. The Chief walked with him to the cathedral side of the square where her own driver was waiting. Around them, the teams of firemen were still working, taking the collapsed ride apart piece by piece, clambering on ladders laid flat and occasionally calling down through the debris and then listening intently. The area had been cleared but a few people waited outside the police tape, close to the battery of press vans.

'I'm glad your own family were found so quickly, Simon. Some of these are going to be waiting for the rest of the night and into tomorrow. Have there been many calls reporting people still missing?'

'Not as many as you might expect. They've got a lot of people out now.'

'Get some sleep. I'm giving a press conference at nine, come in for that.'

Simon nodded. He saw her into her car before walking off towards the close.

Once he had left the range of the arc lights he had looked up and seen that the sky was clear and star-filled with a thin paring of moon over the cathedral tower. It was only when he reached his car that he realised that there was also a frost and he was very cold. He wondered whether to go straight inside, call Hallam House and then go to bed. But he would be flat out all the following day and almost certainly into overtime for the rest of the week. He needed to see them now, no matter what time it was.

*

His father and Cat were sitting at the kitchen table, teapot and cups in front of them. Sam was stretched out on his mother's lap with his legs and feet on the chair beside her. He sat up as Simon came in.

'Do you know how many people are dead? Judith might easily be dead and so might I, it was a lucky escape. The fireman said it didn't have my number on it.'

Simon sat down next to Cat and put his hand on her arm. 'You should be in bed. Are you staying here?'

'Yes. Chris is asleep. I've made the beds up.'

'Do you propose to stay here as well?' Richard Serrailler said. 'If so you could probably do with a whisky.'

Simon hesitated. There was his old room, though he had last slept in it after one of his mother's choral society suppers at which he had been roped in to help.

'You've absolutely scootly got to stay,' Sam said. 'We can discuss how the ride collapsed, I've been thinking about it – you see, probably what started it was –'

'Sam, can we do this later?'

'OK, when? It's very interesting actually, how buildings and things sometimes do just collapse. Occasionally it's a structural defect but it can be an earth tremor. Do you think there was an earth tremor?'

'It's a possibility but I haven't had anything like that confirmed, Sambo.'

'It would be on the Internet, there's a very good seismological website, we could look it up.'

'We could, but not now. I'm going to have a drink with your grandfather and what I really need is for you to encourage your mother to get to bed. She's had a bit of a shock, you know.'

'Right. I understand. Shock can be delayed, did you know that? In older people anyway. Mum, I think you might have shock and need to get some sleep now. When people have had a shock they need rest – I expect even I might need a bit, my arm's started to hurt again.'

'Si, one end of the curtain pole in our room has come down, can you sort it?'

He followed them up. Sam had gone quiet.

'I feel as if I'm climbing the north face of the Eiger,' Cat said.

'I know about that, you see the north face –'

'Save it, Sam.'

'Oh. That's quite a lot of things we have to discuss tomorrow, there's the possibility of an earth tremor, the structural weakness of fairground rides, the . . .'

'Relative steepness of a flight of stairs versus the north face of the Eiger. Scoot into the blue bathroom, I've put all our stuff in there.'

'Oh pooh, I like the big bathroom best, can't I use that, I always did when Granny was here and I know it's Grandpa and Judith's bathroom now but they won't mind and . . .'

'Sam, I've had enough. I'm exhausted and I need my bed. Bathroom. Go!'

He went.

As he was lifting the end of the curtain pole, Simon glanced at the double bed where Chris lay, curled on his side. His scalp looked raw. The hair had been shaved and there was a long line of sutures curving across his head.

'He'll be like this till nine or so. He's on some pretty knockout stuff.'

His brother-in-law looked different, Simon thought, and not only because of his head. He seemed to be far away in another place. Simon looked away.

'Poor Dad,' Cat said. 'Too much to cope with.'

'Dad? Christ, he's not the one you should worry about.'

'Judith . . .'

'Oh, sorry, yes. Broken leg. Nasty that.'

'She was bloody lucky. Sam's right. They were both bloody lucky.'

'I dare say she'll be well looked after here, dressing gown behind the bathroom door and all.'

'You're an A1 shit sometimes. I don't know you as a brother when you come out with things like that. I can't deal with you now but don't even think of saying anything to Dad. Oh, get out.'

He felt as he had felt as a small boy, tempted to say something, knowing it should not be said, unable to stop himself. Something goaded him on. Of course he should not have said what he did, not now, not to Cat. Not ever. But from the moment Sam had mentioned the bathroom he had known that he would. The goad had pricked and pricked away.

He went downstairs, furious with himself.

'Dad?'

'In here with the decanter.'

He went into the study where Richard had stirred the remains of the fire together and was sitting beside it. He looked younger, Simon thought, seeing him as he went in, not suddenly older, which was the way he should have seemed now, but suddenly younger.

'I'd better get back actually, they're bound to call me and I've got to be in for a press conference first thing.'

His father glanced round. 'You know best.'

Nothing more. If he had said, no, stay, I want to talk to you, we don't see enough of one another, we don't talk enough . . . No. He wouldn't stay, not now.

'Goodnight.'

As he turned the car, he saw the study light go out.

In the flat, the answering machine flashed. Simon waited for the cathedral clock to finish striking before listening.

'You have two new messages. First message.'

'Duty Sergeant Lewis, guv. Report that the fire service have recovered another two bodies from the wreckage of the fairground ride. Also, the Chief is bringing the press conference forward to half eight. Thank you.'

'Second message.'

There was a pause. A breath.

'Oh – Simon. Hello. This is Jane. Jane Fitzroy. I've just been listening to the news. I didn't think you'd be at home, obviously, but . . . I just wanted to say how awful. And my prayers and thoughts are with everyone. So, well . . . that's all and I'll . . . I'll catch you sometime. And it's Jane. If you didn't hear that. Thanks. Goodnight, Simon.'

Fifty-seven

He laughed as he rode. He went the back way, not through the town but on a four-mile detour, so that he approached the road out towards the Moor from the far side. Had to. No risks. No one knew him out here. And he laughed. Sometimes he grinned. Sometimes he smiled. But mostly he laughed aloud.

It had been good. Better than good. There they had all been, dressed up and nowhere to go and they'd been waiting for him, expecting him. Had they? Had they seriously thought he would have shot a kid's water pistol at the fair? He hadn't so much as tried the shooting range though he'd walked past it and watched a couple of times, watched idiots who couldn't have shot a barn door at ten feet. Didn't matter. He'd enjoyed it. So had they.

What had it cost and all to catch a sniper who was never going to shoot? That wasn't his way, ripping off into a crowd at random. People who were mad did that and he despised them. Youths in America who walked into a schoolyard and gunned down a dozen innocent kids, college boys who turned on their classmates with a machine gun. They were sick. They were crazy. They needed locking up for life, only they rarely saw the day out, they turned the gun on themselves. Almost always. Which was one thing he was never going to do because he was not sick, not crazy, not a weirdo, not high on drugs. He had a purpose, he had plans and targets and methods. He was different.

It had been good to know he could be at the fair and be certain, absolutely certain, that nothing was going to happen. He laughed.

But then as he accelerated on a straight bit of road, he remembered that eight people were dead and dozens injured because of some moron. He heard the screams again. He heard the shouts for help deep inside the collapsed ride. That sort of carnage was what deranged youths who rushed into churches and baseball stadiums and school classrooms caused. The electric chair was all they were fit for and he despised them for shooting themselves and taking the easy way out.

All the same. He smiled again, remembering.

He had timed it right today. It was cold and bright, no haze, no wind. Clear. He parked the bike out of sight in a dip, took his bag off the back and walked the rest of the way, up the steep slope. At the top he turned and looked out over the countryside. A pair of buzzards soared high, wings open flat and stiff like the paddles of windmills. The distant town was a faint smoky blue line. He thought he could fly himself from here, just open his arms, lift off and soar on the current of air.

He opened the bag and took out the roll-up tin and tobacco. Papers. Licked. Rolled. Struck the match. The smell of the smoke and the taste of the cigarette was like nothing else. Smoking in the open air. Eating something cooked in the open air. Nothing like it.

He never smoked indoors.

He lay on his back and blew a smoke ring at the sky. He thought about nothing, but he felt and his feeling was a diffused warmth and satisfaction which filled his mind and his body. He was happy. Things were going well. He was good at planning, and it showed. It was idiots who tried to do this sort of thing without a plan, opportunists who came unstuck because they had not thought of every possible error. Leave nothing to chance. He didn't.

It was good to lie here knowing that every time he carried out a part of his plan he was doing it because Alison had made him. He was not a violent person. He didn't need some sort of stupid revenge. That was for losers. But what Alison had done to him had caused all of this. Alison was responsible. If the time ever came for him to talk about it, that would be what he would say and he would give details, chapter and verse, so that it was absolutely clear. If he were ever caught . . .

He sat up. He took the roll-up out of his mouth and smiled. Laughed. Laughed and laughed and laughed.

He put the cigarette out carefully and picked up his bag.

It was beautiful inside the spinney. The light came sifting down through the trees and onto the fallen leaves, though there had not yet been one of the autumn gales to strip the bulk of them off. He knew the spot. Nothing had changed.

He opened the bag, took out the small white-painted cans and set them up in a row on the fallen tree. Then he went back thirty paces, carrying the bag.

A minute later he was lying on his stomach, carefully poised. The white cans were bright in the sun.

He levelled. Waited.

Fire!

Fire! Fire! Fire! Fire! Fire! Fire! Fire!

Every one.

He smiled.

Got up and replaced the cans and paced back again. Forty strides this time. The leaves made a soft crunching sound as he lay down. A conker in its prickly bright green ball was beside his hand. He smiled.

Levelled the gun again. The cans were smiling back at him. Beautiful. White.

Fire!

Fifty-eight

Statistics was the only class on Monday. They were out at half eleven.

'Coming into town?'

Tom hesitated, standing beside his Yamaha.

'Cheer you up, man, you need it. Look at you. Listen, your mum's going to be fine.'

'I know.'

'Right then, so, what? Leave the bike, come into town. You got any cash?'

Tom shrugged. He had cash. At the hospital his mother had made him take twenty quid out of her bag. He had been going to say no when Phil had appeared and asked him if he was all right for money. Bloody cheek. Tom had taken the twenty-pound note and left without answering. What was it to do with Russell?

'Where do you want to go?'

'Rattlers?'

He knew what it was. Luke had always looked out for him, since they were in juniors. The only problem now was Luke had a tendency to rib him about the Jesus Gang. When he'd been at the camp in the summer Luke kept sending him filthy texts. Thing was, they were very, very funny. But three nights ago, it had been Luke who'd rung him, Luke who'd fetched him, Luke's dad who'd driven him to the hospital and waited and then taken him back to theirs, Luke's mum who'd fed him and handed him a clean cloth to cry into when it had all hit him. And hugged him.

They'd all hugged him. He hadn't known then if she would be alive or dead the next morning.

Rattlers was in a back street near the bus station and did pie and peas, pie and chips, pie and mash, pie and eggs. It was small and greasy and permanently full.

'You God-bothering this weekend?' Luke asked as they got mugs of tea and ordered food.

'Don't call it that.'

Luke gave him a shove and grinned. They hung about by the counter waiting for a couple of workmen to leave their table.

'Didn't notice God round on Saturday night. Maybe off duty?'

'Yeah, well, my mum might have died.'

'Right.'

'What?'

'Right, she got spared, the other eight didn't.'

'Leave it.'

Luke elbowed his way to the table before someone ahead of them in the queue.

Tom sat down and stared out of the window onto the graffiti sprayed on the wall of the bus station. BRING BACK HANIGN.

'Your mum going to marry that Russell bloke?'

Tom shrugged.

'Be OK. He's OK.'

'It wouldn't and he isn't. He's weird.'

'Does make you wonder.'

'What?'

'What sort of teacher goes Internet dating.'

Tom flushed. 'Who said that?'

'You did.'

'No. No, I never did. I've never told anyone about that.'

'Right. I dunno then. Didn't know it was a secret. Jesse Cole said Mr Russell told them.'

'Phil told Jesse's class?'

Their food arrived. Luke stabbed a knife point into the pastry to release a plume of steam. 'No big deal,' he said.

'Yes it is. It makes her look weird as well and she isn't.'

'I know she isn't. Everybody knows she isn't. What's it matter? What do your Jesus lot think then?'

Tom bent his head. He didn't answer. He never did. That was his. And private.

'Anyway, you'll be off, doing this Bible-bashing course, won't make any difference to you, will it? When you get back what do you do with it?'

'What?'

'This Bible-bashing thing.'

'Don't . . .'

'You going to stand on street corners and that? Come and be saved?'

Tom flicked a pea across the table into Luke's face.

'Right.' Luke flicked a pea expertly back.

When they came into the street, stuffed full, Tom said, 'I hate him.'

'You can't say that.'

'Why?'

'You can go to hell for hatred.'

'I would,' Tom said. 'I'd even go to hell.'

Luke glanced at him. He means it, he thought. He hates him and he bloody means it.

At home, Tom made himself more tea and found a slab of milk chocolate at the back of the fridge. He stood at the kitchen window, biting a chunk of chocolate and then slurping hot tea and sloshing the two around his mouth together. He thought about his feelings with both shame and a certain amount of interest. He had never hated anyone, as far as he could remember. He had hated *things*. The cancer that had killed his father, for instance, but that had felt like a righteous and pure kind of hate. If he thought about it enough he could conjure up that hatred even now and it was like a clean burning flame, straight and steady. What he felt for Mr Russell was messier. A dirty, dingy sort of hate. It was mixed up with too many other things. His father again. Anger. Confusion. A small-boy jealousy. Dislike of Mr Russell's brand of atheism, which scored intellectual points and sneered and jested and talked clever. He could demolish arguments so comprehensively that Tom felt inept and a failure because he couldn't defend his beliefs and speak out convincingly for what he knew as Truth. But what he did most was worry. He knew that it was his responsibility to bring his mother and sister to Jesus, to save them, and he had failed.

He stopped himself. NO. Failed so far, not failed period. When he got to the States and to the Bible college he would learn the way to succeed and when he got back he would begin again. He couldn't bear the idea of them being outside in the darkness of ignorance, condemned. But he knew what might happen while he was away. He'd seen them together. Lizzie thought it would. Lizzie thought it was a brilliant idea, make sure Mum wasn't on her own once the two of them had left. And maybe getting together with someone was a good idea. The right someone. A picture of Phil Russell came into his head, smirking, a sarcastic, superior sneer on his face, and fury surged up inside him. He went and knelt down in front of the cross on his bedside table and closed his eyes.

'Jesus Lord and Saviour, who paid for my salvation with your blood . . .' He stopped. What was he praying for? That his mother would not marry Phil Russell? 'Dear Jesus, make Mum and – and Phil come to know you and ask you to come into their lives and give them new birth. Make them see the light. Take Satan from his heart and mind and wash him in your holy blood. Praise and worship. Amen.'

His heart felt ablaze with love and fervour and hope. Later he was due at a youth worship meeting and he would ask them to pray. He was leading the group for the first time tonight and it set him alight just thinking of it and the trust placed in him.

The front door banged. 'Tom, you up there?'

He got to his feet in case Lizzie came bounding in. He shouldn't feel ashamed and foolish to be caught on his knees in prayer and praise, but that was how it always was.

He went downstairs.

'Hey.'

Lizzie was feeding the toaster. She held up a slice.

'Two,' Tom said. 'Hey, Liz, why don't you come with me?'

'Come where?'

'Youth worship. I'm leading it tonight.'

'Right.'

'It'd be good. If you came.'

The toast jumped up, smoking slightly. 'Bugger, it keeps doing that, it sticks somewhere and then the side bit gets burned. It's only the one side. Can you have a look at it?'

'I did. Couldn't see anything. We just need a new toaster.'

'Jam or Marmite?'

'Marmite. So, will you come?'

Lizzie opened the wall cupboard. 'In your dreams. I'm going to see Mum but even if I wasn't. That's what you should be doing as well, that'd be more Christian.'

'I went this afternoon.'

'Oh. OK. How was she?'

'Seemed to have quite a lot of pain still. They don't come round to check much.'

'Short-staffed, aren't they? You have to speak up for yourself in those places.'

'He was there.'

'Good.'

'Not.'

'Don't start, Tom.'

Tom held up his hands.

'Just heard on the news. Another one died today . . . she was on the bottom level when it all came down.'

'Nine.'

'I'll never go on one of those things again. I'll probably never go near a fair again. Too bloody dangerous.'

'Lafferton's dangerous, right? They haven't got the gunman yet either.'

'The royals aren't going to that wedding now, last I heard.'

'Don't blame them. They've not been married all that long themselves, have they? He might take a potshot at Charles and Camilla. He doesn't seem to go for marriage much, our local sniper.'

'God, I hope they get him before Mum and Phil go down the aisle.'

Tom scraped back his chair loudly and went out of the kitchen.

Fifty-nine

'Another person has died as a result of the accident at Lafferton's Jug Fair last Saturday night when a ghost train collapsed. Today's death brings the toll to nine. Tanya Lomax, aged twenty-five, was on the ride with her husband, Dan, when the cart in which they were travelling was overturned as the ride fell to the ground. Dan Lomax was badly injured and is still in intensive care. The couple were married only last month.'

He stood still in the middle of the bedroom, naked after his shower, transfixed by the radio report. It was ten o'clock. He had been about to switch off when the item had started. Now, he stood while the newsreader blathered on and his mouth twitched into another of the smiles he could never suppress.

So, nothing had happened at the Jug Fair!

And it had happened without his having to lift a finger. Something was looking after him.

He pulled on the old grey T-shirt and shorts which he wore to bed. He would read for a bit before listening in again. There was a local news bulletin on Radio Bevham every half-hour. He couldn't wait.

Sixty

'As abbess of the Paraclete, Héloïse wrote to her former lover Abelard asking for guidance on the observance which should best be adopted by nuns. Her letter hit on a critical problem; the lack of a rule written for women . . .'

The ringing on her desk made Jane start. She had been working for an hour, so immersed in *The Monastic Order in Yorkshire 1069–1215* that for a split second she stared at the phone in bewilderment before picking it up.

'Jane, Peter Wakelin. I wondered if you had a few minutes to spare?'

'Yes, of course.'

'I need to rearrange things for a couple of Sundays in November.'

'Shall I come along now?'

'Now would be good – or I'm free after dinner.'

The Dean's rooms were on the east side of the court overlooking the Backs where they narrowed to flow under the Martyr's Bridge. Orange and brown leaves floated on the current as they stood at the window looking down. A couple of weeks before when she had been here there had been not a soul about. Now, with the new term under way, it was busy with young people cycling, walking, hanging about in groups.

'I like it full of life,' Jane said, 'but I like it when it's deserted too.'

Peter Wakelin nodded.

Before she had met him, she had had an image of a dean which was based on the one in her own undergraduate time, a thin, beaky man with an acerbic manner concealing great kindness and sensitivity towards the young. He had died suddenly in Jane's last year and she had been surprised that he had been only sixty-five. Peter Wakelin had also come as a surprise. He was in his early forties and a Yorkshireman by birth and education.

'I've been asked to go to the cathedral in Washington for ten days in November. It runs over two Sundays so we need to rearrange the preachers and I wondered if you could do the first? I know you're taking evensong that day as well. Is that too much?'

'It's fine. Nice to preach near All Saints' Day.'

'I'm very aware that you have limited time. I don't want to push you, Jane. You have the chaplaincy and your PhD – and then you're doing things here . . . Have some fun as well.'

'I'm fine. I love balancing the three things actually. It works rather well, though I probably like the hospital work best.'

He frowned slightly. 'I was there this morning,' he said, 'with a dilemma. Can I ask your advice?'

'Mine?'

'Why not? You've worked in a hospice, I haven't. Though I know them well enough of course.'

They sat on the window seat. But for some time Peter Wakelin said nothing, only looked out at the mist hanging low over the water. Jane waited. She knew little about him. Wondered what he had to say.

'I was called to an elderly woman,' he said. 'She has Alzheimer's and this morning she had a stroke. She was alive and conscious and they'd made her comfortable. No one had much idea of a prognosis but the quality of her life was certainly very low. Her family – sons, daughter-in-law, had asked if she could be – they said "put quietly to sleep". The doctors refused of course so the family called me. Wanted "my opinion". No, they wanted me to persuade the medics. I couldn't, it wasn't for me to do that, and even if I had they wouldn't have listened. But they were so desperate and what they said hit home, Jane. They said it wasn't that they wanted her to die, because she'd died to them long before, but that if she went quietly to sleep now, she'd finally be at peace and out of distress and pain – and they were right. They were right. No one knows how long she'll last – maybe hours but it might drag on for weeks. They hope it won't but . . .'

Two young men came running towards the college buildings through the gathering mist. They were wearing singlets and shorts, grim-faced.

'What do you think?'

'You mean what would I have said? The same as you because we have to.'

'In the hospice, were you asked this? To intervene? To plead with the doctors to end a life?'

'Yes. Only a couple of times, though I'm sure the medics are asked more often.'

'And?'

'Listen, I understand the request . . . but in a hospice the pain is so well controlled and they make the quality of life as good as they possibly can that it isn't the same. And death is not usually very far away.'

He was silent.

'You think you should have said yes?'

He shook his head and again was silent and then Jane realised that he was crying.

'Peter?' she said gently.

He went on looking out of the window. 'I did it myself, you see,' he said at last. 'I asked them to – to give her something much stronger.' He looked at Jane. 'My wife.'

'Oh, Peter, I didn't know.'

'No reason you should. She had a melanoma.'

'When was this?'

'Oh, it's a couple of years. One reason I came down to Cambridge. Only you never get away, do you? You can't.'

'I'm so sorry. It doesn't help when you have to deal with situations like this morning.'

'Different though.' He stood up. 'Feel like a walk out there before it gets dark?'

*

They went, out of the back gate, over the Martyr's Bridge and along the path in the direction of King's and Peter talked. He talked about his childhood, on a York housing estate, his visit to York Minster, alone one evening during choral evensong, and how he had stood at the back, a boy of twelve, transfixed by the singing and had come sneaking back – sneaking away from everyone – to wander about the great building, looking and sometimes listening and thinking. He talked about his decision to become first a Christian and later a priest – not a conversion, he said, a gradual, inevitable decision. About Alice. About their ten years together, longing for and failing to have children. Her illness, swift and terrible, and her death, slow and also terrible. His first months here, when he had felt lost and out of place, bewildered and uncertain of anything.

'Did you lose your faith?'

'Never. I just became very, very angry.'

They walked back through the streets of the town, dodging posses of cyclists, in the gathering dusk. Jane felt she had begun the afternoon with a comparative stranger and ended it with someone she had come to know rather well. A friend.

They parted at the college entrance. She had to buy a couple of books. In Heffers, finding the shelves she needed, she stood in front of them unseeing, thinking about Peter Wakelin and about living and dying and keeping the dying alive.

They did not have the books she wanted in stock. At the counter, waiting to order, she picked up a new edition of T.S. Eliot's *Four Quartets* and opened them at random.

What might have been and what has been
Point to one end, which is always present.

She did not buy the book because she had her own copy but it reminded her of how much meaning she had always found in the *Four Quartets*, how much there was between the lines, how the poems had sometimes seemed to enrich her as the Bible and the *Odyssey* had.

She came out into the street which was bright and busy with lights and packed with students and shoppers, so that she kept having to walk in the road. Cambridge delighted her. Everything was here and she felt an uprush of gratitude for her work, the college, the new intellectual stimulus, new friends. After a series of stumbles the way ahead seemed smooth.

She wished she had not left Simon Serrailler any message.

Sixty-one

'Daddy's been sick in the bathroom and now he's crying,' Hannah had said, running down the stairs into the study after ten o'clock. Cat was replying to a long email from the practice manager. The fact that she was now off work to look after Chris did not mean she was out of touch and she knew that if she did let go it would be harder than ever to pick up the reins later. Whenever 'later' was.

She had resettled Hannah in bed, cleaned up and gone into the bedroom.

'Chris?'

His head was turned away.

'Oh my love.'

His shoulders shook occasionally. She put her arms round them and held him against her.

'I know.'

'You bloody don't know.'

'No.'

It was true. Whatever it felt like to watch him, to nurse him, to see him in pain and distress, it was different, separate, it was happening to him and not to her. Then he had mumbled something.

'What?'

He pushed her slightly.

'Chris?'

'I can't see properly. It's like a tunnel. I can see straight ahead but nothing else.'

'Since when?'

'Earlier. I don't know. I woke up. It was then.'

She said nothing because she could find no words. After half an hour she had given him a shot of morphine and stayed until he slept before going back to the computer. Oddly, she had finished the notes and sent them off with complete concentration before checking on a query from the junior locum about a patient he thought had Lyme disease – had Cat ever seen a case of it locally? – and reading several articles in the *BMJ*. Her mind was hungry for facts and medical information about anything other than brain tumours and work kept her occupied – kept her downstairs, she thought – though the door was ajar and part of her was tuned for any sound from Chris or, as always, the children.

When she came to it was half past one, and Chris was calling.

He was lying on his back, eyes open and shimmering with tears.

'I can't do this,' he said. 'You'd be better at it.'

She took his hand. 'I can't give you another shot just yet but I'll get you a syringe pump first thing in the morning. You'll be much more comfortable. I think we should have one of the Imogen House girls come in every day – they're so much more used to the dosages and everything else.'

'Don't send me in there.'

She was silent. He had always said that though he had been happy to send patients into the hospice, knew how well they were cared for, knew it was far better than the hospital, he would never want to go there. Cat had not understood and never argued.

'Cat?'

'No. If you want to stay here you're staying here.'

'Do I have to have one of them come?'

'No. But if you could bear to, it would help. They really do know more than me about . . .'

'Dying.'

'Yes.'

'It didn't do any good. Remember that in future. Forget the treatment, it doesn't do any good.'

'Everyone's different, you know.'

'Shit, who's got this thing, you or me? Jesus, you've always got to know best, haven't you? Only you don't. This time I know fucking best.'

It was happening like this more and more, a sudden spurt of rage and vicious accusations directed at her. It was the tumour talking, she always had to remind herself, it was not Chris. But it was the hardest part. Twice he had turned on Sam and snarled, shouted angrily at Hannah, terrifying her. Seconds later he had fallen asleep or simply forgotten. When Hannah did not want to come and say goodbye to him before she went to school or kiss him goodnight, he was bewildered and upset.

She went into the kitchen. Mephisto was sprawled on the old sofa in a deep sleep and did not stir. The wind had got up. She poured a glass of milk and sat down. Something else was worrying her. She had been sleeping with Chris in their bed until tonight, but he had seemed increasingly disturbed by her and was awake or restless so that she wasn't getting much sleep. The children had enough without having her tired and irritable. But how could she tell Chris that she was moving out? Perhaps she could indicate that she needed a good sleep 'just tonight' and then 'just another night' until it became permanent. The spare room was next door to theirs and she could leave both doors ajar.

But something practical and even necessary had a finality about it which she could not face. This was not only about her getting sleep. It was about nothing ever being normal again, about never sharing their bed again, about the end of everything. I have not been a good doctor, she thought now, because this is something that has never occurred to me and which not one single patient who has had to face it has ever talked to me about. Perhaps there is nothing to say, perhaps it is simply unbearable and impossible to put into words, tell someone else, express at all?

There was a sound. She went to the foot of the stairs and listened. Nothing. Then again.

Chris was sitting up, his arm stretched out to the bedside lamp which was lying on the floor. Seeing him, his head shaved on one side, his face and body thin, his eyes full of bewilderment, Cat thought, I cannot do this. I don't know how to be here any longer. And was ashamed and angry with herself, as she restored the lamp, settled Chris down again as she would one of the children, smoothing his forehead, murmuring to him. He had not been fully awake or aware, the morphine was still having its effect.

She went into the children's rooms. Felix, as ever, was sleeping on his face with his bottom in the air. Sam was curled neatly, his Alex Rider book open under his arm. Hannah's duvet was on the floor. Cat replaced it and tucked her in. Whatever else was happening in the house, whatever had upset them during the day, they were all blessed with the certainty of sleep.

Her own body was tired but her brain was so wide awake it seemed to be sending out sparks. She settled on the sofa next to Mephisto, who squeezed his claws once or twice. A pile of books were on the floor beside her, books she had been trying to concentrate on for days. Even when she had been at her busiest stretches as a GP she had never left a novel unfinished or taken so long over one as she was now. She picked through them. The latest Ian Rankin. Ruth Rendell. But she couldn't read about the dark side, violence and distress, nor care who had committed whatever the crimes might be. *Barchester Towers*. Martin Amis. Both loved, neither right. At the bottom was the huge, heavy novel Chris had bought her at the airport on the way home from Australia because, he had said, 'Even you can't say this one's too short for the flight.' *Jonathan Strange & Mr Norrell*. But she had barely begun it when Felix had been sick and Hannah had been frightened of a bout of turbulence and then it had been food trays and sleep and more sickness, until she had put the novel away and read an old Dorothy L. Sayers someone had left in the magazine pouch of her seat.

'Some years ago there was in the city of York a society of magicians.'

She felt herself sink into the book as into a deep soft bed.

She came to when the cat uncurled himself, leapt softly onto the floor and went out through the catflap, letting in a brief draught of cold air. It was almost three and the house was creaking slightly here and there as the wind got under the floor-boards and the roof tiles and around the window frames. Go to bed, she told herself. Now, or you'll be fit for nothing tomorrow.

She shivered. Did not go to bed but instead picked up the phone which was beside her and pressed 3.

'Serrailler,' he said at once.

'I didn't wake you then.'

'Hi. No, that was half an hour ago. Some jerk's running round town in a stolen jeep firing an airgun out of the windows.'

'Nice.'

'Don't worry, he's nicked.'

'Why did they ring you?'

'They ring me if a car backfires at the moment. But that's not why you're ringing me. What's wrong?'

'It's three o'clock.'

'Bleak?'

'Very.'

'Fifteen minutes.'

It was less. He blew in with the wind and came straight to her, holding out his arms. She had no need to say anything. He would have understood if she had gone to sleep but she needed to talk and he simply listened to everything without interruption, passing her a handkerchief, making tea and always listening, listening.

In the end, she sat, drained of words and even of emotions, sipping the tea in exhaustion.

But then she said, remembering, 'I'm sorry I got at you the other night. About Dad.'

He shrugged.

'Si, you have to take this on board. He's happy. Judith is very good for him. Ma would have been pleased, you know. Amazed, but pleased.'

'I know. It isn't that.'

'You think she's taking Ma's place.'

'It's the house.'

'You care about the house more than about Dad?'

'I suppose I do. What a shit.'

'Yes.'

'None of it matters. Not beside this. How long will it go on?'

She shook her head. 'Probably not as long as I expected. They gave him a few months at the beginning but they can never be sure and I guess they were wrong. Not their fault.'

'Why is he so set against the hospice?'

'I'm not sure. He's always been very keen on it for his patients. I don't think it's that he doesn't want to go there so much as that he does want to stay at home. We can manage that. The hospice does home support and Dickon Farley's his doctor – I'm his wife but at this stage it doesn't make much difference. Dickon will make the decisions, I'll be on the spot. I won't send him away. It's a few weeks.'

'The kids?'

'They have to live with it . . . Sam and Hannah anyway. I can't protect them from everything though we'll make sure they don't see him if they shouldn't. But they know. I've talked to them about it. Sam listens and doesn't say much, Hannah says a lot but she hasn't listened and she hasn't really taken it on board. It'll be worse for her.'

'Worst of all for you.'

'Adam's driving his mother down the day after tomorrow. I don't want them to leave it too late but I suspect that actually she can't face it. You know Chris's mother – only looks on the bright side because only the bright side is allowed to exist. I can't talk to her on the phone because she just insists it's a matter of positive thinking. She's a great one for positive thinking, my mother-in-law. I wish I were.'

'You're a realist. You have to be. So am I. I have to be.'

'You're up against it at the moment, aren't you?'

'Yup. I wouldn't admit it to many but he's got the upper hand. He's laughing at us, I can hear him.'

'What do you think?'

'He'll make a mistake. They always do. He'll make a mistake or he'll flip and start running round the shopping centre with a gun and then turn it on himself. But not before there's a massacre. Have you counted the number of times the media uses the word every time they report? They dredge up every American high school and small-town gun massacre in history and scare the daylights out of everyone. Apparently two weddings have hired private security – word has it one lot were armed though we don't know that for sure. Another lot have postponed their wedding until it's all over. Shops say they've never known such quiet Saturday afternoons and the Jug Fair didn't help any. And all the time, I'm looking round, you know? I'm looking round trying to put myself into his head, thinking, would I have a go here, why wouldn't I come and shoot someone there, what would I do next, who would I gun down this week? I can guess. We can all guess. But we can't have a full armed response every time a popgun goes off.'

'I heard the royals have cancelled for the Barr wedding.'

'They've been advised to cancel but we haven't had anything official. The Lord Lieutenant's having apoplexy, his wife's having a nervous breakdown, the Chief wishes they'd skip the wedding and go straight for the honeymoon.'

'Nothing will happen there.'

'Probably not, but thinking so doesn't help lower the temperature.'

From upstairs they heard Chris shouting out at the same moment as Simon's mobile rang.

Chris was standing up beside the bed and when Cat went into the room he said, 'Please . . .'

'I'm here. What is it?'

But he simply sat and then lay down on the bed without replying and fell asleep. Cat pulled the duvet over him and left the room.

The kitchen was empty. She looked out and saw that Simon had driven away. Mephisto was still out. The wind was still blowing hard, stirring the edges of the yellow curtains and rattling the catflap.

She lay down on the sofa, knotted with misery and dread, and waited for first light.

Sixty-two

'This is a situation virtually without precedent,' the Chief said. 'There have been shootings, of course there have – Dunblane. In the United States they are becoming commonplace. Lone gunmen open fire in a school playground or a college or a shopping mall, but in almost every instance they turn the gun on themselves. Not in this case.'

She looked round the table. Faces were grim. The media had returned in force. There had been half an hour about gun crime on the BBC with TV pictures of Lafferton. Awkward questions were being asked in high places. Simon wondered how long it would be before the rest of his SIFT team was called in. Could he head up both? Probably not.

'My –'

A knock. The door opened. Paula Devenish glared. The desk officer brought in a single sheet of paper, gave it to her and vanished.

The Chief Constable read. Closed her eyes for a second. Looked up.

'This,' she said, 'is a message about next Saturday's wedding. The Lord Lieutenant's daughter.' She paused. 'The Prince of Wales and the Duchess of Cornwall will be attending.'

There was an intake of breath. Someone muttered, 'All we need.'

'Quite,' the Chief said.

'But I thought –'

'We all *thought*, John. We were told royal protection advice had been firmly not to come, and that the Prince of Wales had agreed.'

'Buggers.'

'Don't say that,' someone else said, 'PoW's never bottled it before. He knows someone could take a potshot every time he goes out.'

'I'm going to apply for an extra unit from RP,' the Chief said. 'I don't see why all this should be down to us.'

She stood up. 'Thank you, everyone. Simon, can I have a word . . . ?'

They went along the corridor to his office.

'Frankly, I'm terrified. Not something I readily admit to. I know this is a private visit but we are going to organise ourselves as if it were high profile. Gold Command.' The Chief looked at him. 'You've got plenty on with this entire case but no one knows it better. Problem?'

'It's personal and family, but yes. I'm concerned that I may need to be available for my sister at short notice . . . her husband has a brain tumour – he's very ill.'

'I'm sorry, Simon. That's a pig, my father died of one, so I know. But the fact is, it's your brother-in-law, not your wife or child. I can't let you off.'

Tough, he thought. Tough as ever. Station word had always been that the Chief was tougher than a man because she had more to prove. That might have been true ten years ago but now Paula Devenish was one of several female chief constables. She was still reckoned to be the toughest among them.

'I'll fix a meeting with royal protection and whoever else as a matter of urgency. I'll let you know. Any more news on the fairground accident?'

'Fatalities stand at nine – the ones still in hospital are all out of danger.'

'Good,' she said briskly.

Simon went to get a coffee. The royal visit was the least of it. There would be a lot of tedious meetings, the wedding would go ahead, nothing untoward would happen because, whoever he was, the gunman had a brain. He would know that the cathedral would be bristling with armed police.

Patience, Simon thought, closing his office door. It was only a matter of patience and good, careful policing and of playing a waiting game. Sooner or later the man would make a single mistake which would give them their chance. A mistake, a bit of luck, making sure their backs were covered, double-checking everything . . . the tedious stuff. Most of his police life went to prove that he was right. The rest, the serial killers, the major dramas – they were rare.

But in any case, he knew that at the moment he needed the shelter of routine. For most of the day, the thought of Cat and Chris was not at the back but near the forefront of his mind. That was a question of waiting too. The worst sort of waiting.

Sixty-three

'I bought some fish from the new place in the Lanes – apparently they get a delivery straight from Grimsby every morning so it couldn't be fresher. Would you like it just plain grilled?'

'What is it?'

'Dover sole.'

'Oh, Lizzie, what a treat, you are good.'

'No, it's fun. You know I like cooking – sometimes.'

'I feel completely useless.'

'Right. Can't stop you feeling what you wanna feel.'

Helen laughed and winced.

'Hurt?'

'Laughing does. Sneezing does. Coughing does. Moving does. Breathing does. If I keep off those it's fine.'

'Well, you can't have any more painkillers until half past five so you'll have to practise mental diversion.'

'I didn't realise I'd brought you up to be so hard.'

'Yup, you did. Tea?'

'Thought you'd never ask.'

Helen was propped up on the sofa with the French windows open onto the garden. It had been a beautiful day to come out of hospital, she thought, a beautiful day to be thankful that you were alive when you could so easily have been . . .

'Lizzie, how many people have died now?'

'Morbid.'

'No. I want to know. I was incredibly lucky – how lucky was I?'

'Nine people, and four with serious injuries. But out of danger. So yeah, lucky. Too true.'

A squirrel leapt into the ash tree at the bottom of the garden, scrambled down the trunk and bounded across the grass. Beautiful, Helen thought. That is the most beautiful squirrel I have ever seen and the tree is the most beautiful and the sun is shining more beautifully than it has ever shone. I have done nothing to deserve life just as the others did not deserve death. But I am going to revel in it and every moment I am awake I am going to be grateful for it. Her ribs hurt. Her shoulders hurt. Her neck was excruciatingly painful if she tried to turn it so much as a millimetre and none of it mattered, it could be borne. It was the pain of getting better and how different that must be from any other pain – the pain of getting worse.

She remembered very little of the accident. It was like a film flickering through her mind from time to time, in which parts had been removed and parts elided with others so that the time was muddled and the scenes made no sense. She remembered the noise of screaming. The lurch as they tipped or fell. She remembered the feel of the man's strong grip on her wrist as he found her and then his face. 'OK, love,' he kept saying, 'you're OK.'

How Phil had simply crawled out and walked away virtually unscathed was another matter for wonder, though she had not known about that until she was at the hospital and he had turned up with Lizzie. He had not taken a day off but been in school as usual first thing the next morning.

She shifted to try and get comfortable. The squirrel was back, nibbling at a conker among the fallen leaves which Tom had promised but failed to sweep up. It didn't matter. Nothing so small could possibly matter ever again.

She closed her eyes and dozed and was wakened by the sound of the doors being closed. Phil looked round. 'Good to sleep,' he said. 'Lizzie's in charge next door. How do you feel?'

'Stiff. Sore. Very happy.'

He came over and sat beside her. 'Are you going to be able to get upstairs all right later?'

'Oh yes. I can't sleep on a sofa, that's what invalids do. How was your day?'

'Busy. I had a bit of running round to do.'

'They should be keeping you on light duties – I said you should have a week off.'

'I know.'

'Why running round?'

'I had to go into town. Shopping. Bought you this.'

The door opened on Lizzie bearing a tray so she put the package to one side while they set up a table and cloth and helped her to sit up. Moving to an upright position was painful enough to make her catch her breath. Four cushions at her back. Her left arm was in a sling.

Eating was slow but the fish was the best food she had ever eaten, the vegetables perfectly cooked, the bread and butter manna. She wondered if the painkillers were making her high but knew that it was relief, the high of having cheated death. She had said prayers of thanks in her head several times. Phil would laugh. 'No such things as miracles,' he had said.

Perhaps it didn't matter.

She had thought she was hungry and Lizzie had given her only a small piece of fish but she couldn't manage it all. Some reflex made her throat close as she tried to swallow, though she knew there was nothing wrong. She drank tea, ate some bread and butter, expressed great thanks, refused a date slice. Felt faint with exhaustion.

And then Phil handed her the package again. It was the size of a box of chocolates. She hoped it was not. Chocolate was not what she needed.

But inside an empty chocolate box was another box and, inside that, another and another and then the smallest box.

'Will you marry me?' Phil said.

Helen began to cry.

An hour later she was still crying but upstairs in bed. Phil had gone home. Lizzie was lying on top of the duvet beside her.

'I can't stop grinning,' she said.

'So I see.'

'If it hadn't been for me pushing you onto the Internet . . .'

'True. You'll have to wear pink satin, you know.'

The front door slammed.
'He won't,' Lizzie said.
'God, don't make me laugh please, it's so painful.'
'Mum?'
'We're here, talking about pink satin. Where have you been?'
'Giving out leaflets.'
Lizzie groaned and pulled a pillow over her head. She steered clear of what she called Tom's religious mania but when he went into bars and cafés or shops handing out Jesus leaflets she wanted to curl up with embarrassment.
'Shut up. You OK, Mum? Sure they ought to have let you out?'
'Quite sure. Very sure. And I'm fine, thanks, love, never better. Sleepy and sore and never better.'
Tom looked at Lizzie.
'It's OK, it's not the drugs, she's just going to get married. Isn't it great? He brought a ring all hidden inside lots of boxes, I think it was the most romantic thing in the world, I'm really jealous.'
Tom stood half in the room. He did not look at either of them. He looked straight ahead. He seemed hardly to breathe.
'Great news, Tom,' Lizzie said.
Nothing.
'Tom? Don't stand like that, come here.'
Nothing.
'Oh God, if you're going to be childish . . .' Lizzie got off the bed and started towards him. 'If you are, then bugger off before you upset her. You make me really angry, Tom.'
But as she neared him he turned away. He went across the landing, back down the stairs.
'Lizzie, don't, leave him, it's fine, he'll be fine.'
'Tosser!' Lizzie yelled.
But the front door banged shut over the sound of her voice.

Sixty-four

'Tell out, my soul, the glories of his word!
Firm is his promise, and his mercy sure.
Tell out, my soul, the greatness of the Lord
To children's children and for evermore!'

'Alleluia!'
'Alleluia!'
'Praise Jesus' name!'
'Praise the name of Christ Jesus!'
The band struck up, two guitars, two flutes, the electronic keyboard, and Combo on the drums. Tom had backed out. He usually took part playing something but tonight he couldn't face it. He stood towards the back.
'Allelluia, Ay-men!'
The pastor raised his arms. Tom closed his eyes as they began to sing again, sing and wave their arms and sway, row after row. He could feel the woman next to him swaying against him.
'Jesus, sweet Lord,' she moaned.
He opened his eyes. There was a woman with two young boys in the row in front but where the backs of the boys were, one with a blue fleece, one with a red, he saw only his mother's face, lit up with happiness, hers and Lizzie's. Lizzie was grinning at him.
He had walked for an hour around the roads, in and out of cul-de-sacs, down avenues full of houses. Car in the drive, lights in the windows. Car in the drive. Lights in the windows. On and on.

He had come out near the Hill and thought he might climb up there but it was pitch black and he had no torch. He had walked back, veered off, not wanting to go home, walked halfway into the town but changed his mind and walked back again. He didn't want to meet anyone, couldn't talk. What he wanted to do was cry. He wasn't angry with his mother, though he didn't understand her, but maybe it was the shock of the accident, maybe she didn't know what she was doing. Maybe? He was sad and upset. Phil Russell. OK, so he, Tom, was off to the States, leaving home, and would have little to do with him, but the knowledge that Phil Russell was his stepfather, had married his mother and was filling her mind and heart full of atheistic poison, sneering at the Bible, turning her against it with clever intellectual talk, making her feel a fool, probably stopping her going to the cathedral singers . . . He knew in his heart that God was asking him to stop this thing, that Jesus was relying on him to bring his mother to salvation and Tom wanted to, but on his own it seemed impossible.

'You are not on your own, Tom,' a voice said in his heart. 'Behold, I am with you always, even to the ending of the world.'

He smiled. The fleeces of the two small boys glowed.

'For my sake,' the voice said, 'is there not more rejoicing over one lamb which was lost and is now found . . .'

'Yea, Lord,' he said, 'bless your name. I know it's down to me, I know what you're asking me to do. It's just . . .'

'Nothing is too difficult for God. Ask and ye shall receive. Knock and it shall be opened to you.'

The woman next to him clutched his arm and the room was filled with the babble of people speaking in tongues. She spoke in tongues. Her eyes were rolling. Tom tried to move her hand gently from his arm but her grip was too strong.

'Amma jambagrisalamoralamma fornamo jammay jammay canfalabedei.'

Tom opened his own mouth, trying to remember what he had been taught by the pastor after his baptism.

Relax, take a deep breath, let it out slowly, and focus your mind on the God and the Lord who love you immeasurably. Thank them for having filled you with the Holy Spirit, take another breath, and let it rip – speak forth words of praise, thanksgiving, and worship. And that is exactly what you will be speaking. And be BOLD – the words you are hearing are the proof that Jesus is alive and well – and that so will you be – forever! It cost him his life for you to be able to praise and worship God in this wonderful way, so get into it!

He closed his eyes again but by now the pastor was back on his feet, waving his Bible and calling out to them to hear the words of Jesus.

'"Come to me, all ye that labour and are carrying a heavy burden. I will give you rest."'

'Which of you here works hard to pay the rent, to fuel the mortgage, to feed the little ones, to buy the clothes, to run the car? Which of you gets up before light and trudges off to a job they don't much care for and stays at it all day and trudges back home in the evening, tired out? Which of you here? I guess all of you here, those of you of an age to be in work. And those too young, well, I guess you go to school, don't you, you sit through your classes and do your homework, day after day. You carry a heavy burden. Now what does the Lord Jesus say? Does he say I will give you a load of riches so you can stop work and fly to Florida and lie by a pool all day? Does he say, OK, I'll see to it that you quit school and have fun all day and never have to learn a spelling or a chemistry formula ever again, Ay-men? No, he does NOT. What he says is, "I will give you rest," but does this mean idleness. It does NOT! Was Jesus idle? Were the disciples idle? No, they were NOT. The words of Jesus need to be thought through. Rest. I will give you rest . . .'

Feet shuffled. Someone sneezed violently. The boy in the blue fleece pinched the boy in the red one. The woman next to him leaned against Tom. He moved away and she leaned further. She smelled of fish.

He hung about the chapel after they had all left, until the pastor came out from the side room to tidy up.

'Tom? Sorry not to have you up there playing for us tonight – everything all right?'

He came nearer, looked closely. Sat down beside him.

'You don't look good. You hear the words of God just now? "Come to me all ye that are burdened"? Whatever's wrong, boy, take the words to heart.'

'I'm trying. It's just – difficult.'

'I'm here for you if you want to talk, but if not, try Jesus. He's always there for you.'

'Yeah. I know.'

'So . . . I'll just get on with the clearing up, you do what you decide to do, Tom. We're both of us right next to you.'

'Thanks.'

He bent his head. The floorboards were scuffed and dirt-stained. Thousands of feet, he thought, thousands of feet.

He didn't know if he wanted to talk to the pastor or not but he couldn't talk to God, and in any case, why should he need to, he knew his innermost heart, he knew what was wrong. He ought to do something to sort it, that was all, he ought to stop it happening. He couldn't want this marriage, Helen Creedy to a militant, arrogant, atheist who sneered at Jesus and had once drawn a pair of spectacles on his image on one of Tom's leaflets. His mother wasn't reborn yet but she was a good person, he knew it was only a matter of time before she saw the light and welcomed Jesus into her life, but there wasn't any hope for Phil Russell and if she married him . . .

No, you couldn't say there wasn't any hope. There was hope for everyone to turn to Jesus before it was too late. Only just now Tom couldn't see how it would ever happen to Phil. Proud and stiff-necked, he thought. That was him. The Bible always had the right phrase somewhere.

The pastor banged shut the wooden box full of hymn books and paused.

'Tom, I have to go in ten.'

Tom got to his feet.

'You need to talk through something, give me a call. I'm back in later, you ring me, now? No fretting, OK?'

'OK. Thanks.'

'You on your motorbike? Frighten the pants off me those things.'

Tom laughed and followed him out. The bike was parked up

in the schoolyard next door and when he had trundled it to the gate and buckled his helmet he sat for a moment looking down the street. He couldn't have told the pastor but while he had been there on his own in the chapel, he had prayed for the last time to be told what to do and it had come into his head at once, shocking him, taking his breath away. But the voice had been clear. The words had been unmistakable. He didn't understand why this was what he should do because it was so off the wall, he'd never expected anything like it. But the more he thought about it now, sitting astride the machine in the evening dark, the more it seemed the right thing and clear. If nothing else, it would wake her, make her understand, show her the right way, this would. That was why he had to do it. It wasn't for himself, it was for her. The sacrifice was for her. She might not see it straight away but she would see it pretty soon because that was what his answer had been and God's answer could never be wrong.

He kicked the bike into a roar and turned out of the gate. Behind him, locking up, the pastor shook his head and said a word of prayer for the boy not to speed into an accident.

Sixty-five

'You're happy with all of this, I take it?' Peter Wakelin asked again.

'It all seems fine.'

'I'm not very good at delegating, I'm afraid.'

Jane laughed. 'That much I gathered. Honestly, Peter, the place will still be standing when you get back.' She got up and gathered the papers on the table into her folder. It was a mild morning with shafts of sun breaking through the inevitable Cambridge mist. She wondered how many more times the Dean would want to go through the arrangements and timetables for everything due to take place during his absence. Now she had her doctorate supervisor to see and an undergraduate to visit in the acute psychiatric ward, but as she reached the door, Peter Wakelin said, 'Jane – are you busy later?'

'When later? I'm not free for the rest of the day now, I'm afraid.'

'I mean this evening. I wondered if you'd have dinner with me?'

She hesitated. Her plan was for a quick supper in hall and an evening of work. She didn't especially want to change it. But as she glanced at him, she changed her mind. This man is lonely, she thought, and he can't face either a convivial evening with the entire college or one alone. She knew how that felt. She liked her own company but there had been times over the last couple of years when she had wanted anything but.

'That would be nice,' she said.

Something she read as relief lightened his features.

'Shall we meet at the main gate? Seven thirty? I'll bring the car round.'

'Can't we walk?'

'Not where we'll be going, no.'

'Fine. See you then.'

She went out to collect her mail from the lodge. She felt that she had somehow been put on the back foot, and had misinterpreted something without quite knowing what or why. It was a question in her mind as she drove out to the hospital to see the undergraduate who had been sectioned.

Jane did not know Polly Watson, as far as she could remember, but the girl, a second-year student, had asked to see her. Her academic record was impeccable, she had had no reported medical problems prior to this and seemed to have been generally invisible.

Jane had had little experience of visiting psychiatric patients. She had expected security in the wing but the reception clerk gave her an odd look and asked her to take a seat. Why, Jane wondered, do they always have them placed around the walls, in hospitals and waiting rooms everywhere, regimented and rather alarming? Chairs in groups changed the whole feel.

A number of people waited together, heads down, not speaking to one another. A woman alone flicked the pages of a magazine without reading anything. A man came in, gave his name, sat down, got straight up again. Left.

Several people came and went. Jane decided that fifteen minutes was a reasonable time to wait before returning to the desk.

Someone came out carrying two potted cyclamen, put them on the window ledge and went again, tapping a code into the security panel to open the door.

After ten minutes, a young woman in a dark trouser suit came over to her.

'Reverend Fitzroy? Dr Fison. Would you come through with me?'

They went down a corridor. Cream-painted. An institutional corridor. Voices in the distance. A smell of burning milk.

'Do sit down.'

An office. She had expected to be led to a ward.

'I'm sorry you had to wait but as you can imagine when this sort of thing happens there's a bit of a procedure.'

'I'm afraid I don't know Polly at all, but as she sent for me perhaps you can fill me in before I see her?'

A look of surprise. A frown. She put down her pen. 'Oh Lord. They didn't tell you.'

'Tell me?'

'Polly's dead. She had a stash of medication and she also swallowed four razor blades. She was found in the toilet at five this morning. I'm so sorry, there's clearly been a slip-up in communication.'

'Clearly.'

'We've been in touch with her family. Her parents are on their way from –' she glanced down at the papers – 'York. So that's that. You've had a wasted journey.'

'No,' Jane said. 'Would it be possible for me to see her body?'

'Afraid not, unless you want to go to the mortuary. There's got to be a PM of course.' She spoke coolly. She had not known Polly Watson either. One acute admission, one suicide, file closed.

'I will go to the mortuary, actually,' Jane said.

'As you wish. Do you know where it is?'

Handshake. The corridor again. 'I'll leave you here if that's all right – busy day.'

Jane went out into the chilly grey morning. She felt bleak and helpless. She had failed someone without even knowing them. An unhappy girl with who knew what problems and in what distress, a girl who had studied here for a year and was barely known to any of them.

It shouldn't happen, she thought.

It happens.

After she left the mortuary she realised what had been in her mind. Peter Wakelin had asked her to dinner. Dinner was different. She liked what little she knew of him but she also knew that she did not want to go. She was still finding her place and her feet after a bad two years. Calm and peace in which to get on with her doctorate and do her job well were what she needed now.

When she got back she wrote a note and left it in his pigeonhole.

Sixty-six

'If you'd just like to tell me what it's about, sir . . .'

'I said, I'm not telling you what it's about, I want to see the boss.'

'Not sure who you mean by that, sir, but I'm the duty sergeant.'

'I know that. I want to see the one in the suit that's on the news.'

'That would be CID, sir. I can get someone from CID to talk to you if you'd tell me what –'

'No. Tell you what, I'm going to sit over there. Not been out of hospital long, so I get giddy, I'm going to sit over there and wait and you can fetch him and if he's out I'll still wait and if he comes through those doors I'll see him. I don't mind waiting, I got nothing better to do, and when I see him and when I tell him he'll be very glad I did. So you fetch him. The one on the news. Not talking to anyone else.'

'If you mean DCS Serrailler, he's out and he'll be out all morning and he won't talk to you without knowing what it's about.'

'He'll talk to me. I can wait.'

The man walked over to the bench against the wall and sat down. His movements were cautious and he held himself together as if he feared the onset of pain. The hair at the back of his head was shorter than the rest, as if it had been shaved. He was bristly, scruffy, pale. Neither old nor young. The sergeant watched him for a minute. He wasn't familiar. Dosser? Nutter? Hard to say. Bit of both, he thought. The phone rang.

Half an hour later the man was still there, sitting, occasionally closing his eyes but alert every time the doors swung open, looking closely at whoever came and went.

'You'll have a long wait, sir – why don't you let me get someone down from CID? You can talk to them, then maybe if it's important they'll pass it on to the Super. Only as you may have heard we've got some big stuff going on – as you said, you've seen him on the television news, so you can guess he's pretty busy . . .'

He wound down. The man heard him out, looking at him without much interest. Then looked at the floor, not acknowledging anything that had been said.

Two hours later, he was still there. Two and a half hours. Three. In the end the desk sergeant went over.

'Listen, you can't sit here all day and all night. He might not be back for hours. If you won't talk to anyone else I'm going to have to ask you to leave. What's it to be?'

'Cup of tea?'

'You're pushing your luck. Right, here's the deal – cup of tea, you talk to someone else or on your way.'

'Who will I have to talk to?'

'Someone from CID. Whoever's available. If anyone is available, otherwise it'll be someone from uniform.'

The man sat quiet for a long time, weighing it up. Then he nodded.

Ten minutes later, tea in front of him, he was sitting opposite DS Graham Whiteside in the small waiting room.

'Right. Name?' Whiteside looked bored.

The man put his hand to the back of his head but did not quite touch it. 'In hospital couple of weeks,' he said. 'Not good. Left me for dead.'

'What's this all about then? Hit-and-run? Whatever, if it's that long ago why didn't you report it before?'

'Because I was in hospital, wasn't I? Didn't come round for the first four days.'

'Let's get this organised. Name, I said.'

'Matty.'

'Oh, come on, give me a hand here, I'm bad at guesswork. Matty *who*?'

'Lowe.'

'Getting somewhere . . . and when was this?'

'When was what?'

'The hit-and-run or are we making the whole bloody thing up – sir?'

'I'm not making anything up. Why would I do that?'

'Oh, you'd be amazed. When are we looking at? Date and time. If you can manage that.'

'When it happened or when I saw him?'

Graham Whiteside passed a hand over his brow and mopped off imaginary drops of sweat.

'I saw him at the fair. He'd left me for dead, you know, and they say you don't remember anything after you've taken a bash on the head but I do. Not everything, mind, but I remember a bit. Enough to know where I was and that someone blinded me with light and then clouted me on the back of the head here and left me for dead. I came round in hospital, splitting skull, load of bruises. All I remembered was being blinded. At first. Still don't remember much more.'

'If you don't remember anything you're wasting my time, sunshine.'

'I didn't say that. I said I didn't remember everything. I was on the old airfield, in one of the hangars . . . I've been dossing a bit, lost my way. It's all right out there. Better than shop doorways.'

Drugs? Probably. The sergeant tapped the side of his foot against the table leg. 'Get on with it.'

The man sipped his tea. 'Hospital got me a place, hostel on Biggins Road. You know it?'

'I know it.'

'Not bad. Could be worse. Could be better. So. So I got on my feet and walked a bit. Took me time. Skull splitting, leg aching. Two weeks is a long time, your muscles go. I could have walked ten miles before it happened. Often have done. But I got going. So I thought I'd have a wander out to that fair.'

'What's the Jug Fair got to do with your hit-and-run?'

'Right. Nice night, got a quid or two. Thought I'd have a wander and I did, but the lights and the noise got to me, made my skull split again. I wasn't as fit as I thought so I decided to make back.'

'I'm seeing stars, Matty, my head's spinning.'

'Tell me about it.'

'When were you run over?'

'Didn't say I was.'

'Listen up, you answer straight or I'll have you for wasting the time of a senior officer.'

'You?'

'Me. Now, from the beginning.'

'I was in the hangar. I was having a sleep quiet like in a corner and he come over, shining the torch in my eyes, and I got up and he shone the torch about a bit and I turned round and he hit me. Got it?'

'So this was the accident.'

'Terrible that. Couple of weeks in hospital and it was all a bit hazy, then I was in the hostel and I thought I needed some air, you go mad cooped up in a place like that when you've been used to living outside. So there I am. Only the fair was packed, world and his wife, and it's all flashing lights and noise, made my skull split even worse. Bad idea. So I thought, I'll get back. But thinking I'd get back and getting back was two different things. Never seen anything like it. Couldn't move. I was right at the far end of the thing. Push a bit here, push a bit there, worm your way in and out. My skull was splitting, I tell you. And it was then I saw him.'

'Saw?'

'Him. And there wasn't any doubt. It was like a bit of a jigsaw slotting in, a bit more of the memory coming back. Like a light going on. When I saw him. The minute I saw him. Lots of it's still not back, there's like a black fuzzy edge all round, but that bit came up clear as clear.'

He was pushing his cup round and round and focusing intently, as if trying to see the picture again in his mind.

'I know I got a knock but I'm not seeing things. I know it was half dark but he had a torch and that was it! The torch. When I saw him again at the fair, there was a light from somewhere, one of them rides or stalls that have bulbs all round, he was standing by one. It was him.'

Matty Lowe looked at Whiteside in triumph.

'I need a name, I need a description. You could maybe come back in and look through some photographs, see if you recognise him.'

'Don't need 'em.'

'So you know him?'

'No, I don't know him.'

'You know his name?'

'Nope. Only I can tell you what he is. When I saw him.'

Graham Whiteside sighed. 'Get on with it then.'

Matty Lowe got on with it. It didn't take long.

When he'd finished, Whiteside took his empty cup from him, chucked it in the bin, and saw him out of the station.

The DS went up the concrete stairs two at a time, grinning to himself. By the time he was back in CID he was laughing out loud. He needed a laugh around here just now. He was almost grateful to the dosser for having come in with his daft story. As if they didn't have enough on.

Sixty-seven

'This is tough,' Judith said, 'tough on you.'

Her crutches were leaning against the wall and her leg in its unwieldy plaster rested against the sink. She was peeling carrots, looking out of the window of the farmhouse onto the autumn leaves which were spinning down onto the drive. The beef was cut, the onions chopped, stock made. 'Do you have any thyme and a bay leaf?'

'In the bed opposite the kitchen door. I'll get it.'

'There is always a window of wonderful weather around now – quiet weather.' Judith took the bunch of thyme from Cat, and lifted her hand to smell its muskiness on the stalk. 'If he wants to stay here at home, he should,' she said. 'You know I'll help you as much as I can. And Richard of course.'

'I couldn't manage without you. It's the children . . .'

'Don't try and hide everything from them.'

'I know.'

'Sorry, Cat – that was patronising. Any parsley?'

'I'll get it.'

Mephisto followed her, padding carefully between the rows and pushing his face against her outstretched hand.

'Having the nurses twice a day is brilliant, though they treat me like Chris's GP not his wife. I don't want to be his doctor, Judith. I want to talk to him as a husband and see him as a husband who is dying, not as a patient. I know I can do medical stuff if I have to, especially in the middle of the night, but I'm struggling to get them not to think of me as the doc.'

'He doesn't though.'

'True. You're very good at seeing things in perspective, did you know that?'

Judith laughed.

'You're very good for Dad too.'

'Thanks,' Judith said, pleasantly but in a tone that Cat recognised as one barring further discussion. Well, that was fine. She wasn't about to start probing. Judith was happy, the relationship seemed good, her father was less uptight. She didn't need to know any more.

They stood for a few moments – Judith leaning awkwardly against the sink, Cat in the open doorway – looking at the spinning leaves as they caught the sun.

'I want this to be over,' Cat said. 'I can say it to you. I want it to be over for Chris because it's terrible but I want it to be over for me. I never understood this before – patients whose family said it. They couldn't bear them to die and they couldn't wait for them to die. I understand it now. The other thing is I can't say any prayers about this – it's what I've always done and suddenly I can't.'

'Doesn't matter. Let the rest of us do that for you. I think it's probably quite normal.'

'I don't know what you believe . . . It's not something one asks, is it?'

'What, you mean is it isn't PC?'

'Sort of.'

'I'm a Catholic. Not a very conscientious Catholic but I am one. I get a bit fed up with the Pope. Still, the Pope isn't God, whatever he may believe to the contrary. Now, I need to finish this casserole.'

As Cat helped Judith to sit at the kitchen table, Chris was calling and Felix had woken from his sleep.

'Give me Felix, you go to Chris,' Judith said, covering the casserole against Mephisto.

As Cat went into the bedroom she knew. Chris was lying on his side facing her, his eyes closed, but when she touched him he opened them and said, 'I'm so cold.'

She hesitated only for a second, then she lay down beside him and pulled the quilt over them both, and moved closer, to hold him to her as well as she could. He was shivering.

'I love you,' Cat said. 'I love the children but I loved you first.'

He coughed suddenly and took several short, rapid breaths, coughed again. 'Cold.'

'I know. It's cold. Winter's coming. Darling, Sam and Hannah will be back from school in a minute. Do you want them to come and see you?'

He muttered something she could not make out.

'Dad has gone to fetch them.'

His limbs began to jerk spasmodically. Then they were still again. He coughed several times. Stopped coughing.

'Chris?'

'Sam?'

'Yes. Judith has made their supper.'

'No.'

'I know. You're not hungry.'

He moved his head and cried out.

'Let me check the pump.'

But he clutched on to her hard so that she did not move. His body was cold. His body was unbelievably thin. She could feel bone beneath skin. It seemed as if there were no flesh.

'Stay . . . here . . .'

'I will.'

From the kitchen she heard Felix's chatter. Judith's calm voice. Their sudden laughter.

Tears came.

'Sam,' he mumbled.

His legs jerked again. Were still. She lay holding him as the sky outside the window faded from bright to silver blue and then flared golden and red as the sun went down. Autumn, she thought. His last autumn.

They lay still together. The car came into the drive. The children ran into the house. Doors banged. Her father's voice on the stairs calling her name. Then he entered into the room quietly. She had not put the lamp on. The wall opposite her was flushed rose red in the last of the sun. Richard came over and bent down to Chris, touched his forehead, lifted his wrist gently and felt his pulse. Cat turned her head to him. He nodded.

'I'll help out downstairs,' he said and went out.

After a moment, Cat asked, 'Would you like to see the children for just a second?'

But Chris's arms jerked and then he was still again, his head turned away from her. Cat touched the back of his neck and then his head very gently.

'Poor old boy,' she said, 'poor head.' She bent nearer and kissed it.

The sun slipped further down, off the wall. The sky darkened to violet and grey.

In the kitchen, Richard and Judith sat at the kitchen table with Sam and Hannah, tea, juice and toast.

'What's for supper later?'

'Beef casserole and fruit crumble.'

'Can I have the crumble and not the fruit?'

'I'll eat her fruit, she hates fruit and you should eat fruit, shouldn't you, it makes you not get things. Illnesses and things.'

'Hannah likes some fruit, don't you, Hanny?'

'Bananas.'

'See? That's not enough, is it?'

'Bananas are OK, Sam. Do you want some more toast?'

But Sam got up and pushed back his chair. 'I'm going to see Daddy.'

'I don't want to see him in bed, I only want to see him when he's better,' Hannah said.

'Oh, you are so stupid, stupid, stupid, he isn't ever getting better, don't you know that?'

Hannah dropped her toast on the plate and howled. Felix stared at her over the lid of his beaker. Sam went through the door like a shadow and fast up the stairs. Richard got up.

'Let him be,' Judith said. 'Cat knows what to do.'

Richard frowned but then sat down again, and after a second, put his hand on Hannah's arm.

Upstairs, as Cat lay beside her husband, Sam came quietly to the doorway, but sensing that it was different now, that there was something in the silence and the stillness that he had never known before, he stopped just inside the room.

'Sam?' She could hear him breathing. 'Sam, do you want to come here? You don't have to.'

'What's happening?'

'Daddy just died. A few moments ago. He was sleeping and then sleeping more deeply. And then he wasn't . . . he died.'

'Now?'

'A little while ago.'

'Should I tell them?'

'I think I'd better do that.'

'Can I look at him?'

'Of course you can. Do you want me to put the lamp on?'

'No.' Sam did not move. 'Not yet, please.'

'Fine. There's some light from the landing.'

Slowly, Sam came to the bed. Cat reached out her hand and he took it and squeezed it tightly. After a moment, he climbed up and reached over her, his hand hovering and then finally touching Chris.

Cat held her son closely and put her hand over his.

In the kitchen a few minutes later, Judith, putting the plates and cups onto a tray, paused and looked at Richard. He held her gaze. Hannah had gone to feed her hamster.

'There is,' Judith said, 'a different kind of stillness in the house.'

Sixty-eight

'What I don't understand is where people get guns from. And I don't mean field sports.'

Phil shrugged. 'A lot of them are adapted from guns built to shoot blanks, some come from Eastern Europe.'

'But that's gangsters.'

'You've been watching too many B-movies.'

'Seriously . . . I can't understand how kids get hold of guns, kids on the estates.'

'Why are you worrying about it?'

'Because it's worrying of course. Aren't you worried? Don't you wonder if the kids you teach are going to get hold of guns? Maybe they already have, maybe this lunatic is one of them.'

'Unlikely.'

They had just watched the television news and what Phil had called a non-report from Lafferton about the gunman-on-the-loose.

'This guy doesn't just have one gun – if it is a guy.'

'Oh, it couldn't be a woman.'

'Why not?'

'It just couldn't . . . no. It couldn't.'

'And if it is just one man and not two. Or more.'

'I don't think I want to have this conversation.'

'Want to talk about weddings instead?'

'Yes. No. I think I'm too tired.'

'We don't have to wait until you're well, you know. We can get married next week.'

'I can't plan a wedding in a week!'

'What's to plan?'

Tom moved silently away, across the hall and into the kitchen, closing the door with care. But they hadn't heard him. They were too wrapped up in themselves to be bothered if he had heard.

He didn't like himself for listening at the door. He hadn't meant to do it, but as he had come downstairs, they had started to talk and he had, somehow, started to listen.

How do people get guns?

He sat down and fiddled with the salt and pepper, changing them round and round.

How do people get guns?

Lizzie was out with a gang from school. He should have been at a practice for the chapel song group but he'd had a sore throat and his voice sounded weird.

How do people get guns?

Besides, he wasn't sure he wanted to be at the chapel. There was stuff in his head he needed to deal with and it was muddled with the last time he had been there, his conversation with the pastor, the nightmares he kept having.

'We can get married next week.'

They wouldn't. They could. They might.

He pulled a small paring knife towards him and started to make a score mark in the wood of the tabletop, a thin, mean little line, cutting it slowly.

How do people get guns?

Phil came banging in, whistling.

'Tom.'

Tom nodded. Did not look at him.

'How's things?'

'OK.'

'Your mother wants a word.'

Even Philip Russell, Tom reminded himself as he went, has an immortal soul. He doesn't know he has. But he has.

His mother looked pale. She'd almost died. She hadn't died but if she had, what would Phil Russell have done then? He knew what he and Lizzie would have done, which would have been just carry on, because that's what they knew you had to do, that is what they'd done when their father died. It helps to know.

'Hi.'

'Come and sit down.'

'I'm going out actually.'

'Two minutes. Where are you going?'

'Just out.' He sat on the arm of the sofa next to her. 'In a bit. You OK?'

'I'm fine. Tired, that's all. I wanted to ask you something.'

He waited. He could hear the kettle whistling.

'When we get married, I'd really like it if you would give me away, Tom.'

He knew what it meant now when it was said that someone went cold. You did. You did exactly that. You went cold.

'You don't have to answer now. But there isn't anyone else I'd like to do it.'

'Uncle Pete.'

'I never see him. How long is it – three years? Has to be.'

'He'd do it.'

'I expect he would but I don't want him, I want you.'

He got up. Still cold. How could this have happened?

'I'm going out now.'

She didn't say anything but he knew that she was watching him, looking after him, he knew what the look on her face was and how her eyes were and what she was thinking.

He went out. At first he was going to take the Yamaha but then he decided against that. At the gate he glanced back at the house. Something clicked inside him. Odd. He felt odd. He'd never felt so odd.

It was cold. He zipped up his fleece.

Odd.

Why should it matter? Being cold.

Sixty-nine

They reached the top of the Hill at last. It was steeper than she had remembered, took longer. After a while, no one had spoken. Simon got there first and put the cool bag down on the stone which had been there for thousands of years. Or since just after the last war, depending on who you believed.

It was, as always, the most amazing view.

'Three counties,' he said to Cat as she arrived. Hannah was with her, Sam, the best climber, walker, runner, swimmer, all-round athlete, trailed slowly up a long way behind.

'He's all right,' Cat said, following her brother's gaze. 'Really. Quiet. But all right.'

'Can we have our picnic now?'

'Wait for Sam.'

'Why? I want a drink now, why do I have to wait for Sam before I can have a drink? That's cruelty to children.'

They had left Felix at Hallam House with Richard and Judith. Simon unzipped the bag and handed Hannah a carton of apple juice.

'I wanted Ribena.'

'Hannah!'

'Please?' She sighed and sat down on the stone. Simon swapped the cartons.

The autumn sun struck warm on their faces, touched the flying angels on the four corners of the cathedral tower in the distance, and a white horse in a field.

'What have we come up here for?' Sam turned his back on them, looking down the grassy slopes.

'Because it was one of Daddy's favourite places and I thought . . . we should just be here and . . . think about him.'

'I keep thinking about him all the time,' Hannah said, 'every minute and even when I'm asleep I do.'

'You don't think when you're asleep, duh.'

'I do so, I think about Daddy.'

'You dream when you're asleep.'

'I do that as well.'

'He'd like us to be up here.'

'Not without him he wouldn't.'

'I'll open the flask,' Simon said.

In the end, Sam and Hannah wandered off further down the slope and sat together on a tree trunk, not looking at one another, not speaking, but with their arms just touching.

'Don't worry.'

'I'm not. Not a lot anyway. It's good you could get a Friday afternoon for once.'

'I haven't had a day off in weeks and then there's tomorrow.'

'You don't have to be at this wedding, do you?'

'Yes. If something goes wrong I don't want my back to be turned.'

'It won't be your fault.'

'I know, I know. The Chief's going, every ARV in three counties will be in place, royal protection is doubled. All the same.'

'Nothing's going to happen.'

'Oh, I know.'

'How near can the public get? There's usually a big crowd for a society wedding.'

'Cordoned off on the other side of St Michael's Street but they'll get a view. The Lord Lieutenant was adamant. I left him to sort out RP.'

'Wonder what Camilla will wear?'

Simon looked blank. 'Reader,' Cat said, 'she married him.'

She sipped her tea. They had brought old china mugs.

'Have you decided what to do about the funeral?'

Cat sighed. Chris had always said he didn't want any kind of service. If you were not religious, he said, then nothing was better than some made-up humanist event. But that had been long ago. During his illness he had said nothing about it at all and there was no mention in his short, straightforward will.

'I can't bear nothing. Just . . . nothing. Apart from anything else, it's a rite of passage the children need to help them through. And a lot of people have been asking.'

'I think you do what you want . . . because it's for you and the children now and I bet that's why Chris left it open.'

She turned to him in surprise, with a look of something like joy. 'I hadn't thought of it like that. Do you really believe it?'

'Absolutely. Whatever your beliefs are, your funeral is for the ones still living. What do you really want?'

'Cathedral. Of course. Not a great fuss but a proper funeral.'

'Then that's what you should do. Talk to them. What about Chris's side?'

'They'll get what they're given,' Cat said. 'Sorry.'

'I know.'

'There's something else.'

'Say.'

'Dad. And Judith.'

'They'll have to have what they're given too, won't they?'

'I didn't mean that.'

He was silent. Ahead of them, Sam and Hannah were talking quietly, heads together.

'Don't be difficult.'

'No.'

'I think they'll probably marry before long. They're more or less together now. Nobody has said anything, it's just a hunch. And I want you to be prepared so you don't go up in flames.'

'As if.'

'I mean it. Judith's daughter is getting married next spring. She was talking about it yesterday. And weddings sort of breed.'

'Didn't know she had a daughter.'

'Yes, Vivien – and a son too. Judith is going to a wedding fair. Tomorrow, I think it is. At the Riverside. It feels unreal. The world goes on, people are getting married and planning half-term and bonfire night, babies are being born, the supermarkets are full and the trains are running and Chris is dead. I can't take it in. I've been with dying and death all my working life and I can't take it in.'

Simon put his arm round her. She felt light, frail. Vulnerable.

'But I did the right thing, didn't I?'

'With Sam? Yes. You know you did.'

'He doesn't say anything.'

'He said something to me.'

'Oh, Simon, you didn't tell me.'

'No, because he made me promise not to. But he's fine. Truly and absolutely. I promise you that.'

What Sam had said, when Simon had arrived that night, had moved him to tears. 'I'm glad I was with Daddy when he'd just died. It made me feel I'd grown up a lot.'

'Tell me one day,' Cat said.

'No. Never.'

Hannah came back to them. 'Isn't it time to have the picnic?'

It was a good afternoon. They ate the picnic, drank the tea, packed and then ran up and down the slopes and on into the wood where the leaves were piling up and the last of the afternoon sunlight slanted down through the bare tops of the trees.

Simon had not let go of himself so much or relaxed so well for weeks and, watching his sister, he saw that this was the first time she had been able to let go too, not worrying about getting home, not wondering what was about to happen. It had happened. She was dealing with it but this afternoon even her grief seemed to be suspended for this brief hour or so. Her sad eyes were brighter.

Seventy

He finished just after two. It was still sunny, still warm. He cut himself four slices of good bread and made himself sandwiches, one corned beef, one cheese and tomato. He took a banana from the dish and a couple of custard creams. He made a mug of tea and took the whole lot outside. He had an old Formica table there, up against the wall, which faced south. An aluminium chair with a red canvas seat. He took a bite of sandwich, a bite of banana, a bite of biscuit, a swig of tea and then, mouth comfortably full, he sat with his face to the sun, and as he ate, he thought everything through again. He had to get this one right. He would, of course. He always had, always would. But he knew that he must never, ever get complacent, be cocky, make assumptions, fail to plan. That way lay the brick wall and the dead end.

So, he went over each step. He kept his eyes closed and he took himself through it, from the moment he woke, got up, dressed. The clothes were important. Every item of clothing he put on in his mind. He would be laying them out in order that night.

Dark jeans. Dark shirt. Navy sleeveless fleece. Navy woollen hat, fitting close to his head. The usual trainers with the thick polythene wedges attached to the soles.

He packed the gear. He took the bike. At the airfield he got out the new roll of plastic for the side of the van. He rode over to the lock-up on the business park. Got out the van. He fixed the panels. Left the bike. Locked up.

He had left himself two hours. He would need that. He wasn't going to rush anything. Danger in rushing. Ahead there were half a dozen problems, things that might go wrong, however careful his planning. He needed time to sort them.

He would be there by half ten. Too early but better that. He'd timed it well.

He bit into the second sandwich. The sun was warm for November but the forecast for tomorrow was the same and it suited him. You needed clear, bright light to do the job properly at that distance and the sun wouldn't be in his face – he had that one worked out long ago – the sun would be right where he needed it, on them.

He finished his tea. From next door came the sound of a vacuum cleaner. A cat came slinking over the fence that ran along the row of gardens. Looked at him, eyes half closed. Paused.

'Wise guy,' he said. The cat opened its eyes and hopped neatly down onto the soil. Came padding over the grass to where he sat and started to weave in and out of his legs. He bent down. Rubbed its ears. Stroked it. The cat went on weaving. Then settled down on the concrete slabs in the sun and closed its eyes.

He went over everything one last time. A to Z. Then, he put it out of his mind. He'd done. There was such a thing as overplanning.

He picked up the field sports magazine he had bought on the way home and began reading about the effect of climate change on the future of grouse shooting.

Seventy-one

It was almost midnight when Tom's motorbike ran out of petrol in a side street near the centre of the town. He hauled it up against a wall. He wouldn't need it now. Someone could find it. It was a decent bike.

The words that had been filling his head, coming in as thick and fast as snowflakes in a storm and packing in so that they had confused him, began to sort themselves into phrases that he could understand now and the phrases were familiar.

'He will give his angels charge over you to guide you in all your ways.'

'They will bear thee up in their hands lest thou shalt dash thy foot against a stone.'

It was odd. The Bible they read from and studied with the pastor was modern, it didn't go in for thee and thou but the words that came to him seemed to be the old words. He wondered if it mattered.

It was quiet. He walked past the empty shops and there was no one else walking, across the square, past the cordoned-off site where the ghost train had fallen, down into the marketplace towards the new shopping mall and no one else walked there either. A couple of cars passed. That was all. He put his collar up.

'He soared upon the wings of the wind and he went in flight through the air.'

The words had never struck him before but now they were here for him. He felt exhilarated. The feeling was one he had heard described, an ecstasy, the pastor had called it, an out-of-the-body ecstasy. People had experienced it in front of him during services, praying in tongues and throwing themselves to the ground, but before now Tom had always found it rather embarrassing. He didn't know if they felt different or were just trying too hard.

Now he knew. He seemed to be walking above the ground.

He had left his mother and Phil Russell behind him. They would be saved or they wouldn't. Like Lizzie. He couldn't worry about it any more. He had to look after himself and he knew that he was making none of it up, not trying to do it, it was simply happening and all he had to do was go with it and with the words. The flying words.

He started to walk faster, and then to run, and then he turned as he ran. Someone watching him would think he was either very drunk or very mad. Or happy. He turned and danced down the street and across the road. At the end he saw it, like a heavenly castle. It was shimmering and beautiful and he could see figures here and there, pale figures beckoning to him. He ran towards them. The nearer he got the more figures he saw and when he arrived and began to climb up and up, round and round, they came with him, hovered about him, touched him, held out their arms to him.

A car at the far end shone its lights and began to move. He dodged behind one of the pillars and the figures shielded him from sight. The car drove away down the ramps, its noise echoing round the empty spaces and away, and then there was only him, with the figures wreathing and encircling him, protecting him.

'Lest you dash your foot against a stone.'

Below him were sparkling, shining, glistening golden lights. He looked up. Above him, more lights, tiny little pinpricks of stars, thousands of stars.

He wondered briefly what they would make of it, how they would interpret what he knew would be the ecstatic expression on his face. The pastor would know of course, but how could his mother and Lizzie, because they had never seen the lights or known the glory, never had this overwhelming experience of beauty and heard the voices singing and singing to him like sirens and seen the beautiful faces, upturned to him, the arms outstretched to welcome him.

But perhaps when they saw him, it would be given to them. They would know. They would be enlightened. They would understand at last.

He spread out his arms.

'They will soar on wings like eagles.'

He flew.

Seventy-two

Simon Serrailler took a left turn and drove into the country. Six miles out, he turned again, onto the high, winding single-track road that led up to Featherly Moor. A mile on the other side, the tiny village of Featherly clung to the slopes, cowering back from the wind that drove towards it for three-quarters of the year. But now, the autumn sun had returned. He parked beside the pub and went inside. The saloon bar was empty apart from a couple of walkers in the far corner, rucksacks and cagoules in a heap beside them.

'Hello, Gordon.'

'Well, blow me. Haven't seen you here in a while. What'll it be?'

'Lime and lemonade. Can I take it outside?'

'Put the garden tables up now after the rain the other night. Thought winter had come. Bench at the front.'

The walkers were making to leave.

'I'll go over here.'

The pub fell silent. In the summer and at the weekend it was always full with hikers and climbers. During the week, it was generally empty, and although Gordon served food, the Arms had never tried to compete with the gastropubs around Lafferton, preferring to stick to ham and eggs and ploughman's lunches.

Simon took his drink into a corner. Gordon retired into the back. After a moment Simon heard pattering feet. A cold nose was pressed against his hand. Byron, the pub's Labrador, settled at his feet. He was grateful to the landlord for not hanging around to ask him the usual questions about the gunman, tell him how bad it was for trade, make his own pronouncement about what should be done and how. A quiet half-hour away from the station, the phone, the ever-present media pack outside, was something Simon believed in and quite often took. His time was sometimes best spent not doing, but thinking.

Just as he was leaving the station, Graham Whiteside had run after him. 'Sir, don't you want me to come along?'

Simon remembered his previous sergeant. Nathan was constantly at his side and had often been present at his thinking sessions. But Simon's relationship with Graham was different. Indeed, he had no relationship. Graham's personality jarred and irritated.

'Sir, it's about that tramp. The one in the hangar . . .'

But Simon had pretended not to hear and had accelerated away.

Now his peace was shattered as a party of walkers came piling into the bar, filling the room with chatter and the clump of boots on the wooden floor. Simon groaned and finished his drink. As he made his way out, a woman to his left was saying, 'Makes you think twice about getting married, doesn't it?'

He stopped dead. It had happened before, a chance remark or something glimpsed letting light into a dark place. He left his car and walked on up the lane into the village street. Flowers were still blooming in front gardens, apples and plums were heaped under trees here and there. There was no one about. This was another dormitory village for Lafferton. There was no shop or school, though the church was handsome, set up on a high bank and dominating the village. He opened the gate and walked up between the leaning headstones. A rabbit bounced away out of sight, a woodpecker yaffled from a fir tree. The church was locked.

A wedding. Why fire at a wedding party? Serrailler did not believe in random. There was always something.

Makes you think twice about getting married, doesn't it?

He groaned. He'd missed it. How could he have missed it when it was there in front of him?

He ran down the path and back to the car to put in a call.

He pushed the Audi up to seventy on a clear road, thinking, thinking, clicking things into place.

Seventy-three

The ball banged down the wooden slope and the skittles crashed, raising a cheer.

'Ours,' Duncan Houlish said.

Clive Rowley clenched his jaw. He hadn't been to a bowling alley for what, five or six years? Longer? He had not wanted to come tonight, but now he was here, he revelled in it. Roll, bang, smash. Roll, bang, smash.

'Useless,' Ian Dean said.

The whole lot of them had come. It was almost like a ritual of some sort before the big day.

Roll, bang.

'Yesssss!'

Further up, a gang of shrieking girls threw the balls down the aisle and through the gaps or into the skittles, equally hysterical no matter what the result.

'Jeez.'

'Looks like a hen party.'

'Sounds like a parrot house. Why do women shriek?'

'Not all women shriek.'

'Oh yes they do. My sister shrieks, my missus and her girlfriends shriek, my mam shrieks, the girls across the road . . .'

Another lot of shrieking.

They finished a session and went up to the bar at the same time as the girls.

'Must be a thousand of them,' Clive Rowley said.

'Oi, what was that?' one of them said.
'I said happy days.'
'Can I buy you ladies a drink?'
'There are seventeen of us, and no thanks, we'll get our own.'
'That's a relief.'
Ian and Clive came slowly across with three pints each, weaving between the tables and the chairs and the girls. They set the glasses down.
'Look at that. Didn't lose a drop.'
'Great stuff. Cheers. You all right, Clive?'
'What? Yeah.'
'Right. Where are you tomorrow?'
'Top of the tower with Ian.'
'You OK with heights?'
'Love 'em. You reckon it's someone's twenty-first?'
'That lot? They're way over twenty-one.'
'What did you say?'
'Listeners never hear good. Stop earwigging.'
Shrieks. They had five tables pulled together.
Dale groaned. 'Pink feathers coming out,' he said. 'And the handcuffs.'
'I was right. Bloody hen night, innit?'
Louise Kelly, the only woman among the policemen, stuck her head down into her glass. She was married and separated.
'You have a hen night, Lou?'
'Sort of. Mam said they were bad luck so a few of us just went for a pizza. Sort of compromise. Bad luck was, he and his mates walked into the same pizza place.'
'Your mum had a point then.'
'What do you reckon about tomorrow?'
'Keep your voices down.' Duncan. Bronze Command. Conscious they had just the one chance to get the thing right. Or very wrong.
'Be fine,' Louise said. 'I'm going to enjoy it. I'm over on the left where the cars come up. Got a grandstand view. It's uniform I always feel sorry for. Don't get a look, faces to the bloody crowd.'
'I was surprised they're bringing in mounted.'

'They're bringing in the bloody works. Surprised there aren't tanks.'

'Be glad when it's this time tomorrow, me.'

'I'll drink to that,' Clive said. He sneezed.

'Oi, watch it. I don't want your snot in my beer, thank you.'

'Told you I was heady.'

The hen party got up and started the conga round the room, police helmets, pink feathers, handcuffs, maids' aprons, fishnet tights. Shrieking.

'Come on, lads, get on the back.'

A couple of them joined on. The rest cheered.

'Last pint,' Ian said. 'That's your lot. This time tomorrow we can all get bladdered.'

The shrieks went up a few decibels and Clive Rowley sneezed again.

Seventy-four

'I'm sorry but you can't stay here, you'll have to go right back.'

'Where to?'

The special constable indicated the cordons. 'Behind there.'

The women groaned. 'But we won't see anything.'

'Course you will.'

'Well, we haven't brought binoculars.'

'Brought your chairs though.'

'Can't stand for hours and hours.'

They folded the camp stools they had brought and went slowly in the direction of the pointing hand. The area behind the cordons was filling up.

Tactical Team Bronze Command Duncan Houlish looked up to the tower. Two officers up there and it should have been three. He had two men down, Bannister whose father had died the previous night and Clive Rowley who had rung in with a cold.

'I'll bloody cold him. He was perfectly all right last night.'

'Bannister said he could come in, but he won't be focused. Not fair anyway.'

'Look, your dad dying is one thing and a snuffly nose is another. I'll bollock him on Monday.'

'If he's in.'

'Thinks because he was some sort of five-minute hero he can take the piss.'

'Talking of that, you know the woman he rescued?'

'What about her?'

'They found her son's body last night. Bottom of the multi-storey.' His walkie-talkie crackled.

Behind the cordon the women settled down.

'I feel sorry for these,' one said, nodding to the constable facing them. 'They never get a look at what's going on, just at our ugly mugs.'

'Place is bristling with them today.'

'Do you wonder?'

'They still won't confirm whether Charles and Camilla are coming or not. I've asked three of them but they're staying shtum.'

'They'll be here. There wouldn't be all of this . . . helicopter buzzing and everything.'

'I hope so. I like a big wedding but I wouldn't be sitting out here in this cold just for that.'

'Lovely day though, even if it's cold. Just right.'

'I got married on a day like this.'

'Did you? Mine was pouring down.'

Two miles away, Serrailler was arguing down the telephone.

'I know it's a hunch, ma'am, but I have to trust it. It's got everything he needs and no risk. I do urge you to go with me on this.'

'Simon, I can't conjure up an ARV out of thin air.'

'Then take one of the armed vehicles from around the cathedral.'

The Chief sighed. 'And if things kick off at this wedding? I couldn't live with myself.'

'I couldn't live with myself if I'm right and we do nothing.'

There was a long pause. Serrailler tapped his finger on the phone. His adrenaline was pumping. He knew. He just knew. Always follow your gut instincts, his first DI had said. Always go with your hunches.

'I'm sorry, Simon. It's too risky. We've got to keep the cathedral covered.'

He hung up. Waited a moment in thought. Then picked up the phone again.

*

The helicopter dropped several feet and hovered like a gnat over the tower. The draught hit the two marksmen in the face. They did not take their eyes from the direction of their rifles, resting in the spaces between ancient stones.

'ETA three minutes, twenty seconds,' the small black box said.

The marksmen focused. The space in which the royal car would halt was bang on target.

'Two fifty.'

The helicopter swung to the west.

'Bloody racket,' Duncan Houlish muttered.

In the reserve AR vehicle in Cathedral Lane the driver's box also crackled into life.

Houlish listened.

'Confirm please.'

The voice confirmed.

'On our way.' He turned to the boys in the back. 'Change of venue.'

'What's going on?'

'Serrailler says we can leave this lot to the others. We're needed elsewhere.'

'Thirty seconds.'

'Roger.'

'Keep your eyes peeled then,' the constable said and moved an inch or two to give the women the best view.

'I knew it, I knew they'd come.'

'Charles isn't one to be put off.'

'Not by some lunatic, he isn't.'

The car doors opened. The security men leapt out, eyes scanning the crowd.

'I'll say this for her, she's done wonders for the older woman has Camilla.'

'Oh, look at that!'

'Not sure about the colour.'

'Oh, I like that pale sea green.'

'I love those feathery head things – she's made them her signature.'

'I love a man in a morning suit.'

'Look, his tie matches, same sort of green.'

'They're looking over here, they're looking.'

'Wave, Janet, *wave*!'

'Now then,' Bronze Command muttered, 'show your face if you dare.' Tactical Team officers were high voltage.

The Prince and the Duchess walked, calm and smiling, up the path to the east door beside the Dean.

Ten minutes later, the bridesmaids glided into sight.

'Oh. Four big ones.'

'White velvet!'

'I like little bridesmaids, I hope she has some littles.'

Two more cars. Six small girls. Six small pageboys. Velvet. Satin. White flowers. White ribbons.

All around them, unseen rifles were trained and eyes scanned the crowd and every inch of the building. Small children walked self-consciously up the long path.

The duty armed response vehicle with full complement pulled out of Cathedral Lane as the bride, glorious in white and silver, tulle and diamonds and a fifteen-foot train strewn with white roses, was helped with extreme care out of her car.

'Pray now,' Houlish muttered into his mike.

Seventy-five

One of the papers had had a long piece about people like him with a profile by an expert, a professor no less. He had read it with great care and growing amusement.

'Inside the mind of the Lafferton Gunman.' He read it to find out about himself because this woman apparently knew him better than anyone. She knew what made him tick, what his thoughts and feelings were, why he did what he did, what his childhood was like, his father, his mother, how he had grown up. Most important of all, she knew about the women he had had relationships with. Everything, every detail. He read it a dozen times.

She was right. She was hopelessly wrong.

He had a father and a mother. Yes, ma'am. He'd had an unhappy and lonely childhood. No.

An only son. Yes.

No sisters either. That was wrong.

He had a fascination with guns, loved gun movies, westerns, reading books about men who had gone on the rampage with a gun at schools and colleges. To a point. But she was wrong about the books.

He had served in the armed forces and seen armed combat, in the Gulf probably. Wrong again, ma'am.

He was probably unmarried, after a painful divorce. Wrong.

He hated women. Wrong.

He had been let down by a woman. Correct.

He had never been able to have a full sexual relationship with any woman.

He had started to laugh.

He lived in a meticulously clean and tidy house and planned every detail of his life as well as his crimes with extreme care. Spot on.

He bore a grudge. True.

He loved killing. The more he killed the happier he found he became.

He had set the paper down at this point because he was troubled by what he was reading. She had sent the thinnest but sharpest of needles through to the right place, this woman expert, this profiler who had got so much wrong and then, bingo. He sat in a chair by the window looking out at nothing – darkness, the neighbour's outside light – nothing of any interest to him because what was of interest was in his head.

'He loves killing,' she wrote. 'This man started with one and it escalated and maybe now he is worried that he has an addiction to killing. No one who becomes addicted to anything – alcohol, drugs, cigarettes, beating up their partners – no one actually enjoys it after a while. Maybe it was good at the beginning but not now. Now it is a strain and a burden, something he cannot stop, cannot get away from, but in his heart of hearts he hates it and hates himself even more. He doesn't want to go on doing this. Every time, he says to himself that this is the last one, the very last, that he's giving it up, has done with it. It has served whatever purpose it had – though he can't remember clearly what that was. What was its purpose? Why is he taking out his hurt feelings and his desire for revenge on all these people who have had nothing to do with it, are innocent and blameless and deserve none of it? He doesn't know.'

She ended by talking to him.

'Jim,' she wrote (she called him 'Jim' for no reason, it was just a name), 'if you are reading this, and I am sure you are, then you know I'm right. It doesn't make sense any more, if it ever did. And a lot of people have suffered who you didn't really want to suffer. So stop. You can do it still. You still have the will and the strength to stop right now. And when you have, give yourself up.

Until you do that you will go on carrying this dreadful knowledge, the burden of this addiction. Until you stop and give yourself up, put an end to it all, you will go on hating and loathing yourself. Just listen to me, Jim. Think about what I have said to you. Then do it. Do it now.'

He thought about what she was asking him. He'd been thinking about it for some time. But if he agreed it would mean his plans for today would go up in smoke and he had been looking forward to today. It had been a long, careful time in the planning.

It seemed a waste just to abandon everything now.

Maybe after today.

Yes. That was it. He stood up, leaving the paper on the table. Today. Then he would do what she told him. Stop. Not give himself up. Why would he do that? What would be the point of one more body in prison? But he would have today, which he had been working up to and planning, today would be his parting shot. Then stop.

Just stop.

He felt pleased with himself. He had strength of mind and character, he was not the weak addict she supposed. He could and would stop and when he had stopped he would be clean and clear of it all and able to get on with his normal life. He was looking forward to that.

Seventy-six

As they walked through the hotel foyer and into the ballroom and dining room leaflets came at them from all sides.

'Are you a bride-to-be? Are you a bride-to-be?'

'Yes,' Georgina said, 'yes, yes, yes. Bring it on.'

Chocolate fountains, confetti, marquee hire, jewellery, wedding dresses, hats, favours, bridesmaids' gifts, photographers, wedding planners, hairdressers . . .

'I don't know where to start,' Georgina's mother said.

'Dress and caterers. Get the big stuff sorted.'

'And they say people don't bother to get married any more.'

The stalls filled both rooms and carried on out of the open side of the dining room into the gardens. Florists. Beauticians. Fireworks. Pig roasts. Balloons. Honeymoons.

'Are you a bride-to-be? Are you . . .'

'Good job we've got all afternoon.'

'Real flower petals and those little paper cones. Love it.'

The hotel car park overflowed into a field next door.

He had been set up on the other side of the river since early that morning. The time of year meant that the trees were almost bare but the shrubs and undergrowth along the bank were still thick. He had sussed out the exact spot two or three times and it was perfect. He was well concealed.

First he'd parked the van at his getaway point. 'JOY'S FLORISTS'.

Then he'd strolled across the bridge from the other direction, carrying fishing gear.

The place was busy from the moment he got there. Stands. Tents. Setting up. Buzzing about. He watched. His rod was angled carefully into the water, fishing umbrella carefully placed. Camp stool. He ostentatiously unwrapped his sandwiches. He waited. Watched.

This was it. The last time. His promise. And there was only to be the one. No more children. That haunted him. That had never been part of any plan.

He would watch and when he saw the right one he would know. She had to be pretty. Dark hair. Not tall. There would be one like that. One. Then out of here. Leave the rod. Move. He'd be back in the van, hitting the road. At the airfield in twenty. Not breaking any speed limits.

JOY'S FLORISTS.

It was deserted on this side. The occasional voice floated over. 'Back up to me.'

'How many more tables?' A sudden cheer.

He sat quietly. The float bobbed on the water. The sun was bright. He wondered if fishing was something he might take up. After this. When it was over. It was nearly over.

Outside the cathedral the crowd heard the occasional few notes from the organ, and the ebb and flow of the hymns. The armed officers did not relax but the music was pleasant, what little they could make out. A breeze ruffled the trees up the long path to the east door and sent some late leaves spinning down. A squirrel jumped from branch to branch.

'How much do you think it would cost,' one of the women asked, 'a wedding dress like that?'

'Designer.'

'Oh yes. Well, thousands. Ten thousand?'

'Easily. And the rest.'

'You could do an entire wedding for ten K.'

Someone passed round a bag of Mintoes. Offered one to the police constable who looked tempted. Shook her head. Smiled.

'You'll be glad when they've all gone.'

She nodded.

Just the one.

He had said it to himself, and he'd keep his word.

He watched carefully. A lot of people were still inside but as the time went on they drifted to the outside stalls on the lawn that led down to the river, a few here, half a dozen there. You could tell the brides easily enough, and the mothers and mothers-in-law and sisters. Almost no men apart from the stallholders. Not a man's thing, a wedding fair, which made it easier.

Which one he picked out depended on the exact timing, the perfect position. Luck. Or bad luck, depending on your point of view.

And then, as the lawn began to fill up, he saw her.

She wore a pair of cream jeans and a skimpy top and her hair was pinned up and he went sick. Georgina. He looked for Alison but Georgina was on her own.

Then their mother, her mother and Alison's, came out to join her.

Georgie getting married? Who to, when, where? The words jumbled in his head and he cleared them out of the way because he didn't need questions, he needed to focus and he couldn't. He felt different. Always, before this time, he had felt icy calm. Icy. Calm. Focused.

But something splintered inside him and anger, anger mixed with a terrible sense of betrayal and rejection, took over and he was no longer icy, calm, focused, he was an uncontrollable mess of emotions. His hands shook. He had brought the deer rifle, but the Heckler & Koch carbine was in his bag too. He put the rifle away. His hands still shook because he was trying to be quick but more because he knew that he was losing control, he was angry, he was not going to follow the plan. How could he follow any plan now? Plans didn't matter any more.

He picked up the G36, looked, saw Georgina and her mother, standing talking to some girl with a load of floral displays. There were others. Other girls. Other mothers. Other women. Alison might even be there somewhere. He took a single deep breath and ran with it, the handgun held correctly, up under the nose, close, tight, not like some amateur kid. He wasn't an amateur. He knew what he was doing. He ran over the bridge towards the lawns. Silently. He would start shouting to Georgie any second. Shoot first, then shout, shoot first . . . not the other way round, not what he should do.

Shoot. Shoot. He saw Georgina turn. Her face. Horrified. Disbelieving. Hands coming up to either side of it. Saw her mouth open. It seemed to take forever. He had all the time in the world now. They were all looking, they all saw him, though not all of them knew what was going to happen, they looked confused. Someone even laughed.

Shoot and shout.

He shot. It went anywhere.

Shouts. Shouts that were not coming from him, though they were words he had used often enough.

'Drop the gun, drop the gun. Drop the gun. Put your hands above your head. Put your hands . . .'

The lawn and the gravel area in front and the bridge were trampled by thousands of them, thousands, feet, boots, shouts. Screams.

'Drop the gun, drop the gun. Put –'

A voice he knew, close up. 'Fucking hell, it's Clive Rowley.'

'Rowley. Clive Rowley. Clive Rowley. Rowley, Rowley, Rowley.' His own name went round and round in his head as he dropped the gun and was on his knees, then on his face, flat on the grass, pressed to it, a foot in his neck.

'Fucking hell.'

He closed his eyes. He was calm. Glad really. He'd stopped. Like he said he would.

Stopped.

Seventy-seven

'Can you wait five minutes, Superintendent? The Chief is just on a call.'

Ellie, Paula Devenish's pleasant secretary, smiled but Simon was not reassured. He did not feel that the call, whatever it was, could not be interrupted, he felt that he was being kept waiting so that the Chief could score a point. But he nodded and smiled back at Ellie, and sat down and got up and looked out of the window onto the station yard. And sat down again.

'Can I get you a cup of tea?'

'No, thanks.'

Ellie went on with her work. From other rooms, other sounds of HQ at full stretch in the middle of a normal afternoon. From behind the Chief's door, he could not even make out the murmur of her voice.

The last time they had met had been at the press briefing following the arrest and charging of Clive Rowley. Paula Devenish had spoken, Simon had sat beside her and said nothing; she had fielded the questions to which, inevitably, few answers could be given. She had gone into the conference room and given a pep talk, praised everyone, left immediately. Since then, there had been silence, until this morning when she had asked Serrailler to come in.

He was glad to get out of Lafferton. The atmosphere at the station was strained and quiet. That was always the case when a member of the force had been charged with an offence, but although the DCS had known it happen a couple of times in his career, nothing any officer had done had ever been as remotely serious as this. Clive Rowley would go into police history. The other members of armed response were still stunned, still unable to take in that one of their own, a man they had worked with in the tight bond of trust and mutual reliance which was so essential, could have used his skills and training, as well as his weapons, to kill so many. Every incident was being analysed, there was talk of nothing else. What kind of man Rowley was, whether he had ever said a single word which might have given them a clue, every what, when, how and why was being talked over and over and Serrailler had no intention of stopping the post-mortems. Not yet. They needed to talk and that was fine by him so long as the talk stayed within the station walls.

Rowley had been denied a final killing. The mother was injured, not seriously. And the girl was unscathed. Rowley was a trained marksman. However disturbed he was, he could never have missed her. Not at that range. He must have deliberately aimed away.

On arrest, he had said nothing. He had not spoken a word or looked directly at any of them. The whole thing had been over in some highly charged but also highly disciplined minutes.

Time went on. Ellie left the room. Came back. Smiled at Simon again. Answered the phone. Went back to her computer. After a further few minutes she had got up and put the light on. It was a gusty, wet day of low sulphurous-looking cloud. The autumn had changed.

Ellie glanced up. 'Sorry about this.' She smiled.

They had had Chris Deerbon's funeral the previous day, in this rain, this wind, this gloom. Cat had made her own decision. The service had been in the lady chapel of the cathedral, which was full – but it was small. The notices had said 'Family' but patients and colleagues had come and they had all been glad of it. Sam had walked, white-faced and serious, up to the front, and stood beside his father's coffin to read a short prayer. And, for once, Hannah had made no fuss, demanded no attention, but only looked at him intently. He had asked to do it, Cat had said. The whole occasion had seemed over too quickly. Weird and unreal. Any moment, Simon had thought, Chris would be there, after all, standing among them and none of it would have happened, this would be someone else's funeral, a stupid mistake.

Cat had gone with Chris's mother and brother to the crematorium. Richard and Judith had taken the children back to Hallam House. There was no wake.

Simon had watched them all leave at the side door and then walked, through the rain, back to work.

He sat on the hard chair in the Chief's outer office and the funeral was in his head, his nephew's white face, his father's sudden look of old age, Cat's eyes heavy with weeping, the smell of the candles being snuffed out by the verger, the sound of the footsteps of the bearers on the stone floor. Chris. Simon had had such a good, such an easy relationship with his brother-in-law, who had been part of his life for so long; they had been friends and family, like brothers but without the strain of being siblings. And Chris had been the best husband to Cat, the best father, the best doctor. The best.

'Simon?'

He looked up, startled for a second, before pulling himself together ready for a battering.

He didn't get it. Nor was anything said. Not explicitly.

'I knew I was right to trust you,' the Chief said with a wicked smile.

'Thank you.' Simon grinned back. 'I had a hunch about the wedding fair. But as soon as I'd taken the armed chaps off the cathedral, and rushed them to the hotel, panic set in. Not about the royals. About you. And your reaction.'

'We had thanks and compliments from the Lord Lieutenant and thanks from the Prince's office. The cathedral couldn't have gone more smoothly, though I'm glad we don't have that sort of thing often, it puts a huge strain on the system. How are the team?'

'Shaken. Can't get their heads round it. But Rowley never put a foot wrong you know, there was nothing. Not a thing.'

'So how do you account for this? Your desk sergeant has a visit from a man called Matty Lowe who said he'd been attacked.

Then he saw Rowley at the Jug Fair and recognised him. Rowley was his assailant. Mr Lowe went into Lafferton station wanting to talk to you but ended up with DS Whiteside.'

'I didn't know anything about this.'

'No,' said the Chief drily. 'Whiteside claims you refused to listen to him.'

Seventy-eight

There were no messages on his answerphone when he got back to the flat. He opened the windows – it was a mild autumn night, cloudy and still. The lights were on in the cathedral for a service.

He rang Cat.

'I'm fine, Dad and Judith have been here all day and Judith is staying a couple of nights. It's not for me, it's the children – they need a lot of extra attention. Sam's gone silent. He might need you, but not yet. Go away, Si, you need a break.'

'If you're sure . . .'

'I am. I'll need you too, but for now it's OK. I'm numb. Really. Go.'

He was about to ring off, then said, 'Listen. Clive Rowley.'

'What about him?'

'There's one word everyone has used about him – I've used it – it seems to be the defining word.'

'What's that?'

'Loner.'

'Does it fit?'

'Oh yes. But – is that the word you'd use to define me?'

There was a long silence.

It had struck him just now as he had run up the stairs to the flat. Loner. He had been longing for his own space, his beautiful rooms, his haven, his peace and solitude.

Loner.

'Well, there are loners and loners. Obviously.'

'You know what I mean.'

'If you're asking me are you a weird loner and likely to turn into a maniac with a gun or a serial killer, then no. No, of course you're not. Or a crazy recluse or one of those people who go along the street talking to themselves. No.'

She was talking seriously. She had not made light of his question.

'Is this really worrying you or is it just the aftermath of the gun business?'

'I don't know,' he said truthfully.

'If it's the latter I'm not surprised. If you're really worried . . . listen, don't take this the wrong way, love, but I'm not sure I'm the right person to talk to about it.'

'You think I ought to see a shrink?'

'I didn't say that.'

'Didn't need to.'

'Stop it. I can't take it.'

'I'm sorry.'

'You asked. It's been a bad night. Helen Creedy rang me.

'What was she thinking of?'

'She didn't know about Chris. Not everyone does. Why would they? I had to listen, I couldn't tell her, but I'm pretty much drained. Her son Tom killed himself.' She paused, gulped and then said, 'Anyway – if it doesn't worry you, then it's fine. If it does, do something about it. That's good advice about quite a lot of things, from warts on the nose to liking your own company. Make the most of your time off.'

Seventy-nine

The roads to North Wales were easy for the first fifty miles, after which Simon ran into a series of hold-ups and an accident which created a particularly long detour. He switched the car radio from channel to channel until he found some news, started to listen to a long report on police corruption and switched to Mozart. It was dark and wet and, after half an hour, he heard a weather forecast which indicated that the area he was heading for would be subject to a higher than usual rainfall with gales and the likelihood of landslips.

He pulled into a garage which had a dismal café attached, drank a decent coffee, bit into a disgusting sandwich and had a sudden picture of himself, sitting alone at this plastic table in front of squeezy bottles of ketchup. The windows were steamed up but outside the weather was worsening.

He drank up, left most of the sandwich and ran through the rain. His plan was madness: he would have to retrace part of the route and probably stay somewhere overnight. He didn't care.

Right, he thought. It's the right thing.

He put a Bruce Springsteen disc into the player and drew away from the forecourt and out onto the road.

He stopped once more and then, an hour later, found a large corporate hotel off the motorway. It was bright, warm and dry, he had a clean room, two large whiskies and a good steak, before dialling the farmhouse number.

'Hi. Me.'

'Where are you? I hope you haven't gone to North Wales, the forecast is seriously bad.'

'I heard it, so I turned round.'

She sounded relieved. 'What will you do?'

'Might head for London.'

'Better than the Welsh mountains.'

'Might go across country, instead.'

'Right.' She knew better than to ask questions.

'How are you?'

'Oh, you know. It's Sam I'm worried about . . . He went for a long walk with Dad and didn't say a word apparently. Not a single word. Judith has been playing board games with Hannah. I just feel shattered but I can't sleep. Normal. That's normal.'

'I'll be back on Tuesday. Maybe Sambo will talk to me . . . I could take him somewhere. I'll think.'

He slept better than he had done for some nights, in spite of the traffic nearby and the soft mattress, woke at six and was on the road in half an hour. Breakfast later.

He switched on the radio. Off again. The sky lightened to a seagull grey but the rain had stopped. The roads were open and straight, the land flattened out. He speeded up.

Was this the way? He didn't know. The right place to be going? Nor that. But he knew he had to try. If it wasn't right, he could draw a line in the sand.

'Follow your instincts.'

It was just after eight. He drove to a hotel where he had stayed some years before. Still there, still the same. They had a room but it wouldn't be ready until lunchtime. He left the car.

It was chilly. But beautiful. He had forgotten how beautiful the buildings were. The last time he had been here it had been springtime with daffodils and crocuses studding the grass. Now the last few leaves hung on to the trees and the wind ruffled the surface of the water. Bells chimed the half-hour.

He walked. Past Peterhouse. Past King's. On. At first he could not find it, but then he remembered that it was tucked away, cloistered behind larger, more imposing facades.

He went through the gateway. Under the arch. Stopped at the lodge for directions. Across the court. Another arch. The sudden silence.

He pushed open the wooden door.

There were twenty or so people in the college chapel. The lights were on. Candles lit. He hesitated. Chapels and churches were not regular haunts of his in spite of living in the shadow of the cathedral. But this was where he had been directed. He slipped into a pew, at the end of the row. Bent his head briefly. When he looked up again Jane had come into the chapel to take the morning service. She was standing at the front a few feet away and staring, with astonishment, into his face.